The
CHOICE

P.D. VINER

hera

First published in the United Kingdom in 2022 by

Hera Books
Unit 9 (Canelo), 5th Floor
Cargo Works, 1–2 Hatfields
London, SE1 9PG
United Kingdom

A CIP catalogue record for this book is available from the British Library.

Print ISBN 978 1 80436 032 3
Ebook ISBN 978 1 80436 073 6

Cover design by THE-PARISH

Look for more great books at www.herabooks.com

Printed and bound in Great Britain by Clays Ltd, Elcograf S.p.A.

1

To all the children who have had to run from harm, and to those who have kept them safe.

Chapter One

Sunday

'Please don't, Sarah. *Please*,' he begs, but I can't stop. My fingers are curled around the hilt of the knife. I see his beautiful brown eyes – they absolutely burn with life and hope. He desperately wants to live.

'Please, I didn't mean to betray you,' he says, but it's too late. The blade is at his throat and – *Oh god* – it snicks through his artery and the blood sprays across my naked body. A moan escapes his lips, soft like a butterfly sighing at the end of its life, and his hands go up to try and stem the tide of blood. 'Please,' he begs, but the blade is red in my hand, it pulls back, and then... *I'm so sorry, I have no choice...* it slides into his heart.

His eyes are wide, their fire burns bright as the sun as his life flashes at warp speed across them – the memories, hopes and fears of a lifetime re-told on the point of death – and then they flicker and begin to fade. He's burned, from the inside out, leaving a black hole where a man once was. Dead. Gone forever.

I love you, he told me just moments ago. *I love you too*, I'd said, and I meant it. For the first time in years I'd fallen for another human being, trusted a man with my heart, but now he's dead and in my hand is the knife that killed him. It looks bad, but I'm not his killer. I wasn't in control of myself, I swear it on my mother's grave. But who'll believe me?

I feel nothing. I'm light as air, the size of a human soul, as I float outside my body. I've escaped, closed myself down to the horror of what's just happened so nothing can touch me. I can't be hurt. I'm merely an observer, looking down on myself, seeing the tears that streak my cheeks, and the scream etched on my mouth. I guess that, if I could actually feel something, the blood on my skin would be warm, like summer rain, but I can't feel anything touch me.

I look down on the dead man, his name is… was… Theo. Theo Tellner. He's only the second man in my entire life that I've said *I love you* to. Only the second man that I've ever made love to – just once – and just now. My skin is still cooling from the intensity of our lovemaking, the air still heady with the scent of our passion, though now that's undercut with fear and the stench of blood. I'm sorry Theo… I told you I loved you and then I stabbed you through the heart. *Christ*, it's all happened so fast. Only an hour ago I was happy and I thought my life had finally changed, that after so long I could stop hiding. I thought it was over. How did that joy turn into this hell so quickly?

In the distance I hear the wail of a banshee morph into the call of a siren, as the police and ambulance are almost here. They'll be downstairs, at the front door, any second now. They'll have to force it open of course, smash it down, but that won't take them any time at all. Then they'll rush upstairs and find us both naked, Theo dead, and the knife that took his life in my hand. There are no other doors in this room, just one way in and one way out, and that door is locked. The windows have shutters

2

and metal bars on them – there is no possible escape – and when they find me, the police will have no doubt as to what happened; that I killed Theo in cold blood after we had sex, and I will be lost. I will be locked up for the rest of time. Unless—

Bang—Bang—Bang—

Oh my god – the police are at the front door already, hammering on it. Any second now it will fall, and they will rush up here and—

What… what can I do?

There's a crash from the floor below me – the front door has been broken down. There's a roar of sound, boots stampede inside the house and officers shout orders as they swarm inside, buzzing like hornets. *Oh god* – any second now they'll storm upstairs and find me, covered in his blood.

'We're inside the property, ground floor secured and empty,' a voice calls from downstairs. 'Now heading up to the first floor.'

I hear the clunk of hob-nailed boots on the wooden stairs.

'Upstairs there's a bathroom and the door is open…' There's a pause, before his voice booms out once more. 'It's clear.' Then I hear the footsteps get closer and stop right outside the bedroom door. *Oh god*, he's just a few feet away from me, there's just a door between us.

'Door at top of the stairs. It's closed and maybe locked. I assume it's the bedroom. I'm trying it now,' the voice yells back to the officers behind him, and then I watch the door as the handle rattles.

'Locked,' he shouts.

There is a blast of radio static, and then a flurry of voices, but I can't make out any words; they're swallowed

3

up in the white noise and blare of sirens, as more emergency vehicles pull up in the street outside. The handle rattles again, even more insistently than before. The door shakes, it feels like it'll be ripped off its hinges any second.

'Is there anyone inside this room?' the voice yells through the inch and a half of wood that stands between us. 'If there is, then open the door now, put your hands above your head and step back into the room.'

Any second now.

'We have a locked door we need to force,' he calls out, and I hear more men rush up the stairs. I hold my breath and wait for the crack of wood as the door is rammed and— *crunch*.

It breaks, right down the centre and splinters inwards, caving in, as bodies surge into the room. They hold shields and guns and they're covered in tight black body armour. They look like flies.

'Man down, we have a body,' someone yells. 'Get paramedics in here fast, there's a lot of blood.'

I hold my breath and wait. I hear officers scramble around and pull at furniture. Something's dragged across the floor. I hear breathing and hitting – the *slap, slap, slap,* of fists on Theo's chest as they try to revive him. There are more footsteps, more static… and all the time my own heart is hammering in my chest – they must be able to hear it. They'll find me, and all of this will be over. I only wanted to be held and loved, was that too much to ask?

Please… please… please… I fill my head with the mantra of *please*, so that I can't hear them trying and failing to resuscitate poor Theo. I don't know who I'm asking help from, or what I want… to go back, to make a different choice? But of course I know that can't happen, that wishes and prayers are meaningless, and yet I can't stop asking: *could we start again please?*

'I'm calling it,' a voice cuts through the buzz of the room. 'Time of death: 21.14 hours. Cause of death is a stab wound to the heart. Given the angle, I don't see that this could be self-inflicted.'

'Anyone else in the room?' a woman officer calls.

'No, there's nobody else here. It's a locked room, no assailant – just the victim.'

Silence falls on the murder room. I feel the weight of it pressing down on me, so heavy I want to scream: *Here I am, here I am*. But I can't. I mustn't. I have to stay free, so I hold my breath until the quiet is blown apart and the wall of sound crashes back down on top of us. Police officers pile in, crime scene tape is ripped from rolls to cover doors and windows, and these men and women begin the job of finding a killer… searching for me. They may discover me at any moment, but perhaps I have a chance to stay hidden, and if I do, then I must make it count. I have to get away, stay free and run, but this time I have a destination… *Aberdeen*. My first clue in all these years. Finally, I could discover the truth, I have a gossamer-thin thread, leading into the labyrinth of the past, and if there is any way to save myself from rotting in prison I have to follow it down the rabbit hole, all the way into the dark. I'll have to go back, but I'll take baby steps to begin with, and go back one hour. One, isn't that crazy? How can it be only one hour since we arrived here? How has everything been shattered in so short a time?

Think back… remember… one hour.

Chapter Two

One Hour Earlier

'Drumroll…' Theo announces, his fingers tapping on the steering wheel, getting faster and faster. 'We're almost there. Just over the top of this hill, and then you can see it in…' He drums more insistently. 'Five… four… three…'

We crest the hill and… *Oh my god*, it's so beautiful that I actually gasp. I can't believe I'm looking out over the sea for the first time in my life. I'm so excited by all this. Is that a little sad? For a woman who will never see thirty-five again, to be at the coast for the first time in a land-locked life? Maybe, but right now I don't care about what poor little old me has missed out on over the years. Instead I just want to bask in the autumn sun, and the view of the water as it sparkles as far as I can see. I feel something in my chest − or rather, it's the *lack* of something that normally sits there, like a malign gremlin. Right now, it's gone and I'm not feeling anxious. I don't want to run. I choose to be here, with Theo. *Wow*, that feels good.

I look across at him. Even though I can only see the side of his face, I like what I see. He's handsome − tick − and has really nice hair and beautiful eyes (soulful like an old bloodhound, but sometimes playful like a puppy too) but that isn't really what I like about him. I think he's a good man, and that's all that matters in the end. I trust him. *Finally* I trust him, though it took quite some time for me to be able to say that.

It's been six months, from the first time he came into the café to this – a trip to the seaside and an Airbnb with a single bedroom. Single bedroom, one bed and I've got new knickers and a skimpy nightdress and— *Oh my god*. I feel myself turning beet red. I could back out, I could, but… but I don't want to. I want this; to be here with him. I want to stop running away from life.

'You don't see anything like this in South London,' he says, looking out over the dazzling sparkle of the sea. I can see he's pleased with himself. I told him on our second date – when he took me to the Sea Life centre (and I drove him crazy by humming the *Jaws* theme incessantly) – that I'd never actually seen the ocean, and so here we are. He listened to me and made my wish come true. It makes me feel really special and… *bloody hell*, I can't stop blushing.

'We used to come here every summer, the whole family,' he says and a nostalgic note falls into his speech, making it sound a little dreamy. 'The five of us together. Sometimes it was just a day trip, but we got a hotel one year and stayed for a few days.' He makes a little sighing sound in the back of his throat. 'We walked on the Devil's Dyke and on the South Downs, we cruised through the lanes and had ice cream on the beach. It was wonderful… but…' A cloud scuds across his brow. 'It must have been the last holiday we had when we were all together, before Dad died.'

He's silent again, lost in the memory of his dad, and I hear how bittersweet it is for him. Sadness at the loss – but joy at remembering his dad and the fun they shared and— *ouch*. I look down at my hands and they're bleeding

7

from where I've dug my nails into my palms, making little crescent moons of scarlet blood. I wipe them away, hoping Theo hasn't seen.

I turn my head away from him, over to the shimmering water, as our car follows the undulating curves of the cliffs, and heads into Brighton. I think about my own dad and… *Christ, don't go there*, I tell myself; *forget the past*. All I want is to be normal, and I like Theo because he's a regular guy. I like that he misses his dad and loves his mum and his sisters… that's real life, isn't it? Family is special to most people, and of course it's only natural that Theo wants me to meet his mum and sisters at some point but… but… it scares me. I've spent fifteen years on my own and… *ugh*, I don't understand why Theo likes me so much anyway. I don't get it. It's not like I'm pretty. I used to be, once upon a time maybe, but I'm small and skinny like a teenage boy, and I don't do things like have nice haircuts or wear make-up and stylish dresses. For so long I've wanted to be invisible, I have a head-down, don't-look-at-me vibe. I wear shapeless clothes and no make-up and—

Okay, so I did go out and buy some nicer things yesterday. Ayo helped me choose them – she works in the café with me – and it's really her fault I'm here, and that I let Theo into my life. She encouraged me to go out with him. She pushed me into it and maybe I'm glad she did. Oh god, I feel the blushing start in my toes and shoot up my body. I turn red so easily now; ever since he appeared on the scene.

He came into the café one night, about six months ago. It was late, like nine thirty, and we close at ten p.m. He ordered a strong black coffee and sat in the window and read a book. The next night he came in again, and the same thing happened – coffee, window, book. And the night after that was the same. And the next – it was the same deal all week.

'Almost time for Mr Nine-Thirty,' Ayo said after about the sixth time he'd come in, then she smiled this weird knowing smile and said, 'You know he likes you.'

'No.' I winced at the suggestion.

'Oh yes.' She giggled a little. 'He'll only sit at one of your tables, and that book he's reading – he's on the same page he was the first night he came in. He don't read nothing; he just watches you over the top of the page. He *likes* you.'

I didn't believe her, I thought she was crazy, but I waited to see what would happen when he came in. Dead on nine thirty he arrived, and I watched him as he watched me. Ayo was right; he didn't take his eyes off me.

The next morning I asked our boss, Lillian, to move me to the day shift. I was freaked out – why was he watching me? It made me feel really uncomfortable, and on top of that I was anxious about Ayo – why was she suddenly being so friendly? I felt hemmed in, trapped by all the attention. The reason I worked for Lillian was because there were no questions, no forms or papers to sign, just cash-in-hand work with no one prying into my life. Early on Ayo had asked stuff, but I just avoided answering her. She gave up asking after a while, but she did talk a lot about her own troubles with her daughter and her parents – legal problems and custody issues – though I didn't really listen. She jawed and jawed for a long time, months and months at least, but slowly it faded. She stopped telling me personal things and we just worked together. We got to be the perfect team, I liked that, but it all changed when Theo came in. Suddenly she started being all gossipy – like we were sisters or something – but I don't have a sister, or a friend; I didn't trust anyone. It was crazy that he liked me. So I asked Lillian to move me an—

'What about you?' Theo breaks into my thoughts. 'What holidays did your parents take you on when you were a kid?'

I hear his question, but I don't reply. Instead, I watch the architecture change, as Regency squares and impressive town houses lure us deeper into Brighton.

'What about boyfriends? Did you go on—'

'I hope Hobnob's okay.' I cut him off, and see him wrinkle his face a little in disappointment. I know he wants me to share my stories with him, he wants to know the *real* me but… UGH. We have been on nine dates, and he has told me everything about his former girlfriends (way more than I wanted to know) and about his sexual life (he once gave himself love bites with a hand-held Dyson, and then tried to use it to – you know – which has made me never want a vacuum cleaner in the house) but I've told him almost nothing about me. Not one word about love, or sex, or exes, or anything about any romantic past. I can't. I won't.

'I'm sure the hamster's fine,' he says. 'Ayo will feed him tonight, won't she?'

'I guess…' I've given my spare door key to Ayo so she can look after my hamster, Hobnob. I've never given my key to anyone before. I don't like the thought of someone being in my room when I'm not there. I'm not sure I trust her in my space and—

'Did you ever go away with any boyfriends?' he asks.

'Oh, did I tell you that Edan – he's the cook at the café – well, he said I could try helping with the lasagne next week. Isn't that brilliant?' I smile.

'Yes, that's fantastic, I can't wait to try one,' he says enthusiastically. Does he realise that I changed the subject, so I didn't have to talk about old boyfriends? The truth is that I don't want to tell him outright that I won't talk about the past, because I'd like him to drop it; take the hint. I understand why he wants to know this stuff; it's what new boyfriends ask new girlfriends – he wants to know what he's getting himself into. To know all the baggage I'm dragging around with me – the skeletons in my closet. I get that, but I don't want to look back. I want to go forward and – *please don't blush* (I tell myself) – the truth is that I like him. I like *like* him. That's why I'm here, isn't it? On what I think is a dirty weekend (Sunday to Tuesday anyway) in Brighton? Isn't that enough for him? It should be, it's the most I've been able to give to anyone in fifteen years, he should be happy with that. We can be together in the here and now, we can talk about how great tiramisu is (my absolute favourite dessert), and we can play Scrabble (he always wins but I'm getting better) and we can have actual kissing and touching and sex. Tonight, in our Airbnb. It's amazing. I'm actually looking ahead and feeling optimistic for the first time in so many years – and that is because of him. It's all good, except for the fact that I don't want to look back. I don't want to tell him about my past. I just want a relationship in the present, with a man who likes me… and who I like. And I do like him, even though I ran away from him at first, and moved my shift to the mornings as soon as I thought he was interested in me. As usual, my first response was to run and hide.

Moving to the morning shift was a mistake, though. I'm no good at getting up early, so I was late most days, which annoyed everyone, and after two weeks Lillian told me I had to go back to working evenings or quit. I moved back to the late shift. Ayo was glad to see me (which I didn't expect, but I found really nice) and when I asked about nine-thirty guy, she said he'd stopped coming in. I was glad. I was… really I was… though a part of me wished he'd kept dropping in to see if I was there and – this is really embarrassing – but I'd found myself thinking about him a little over the past couple of weeks. One night I'd woken up and he'd been in my dream. He hadn't been chasing me, though, like in my normal dreams. He'd been… you know… doing sexy things.

But it was good that he'd stopped coming in, as it meant I could get back to normal and stop daydreaming about him. Except, at nine thirty that night, he walked in. I felt my stomach flip (and not in the bad way, but in some new kinda good way). He ordered his coffee, said nothing more to me, drank it and was gone… but he left a package on the chair. It was a book of poems. Inside, it said: *Welcome back to my waitress*. Of course I gave it straight to a charity shop – what room have I got for poetry in my life? – but I was… *pleased*… by his gesture. Ayo had been right, and now he was wooing me, and that felt nice. Really nice.

He was back that next night, and when I saw him I realised that I'd been waiting for him to come in. He ordered his normal coffee and when I brought it over I stopped at the table and I said, 'Don't you find it bitter?' I actually spoke to him – *oh my god* – and it wasn't like I said *please fuck me*, but I hadn't started a conversation with a man in fifteen years. My stomach was full of butterflies.

'Life needs a little bitter or sour sometimes,' he said. 'If everything's sweet, it can be too much.' He smiled this really nice, slightly wonky smile.

'I-I have to go,' I stammered and ran back to the kitchen because I could feel myself turning bright red. Idiot. I stayed in the kitchen until he'd gone, fanning myself with menus like old Spanish women do.

He came in loads of times after that and, little by little, we began to talk – no pressure – and after a couple of months he asked me out.

'Ice skating,' I told him. I wanted our first date to be ice-skating (I had always wanted to go as a kid, but never had) and he agreed. Even after he fell and badly bruised his coccyx (I couldn't help myself, I laughed so much, even when he had to be stretchered off the ice) he was nice. I thought he'd hate me for laughing, but he still liked me (though he said no more ice skating) and he invited me to dinner next time (I love going to restaurants where I get waited on and not the other way around). After that it was the movies, and then a long walk in the park and… he romanced me. Nice and slow, so that eventually all the anxiety left me, as he proved time and again what a nice guy he was – we even went to a soup kitchen to work for a weekend – and finally I was ready to… well, do this. To come to Brighton with him, and I actually think I might—

'Here we go.' Theo swings the car into a square of incredible Regency town houses, with a lawn in the centre, and a statue at its heart. 'That's our Airbnb.' He points at a grey stone house that's tall and thin and looks historical and important. 'I hope…' he starts but doesn't finish his thought.

'Me too,' I say with a sly little smile, and slide out of the car. *Oh*. I gasp as I hear the sea for the first time, surging and then breaking, a whoosh and a clatter, and then it's pulsing up again… and then crashing back down.

A rhythm, like a heartbeat. Alive. It's amazing. I walk towards it. I can't stop myself, I've been mesmerised. I stand on the edge of the beach. It's made up of stones, which is a little disappointing as I expected sand, but it still makes my heart sing. *Wowsers*, it's so hard to admit it, but I feel… happy. I am happy for the first time in so many years. *Enjoy it*, I tell myself. *Don't mess it up.*

Behind me, Theo is getting the bags out of the car but I can't take my eyes off the water. In the far distance I can see an army of wind turbines, like sentinels, standing guard over the coast, and just off shore there is some kind of metal structure, like a black iron spider standing in the waves. It looks sad and old and broken.

'What's that?' I call back to him.

'What?' he says, and turns and walks over to me with our bags and – *oh hell* – I see that mine still has the price ticket on it. I hope he hasn't seen it. I don't want him to know that I didn't even have a suitcase before this morning, and had to go out and buy one. My clothes have only ever moved in a cardboard box before this, not a shiny pull-along case (half price in the sale), and just owning a case makes me feel a little more grown up than I normally do. And I like it, because that's what real adults do, isn't it? Go on holiday with their special cases and swimming costumes (yes I bought my first grown-up bikini with Ayo's help) and they go with their boyfriend or girlfriend and they drink alcohol and eat at restaurants and have a great time. And that's what I want, to be a normal grown-up, make my own decisions as an adult. So I treated myself. I spent some of my emergency escape money.

And truthfully I had to; I couldn't go away with Theo and take my regular underwear (too holey), or the nightclothes I've worn for years and years, and my tooth-brush was bald and I hadn't shaved my legs in more than ten years and Ayo said I should trim *down there* and… *oh*, I feel myself blush even thinking about that.

He points across the water at my iron spider. 'That's the old pleasure pier. In Victorian times it was like Disneyland and Vegas all rolled into one.'

'But now it's just a wreck?'

'Pretty much. There's a newer pier down that way.' He points off to the left. 'This one's left just sitting here, being slowly eaten by the sea.'

'And one day it'll collapse into the water?'

'Some day, maybe. I don't know, I'm not a structural engineer.' He laughs. 'But maybe that should be our next holiday, Vegas, baby.'

'I don't… I… not… I'm…' I stumble over my words and he tilts his head like a puppy. 'I don't think I could afford it.' I say lamely.

He wrinkles his nose. 'I'm sure we could find some-thing down the back of the sofa?'

'I… I…' I feel awkward all of a sudden. Talking about money makes me uncomfortable.

'Anyway, let's not plan the next holiday before we've even had this one,' he says with a smile. 'We have a perfect Airbnb just over there and a reservation for a fancy-shmancy dinner in two hours.' He leans in and kisses me, so softly it's like a whisper on my lips. 'Come on.' He turns to walk away with our bags.

I watch him, as he passes the car and gets to the front door. He puts some numbers into a code box and unlocks it. He pushes it open with his foot, before disappearing inside with the bags. The door stays open, inviting me in. I know I should go, but instead I turn back to the sea, as the sun finally touches the horizon, on its way down to Australia to spend the night. The sea is alive with slivers of gold that shimmer and shake like an exploding disco ball, and above me, birds start to dance and sweep across the sky like some giant flash mob, all synchronised and flowing, beautiful, just—

'Sarah?' he calls and I turn to see him waving from a first-floor window. He's smiling broadly and he looks so handsome. Why does he want me?

'Come on up,' he calls. And I nod and… (I feel myself blush – again) I am going to go inside and make love with him. He has been an absolute gentleman these last few months, no pressure and no demands on me. But now, I'm ready. I am pretty sure I am going to have sex for the first time in fifteen years. Pretty damn sure.

Wow. Sex. Wow.

I have to remember to send a postcard tomorrow. I haven't sent a letter or anything by post in so many years, but I should send a card to the café. They can put it above the bar. It'll prove I have a life, that I'm the kind of person who can go away for the weekend and have sex (I might not write that on the card, though). Finally, I am alive again. No more hiding and running. This is the start of my new life.

I walk into the house and shut the front door. There's a large, open-plan living room and kitchen. It looks flashy and modern. At home I just use a microwave and kettle. I'm not much of a cook, more a Pot Noodle and tea kind of girl – even though I do love watching a bit of MasterChef – and Edan is teaching me some of the recipes at the restaurant. He even lets me cut up veg and help make sauces on busy days. Through the living room and kitchen, past shelves stacked with books that have broken spines – like someone's actually read them – are stairs that lead up to the bedroom. Butterflies flutter in my tummy. I'm ready. *He isn't going to hurt me, he's a good guy. I'm safe. Breathe.*

'What would you—' he starts, as I enter the bedroom, but I stop him with my tongue, as I slide it into his mouth. We have kissed before. The first few kisses were chaste and then they started to get progressively hotter as they moved from English to French. There has been some stroking, like knees and hair – maybe a cheeky thigh – but no major erogenous zones. He's waited for me and now… now I'm ready. I kiss him. Hard. I want him. Just that thought makes me want to cry. *Oh my god, this is really happening…*

'What's the matter?' he says, as he kisses a tear off my cheek. 'Have I done anything wrong?'

'No, no it isn't you. I just… I just haven't felt anything like this in so long and—'

'I love you,' he says.

KABOOM.

Love… did I hear him right? He's gone with the nuclear option right away? *Love* – the Manhattan Project of emotion – but what do I say? How do I follow that? *Love you…* I mean, it's too soon… isn't it? How can he know how he feels? *Love…* how can he love me? *ME.* What do I do? I like him but… *love…* how do you know stuff like that? How the hell do I know what I feel? I'm so rusty at this. It's been so long since I felt love for a man and I do feel something for Theo, but is it love? Is it?

'I… The thing is…' I start, and I see the smile turn to sadness on his lips. He thinks I'm going to knock him back. Am I? Am I that cruel? Because he's a good man and I need some good in my life, don't I? Don't I?

'The thing is…' I start again and… *oh what the hell.* 'I think maybe I love you too,' I tell him, and it might be true. It certainly isn't a lie and maybe if I say it loads of times it will be true. He is lovable, and if I take a leap of faith…

He smiles a beautiful warm smile, and leans forward and kisses me. His hand slides over my body, and all thoughts of love fall away as all I know is that I want him to touch me… everywhere. I fall into him. I straddle him. I want to be on top, to be in charge, so that if it becomes too much I can stop it.

'I don't have any condoms,' he says. 'I didn't think—'

'I don't care,' I tell him, and know that I shouldn't be thinking this, but wouldn't a baby be just wonderful? To love another human being with no reservations, no ulterior motive, just unequivocal love – wouldn't that make everything all right? Love a baby and then love the man too… wouldn't that make all the fear and all the running worthwhile? I'm only thirty-eight, and a baby— *no, don't think like that. It's too much pressure to put on this whatever this is. Just enjoy the moment. Live for now. Just live.*

And I move on top of him and lean down and grasp him to guide him inside me. It feels beautiful, and I want to cry and laugh – I am so happy.

'I love you,' I say as I move on top of him, feeling him inside me, and all around me. We are no longer separate but one being. For a few beautiful minutes there is bliss, as I feel an orgasm build and build and then rush through me, as I moan so loud I could wake the dead. Then Theo stiffens beneath me, groaning along with me, and I feel him explode, he fills me, and together we sigh in satisfaction. My chest is full of light and there's a choir singing in my head. *Oh my god, that was amazing.* I am happy again, at long last. I thought I would be alone forever, I thought—

'I love you, Sarah.' He tells me and I blush. 'I think you're good and kind and funny and beautiful – so beautiful. Being with you will make me so happy...' but as I look into his face I see it start to crumble, as the happiness can't last. I can see it's already started to rain, as a tear slides from Theo's left eye and rolls down his cheek. I want it to be a tear of joy, but as it falls off his face I know it isn't, as other tears join the first to fall down the crags of his cheeks, like lemmings tumbling off a cliff. I don't even get a minute to enjoy the love, before it all comes crashing down. Not even sixty seconds.

'I love you, I want to be with you b-b-but I have to...' he stumbles, screwing his eyes up tight, maybe trying to suck the tears back up into his head, but it doesn't work as they flow ever more freely.

'You're scaring me,' I tell him – and he is.

'I just... you know that was amazing and I l-l-love you...'

I hold my breath.

'There's something you should know. I didn't lie or anything, I just didn't tell you everything... I want to be with you forever, I want to share everything with you.'

'Share,' I repeat dully.

'Yes, I want to share with you – what's mine is yours and what's yours is mine; that's what couples do, they share everything. So there's something I have to tell you.'

I feel nauseous all of a sudden, as my head fills with a dozen terrible truths he could be about to *share* with me. He's married; he's a murderer; he killed his wife; he killed his kids; his wife killed his kids and is getting out of prison today; he has a month to live— *bloody hell, just tell me.*

19

'I didn't *just* invite you down here for a romantic weekend,' he says and I feel my jaw clench so hard it might snap. 'I wanted to be with you and show you the sea. I wanted to make love with you but… but I also had to get out of London. I couldn't stay there.'

'Why?' I ask, my throat incredibly dry all of a sudden.

'It's nothing, nothing really. Nothing as important as us… it's just that,' he pauses, 'I-I-I owe some money.'

There's silence. I can't tell if that was the terrible thing he was going to tell me or if there's something else. 'Money?' I repeat.

'Yes… I mean it's crazy to get upset about money, I know that – but it's more than I can pay back and…' His eyes are wide and huge, like in some Japanese kids' cartoon, but I'm not finding it cute at all. 'I was really dumb and… they… they…'

'What?' I say in barely a whisper.

'It's stupid, Sarah, just an idle threat, but they said… they said they'd hurt me.'

I pull back from him, and put my arms across my chest. I suddenly feel more than naked. 'Hurt you?'

'I'm sorry, I should have told you before we left, but I was afraid you wouldn't come and…' He pauses and I see how he's trying to stop crying. 'I love you, Sarah. I'm afraid of losing you, of losing the best thing in my life and I can't do that. Together we can get through this… together.' He turns those enormous sad eyes on me again and I feel, just for a second… that I want to scratch them out of his damned head. He's a liar.

'I love you Sarah. Losing you would be worse than any beating they might give me,' he says, thinking it's romantic, but all I hear is one word: *beating*. I don't hear his *I love you*, or how losing me would be so bad – all

I hear is *beating*. My skin was so warm just seconds ago, flushed with the heat of lovemaking, but now I shiver. Goosebumps prickle all over me. Somehow violence has crept into our lives. It's happening again.

'They just want their money, that's all. I pay them and it all goes away. I've been such an idiot. I'm sorry, will you forgive me?' he asks but I can't say yes.

'Who do you owe money to?'

'A businessman.'

'What kind of a businessman?'

'It's all just a misunderstanding. He knows I'm good for it, it's just a cash-flow problem. I can sort it out.'

'You told me you worked in recruitment.'

'I do, I earn good money,' he tells me, puffing out his chest proudly.

'So why do you—'

'It's just I… you know…' He looks pained. I think he's desperately hoping that I'll stop asking questions and end his suffering, but I have to know the details.

'Why do you owe money?' I ask.

'It's nothing, just a little gambling,' he says and drops his head, shame radiating off him.

'I have to…' I say, feeling panic start to build in my chest. I want to get off him, but as I move, his hands grab at my wrists, holding me there, on his lap. I can feel his penis under me. Just minutes ago it excited me but now it scares me. 'Theo, let me go,' I say, my voice quivering.

'I'm sorry, I don't want to hurt you, but you need to understand.' And he holds my wrists so I can't escape from him.

'But I do understand. You owe a bookie some money?' I try and be breezy, to keep it light, but deep down I am starting to unravel and I need him to let me go.

'Yes, you get it.' He smiles. 'I was on a roll, I wanted to win some money so that I could take you away somewhere nice – like maybe Thailand.'

'Here is nice.'

'This is just Brighton. I wasn't going to get you a staycation. I think you deserve the best; a five-star hotel on a beach where the sun never stops shining. That's what I want for you.'

I can see he means it, and I'm touched that he wants to give me something so special, but I didn't ask for that. All I want is someone kind, and to feel safe, but I see now that man isn't Theo. He hid it well, but he isn't a completely *good* man. He won't keep me safe. I can't trust him. How did I fall for that again? What's wrong with me?

'How much?' I ask. 'How much do you owe?'

He looks upset, like I don't care that he loves me – but I need to know the truth. So I ask again. 'How much do you owe?'

He pauses, and I think he's wondering how much of the truth I can take. Then he sighs. 'Forty thousand.'

I suck in air through my teeth, shocked. It's way more money than I thought it could be. I feel panic in my chest, like a bird's trapped inside and is beating its wings to get out. I want to get away, but he still has my wrists.

'But I can get it, easy-peasy. I just need some time, that's why we came down here.' He says it like a little kid who's convinced that, if you believe in Santa hard enough, you'll get your heart's desire.

'When do you need to pay it back?' I ask, and he looks sheepish and doesn't reply. 'You're already late, aren't you? You've run out of time,' I say, and I know I'm right; I see it in his eyes. He's running – vicious men are on his trail and he wants me to run with him – but I can't, because

22

he isn't good enough at it. I know what it takes to truly run away, and the trick is to leave everything and everyone behind. Running is brutal, it's callous, and Theo doesn't have what it takes. He doesn't have that strength, so he's going to be found and he's going to be hurt, and anyone with him will get hurt too.

'I should—' I move to slide off him. I want to get dressed and go before the men hunting him arrive, and I've already decided that I'm not going back to my old life. I thought I was done with running and hiding, but now I have to start again, cut the ties that bind and disappear. I have to put some distance between Theo and me. I have to run.

'Let me go, Theo.' I try to pull away from him.

'No, please. Don't go. I need you, I love you.' He holds me tightly, as his face screws up with pain. Ten minutes ago I would have helped him with almost anything, but I don't feel any emotion for him now, none at all. Not even pity. I have to get away from him; he's too weak to have in my life.

'Let go of me. I'm cold and I want to put some clothes on.' I eye my new case by the side of the bed.

'No, not yet, I have to tell you something. It's you and me, Sarah, I know that so deeply now. I was even thinking about proposing, because you're the one. I know it.' He says it like some evangelist in the pulpit, so sure of his own cock-eyed worldview.

'I want to go.' I hear the coldness in my voice. I see that it shocks him.

'Go, but—'

'I want to go.' And I tear my right hand out of his grip.

'What the fuck?' he snarls and his normally soft brown eyes harden as his face creases in anger. He scares me, and I stop moving. The animal in him is only there for a heartbeat, and then he softens again. 'You can't go, I need you. You have to help me, you said you loved me, Sarah.'

I can't answer him. He isn't the man I thought he was. I fell for a gentle and kind man – but that isn't Theo. I know that now, I've seen the mask slip.

'I need you,' he says, but not kindly. 'I can get the money, that's why we're here. There are two casinos and they don't know me. I have three thousand to start, but it would be good if I had some more.' He looks expectantly at me.

'I... I don't—'

'I just need a break, that's all,' he says all lovey-dovey again, and then he lays his head on my shoulder and I feel the tears run. They course down his cheeks and onto my shoulder; they run down my back and over my breasts. I don't like it. Can he just turn on the waterworks, like an actor, or some cheap gold-digger? Was this all an act?

'I need you, Sarah, I just need a little help. That's why it's amazing we found each other.' His wide puppy-dog eyes are back. 'If I had another few thousand, then I'd get the forty for sure. By the end of the weekend we'd be safe and we could be together. Don't you want that?' He looks at me, pleading, and he slides his hands across my back – just like he did when we were making love – but now his hands burn me. I flinch, and his brow creases into a frown.

'What's the matter? I love you. Surely you want to help me. We're a couple. We share, don't we? What's mine is yours, and what's yours—'

'I would help, I really would, but I can't.'

'But you can,' he says, a little frustration in his voice now. 'I know you can help. Just a little, to keep *us* together and safe – because it's all for you, Sarah. Everything I do is for you, to make *us* secure. I love you, I truly love you.'

'No,' I tell him, feeling scared. 'I can't help you. I don't have anything.'

'Nothing?' He looks hurt and a little confused. 'No, no, darling that isn't right.'

'It is Theo, I don't—'

'But you must have something, Sarah, a little squir-relled away for a rainy day? You must, you have to. Please, darling.'

I shrivel inside. An hour ago, the word *darling* would have filled me with joy, but now I shrink from the desper-ation in his eyes… and there is something else in there too, buried deep down. I see a feral cunning – like another man is inside, hiding in the shadows.

'Please, Sarah, if you don't help, they'll hurt me.'

'I have nothing, Theo.'

'Oh come on, Sarah, you do have money. You have to help – I love you, Sarah, I love you. Help me. I beg you, for our love, help me.' And he grabs me.

I shake my head. 'I'm just a waitress.'

'No…' His fingers dig deep into my arms. 'You can just give me a little. Come on, let's go to the bank and get it, or wherever it is – in your mattress or a biscuit tin. It's just a loan, an investment in our future. That's something that's worth making isn't it?'

'I have nothing, Theo.' He's hurting me, and I start to fold into myself, getting smaller and smaller – just like I used to when I was a kid and I needed to escape. Soon I'll be able to leave my body and float away, feel nothing. *I'm sorry…* My voice is little more than a breath on the wind. I fold into an atom and I float outside of myself.

'You fucking liar,' he screams. He leans in to me, his nose almost touching mine. 'You have the money, everything your husband stole – what about that?' He shakes me. 'What have you done with it?' he bellows into my face.

But I'm gone. I'm shaken free from the flesh and bones carcass I drag around all day. I am light, I am air. I am just my soul – my essence – free.

'You bitch,' he snarls like a rabid dog, as my empty body flops over on top of him, like a ragdoll. I see him push me back – I feel nothing. I see him shake me, my body undulating with the force of it – I feel nothing. I'm not in there. I'm out in the cold. I really know how to run away.

'Fuck. Fuck.' Theo spits, anger pulsing all around him. 'Tell me where the money is, the bank robbery money. Where the fuck is it?'

I can hear the panic building in his voice.

'Where's the fucking money, Rebecca?'

Rebecca... He used my name – my birth name – how does he know it? How can he know I was once Rebecca, because I killed her when I became Sarah. Sarah with no surname, no middle name, no parents, no past – nothing – just Sarah, the cash-in-hand waitress. How does he know I was married? How does he know about the bank robbery? *How?*

If I was in my body I think I'd be sick, but instead I'm a ghost and I can only watch him, flecking my naked body with saliva as he rants at me, in a tempest of anger and bile and frustration. I see his fingers bite ever deeper into my arms, but there is no sensation in them, I feel nothing – and then my ragdoll of a body pitches to the side and topples over, falling off him and onto the floor, to lie there unmoving. I watch myself. I think I have fallen as far as I possibly can… but that is not true. I have so much further to fall. Theo lies on the bed, shocked by what's happened, then he slides off and kneels down by my side, close to my face.

'You said you loved me, but you wouldn't help me.' He sounds aggrieved and disappointed, like he's the victim here. And then he drops his voice even lower, whispering into my ear.

'They're listening to us, the room is bugged. They said you'd give me the money if I made you fall in love with me. They hired me. I'm just an actor. It wasn't anything personal; they offered me a lot of money… they wanted to do this the easy way, but now they're going to come and hurt you.' He touches my shoulder. It looks like a gentle touch, but I feel nothing.

'You need to give them the money back. It's theirs, after all. Don't hold out on them. They'll—'

His head snaps around as he hears the front door open downstairs and footsteps clump across the floor as someone enters the house. Theo turns pale as he hears the sound of men climbing the stairs.

'Don't be stupid. They'll hurt you,' he whispers.

Hurt me? I think. *They can't hurt me, I don't feel any—* but my thoughts fade to nothing as the door opens and a man enters the room. *Oh god…* it's him, the man who started all this, the man who made me run. Gene Vincent. And that means his brother Michael won't be far behind. *Christ*, they've found me, after all this time. I remember the fear and the pain from back then, but I don't want to— I don't want to think back to that time, fifteen years ago. I don't want to… *Please.*

Chapter Three

There was a rainstorm.

It was one of those storms where a year's worth of rain falls in a few hours and causes flash flooding. The kind that makes religious idiots jump up and down and blame gay marriage for the tempest. It rained for forty-eight hours. I was worried when Drew didn't come home the first night, but by the second night I was bouncing off the walls. I called the police to report him missing, and that was when the sky fell in. They came immediately – within an hour – but they weren't worried about him being hurt somewhere. Oh no, they had different questions in mind, and it was clear that they knew a hell of a lot of stuff that I didn't.

A bank had been robbed and a lot of money stolen. It was the Salford branch that Drew had started working at a few weeks before. It had been broken into out of work hours. Everything pointed to an inside job, and all the current and recent employees were accounted for – except Drew. Of course that made him their number one suspect, but I told them they were wrong. He was innocent.

So where is he? The innocent don't disappear, they said. And I didn't know how to answer that, except to keep telling them he would never do anything like that, he wasn't a thief, he was a good man. He didn't even dip into the stupidly expensive pick-'n'-mix at the Odeon and take a couple – *Christ, everyone does that – but not Drew, he's honest*, I kept telling them. But they didn't listen. Instead, they asked about other jobs he'd had; were other employers satisfied with his performance, had money ever gone missing, was he ever fired for stealing? They asked all these questions, and of course all I could keep repeating was that I knew he was a good man. *A good man.*

'Drew didn't do anything wrong, you have to see that, and now he's missing – maybe the real bank robbers abducted him. You should be out there looking for him,' I told them, but they just looked back at me with a kind of smirk that said *we know the kind of man you're married to*. And even though I kept telling them we were both innocent, I could see they thought I was either cold and calculating, or naïve and stupid. It was pointless trying to change their minds.

Finally they gave up asking the same question, over and over again, and they got up to leave.

'If he makes contact—'

'He will, he's my husband.'

The inspector gave me a weary smile. '*When* he makes contact, you have to call us immediately. You understand?'

'He didn't do anything wrong,' I said for the hundredth time and he sighed and shook his head. I guess he'd heard a thousand wives say that a million times before.

I showed them out, back into the rain that was still falling. In other parts of the country people were being flooded out of their homes. *Lucky bastards*, I thought. Water damage is easy; it makes a mess but after a while it'll recede and dry, it isn't the end of the world. It's not like losing the love of your life. I lay down and curled up on the sofa, listening to the drumming of the water and praying – like a bloody hypocrite – for Drew to be safe. *Come home to me*, I begged the universe, *come back, my darling boy*.

—

Knock, knock.

I jumped up, ripped from sleep, and rushed to the door, even though I knew it wasn't him. He would have used his keys, and he'd never knock that softly, but I ran to the door anyway. I wanted a miracle. I pulled it open and… there were two police officers on the doormat. They were soaked through, like drowned rats.

'You found him?' I asked hopefully but then I saw the look on their faces, like people paid to be sad at a funeral, and I noticed their hats were in their hands, even though the rain was bouncing high off their heads – and I knew the truth.

I'm sorry, Mrs Anthony, the police officer said, but I'd stopped listening by then. I basically lost it… My empty body hit the ground before I even knew I'd begun to fold out of it.

—

Do you have any idea about the kind of deal you might make with the Devil, after God has let you down and Lucifer has become your last hope? Have you ever woken in the early hours of the morning, having dreamed that the man you love, or the child you adore, is dead or dying and you can make everything all right… you just have to sup with the lord of hell. Do you know how far you would go for the one you love? Because I do. I know that to have my Drew safely home, I would have sold the entire human race down the river. I'd have let everything burn – allowed hell to come to the Earth, just for him to be alive and safe. I would have killed for him and I would have died for him. But there are no deals to be made with either God or the Devil; there is only life and death, and there are no do-overs, no second chances. Dead is dead.

–

When I finally came to, they told me they'd found his body, bones broken, behind a wall on some small obscure road, hours north of here. A dog walker had found him. They thought he must have jumped in front of a car and… Suicide. Guilt. Remorse. *Christ.* They asked me to come and identify his body at the morgue. I said yes but then thought: *what the hell do I wear?* I didn't have anything in black, I had clothes for work and T-shirts and jeans – but that was pretty much it. *What can I wear to show the world how much I loved him?* I thought. *What are widow's weeds when you're only twenty-three?* I had to ask the police officers to wait for me, as I went next door and asked to borrow something. I got a black skirt that had been their daughter's, and a white school shirt. I wore black Nike sneakers. All dressed up for the morgue.

–

'I am sorry for your loss,' they said after I'd identified my beautiful husband's body.

'Can I sit with him?' I asked.

'Yes, but I'm afraid you can't touch him,' one of them said, trying to be sympathetic but at the same time knowing there was an on-going criminal investigation. He pulled a chair over, and motioned me to sit alongside my Drew. Then the two of them left the room, giving me some privacy to grieve, though they stood just on the other side of the door. I assumed they were listening out for any confession I might make, or any clue I could give about Drew's part in the robbery – but what did it matter? He was innocent, but he was dead. Nothing mattered anymore. Nothing.

–

A very kind police officer drove me home. She offered to come in and sit with me, make me a cup of tea and a sandwich. I said no, I didn't think I'd eat anything ever again, and I just wanted to be alone. I told her I had a sleeping tablet to take. She scrunched her nose up at that – she'd probably seen a lot of people harmed by prescription medicines – but she didn't say anything. Instead, she described all the different kinds of counselling I could get for my grief. All I had to do was ask the family liaison officer who would come and see me tomorrow. Then, with a warm smile, she touched my shoulder and walked away. I stood on the doorstep of our house for a long time after she'd left, scared to go inside. I wished on a star, I even prayed as I stood out there. I felt desperate. I didn't know what I would do without him. I was alone in the world now... totally and utterly alone.

Finally, when I was too cold to stay outside, I opened the door and went in. They were waiting for me, in the dark. They'd already ripped the place apart, but they hadn't found what they were looking for. So they waited... I remember. I remember like it was yesterday.

'Don't struggle,' a voice hisses and I'm shoved into a chair. My feet are tied first, then my hands, and lastly a gag is pulled tight across my mouth. I start to retch, but a hand hits me hard on the cheek. 'Don't,' the mean voice tells me. They pull the rope tight, so tight it hurts, and then they turn a light on. The curtains have been pulled across the windows and taped in place so no light seeps through.

'That's better,' says the older of the two men. He looks to be in his mid-forties, but not a healthy mid-forties. He has dark hair that has already receded past the point of no return and his face is rodenty, long and thin, with a small mouth full of pointy and discoloured teeth. He looks worn out and worn down. The suit he's wearing looks like it's seen better days, as if it was bought for a funeral at least twenty years ago, and has been worn for a lot of court visits in the intervening years, but never been ironed or dry-cleaned. The cuffs are worn through and the left sleeve has lost both its buttons; the thread just hangs forlorn. He reminds me of a dodgy uncle, who'll bounce you on his knee at Christmas, until one year it isn't so playful, and his lap doesn't feel quite the same as it did before.

'Gene Vincent, pleased to meet you,' he says with a smarmy warmth that seems odd, considering he's tied me up. 'And this is my brother, Michael.' Behind him, mostly in the shadows, is a younger man who looks nothing like his older brother. He's in his late twenties, I'd guess, and is wiry and strong with sandy hair that curls on his head like a statue of a Greek god. His face is ruddy and could almost be handsome except for the fact that his jaw is set in a grimace and his mouth is cross-hatched with thin white scars from some childhood accident.

'We don't want to hurt you,' the older one says, and manages a kind of half-smile (which I do not find reassuring). 'We have some questions. If you answer them truthfully, we'll go and you'll never see us again.'

The younger one leans in and growls. 'But if you don't—'

'She will,' Gene says to his brother, like it's a warning for him to be calm. Gene turns back to me. 'You will, won't you, love? I can see you're the smart one.' He smiles. 'You aren't stupid, are you, Rebecca?'

I whimper – he knows my name. This isn't just bad luck, not some opportunist burglary; they came looking for me.

'If you promise not to scream or call out, I will remove your gag. Do you understand me?' he asks, and I nod.

Gene leans in to undo the fabric gag. I can smell his breath; strong mints that mask a base scent of sweet decay and cigarettes. 'Don't scream,' he tells me in a low whisper. 'I wouldn't be able to stop him if you do.' And he angles his head, ever so slightly, to indicate his brother. Michael frowns, his mouth puckers and the white scars gather, like a thread's been pulled together. He looks like a shark. I feel a river of sweat run down my neck and onto my spine.

'Okay, then.' Gene pulls a chair over, so he can sit down opposite me. 'My brother and I were friends of your husband,' he tells me.

'Your dead husband,' Michael adds.

'Yes, and we are sorry for your loss,' Gene says seriously, but there is a giggle that breaks from the broken mouth of Michael, that makes me think there is no real sympathy here. 'We had entered into an… arrangement with him – your husband I mean, with Andrew.'

34

'What do you mean, *arrangement*?' I ask, trying to keep any fear out of my voice.

'He didn't tell you about it? About us?' Gene tilts his head and frowns.

'No, he didn't say anything about you, either of you.' I can feel my whole body shake. The two men steal a glance at each other; there is anger and disappointment… but there's something else in the older man's eyes – it looks like a sudden sharp fear has hit him – maybe he's wrong. Then I see his eyes darken as he looks back to me.

'You know where he was working?'

'He just started a new job.'

'Yes, in a bank.' Gene sounds a little irritated.

'You know about the bloody bank!' Michael yells at me. The anger makes me flinch.

'Keep your voice down,' Gene warns, but Michael sneers at his brother and keeps his eyes locked on me. He looks like a cat watching a bird, getting ready to pounce and bite its head off.

'Rebecca,' Gene's voice is like honey all of a sudden. 'Your husband started work at the bank three months ago. You know that, don't you?'

'Of course.'

'And you know what happened at the bank two days ago?'

'I know it was robbed.' I say. 'The police questioned me.'

'Of course they did, because they're convinced it was an inside job, and they think Andrew was that guy.'

'Yes…' I suddenly feel relieved. These two men obviously know something, maybe they can clear his name. 'The police were convinced it was him, but they have no idea. They didn't know him.'

35

'What did they ask you?'

'Did he have a second phone, had he brought new people over to the house, did he seem strange, had he spent any large amounts of money?'

'Yeah… those would be the kind of idiotic questions the police would ask when they have no ideas.'

'Then what ideas should they have? Who else should the police be looking at to find the inside man?' I ask, desperate for anything that could prove Drew's innocence.

'Who else?' Gene's face cracks open and he laughs hard. He looks across at his brother like it's the funniest thing he's heard in years. Then he looks back to me and the laughter drains away. 'No one else, Rebecca, they got the right man. Drew's guilty.'

'No…' I feel cold in my belly. 'He didn't—'

'Of course he did.' Gene snaps. 'Don't be stupid, Rebecca. You must know, deep in your heart, that he did it.'

My mouth opens but nothing comes out. I sit there blankly, as the two men light cigarettes. Finally I ask them, 'How are you so sure?'

'Because we're the guys that robbed the bank, and it was your husband who gave us all the information we needed.' He grins at me, like the cat that got the cream. 'And do you know how much money was stolen, Rebecca?'

I don't reply. The police told me earlier, but the number didn't stick in my head.

'It had fifty times more cash than that branch has normally. It had the bonus money for a local business that was celebrating 100 years.' Gene grinds his discoloured teeth. 'We stole eight hundred and seventy-five thousand pounds.' He stops and stares at me, his eyes burning with lust and desire, for the money and whatever he imagines it will bring him.

'But Drew isn't a bad man.'

'Bad?' he laughs. 'What the fuck are you, a primary school teacher?'

'I…' Doubt pricks at me for the first time.

Gene sees my doubt and grins triumphantly. 'There it is, I can see it in your eyes; you know he did it.'

'I just…' and I burn with shame, because I know he's been distant lately, seemed bored sometimes, and I know he doesn't like the job… Maybe I could see him steal, but I can't believe he wouldn't have told me about it. I'm sure he would have asked me to help, because we're a team, we share, we do things together… or at least we did. Has everything changed and I didn't see it? Have we drifted that far apart? I feel tears coming and… I want to be sick.

'That's it, Rebecca, no more lying to us or to yourself.' Gene moves in close to me, sliding in like a lover might. 'You knew about him, I was right… just like I'm sure that you know where the money is.'

'What?' I feel like I've been dipped into freezing water, like a witch about to be drowned. 'I-I-I don't know where any money is, don't you have it?'

'If we did, do you think we'd be here talking to you?' Gene moves away. I'm glad I can't smell the stale cigarettes and sweat that hangs off him anymore.

'Costa del Sol,' Michael says in a sing-song voice as he lights another cigarette off the stub of the first. 'We'd be in the sun.'

'But I don't, I have no—'

'*Liar!*' Michael screams at me. 'Your fucking husband stole from us.' He jumps forward, right into my face. 'And you're going to tell us where that bastard stashed it.'

'I don't—'

He pulls my sleeve up and presses the burning end of the cigarette into my arm an—

Aggghhhh... Fireworks go off in my head – a spike of pain – and I am folding down and down, out of my body. I watch it fall forward. If it wasn't tied to the chair I would have hit the floor. Both men are stunned for a second, then Gene screams at his brother.

'She's unconscious. Fucking hell, you idiot, stop. It might be her heart or... fuck.'

'She's faking.' Michael punches me, hard. From above it all, I watch my face contort. Later I will find out that there is a crack in my eye socket, but I can't feel it now.

'No, Michael don't... you'll bloody kill her.' Gene forces his brother back, away from me. He cuts my hands and feet free, and my body tumbles to the ground.

'She's... oh, Christ.'

'I'm sorry, Geney.' Michael sounds like he might cry.

'You idiot.' He starts to pray under his breath. '*Oh sweet Lord God, let her be alive, let her be...*' He checks my wrist for a pulse, but there's nothing there.

'*Christ*, Michael... you've killed her... *Jesus*... call an ambulance...'

'But the money—'

'Ambulance.'

Michael is breathing hard. He looks like a toddler who's been scolded for pulling the wings off a fly, but doesn't understand what he's done wrong.

'We need her alive, Mikey, she's the only one that knows where our money is. If she dies then we've got nothing.' He prods at my chest and feels for a pulse again. I can see the panic rising in him. 'We need her, Michael.'

'I just wanted to force it out of her quick, Geney, I thought she'd tell us in a second if I hurt her.'

'Well she bloody didn't, she had a heart attack, and now we've got nothing. What the hell do we do?'

I can see the desperation sizzle in the older man, like bacon on a grill, and he lurches away from his brother.

'All we've done, all that planning… it can't come to nothing, Mikey. It can't. *It can't.*'

And I watch this sad man drop to the floor and try to revive me. He gives me chest compressions to 'Stayin' Alive', and the kiss of life – but he can't find a heartbeat.

'Call an ambulance, Mikey – call a fucking ambulance.' He screams at his brother who skulks away to find the phone. 'Don't die, don't die…' he whispers to me, over and over as he pushes down and up, down and up. He keeps going until he can hear the wail of the ambulance siren and then he stops, just before the paramedics arrive. Then they leave.

–

I was rushed to A&E. The paramedics couldn't find a pulse when they first examined me, but by the time we reached the hospital I was breathing again and my heartbeat was steady. They couldn't understand what had happened, but they saw the cigarette burn on my arm, and my broken cheek, and they brought me in.

At the hospital, a doctor looked me over. Of course he asked what had happened, but I played dumb. He said I should stay overnight for observation but I knew that in the morning the police would be called in to ask questions, so I gave a false name and said nothing about the death of my husband, or the torturing brothers from hell. I could have asked the nurses to call the police and then told them about the Vincent brothers – but I kept my mouth shut. I know the police, I know how they think, and I don't trust them.

My mum called them twice when I was a kid, and she was scared for her life, and both times officers came to the house and were met on the doorstep by my dad. Both times they talked to him, laughed with him, and on the second visit they even joked with him about how erratic women can be, how they can make a mountain out of a molehill. *Periods*, one of them said, *or menopause, it drives 'em crazy...* and my dad just laughed with them. We were inside the house, locked in the living room, but we heard the policemen loud and clear. They didn't ask for my mum to come to the door, even though she'd been the one that called them. Instead, they took his word that nothing was wrong. After all, my dad was well educated, respectable and a good Christian man.

So I know the police, and I know how blind they can be, and I don't trust them to keep me safe. They might even think, like the Vincent brothers, that I must know where the money is hidden, and arrest me. Even if they did believe me they wouldn't help much, and the newspapers would still crucify me, and my neighbours would always look at me funny. Everyone would gossip about how my husband had turned bad, and maybe I was to blame. Maybe it was my idea for him to help rob the bank.

People are like that; they always think the worst of people, and I couldn't bear that. The thought of being watched and leered at, gossiped about and scrutinised... that was too much for me. I had nothing to keep me in Manchester, no family now and no Drew. His mum never liked me much and the feeling was mutual. There was nothing for me here, so I decided to go; to run and not look back. It was the only way I could keep myself safe and allow myself some privacy to grieve for my Drew. I had to run. I had to.

–

At three a.m. I slipped out of my hospital bed. I was wearing one of those stupid paper gowns designed to embarrass you into staying put, but I wasn't deterred. I left the private room and padded down the ward. It was dimly lit and there was only one nurse sitting at the desk, and it looked like she was asleep. I found the staff changing room and there was a locker without a padlock. Inside, were a pair of the skimpiest underwear I'd ever seen, alongside a massive tent of a dress. I didn't understand how the two could co-exist, but beggars can't be choosers. I found a pair of slip-on shoes by the door. They were a little too big but not bad. I put them on and headed to the stairs.

I was scared that Gene and Michael would be out there, watching to see if I came out, but I had to take the risk. I didn't have any kind of a plan. I knew I had to get home quickly as I had to grab my treasure box – I couldn't live without that – and then I would run. London was probably my best bet, a city that would welcome me with open arms, and hide me in the millions and millions of others who have run there to hide. Yes, that was what I'd have to do. It was an obvious decision, I don't really think I had a choice.

At the main entrance to the hospital, I stopped and looked up at the CCTV camera on the door. I gave it a feeble wave, and walked out into the chill air, to be swallowed by the night.

That was fifteen years ago.

Chapter Four

Now

The memories of that night, all those years ago, fades and I'm back in the bedroom of the Brighton Airbnb, as Gene Vincent walks in. He looks old, not just fifteen years older than when I last saw him, but really old (even though he can only be in his mid-to-late fifties now). Tonight, if I was seeing him for the first time, I'd guess he was in his seventies. He stoops a little and… is that the same suit he had on fifteen years ago? If it isn't, then it's the same style (charity shop chic at best). His eyes look sunken, like they're trying to burrow back into his head, as if they can't bear to see any more of the horror that's before them. If I saw him on the street, with a cup in front of him, I might even stop and drop a pound in it. He walks up to my prostrate body and looks down. His already thin lips look like he's sucked a truck full of lemons in the last hour.

Behind him there's more movement, and another figure enters the room. Shorter and bigger, wider, more muscular… *oh Jesus*… it's Michael. I feel his cigarette burn me again.

'I'm sorry, Gene,' Theo says as he stands, his hands moving to cover his most private parts. 'I didn't—'

'Shut up!' Gene yells at him, his voice a mix of anger and disappointment. I understand it now. It was all a set-up. Theo never loved me, I was never lovable, I knew it couldn't be right, but I so wanted it to be real. I'd hoped it was the start of something, of love and security and a family... but it wasn't. It was the end of something. The end of me.

'Jesus Christ, Theo, all that time and effort, months planning our moves and setting you up to meet her, so what do you do?'

'I tried... I...' Theo looks like he wants to cry.

'All those bloody dates: ice skating, movies, dinners, everything geared to make her fall in love with you.'

'And she did, Gene she did... she said she loved me – I got her to love me – I did what you asked.'

'Then where's our bloody money?' he moans, sounding heartbroken. 'You were supposed to reel her in slowly. Make her fall in love with you, make her trust you, and then show her that you needed her.' He kicks the bed hard. 'You were supposed to make her feel scared for you, afraid you'd be really hurt. The whole point was to get her to give you some money, so we knew where she'd stashed the rest of it. Jesus fucking Christ, it should have been easy, but you blew it.'

'I didn't, it wasn't my fault. I asked her, I begged her, but she just wasn't going to give me any money. I don't think she has an—'

'It isn't your job to think!' Gene yells angrily. 'You're the fucking lure. You should have charmed her slowly, teased the information out of her, but you panicked, you had no patience. You threw it all away by threatening her. You gambled everything and lost.'

'I really don't think she—'

'She has our money,' Michael Vincent explodes from behind his brother. 'You screwed everything up. I want to kill you.' He pushes forward, his hands clawing into fists but his brother steps between them.

'It's okay, it's okay, Michael. You know that isn't what we need to do. It's okay, I've got it, calm down.' The older man soothes his brother who looks wild, demented by rage.

'But Gene—'

'Leave this to me, Michael, okay?'

'Gene, he doesn't deserve—'

'I know what he deserves, trust me, brother.'

Michael glares at Theo, his jaw clenching and unclenching, until he finally walks away.

'Can I get dressed?' Theo asks. He's covered in goose-bumps, but it's hard to tell if they're from the cold or fear.

'No,' Gene tells him. 'Not yet.' He walks over to my body, still lying curled on the floor. He prods me with his shoe, gently, like I'm a bomb that could explode at any moment.

'You told me her husband helped you rob a bank,' Theo says.

'Yes, yes, he did.' Gene turns to him. 'He worked there, he fed us all the security codes, showed us how to bypass the CCTV, and he gave us the nod when the big haul was ready.'

'Andrew, that was his name,' Michael says from the shadows at the back of the room. 'Andy... He said he was one of us, but he took it all for himself.' He spits on the floor. 'No one likes the boys that don't share.'

'You said there was an accident,' Theo says, and I can't help myself as I feel my heart flutter and, for a moment, I'm back in my body. My eyelids flicker. It's only a moment, and then I'm outside again, but in that instant when I'm back in my own skin, I feel myself burn with the need to know what happened with the robbery. What happened to Drew, how did he die? Was he coming for me? Were we going to ride off into the sunset together with all the treasure? Was I right or wrong about the kind of man he was?

'Accident?' Michael giggles.

'It wasn't an accident exactly,' Gene says.

I feel my soul shudder as he looks at my empty shell; my spirit darkens like a storm cloud. *Not an accident… what happened?*

'Her husband took our money and ran, but we tracked him down. It took a couple of days and by the time we'd found him, he'd already stashed the money somewhere. We asked him nicely where it was, then not so nicely, but my brother doesn't know when to stop asking.'

'He was laughing at us, what was I supposed to do?' Michael glares. 'He was a flashy bastard, funny guy, I didn't like him. He was weak. He snapped when I asked him where the money was.'

'Asked?' Gene sneers.

'Serious asking… I thought he'd take more, but he couldn't. He was too bloody soft.'

'It was still stupid to kill him.'

I feel like the knife is in my heart now, twisting inside me.

'Kill… you killed him?' Theo shrinks away from the two men. Maybe he'd thought them just a little desperate and sad before, and he'd been happy to take their money. Probably thought it was a fun challenge, to see if he could make an unknown woman fall in love with him, but it isn't fun now. He's realised how dangerous the Vincent brothers are, and I see the fear in his eyes. For me, there's no fear anymore. I am raging… They killed Drew. They broke his body and left it behind a wall for a dog to find. I want to kill them. I want to make them pay for what they did to him. But right now I can't do anything – I'm just a soul floating in air.

'I need to—' Theo tries to make a bolt for the door – he's shaking with fear – but Michael has him in an instant.

'Easy, brother, easy,' Gene says and gets Michael to release his grip on Theo. 'We don't want our boy hurt.'

'I won't tell anyone, I swear.' Theo shakes all over.

'We know that, don't we, Michael? We know you're a good boy.'

'I bet he loves his mum,' Michael sneers.

'And we still need his help, don't we? So let's not hurt him.'

'What do you want me to do, Gene?' Theo asks.

'Look at her.' Gene points at my body, still curled like an infant on the floor. He kicks me, hard. I watch him. I can't feel the impact but I see the bruise almost immediately start to darken on my skin. He puts his boot on my face and rocks it back and forth.

'Is she… Oh god, is she dead?' Theo asks fearfully.

'Dead.' Gene laughs and Michael sniggers. 'That's what we thought, fifteen years ago, when we first asked her where her husband hid our money.'

'What?' Theo looks from one brother to the next, completely confused. 'You talked to her already? Then why—?'

Gene lunges for Theo and grabs his chin with his hand, squeezing it tight. 'It was your looks we employed you for, not your brains, so keep your mouth shut and get back on the bed.'

'I—'

'On the bed.' Michael growls at Theo, and he goes and lies down, grabbing a pillow to put over his exposed penis but Gene knocks it away, leaving him naked.

'Pick her up,' Gene tells his brother, who scoops me off the floor like a dropped ice-cream cone. 'Put her on his lap – just like when they were consummating the deed.'

'Screwing…' Michael sniggers, as he drops my body onto Theo, so I'm astride him again, but this time I feel nothing.

'You see, Theo, fifteen years ago we asked Rebecca where her husband hid our money. We asked her nicely, then we asked her not so nicely.'

'And she… she passed out?' Theo is shaking.

'That's right, she collapsed before she told us anything, like she did tonight. We felt for a pulse and there was nothing there… and I bet if I try to find a pulse now…' and Gene Vincent reaches across and lifts my wrist, placing his fingertips on the delta of veins that meet there. 'Yeah, nothing tonight, either.' He smiles, showing his vicious, discoloured teeth. 'But she isn't dead… she's very much alive.' He prods at my prostrate body. 'You aren't dead, are you, Rebecca?' he sneers, and then turns to Theo. 'You're a smart kid Theo, let me ask – have you ever heard of a dissociative state?'

Theo shrugs. 'I don't know what that is.'

'It's the ability for someone, in a position of extreme danger or stress, to let their body go, for their mind to leave so they can't feel any pain. To be lost outside one's self,' Gene says, like he's a lecturer at some third-rate sixth form college. 'It's a form of PTSD. I read about it, after I talked to the doctor who saw our Rebecca that night. He said it was the only answer – but he still couldn't believe that someone could escape themselves so deeply

48

that their pulse was gone.' Gene stops and looks around, as if he thinks I'll suddenly appear to him like the ghost of future-yet-to-come. 'It's rare, but it does happen. The books all say it's normally people who suffer great pain as children... like torture.' He stops and now speaks to the air. 'I looked into your family, Rebecca. That dad of yours... I asked about him especially and some people said he was a religious nutter.' He pauses, his eyes bright and alive now. 'I don't like men like that, they can be right hypocrites, think they're above the rules us common folks need to follow. And they can be right vicious bastards.' He drops his voice and leans in to my face. 'Was he, Becs? Did he hurt you? Was that how you learned you could leave your body? Did you run from him, from the slaps and the punches? Did it happen night after night?' He stops. I think he expects the truth to force me back into my body, but he doesn't know me, and he has no idea about what pain the body can absorb and still hide away.

'I know that physical pain is nothing to you, Rebecca. I know that I can't hurt you; no pain will force you to tell me where the money is.' He pauses, and slowly sighs. 'We lost you for a long time... we had other things to do, places to be.' I see a look of pain and anger shoot through him and I bet he spent a lot of that time back in prison. Maybe they did another bank job and got caught. I hope so; I hope their last fifteen years have been as miserable as mine have.

'It was providence that we found you again; Michael saw you from a bus,' Gene laughs. 'A bloody bus, in a place we'd never ever been before, it was fate. He followed you, found out where you lived, and then we watched you. We watched you for weeks. It was pretty fucking sad, actually. That shitty job and no husband or boyfriend, or even friends really – just a fucking hamster. Pathetic.'

'Sad cow,' Michael cackles.

'And we knew we had to play it smart, get you to trust someone… so we found ourselves a lover-boy for you.'

'This is crazy,' Theo yells, making Gene swing round to look at him, angry at being interrupted. 'If you watched her for weeks, you know she doesn't have anything. She lives in a one-room hovel; she can't possibly have your money.'

Gene looks at Theo like he wants to flay him alive. 'Then why would she run and keep on running?' He glares at Theo. 'She didn't even tell the police about us, she just disappeared off the face of the earth. The innocent don't run, Theo.' He looks down at me. 'They don't run, do they, Rebecca? That's how come I know that you have our money.'

'She knows…' Michael says, and I watch him jab a finger into my flesh. I wish I could spit in his face, but I can't go back to my body. If I do, they will kill me. I won't let them win.

'You have it, even if you're too guilty or ashamed to spend it, you have it.' Gene says. 'I knew I couldn't force it out of you, that you have to give it up willingly. Violence is useless on you—'

'That's why you made me woo her,' Theo says, fear spiking in him.

'Yes, so she had someone to lose.'

'Yeah, but stupid Theo screwed it up,' Michael spits.

'No, I didn't. I did everything you said. I made her fall in love with me and got her to come down to Brighton. I played her, just like you said, but she still wouldn't help –

even though she said she loved me, she wouldn't give me money. I don't think she has an—'

'Think, I don't give a toss what you think.' And in a movement quicker than I would have thought possible, Gene lunges forward and grabs Theo's throat. 'You're a moron – all that time and effort, and you screwed it up.'

'No… she wouldn't save me, even though she said she loved me.'

'You could have worked on her more; you should never have told her that you knew about the husband and the money.'

'But she doesn't have anything, she's just a waitress in a shitty diner.'

'She has it. She has our money and you were supposed to get her to trust you.'

'And I did. I didn't mess it up, it was the plan that didn't work.'

'Maybe – or maybe the danger wasn't enough.' Gene curls his lip.

'It can't be any more dangerous, can it?' Theo asks.

I can see the goosebumps rise on his skin again.

'Not physical danger anyway. We can't hurt her,' Gene says.

'Look, c-c-can I get dressed now?' Theo stammers a little. 'And get this thing off me,' he motions to my body. *Thing*. He called me a *thing*. I hate that I said I loved him. I will never be able to forget how he fooled me. I think I could kill him if I had the chance.

'No, not yet,' Gene replies.

'But I did my part and I was bloody good. Now I want to take my money and—'

'We don't have the spoils yet,' Gene says softly. 'Your money is coming out of the bank money, when we find it.'

'No way, that was not the—'

Michael hits him. He shuts up.

'Thank you, brother,' Gene says. Then he opens his arms like a third-rate preacher and talks to the air in the room.

'Rebecca, I know you can hear me. I know I can't hurt you physically, I can't make you tell me where the money is.'

'But we could cut her hand off?' Michael says with glee.

'We could, but that wouldn't get us what we want. But I have thought about what we can do.' Gene bends down to my body, and drops his voice so that neither Michael nor Theo can hear him. He whispers into my ear.

'You're a smart girl, Rebecca – or Sarah, or whoever you want to be. We tried pain, we tried love but neither worked, so now we've only got one option.' He actually looks upset for a moment.

'If you don't tell me what I need to know, then it's on you – his blood will be on your hands. Only you can save him. It's your choice.'

Oh god… I know what he's going to do.

Gene pauses, he looks expectant for a moment, and then whispers again. 'You have the power of a man's life in your hands. It's your fault if you make the wrong decision.' He waits, and slowly sadness creeps into his face. 'You won't save him? You choose to let this happen, it's all on you.'

Gene stands bolt upright. There is a shift in him. I see Theo start to shake; his eyes are wide with fear.

'Gene… please,' he whimpers, but the older man ignores him, instead he turns to his brother.

'Get the phone out Michael, film this.'

Michael holds his phone up to video his brother.

'Action,' Gene says, and there is a soft beep as the camera starts. Gene stares directly into the lens and starts to speak.

'My name is Gene Vincent. Fifteen years ago I, with my brother Michael, and an ex-bank employee named Drew Anthony, robbed the Salford branch of a major bank. We stole eight hundred and seventy-five thousand pounds. My brother and I were double-crossed by Mr Anthony who took the money. For fifteen years we have searched for it. The only person who knows where to find it is his widow, Rebecca.' He nods to Michael, who stops the recording and drops the phone.

'Last chance, Rebecca: last fucking chance to stay clean. Tell me where my money is.' He looks like a wild animal.

'Please…' Theo begs.

'Shut up kid, you've forced me to do this.' Gene sneers at him and then turns to my body. He takes a small capsule from his pocket, like an empty paracetamol, then writes something on a tiny piece of paper and places it inside. 'This is my telephone number,' he tells me as he opens my mouth and puts the capsule, with the phone number inside it, into my gullet. 'Swallow,' he orders, and massages it down my throat.

'You're gonna poop that out in eighteen to twenty-four hours, then you can use the number to call me. It can be your one call that the police allow you.' He leans in close, almost as if he were about to kiss me, and he whispers, 'You tell me what I want to know now, and this ends. Where is the money, Rebecca?'

Nothing.

'Tell me.' He burns with righteous anger. 'Andrew took it somewhere, didn't he? That's why he hired the car in Aberdeen.'

What?

I feel my soul flicker into my body again, I can't stop it. My eyelids flutter open and I am looking directly into the eyes of Gene Vincent. He sees the life spark back in me.

'What, what does that mean?' He grabs me. 'You remembered something, didn't you – about Aberdeen? You know what it means, tell me.' He shakes me, but I fall from my body again – there's nothing there. Gene snarls in anger and frustration, and then looks back to his brother. 'Camera,' he barks and Michael starts filming again.

'I had an actor, Theo Tellner, get her to fall in love with him. I hoped to use that to get the truth out of her, but she didn't play ball. I've given her every chance to make this right – return our money – but she's refused, so this is the only option left to me. This is on her head.'

Gene takes the knife handle and places it in my hand.

I see what he plans...

'No.' Theo yells and tries to jump away but Michael reaches out and slams him back down, holding him in place.

'Please, I didn't mean to betray you.' He pleads with Gene – I think at the last second he understands the danger he's in – but it's too late. Gene uses my hand to stab Theo in the neck. Blood arcs over me as I sit astride him. Then he takes the knife, still in my hand, and plunges it into Theo's heart. I look into the dying man's eyes and see the promise of his life burn up right before me. I see his soul shrivel.

Oh god… I'm so sorry, Theo… so sorry… it was all because of me… please forgive me… please.

Gene turns to the camera, not a drop of blood on him. 'Here is the proof that Rebecca Anthony, née Waite, is totally innocent of the murder of Theo Tellner.' He finishes with a look of total sincerity, so good it would have got him a job on *Blue Peter* if he was auditioning. 'Stop filming.'

His brother hits *end* and pockets the phone.

'I know you can hear me, Rebecca,' he calls into the air. 'I can't physically hurt you, but I'm going to get you locked up for the rest of your life – and you have no idea what life is like inside prison. The misery of being locked in a cell for twenty-three hours a day, the constant stench of shit, and food that's so bad you wouldn't give it to animals. It's not like on the TV; it's not *Porridge* or *Cell Block H*. It's the loneliest and scariest place on earth.' His face is twisted and his eyes are red and bloodshot. 'That's where you're going. And it's such an awful place that I'm sorry for you.' He almost sounds sincere. Almost. 'You've got my number, Rebecca, even if you can't access it for a while.' He gives me a big shit-eating grin.

'But a couple of days in a cell should prove just how screwed your life will be, unless you give me what I want.' He pauses, letting the threat contaminate the room. 'Call me and tell the truth at last… it will set you free. When we have the money and are safely out of the country, I'll email the film to the police, and it'll clear you of Theo's murder. All you have to do is tell me where the money is and you get your life back.' He smiles, and up close, I can see how rotten his teeth are. He hasn't been to the dentist in the last fifteen years, that's for sure.

'Aberdeen, baby,' he says and licks his lips, like he can taste the money. 'Call me.' He winks. 'Come on,' he says to his brother. 'Make sure the windows are locked and there's no way she can get out. We're going to lock this door and the front door, so there's no way the police don't find her with the knife and his DNA all over her. That will sink her. Rolling up and playing dead won't save her from this.' And he laughs, like a mean kid at the circus, watching the clown bully someone until they cry.

I watch them, trying to keep my eyes away from Theo and the seeping blood and— *raindrops on roses and whiskers on hamsters...* come on think of my favourite things. Red sky at night... the smell of bacon frying... a long hot bath... kissing Theo... *oh god...* don't go there, that's where the monsters are. Fresh baked bread, coffee, clean sheets, a baby smiling at you on the bus and... how do I live with Theo's blood on my hands? Is it my fault? Is it?

I force myself to concentrate on the brothers Grimm, as they secure the flat so there's no way out. I watch as Gene calls 999 to say he heard a scream at this address. They wait in silence, until they hear the first siren – just like all those years ago when they thought I was dead – then they make to leave.

'You've got my number, Becs. Don't be a stranger.'

They lock the door behind them, trapping me here with Theo's dead body. They have me right where they want me. The police will see this as an open and shut murder case; they won't believe it was the Vincent brothers, not for a moment. Without proof that they were here, I'll go to prison for a long time; maybe for the rest of my life. Is this the end, is this what I deserve? I could have chosen another path – I could have – but I didn't. I let Theo die when I might have saved him. But it was his choice after all, to work for those evil men, and he lied to me, he pretended to love me and… *oh god*. I can't hide anymore. If I don't fight back, I'll rot in prison and that can't happen – I won't allow it to happen.

'Come on Rebecca, or Sarah or whoever the hell you want to be today,' I hiss to myself. I feel myself drawn back into my body as my spirit ignites at last, like the pilot light in a dodgy boiler. It's time to fight back and not just bow under the pressure. I won't go to jail, and I won't let the brothers get away with this. Gene and Michael have to pay for what they've done to Theo, to me, and to my Drew. My poor beautiful boy… they tempted him, they corrupted him, and finally they killed him. But I think their worst crime was that, for the last fifteen years, I've believed that he abandoned me, but now I know that he was coming to get me. My Drew was coming for me, and he sent me the key to what happened, to where the money went – *Aberdeen*. I think his plan was to get the money and then run away with me, but they stopped that. They have stolen fifteen years from me, they stole my one true love from me – and they have to pay.

I have what they want, the clue to their lost treasure. I have it, but I'm not giving it up to them. If I do, they'll have won, and I bet they'd still leave me to rot in prison. So I won't give them the clue, instead I'm going to follow where it leads. I'll find the money and then I'll lay a trap for them. They will pay for all of this, I swear it.

The siren is loud now. I hear police officers arrive and push at the front door. I might have a clue to find the money, but I'm still trapped in this room with a dead body. I need a plan to get ou—

There's a crash, as the front door is broken down and officers rush into the house.

How do I get out of this?

Chapter Five

Back to the Beginning

This is my earliest memory.

I was little, I think I was about three or maybe four years old. Back then I went to a nursery a couple of days a week, so my mum could go shopping and get her errands done. She'd drop me there at nine a.m. and collect me at noon. She'd always turn up with lunch, which was either a cheese and pickle or Marmite sandwich, and a Club biscuit. Sometimes it was an orange one, but I was always happiest when it was a mint Club. Plus, there would be a little bottle of squash. We'd go over to the park, opposite the nursery. She'd sit on a bench, I'd sit on the grass, and we'd eat together, as I told her what I'd been doing that morning. Afterwards, we'd walk back home, past the little boating lake, where we usually stopped to feed a stale slice of bread to the ducks (they say that's wrong nowadays, but the ducks always loved it back in the day) and when we got home my mum would let me watch an hour of something on TV.

Though I should confess here and now, that most of that isn't from my memory, at least, not really – it's mostly stitched together from talking to Mum later on, after I'd started school. I always loved to hear stories about baby me, toddler me, and little kid me. I don't actually recall the day-to-day events from those early years, but I do remember the feeling of safety and of always being loved by my mum. Back then I wasn't afraid – not like later – and maybe that's why my first *real* memory isn't of my mum, but of the day my dad collected me from nursery instead. I remember that, as it's been branded onto my brain. That was the beginning – when I learned to escape.

-

My mum had dropped me at nursery that morning as normal. There was no sign that the day was going to get messed up, and there was no message to the teacher to say anything was going to be different. But just before noon, my father rushed in. He looked around wildly for me (he didn't know the layout of the room as he'd never been there before) and when he saw me he huffed, like I should have been ready to go that second. Grabbing my hand, he pulled me off the floor. He told me to get my coat and yanked me out of there – *I'm in a hurry*, he snapped. He was always in a hurry. He was a busy man, as he often told us.

He had no lunch packed for me, not even a bag of crisps. And we didn't walk home because he had the car. *Time is money*, he used to say. He put me in the back. We didn't have a car seat or anything, so I was wedged in place with his briefcase, so I wouldn't slide around. Riding in the car was a real treat – I loved opening the window and feeling the rush of the wind on my face; I loved seeing cars whizz by, especially brightly coloured ones. That morning I was so excited by the novelty of seeing my dad in the daytime, as well as a rare trip in the car, I started singing – *a million bottles of beer on the wall, a million bottles of beer, take one down and pass it around*… you know the song. We had just learned it at nursery (I doubt they say beer these days, maybe it's ninety-nine cartons of juice on the wall) and I was giddy with the thrill of singing for my dad. I couldn't really count back then, so I was just plucking numbers at random – eight beers, a million beers, three hundred beers, it didn't matter because I was happy and was showing off how clever I was with these big numbers. I sang at the top of my lungs.

'A thousand bottles of—'

His fist swung from the front and smashed into my cheek. I felt his ring cut me deep; there was warm wet blood on my face. There was a second of shock – and then snot and wailing and tears.

'Don't you dare cry,' my dad yelled at me. He waved the fist again and lashed out. He didn't look back – kept his eyes firmly on the road ahead like an excellent driver should – so this second punch just hit my shoulder, as I tried to squirm away from him.

'You deserved that. Don't bloody cry. I don't want to hear a peep out of you, not now and not ever. Kids must do what they're told, keep quiet and stay out of grown-ups' way. I don't want to see you and I don't want to hear you, you got that? If you wilfully disobey that rule you will get hit again – and again. Do you understand me?'

I nodded, scared, and all that time he still looked straight ahead, watching the road. He never turned his head, but I could see his face in the mirror. It was red and fierce like a tiger – not friendly, like the one who came to tea, but like one in the jungle who would bite your head off. From that moment on I was always afraid of my father. He demanded I stop crying, but the only way to stop the tears was to escape. So, in that car, with my body trembling and blood on my face, I tucked my chin into my chest and imagined folding in on myself, like the paper we folded and folded at nursery, until it was barely there. I did that – inside, I became smaller and smaller and smaller and smaller until I was the size of an atom – even smaller than an atom, the size of the human soul – and then I could leave my body and feel none of the pain, or loss, or hurt. None of the blows that rained down on my skin that day or over the subsequent years could touch me; not after I learned to become smaller than small. Then I was free.

–

Over the next few years, my ability to escape my body was like my superpower, as my dad was never a *spare the rod* kind of man. But his real brutality was always saved for my mum, and she protected me as much as possible from his anger, until she couldn't anymore.

She said *sorry*, in the hospice – she said sorry, but that was all she said, because there were nurses around and she was a very private woman. But I knew what she meant. Sorry for leaving me alone with *him*.

My dad had always been authoritarian, but when Mum died it got even worse as he found God. And it wasn't your nice, fuzzy, love-thy-neighbour God. No, my dad got all excited by the fire and brimstone. His kind of God demanded an eye for an eye and that you smite everyone different to you. I was twelve years old (and tiny) and mourning my mum, and he got angrier and more Old Testament every day. I was getting my mouth washed out with soap (literally) three or four times a week, and I was being grounded so much that if I laid it end to end, it would stretch into my thirties. I was also getting the strap most days. He'd hit me on my backside and my thighs. He said he had to beat the beast out of me, and he tried. He beat me so hard, but I would escape it. I'd fold, leave my body, and watch him hit me as I floated above his head. I hated him. I wished he was dead.

I was lonely, I was scared, and life got even more screwed up when, about a month after Mum died, I got my period. I couldn't tell my dad. Of course we had no sanitary towels in the house, so I had to wodge up toilet paper. I couldn't talk to anybody about what was happening and I was full of hormones whipping around inside me (worse than a werewolf during a full moon) and I felt so alone. I couldn't get close to people, I didn't really have any friends, not with my dad like he was. I kept to myself at school and didn't go to clubs or play sports or anything. I didn't want anyone ever coming to my house and seeing him. I didn't want to have to explain him to anyone, make excuses for him. I didn't want people to pity me.

I was a classic loner, and it made for a hellish few years, until I was sixteen, and I knew I couldn't bear it much longer, I had to get out. I thought there was only one thing to do – to get pregnant. Then I'd tell my dad, and either he would kill me (I guessed that was about thirty per cent likely) or he would force a shotgun wedding (about sixty per cent likely). The final ten-per-cent scenario was a shotgun wedding first, and then he'd kill me after.

The plan was that I would start dressing like... you know, provocatively. Making sure the boys knew I was up for anything. It scared me – I didn't want to make it seem that I was *easy* – but staying in this house with my dad scared me even more. I could cope with being a social pariah, talked about like I was a slut, as long as I could get free of him and away from the beatings.

On my calendar I drew a big circle around September sixth, the first day back at school; that was when the endgame would begin. I'd have a final few weeks as a child, before getting pregnant and having a kid – oh yeah, I planned on keeping my child. I hated my dad, I desperately wanted to be free of him, but I also wanted to be loved. I knew that whoever got me pregnant wasn't going to stick around – and I didn't actually want them to. I just wanted to get away from my dad... and have a kid to love, and be loved by. That was it, just a simple plan. Just simple.

But you know, the best laid plans, they can crash and burn. That's what happened on the first day back at school. There was a new kid – Drew Anthony – and he was Brad Pitt and Orlando Bloom (with some bad-boy Johnny Depp) all smooshed together in one knock-out, hunka hunka burning love. I had read about sex appeal, I had even seen it at the cinema and in the pages of swanky magazines I was never allowed to buy (they had them in the library), but I'd never seen it in real life. Not in my town, and definitely not sitting in my classroom, just three seats away from me.

It was love at first sight. I think I even squealed, like an over-excited guinea pig, when the teacher introduced him to the class. And you'd think that would be perfect for my plan – but it wasn't. In the plan I was going to go all super-skank and see who took the bait, but now I wanted *him* and nobody else, and there was no way I was going to slut-up for *him*. Not for Drew Anthony. I wanted to win him with my sparkling personality and charm and not just sleaze myself into his pants. I loved him... and of course

64

that's great – we all know that love is all you need, that it conquers all, and you can soar higher than a seagull – but the awful truth was that I didn't know if I actually had a sparkling personality, because how charming can you be when you're brought up to be seen and not heard. But the worst thing was that I wasn't the only one besotted by him. Every other girl in school was drooling like an idiot too, and smarming around him like bees on a dropped ice-cream cone. How was I going to win the most beautiful boy in the world, when every girl at school had the same idea (I'm guessing that the sales of Wonderbras in Salford went through the roof that summer)?

I had no clue. I practised looking alluring and interesting in the mirror (I'm not sure I ever managed it) and I followed him around school, waiting for any opportunity to get noticed. I sat close to him at lunch and sometimes just broke out in wild laughter, hoping he'd look over and see how captivating I was. I bought nerdy glasses (with clear glass in), so I could take them off and flash my seductive eyes at him – right at the moment he looked at me across a crowded room – but I don't think he ever looked directly at me. And then the worst thing happened… the apocalypse… after only five days at our school, he started dating Lara Travers, who was the prettiest girl in our year. I was destroyed. I bet she didn't practise writing *Mrs D Anthony* every night, and hadn't covered an entire exercise book with pictures of wedding dresses and hearts that said: *AD loves RW TRUE*. It was awful. In class, I watched him every second. I knew it was bad, but I couldn't stop. I loved him. Argh. I loved Drew bloody teen heart-throb Anthony.

Sweet huh? True love you might think, because you know we did marry in the end? But no, it was stupid.

Let me tell you that this is not a happy-ever-after love story; unless it's in the tragic Romeo and Juliet tradition with dead teens everywhere – or the Bonnie Parker and Clyde Barrow dying-in-a-hail-of-bullets happy ending. Our love story is one of those messed-up ones. When he started dating Lara, I realised that plan A had failed, so I moved to plan B – to kidnap Drew Anthony's dog.

I went to a supermarket and bought meat (actual steak was way too expensive so I got two packs of 'family-style' sausages from the discount aisle). I went to Drew's house and lured the pooch back to my place with the sausages. Don't worry, the dog wasn't harmed, he was only there for a few hours. I rang Drew and told him I'd found his dog and he should come and get him at six fifteen p.m – it had to be when my dad was getting home from work, and that was always at six twenty-five p.m. every day like clockwork. And when he walked through that door he expected food on the table, just like he had when Mum was alive. I was his skivvy, his cook and his cleaner, as well as going to school. I was his daughter and his wife – I had to get out.

So this is what happened: on the dot, at six fifteen, the doorbell rang. I answered it wearing only a dressing gown.

'Oh it's you,' Drew said. He seemed surprised when he saw me, even though I'd told him my name on the phone. 'I didn't figure you for a dog-napper.'

'Come in,' I said. In my head it was kinda sultry and provocative, but it probably just sounded like an insane teenager babbling.

'No thanks, I just want Buster.'

'Buster? What kind of lame name is that for a dog?'

'It's a classic.'

'If by *classic* you mean unoriginal – then I guess you got that right.'

He frowned at me. 'Why do you have my dog anyway?'

'I stole him.' I crossed my arms, giving him a hard stare.

'Why?'

'To get you here.'

'Why?'

'Sex.' I cringed inside. It did not sound sexy in any way. I just hoped he wasn't going to laugh at me.

'Is this some kind of prank, are there hidden cameras?' He laughed and looked around.

'No.' Shame suddenly burned through me; he didn't even know who I was, and having sex with me would be a *prank*. I felt like such an idiot. 'I'm sorry, Drew, this was dumb.' My face turned beet red. 'I'll get Buster.' I turned around and went inside. In my bedroom Buster was sitting calm as you like and wagging his tail. He'd finished the sausages.

'He likes you,' Drew said and I turned to find him behind me. He must have followed me in. At that exact second, the front door opened and my dad walked in. *Okay – it's now or never*, I thought. I dropped my robe, I was butt naked underneath, and I called out as loud as I could.

'You can come round and fuck me anytime you like, just make sure my dad's at work.'

Drew looked horrified, as my dad rushed in. Without breaking stride my dad pulled his hand back and punched me in the face, sending me reeling into the wall, hitting my head hard enough that blood smeared my face.

'I am going to—' my dad started, but Drew stepped in his way and pushed him back. No matter how angry my dad was, he was still a thin and weedy man, and he couldn't get past Drew.

'You need to calm down man,' Drew told him.

'She's a sinner. There's a demon in her,' my dad yelled, like a televangelist on steroids, but no matter how he tried to squirm past Drew, he couldn't. He just got angrier and angrier. I could see the veins stand out like ropes on his head and his neck. 'You are going to Hell my girl... to *Hell*.' He turned purple with rage and then... *pop*. Something exploded in my dad's head and he wasn't in his body anymore, but he hadn't folded himself into nothing, like I did. He'd just blown himself out, like a candle. His soul just exploded with anger, and he was gone.

'Oh shit,' Drew yelped as my dad crumpled to the floor, stone dead.

—

The police didn't ask anything, not even about my head. I had a story all worked out, but I never had to tell it. They accepted the fact that my dad just dropped dead. Boom.

'An embolism,' the doctor said later. The layman's description: something in his head just went *boom* and he was dead in a second. 'Probably caused by some intense stress or strain,' the doctor nodded.

'Really?' I said. 'But he was such a calm man.'

—

I was left an orphan, but I had the house and a pot of money from my dad's life insurance. It was an under-achieving, never-going-to-university kid's dream come true. Two kids actually, as I married Drew Anthony the moment it was legal. Total love story, love really did conquer everything, but to be honest, I don't know if he really loved me. I certainly loved him, but I don't know that he ever considered love and what it meant. We were bonded by my dad's death, tied up in the secrets and lies of it all, and we had no one to talk to except each other. It was so bloody exciting, and scary because if either of us even hinted at anything being wrong, then both of us would get caught. Dad's death tied us together, brought us close. But the most important thing that bonded us was the life insurance money and what it allowed us to do for five years: not work, eat take-aways and play video games. Drew was happy to leave his irritating sister and deadbeat parents and move in with me and get married. We had a good time and we laughed a lot, and the sex was always lovely. God, it really was. I hoped I might get pregnant but it didn't happen. And maybe that was for the best. Drew was nowhere close to being ready to be a dad, and me... I was still just a kid really. A messed-up kid at that.

The insurance money lasted a good time, but when it ran out we had to get jobs. I didn't care what I did as long as I was with Drew; he was my patricidal Disney prince. It was great while it lasted, but after the nest-egg was gone, he started to get antsy. He felt a little trapped and he hated the crappy jobs he got. None of them lasted very long, because neither of us had taken school seriously after dad died, so all we found was low-skilled and badly paid work. I didn't care, I was happy, but Drew didn't want that life. He signed up to loads of recruitment agencies, he lied about what experience he had, and bought forged GCSE certificates online. That was how he managed to get the bank job, even though he hadn't even taken his Maths GCSE at school. And that was when it all fell apart. When it crashed down on us. When he met the Vincent brothers.

Chapter Six

Monday: Now

Do you know that hamsters can fold their spines back on themselves, so they can turn around in the tightest of spaces? Humans can't. That's why I'm in so much pain, as I've folded myself into my pull-along suitcase. If someone else had hurt me like this, I'd have escaped my body, avoided all the agony, but I've done this to myself, so there's no big bad wolf to run from. I have to take the punishment.

I guess my case looked way too small to hold anyone, so none of the officers thought to look inside, even though they wondered about the *second* bag. They talked about it, they knew that two people arrived, and that the other person was a woman. *She's put toiletries in the bathroom and her clothes are in the wardrobe and on the floor by the bed…* they'd said. *But where was she?* They had no idea, and all I could do was hold my breath and lie still, folded in half, like an origami corpse, while they walked around me. I almost screamed in terror, when someone stuck a metal pin through the side of the bag and almost stabbed me… but I didn't, I kept quiet.

And now the police have finally left, after bagging their samples, taking about a billion photographs, and then removing Theo's body. Once the murder room was secure, they taped up the front door and all lower ground windows and positioned a lowly constable to stand on the doorstep, until the next shift takes over. I hear him, tramping about on the front step trying to keep warm. I hope they gave him a thermos of tea or coffee or something, as it must be freezing out there. Then I heard the officers load all their stuff, and themselves, into cars and vans and leave.

For the first time tonight, the place is silent.

I move and… *Arrgh*… I whimper from the pain, as I force my muscles to work again. Slowly, breathing through the agony, I manage to poke a fingernail into the metal mesh and slowly inch the zip along, until there's enough of an opening for me to slide through, out into the darkened room and onto the floor.

'Oh my god…' I moan, all twisted like a Barbie doll with its head turned all the way around. I beg the blood to circulate round my body again. I've got pins and needles to crucifixion level (sorry Catholics) but I have to move. I part roll, part crawl over to the bed and use it to get me up. I shake with the effort of standing. My feet and legs hurt so much, I don't know if I can do this – but if I'm staying free, I have to move. I've only got a short time before the police return; but I have a plan.

That's the only good thing about lying scrunched in a suitcase for hours; you get time to think and scheme, and finally I have something to tell me what happened all those years ago. I have a clue to what Drew did, why he did it, and why he had to die for it. Before tonight I had no idea about where the money was, but Gene said that my husband hired a car in Aberdeen, and that's the key. I have something now, I can get to the money and… and what? I could use it to get away, buy a fake passport and hide somewhere exotic. Or I could give the money back to the bank to clear Drew's name, or give it to Theo's family and... *Theo*. I'm still covered in his blood, though it's dry and stale now. I am ashamed of myself because, even though I have silently wept for hours tonight, none of my tears have been for him. He died because of me, but I haven't cried for him. He lied to me, and betrayed me, but he was a human being and he died in front of me and... I had liked him. I'd started to care for him, maybe that would have grown into love... but it was all wrong, a lie, because I'd started to fall for a man who didn't exist. I didn't know the real Theo. *Christ*, I don't even know if that was his real name, he could have been a Bill or a Tom. I have no idea how deep the lies go. I swallowed them all, hook, line and sinker – *Jesus, how dumb am I?* But I can't stay stupid, I have to be smart if I'm going to keep ahead of both the police and the brothers. I have to think clearly now. I have to... breathe... and then I have to get away from here. I can do this.

I need to get dressed. When the police arrived earlier, I just had a few seconds after I came back into my body, to dump the clothes out of my case and get into it. I don't know if the officers have moved anything, so all I can do is inch my hands across the floor, patting the wood until... *yes*. I find what I think are a pair of leggings, a T-shirt and a thin hoody. My shoes are downstairs, and there's no way I'm going down there to retrieve them, so I guess I'll be going barefoot for a while. I dress in the dark, listening to the quiet in the room. It's so still; you'd have no idea a man was brutally murdered in here just a few hours ago.

The policeman standing guard on the doorstep means I have to be quiet as a mouse, and getting out of the house will be difficult with him there. I know all the windows are barred and locked – Michael and Gene did that before they left – so there's no *regular* way out. But I have my plan, to go up, into the loft. I saw it in the hallway when we arrived, a hatch in the ceiling that must lead into a loft or attic space. That's my escape route, though when I step into the upstairs hallway it's so dark I can't see a thing. This is going to be much more difficult than I thought. *Okay – first step.*

There's a chair in the corner of the bedroom, I remember it from earlier, so I do my blind zombie walk, arms outstretched, until my fingers find it, and I take it out into the hall. Damn, it's dark and I don't know where the hatch is, so how the hell do I put the chair under it? *Jesus Christ* – I start to get angry. I have to calm down, or I'm lost. I stand in the dark hallway, trying to recall the layout of the floor and how close the hatch was to the stairs and… eenie, meenie, miney, chair. I put it down, but it's just a guess.

I stand on it and reach up, stretching as tall as I possibly can (which, given my height, isn't that high) and I can just manage to touch the ceiling with my fingertips. I let them do the walking, stretching them out as far as I can and—

'Arrgh—' I half scream, but bite it down, as the chair tips back and my heart jumps into my throat. *Jesus…* I throw myself forward, and just manage to wobble the chair back into place. My heart hammers in my chest. This is crazy. I could have fallen and broken my neck. As I get down off the chair, my legs are like jelly. I sit on it and I start to cry. This isn't fair. This isn't right.

You stupid, evil child. I hear my dad in my head. *You can't do anything right, no wonder you're alone. No wonder everyone you ever loved has died and—*

'Shut up, Dad,' I hiss. 'I don't need your nagging and negativity now.' Inside I feel a cheap thrill; saying *shut up* to my dad makes me feel like an outlaw.

I move the chair a foot or so and get back onto it. On tiptoe at full stretch, the pads of my fingers feel the rough Artex of the ceiling. Maybe I'm wrong, maybe I didn't see a hatch, maybe I imag— Ha. There it is. I feel the catch, I was right. I push with all my might, but the damn thing won't give.

'Arghhhhhhhh,' I moan softly as I push again, so hard that my arm spasms, but the bloody thing won't budge. It's probably been painted shut. Maybe it's had fifty coats slapped over it and nobody could shift it. *Damn.* I reach up and try to loosen it by moving it the other way and—

'*Fu*—' The hatch falls away and the ladder hits me in the chest. I fall back, the ladder falling with me and smacking me to the ground. The chair flies out from under me, and clatters down the stairs, making enough noise to wake the dead. *Shit. Shit, bloody shit.*

There's a crackle of static from a police radio, as the officer on guard outside is reporting back to base. I can't hear what he's saying, but it's pretty bloody obvious isn't it? He's telling them about the commotion inside the house. I'm busted. I don't have any time, I'm going to get caught. I push the ladder off me and guide it down to the floor.

Screech – I hear the crime scene tape being ripped off the front door. *Jesus Christ.* I clamber up the ladder and into the black maw of the loft. It smells of mould and rot, the air full of dust that catches in my throat. I want to cough but I mustn't. *Silence.* Behind me I pull the ladder back up, as the front door opens and a torch beam lights up the rooms downstairs.

'Who's there?' the policeman calls and the torch beam jags ahead of him, lighting the upturned chair.

Oh my god. My heart thumps as I slide the ladder into place behind me. I have to close the hatch too, but I can't see it; it's hanging down into the hallway like a giant billboard reading: *the killer's in the loft.* Oh my god. I'm going to get caught.

'I know someone's there,' the policeman yells from the foot of the stairs. I anchor my foot in the top rung of the ladder and lean out, feeling every muscle threaten to tear in half. I reach into the darkness, desperately feeling around for the hatch, as a footstep clunks on the stair and echoes up towards me like a gun being cocked. He's coming upstairs.

'Show yourself,' he yells and the torch beam spills up the stairs like a spotlight. All he has to do is get halfway up, and he'll see me hanging out of the ceiling. Where the hell is the hatch? I flail about, my shoulder nearly dislocating. If the light catches me, he'll see me any second, there's no time. No time at all.

'Arrgh,' I groan as my fingers find the edge of wood, just as the top of his head rises above the top step. I will be caught if I can't... my stomach muscles burn as I flip back into the crawl space, bringing the hatch up with me, but I can't lock it in place. I strain to hold it as close to the ceiling as possible. My fingers are curled around it, visible if he looks up... *Please God, don't let him see me.* I hold my breath.

'I know you're here,' the officer calls, as his radio crackles.

'Don't enter the premises until back-up arrives.' A voice is barely audible through the static.

'I'm already inside, guv, there's a chair on the floor downstairs that wasn't there bef—'

'Get out and wait for back-up, Stevie. It's on its way. It'll be three minutes.'

'But guv I'm in here and—'

'Now,' the voice orders him.

'Okay,' he responds petulantly and backs down the stairs, still swinging the torch beam like a searchlight in a prison breakout. In the distance I hear a siren; the back-up is almost here. Officer Stevie mumbles something that sounds very vulgar about his DI copulating with farmyard animals, and then the front door slams closed. I have a couple of minutes if I'm lucky. *Christ*.

I pull the hatch into position and manage to slide the lock into place. Maybe I've just got out of the frying pan and jumped into the fire. The police will be here in minutes, and this time they know that someone is in the house. They'll crawl over every inch of the place. I can't hide; that won't work this time. My only chance is to run. I have to get out now. *Oh my god*.

On my hands and knees I scuttle into the dark until I reach a wall. I feel the surface. It's brick. Okay. This is the biggest gamble of my life, but I can do it. Drew's Uncle Dan was a burglar, though he wasn't a master criminal, as he spent most of his twenties and thirties in prison. But the one Christmas he was out, and not at Her Majesty's pleasure, he came for Christmas dinner and entertained us with his stories of how he broke into places. He would find empty terraced houses, where people had moved out to go overseas or the owner had died, leaving the place vacant. They were easy to get into, sometimes the doors weren't even locked, but they weren't his real target. No, he planned to rob the neighbouring houses. He would go up into the loft of the empty house; he said that at least half of them had a shared loft, or maybe there'd just be a cheap plywood wall that separated one loft from another. Then he'd crawl into the loft next door and wait for that family to leave. Once they were out, he'd go down the ladder, steal what he wanted, and then go back into the loft and squeeze through into next door. Then it was easy to get away from an empty house, and if he was stopped he'd just say he was an estate agent in to assess the place. He could rob entire streets of houses sometimes, because they were all linked. That's what I'm banking on – what I'm gambling my life on now – that I can get into next door's house and run from there. *Wish me luck, Uncle Dan.*

Outside the house, I hear a police car stop, and at least one officer gets out and talks to the man on guard. *Come on, faster.* I find the central beam and trace my hands along it and touch a wall, but this one isn't rough – it isn't brick. I run my fingers up it. It's wood and – yes – it doesn't go all the way to the top. I grab the lip and haul myself up, just about managing to squeeze myself over the partition and into next door's loft. I can't believe how easy that was. *Thanks, Uncle Dan.*

From the house I just left, I can hear policemen enter and start to search. I could stay up here, but maybe the police will cordon off the street now they know the killer is somewhere close. I have to run straight away, while I have the chance, before more police arrive. It's the middle of the night, so I'm hoping that whoever lives here is asleep, but with the police sirens blaring, they might get woken at any moment. Either way, I have to take my chances now.

I crawl through the loft and try to find the ladder, hoping that this house is set up in pretty much the same way as next door is. And… yes, I'm lucky – as I find the ladder in the same place, and it's the same mechanism. My fingers find the hatch and I slide the catch back as softly as I can. It's in a better state of repair than next door and the hatch opens easily. Slowly, I lower it. I can't trust the ladder, so I wriggle my legs into fresh air and stretch out as far as possible, holding onto the lip of the hatch – I want to shout *Geronimo*, but someone might hear – so I just let go and drop into the darkness. It isn't far, just a few inches, so it's pretty easy, but I do have to leave the hatch open as there's no way that I can close it without one of those stick things that people use.

What now? I don't think the front door helps me, as it's right next to the entrance of the murder house. There'll still be an officer on guard, and more police will arrive soon. Maybe there's a back way out, but I think a first-floor window at the back of the house is probably best. I try and recall the room layout next door. There was the main bedroom, off to the right, and there was another room on the left, maybe another bedroom. In the distance I hear another siren that gets louder and louder and—

Click.

A light flicks on in one of the rooms. I see a band of light at the foot of the door. *Damn*, the police siren woke someone. I have to take a risk if I'm going to get out of here alive. I put my hand out to the door handle of the other bedroom door and twist it. The door opens quietly, but inside it's pitch black. There's no other way out, so I shuffle inside the room, closing the door and plunging into utter darkness.

A soft snore vibrates through the room, and there's a stale sweaty smell like a second-rate gym in the summer. The curtains have been pulled together, but as my eyes get used to the black, I can see that there's a zig-zag of light where they don't completely meet. Maybe I can get out of the window without waking the snoring man. I head towards the thin band of light. I'm going to have to hope that the window opens when I get to it and—

'The bloody police are back next door,' someone shouts from the hallway. *Shit*. I panic, and as I stumble forward, my foot gets caught in something and I trip.

'There's at least four coppers next door,' the man in the hall shouts. 'Something's up. You need to wake up, Gene.'

What? I'm suddenly cold as ice, as I lie on the floor, tangled up in clothes. He said *Gene*.

'Get up, the police are here.' The man in the hallway yells again and then I hear him stomp downstairs. The figure in the bed sits up, he moans a little and stretches. His face tips into the zig-zag of light, and Gene Vincent yawns and then shouts for his brother.

'Go out and see what's up, Michael. I'll be there in a minute.'

Oh god… I want to fold away, to escape… but if I do that then they'll find me. They'll turn me over to the police and… I have to stay in my body. I have to chance the pain and face the fear.

Gene Vincent slides out of bed. His foot almost kicks me, and I back away quietly. If he turns a light on then I'm sunk. I push myself into the floor – I want it to swallow me up. Theo had said they were listening to us, but I never thought for a second they'd be next door. No wonder they arrived so soon after Theo blew his cover. They were here and listening to everything, maybe even watching, too. They might well have put cameras and mics in the walls or… *concentrate on the now*, I tell myself as Gene fumbles for something in the dark. *Please don't turn the light on…*

please just go, I beg whatever deity is out there… but as I already know – there is no God.

Click. He turns the light on. It burns like the sun, and I see Gene is naked. *Jesus Christ*. His legs are covered in scars, where flesh has been cut away. I guess that tumours have been removed, but the scars are so vivid, like they've been drawn in purple and red Sharpie pens. I see the catheter, and the bag that's strapped to his side collecting his urine. Behind him there is a shrine that covers an old Victorian fireplace and on it are rosaries and offerings to the pantheon of saints. It looks so out of place, in the room of a man who causes so much pain. But I can see from the scars that have eaten him away, that he knows more pain than I can imagine.

Then he turns and sees me on the floor, backing away from him, half covered in his clothes. He opens his mouth but nothing happens. He's shocked – rendered mute. Maybe he's trying to work out if this is all a bad dream or if I'm a ghost come to haunt him – like the Ghost of Christmas Yet to Come. I see total fear in his eyes. This moment of hesitation is all I have, I must make the most of it. I leap for the window. If it's locked I'm dead… *ugh*, I grunt as I twist the latch and push it open. I can make it. He's shocked, slow; if he moved right away he would get me but he doesn't… not quite. I'm halfway through the window when he lunges, his fingers latching around my left ankle, trying to drag me back inside.

'*Michael, come quick.*' Gene screams for his brother, then turns to me to spit: 'You aren't going anywhere, you bit—'

I kick out with all my might. My right foot catches him in the chin and he stumbles back, desperately trying to keep hold of me but he can't. He falls, hits the bed and bounces. I see bruises covering his arms, where a cannula has been placed time after time.

'Michael,' he yells again and jumps forward, but I'm out and onto the ledge. There's a gutter above me, and a rainwater pipe to the side. I reach forward to grab the gutter but as I look down – *oh god* – I freeze. There are sharp spiked railings below me; if I fall I will be shish-kebabed to death.

'Argh,' I yell as long bony fingers snag my hair and yank my head back. I'm on tiptoes, straining back like some crazy contortionist in a circus.

'Come inside or I'll let you fall,' he hisses.

I turn around to face him, as his brother storms into his room. 'What's up?' he calls and Gene turns to him with a gloating look of victory.

'I got her Michael, and she ain't gonna escape this time.'

He holds me tight, as I try and twist out of his hands, but it's futile. In a second, he'll drag me back through the window and throw me to the floor… and then they'll kill me. So I stop struggling and instead push myself into him, I slide my fingers into his belly and I rip.

'Noooo,' he screams as I tear at the strapping and the catheter bag flies out of the window and tumbles down into the street. The smell of piss is overwhelming as it spills down onto the railings. Gene has to let me go, as he tries to catch the rubber tube spiralling away from him. I pull away and jump for the drainpipe. I feel it crack as I hit it, and it shears off the wall and dips down, but slow enough that I can ride it down, like a camel bowing to the earth. I manage to jump just before it hits the ground and luckily for me, the grass is soft and I roll. Nothing broken. I'm filthy, but I'm alive.

Above me, I see the Vincent brothers in the window, both their faces are frozen in a rictus of murderous rage. Suddenly a light comes on – a security light or maybe a police searchlight – and traps me in its beam. I must look like a caged animal. I think I actually snarl at it, like a vampire in a seventies Hammer film, then I'm up, and I run. I run like the Devil is at my heels.

I used to run as a kid. I'd imagine my father was chasing me and I'd run like a tracer bullet. That's what I do now, even though I can feel my bare feet start to blister; I run like my life depends on it... and it probably does. I keep running and running. I have to get away from them. I have to stay free so I can get to London. And then on to Aberdeen. I run. I'm coming to find the truth. I promise you, Drew, I will find out what happened.

Chapter Seven

I don't know where to go, I'm all turned around. I ran, blindly, through these twisting streets, and now I don't know where I am and— *hell*, sirens, more bloody sirens. They seem to be coming from everywhere, all at the same time, bouncing off the walls and filling my head, so that I can't tell left from right or up from down. The police are searching for me, and Gene and Michael are hunting me. I have to run from them both, but I can't work out where anything is. I don't know this town. I don't know where to hide, or where to go. I don't even know what the bloody time is. How long do I have before the sun comes up and... I feel sick. From somewhere behind me I hear singing, and I see a naked woman flying in the air and—

'Oy, you, zombie. Show us your tits, zombie,' a group of men yell at me. It's a stag group with an inflatable sex doll that they're throwing up in the air like a balloon. '*Zombie, zombie, zombie – tits, tits, tits,*' they scream and laugh again, before they disappear down a side street. I'm shaking. What the hell is going on, is this real or am I in some nightmare? I want to stop, just sit down and cry... but I can't. If I stop, I'm dead. But where do I go... where the hell am I? I look around, this street isn't residential, it looks mostly touristy with closed businesses and shops. Are there cameras watching me? I look at the tops of streetlights – is that a camera? I don't know, this is crazy. Across the street I see a place that's all lit up, it's a take-away kebab place, I could ask for directions to the station... maybe... is that safe? I don't know, but I have to get away, leave Brighton... I need to get my bearings and... my stomach growls loud enough to wake the dead. I can't think when I last ate... but I don't have any money, I don't have anything. *Christ*, I need help, I need... Slowly, like a frightened animal, I walk towards the brightly lit kebab shop. Maybe I can beg, or promise to— but it doesn't matter anyway, because the door's locked and the *closed* sign is up on the door. I peer through the glass, all the way to the far wall, and I can see a clock that reads four thirty a.m. *Jesus*, no wonder everywhere's closed. There's only two hours until the sun rises. Two hours while I still have the darkness to hide in and... *oh Christ*... I catch my reflection in the glass and I see I'm covered in blood. No wonder those drunk idiots called me a zombie, I look like I just ate a football team. I have to get clean, wash the blood away. Which way is the sea?

From behind me there's a flashing light and a police car streaks past, going at about a hundred miles an hour, it must be heading towards the house Theo died in. So, if that's right – I turn myself around trying to remember the geography of the place – then that means the sea must be *that* way. I turn and run. My feet hurt so much, but that doesn't matter; this is life or death. My life. Or my death.

I turn down into a small gloomy street but at the end of it, I can see bright streetlights. I walk carefully through the darkness, and come out onto the coast road. I actually have to shield my eyes from the intense lights that illuminate four lanes of highway. And past that... *Christ* it's so dark, like I've reached the edge of the world and could just fall into space. There is absolutely nothing, but it must be the sea, as I can hear the lapping of the water. It sounds like a million kittens drinking from an enormous bowl of milk. I'm close – only four lanes of traffic covered by CCTV cameras to cross. Should I just go for it and hope they're blind… there can't be people watching this boring road live all night, can there? But it doesn't matter if there are, because the truth is that I'm covered in blood, and as soon as the sun comes up I'll be spotted and arrested. My priority has to be to get clean. I can't pretend to be a zombie forever. So I need to get to the beach and wash the blood off. *Okay, I can do this.* I drop my head, pull my hoodie up (in my head I yell *Geronimo*) and I run. I sprint as fast as I can, no matter what the blisters are doing. I fly across the four lanes of highway and hit the other side of the street. I vault the little wall onto the beach. The stones are cold and I step onto some slimy seaweed, but it feels good. I walk forward, following the in-and-out breath of the ocean. When my toes touch the water I stop. The salt burns my cut and blistered feet, and I strip off my clothes and leave them a little way up the beach. Then I go into the water and push down into it.

Oh my god, the cold feels like I'm being electrocuted; the pulse of the water surges into me, shocking me awake while it washes the blood off my skin and out of my hair. I feel alive again. Alive.

–

I drag myself out of the water. The salt fizzes in all the cuts and scrapes that cover my body, but in a good way; a healing kind of a way. I hope all the blood has gone. I wish I had some soap and shampoo, because I still feel dirty, but as long as I don't look like a reject from a 1980s slasher movie, I can survive the oncoming dawn. I can already see that the light is starting to change on the horizon. There has been a tiny drop of milk added to the espresso of the night. *Christ*, I can't remember the last time I stayed up all night, but the adrenaline and the cold water has charged me up again, like a battery. I'm wide awake, maybe the most awake I've been in fifteen years. The holy trinity of shock, fear and grief has kept me sleepwalking through life since I lost Drew, but tonight I'm wide awake again. And I'm angry.

I sit up. The cold is biting hard now. I have to think and plan and—

'Shit,' I hiss as a pulse of torchlight sprays across the pebbles. I shrink away, worried it'll be the police, but it isn't. It's only some drunk idiot with the light on his phone. He's looking for something, and then I see, down by the water, a body face-down in the swell. I think it's someone drowned and I almost scream, but then the drunk guy yells that he *found it*, and he runs down to pick up the inflatable sex doll. Then he trots away to find the other guys from the stag party.

It's funny, kind of, watching drunk young people as they meander along the promenade. I never really had that young and carefree lifestyle – boozy parties, playing spin the bottle, and talking drunken crap into the early hours of the morning. I lost the best years of my life... and I want Gene and Michael Vincent to pay for what they did to me – to Drew and me. I don't know if they truly corrupted my husband; I think he was already sold on the dream of *get rich quick* before he met them, but he wasn't a criminal. They made him that, and they have to be judged and punished for it. Plus – and this is the part that makes me most nervous – there's eight hundred and seventy-five thousand pounds hidden some place. I should find it and then… I'm not sure, but I'll be damned if the murdering brothers ever get to touch a single pound of it.

I put my clothes back on, having pretty much drip-dried while I've sat here thinking, but I have no shoes and Aberdeen's a hell of a long way. I also have no money, no phone and no transport. The police will find my finger-prints at the Airbnb and, at some point, they will work out who I am and start searching for me. *Christ*… I have to get away, but that's a lot bloody harder when you're barefoot and have blisters formed on top of other blisters that are sitting on top of even more blisters and… *hang on*. I see a sleeping bag, tucked under a bin on a concrete walkway ahead. I think for a second that it's been dumped, but then I see that there's a figure inside it. There are probably a lot of homeless people sleeping along this beach. I stop, level with him and… *huh*. Next to his pillow I can see a pair of boots. They'll be much too big for me, but I think I need them more than him, and if I'm quiet, I can just reach in and take them and… *No, what have I become?* I'm actually thinking about stealing from a homeless man, just hours after a man died because of me… because of—

And I can't stop them, snot and tears and choking, hacking sobs. They just explode out of me. They're so hard that I have to drop onto my haunches, and as I squat there with the tears and shame and guilt and anger rolling through me, I look straight into the homeless man's eyes. There's a tear in them too.

'Don't cry, kid, this isn't the worst. There's so much worse than this, take my word for it. Buck up, we're by the seaside.' And he gives me a gap-toothed, nicotine-stained smile. I nod back, unable to find a word to say and then he puts his head back down to sleep.

He's right though, this isn't the worst... I saw the sea for the first time yesterday and it was so beautiful. And just now I actually walked into it and let it wash the blood off my body. That's something they can never take away. And even if I'm scared out of my mind, I do have one thing I can hold in my heart: that after all these years I know that my Drew was murdered, and that he didn't leave me. He was coming back to get me. He sent me the key to unlock all this. He loved me. The old man is right, it could all be so much worse... and I do love to be beside the seaside.

'Thanks,' I say softly, but I think he's already drifted into sleep. I wish I could follow, but instead I have to walk. Barefoot. The blisters catch and bubble under my feet, but that's okay. I've coped with worse.

–

I get about a hundred yards farther on, and there's a whole mess of bins and giant recycling skips across the path. They've been pulled out of their regular places, and there's a lot of smashed glass on the walkway and spreading onto the rocks and stones. It looks really dangerous to walk on and... *Oh.* Right in front of me, leaning at a slightly drunken angle, is a fabric and shoe bin. Around it are loads of plastic bags of donations that have spilled out. I open three of them, finding nothing special, but in the fourth there's a kick-ass pair of cherry-red Doc Martens boots. Wow – they are so beautiful. I've always wanted a pair of DM's.

As I turn them over, I can see that the soles have been worn through in a couple of places, and the eyelets are broken, but they are still awesome shoes. I hope they fit? I put them on and... wow. My feet are small, but these are perfect. They have to be kids' shoes, or some pixie magic or something. I lace them up (I feel about a foot taller in them) and walk across the broken glass, hearing it snap under my feet. That's the good karma you get from not stealing off the homeless. With the tiniest spark of hope in my heart, I head towards the pier in the distance.

When I get close to it, I see a signpost that tells me where the railway station is. That will have to be my way out. A train is probably the easiest to sneak onto without paying. *Come on, shoe karma, stay with me* I think as I try to block out the idea that Gene or Michael will be at the station waiting for me.

'But they'll probably be ther—'

'Shut up,' I tell myself, and I turn inland and walk on.

Chapter Eight

My legs are shaking by the time I reach Brighton station, and I don't know if it's from the steep hill I've just climbed, or the fear that makes me bob my head around like a meerkat at the slightest noise or movement. It's still not quite dawn, but the sky is lightening. The train to London takes less than an hour, this is prime commuter belt, and the station is buzzing with the suit and briefcase brigade. It's a large station with a roof of glass and Victorian ironwork. It's like I'm in the belly of a massive steampunk whale that's swallowed me whole, making me feel like I'm Pinocchio's sister – desperate to be a real girl.

The concourse is large, but even so, I can't believe how many coffee places there are, and that each one of them has a queue snaking from it and out into the main station. As well as the queues of caffeine junkies, there are hundreds of other people, whizzing here and there, and most of them are holding giant coffees as well as bags and cases. It makes me feel nervous; they move so fast and in some dance that is both beautiful and frenetic – like a crazed tango – but nobody collides or crashes. I shrink down a little and bow my head. The anonymity of the crowd is good, makes me feel safe, and it's the best opportunity to make it onto a train, given that I have no money, so I can't buy a ticket.

The barriers stretch across one end of the concourse but there's only one guard there, helping people through with large cases and bikes. If I get into the slipstream of somebody going through, I can dodge the gate without paying – but I will have to hope no one sees me or makes a complaint. I'll only get one chance at this, so I should select the person wisely. I want someone thin and not too quick, maybe someone holding a bucket of coffee, as they won't want to jerk their arms about.

I flick my eyes across the queue at the coffee kiosk that's right in the centre of the concourse. It's all grey suits and turned down faces except… there's a kid. He's short, about the size of a ten-year-old, in faded jeans and an old T-shirt that may have once been black but is now fifty shades of grey. He's wearing a baseball cap that's pulled down over his face but, as I watch him, his head tips up and I can see he's actually older than I first thought, about fourteen. In that moment he turns to look at me and… his eyes are old, like he's seen terrible things in his short life. He's handsome and lean… and then he looks away from me and dips into the crowd. He moves like a dancer, or maybe a graceful cat, weaving through the crowd. I feel something gnaw at my stomach for a second, a memory of fear from when I was his age, a feeling of desperation – but it's quickly gone as my gaze progresses down the queue once again, and I forget the ancient-looking kid.

As my eyes reach the front of the snaking coffee queue, I see the perfect mark for me. He's turning away from the cashier, holding an enormous coffee in one hand and a bag of pastries in the other. He isn't as thin as I might have liked, but he's tall, and wears huge noise-cancelling headphones. I'll be able to slip in behind him and get through the barrier without him having any awareness of me. My eyes flick to the departures board and I see there's a train to London in four minutes. This is perfect. I step forward, matching my pace with my chosen target. My head only comes up to his armpits, and he doesn't turn as I fall in behind him. I'm three feet back and I can get in close as he reaches the ticket barrier and—

'You bloody idiot,' my tall man yells, as coffee arcs away from him and pastries rain down like manna from heaven.

'I'm sorry, let me…' The ancient-looking kid grabs a napkin off the floor and dabs at the man's suit, trying to clean away the coffee and Danish crumbs.

'That's… I mean… well… bloody…' The man's face is red and he looks like he'd explode at anyone else but he keeps a tight lid on his anger at a child.

'I'm so sorry…' The boy starts to cry. 'I was trying to get to my mum and—'

'No, no, that's fine. I'll dry off. It's okay. My train is ready to go so I'll…' and the man waves the kid aside and walks past him to the barrier. There's no way I can get in behind him now, and the kerfuffle has drawn a lot of eyes towards us. It isn't safe to try and breach the barrier with so many watching, so I'm stuck here until the next train. Damn it. I catch the eye of the kid as he starts to walk away. There's something wrong. For a start, he didn't look like the kind of kid who would cry like that, and why does he look so nervous now? I see he's still watching the man he ran into, and my eyes turn to look at him too, as he gets to the barrier and stops. He pats his pockets and then furiously starts to dig into them.

'Hey, my ticket… my wallet.' The tall man is stuck at the barrier, searching his pockets like a maniac. Then he swings around, his arm out and pointing right at the boy. 'That kid there, he stole my wallet.'

All the blood drains out of the boy's face and his lip quivers. I see the desperation in his eyes and I can also see that, tucked inside his sleeve, he has the tall man's wallet.

'Grab him, that little shit,' the tall man yells and I catch the movement of hi-vis jackets out of the corner of my eye. Transport police, all rushing towards the boy. There's no way he'll get away – not even Usain Bolt could make it out of here. I step forward, right into the path of the kid and I grab his arm and lean in to him. I hiss, 'Give me the wallet.' And I go to take it but he holds it firm. 'Push me away hard and then run,' I tell him.

'Hold him!' the tall man yells, and then the kid pushes me away with all his might, and takes off like a bat out of hell. I hit the floor and roll. I put a bit of extra oomph into it, so I really get out of the centre of the concourse as hands reach out from all over to grab the kid, but he's fast and slippery. For a second I think he might actually make it and get away, but then a mountain of a man steps out from nowhere and the kid crunches into him and falls to the ground, winded. Within seconds, the boy's been hauled up onto his feet by the crowd, and held tight as transport police rush to grab him.

'I ain't done anything,' the kid protests. 'I don't have anybody's money. I just knocked into him, I'm sorry.'

'Bloody refugee from the look of him, ain't English,' someone says behind me. 'Gangs use kids all the time, little crooks,' another voice says, as about a hundred people crowd around the child they think is suddenly wanted criminal number one.

I'm still on my back on the ground, but I slowly get up, as people pass me, and head into the centre to see the arrest. I take a furtive look, and can see that nobody's watching, and then I drop the wallet on the floor. I take a

94

few steps back and then walk normally, kicking the wallet into a small group ahead of me.

'He stole my wallet, he stole it,' the tall man is insisting. 'He needs to be charged. This is not something that warrants a mild slap on the wrist. He needs to feel the full weight of the law.' Someone cheers and others murmur their agreement. The transport police officer looks hassled and finally agrees to call the local police to get someone in from child services.

'At last, these hooligans need to be locked up and maybe even sent back to where—'

'Is this it?' a woman calls out and holds up the tall man's wallet from where I kicked it. 'It was on the floor here. A wallet.'

'I told you I ain't done nothing,' the kid says and tries to pull himself out of the policeman's grip, but the man holds him steady.

'Can you bring that here please?' the policeman asks and the woman walks over and hands the wallet to him. 'Is this your wallet?' he asks the tall man who turns a bright shade of purple.

'I… em…'

'Your *stolen* wallet?' the policeman asks, and the man drops his head, ashamed.

'I told you.' The kid pulls himself out of the policeman's hold and backs away. The officer hands the wallet back to the tall man and all around, people peel off and move back to the coffee shops or through the ticket barriers to wait for the next train. There is no apology. The tall man looks daggers at the kid, and then turns and walks towards the ticket barrier. I should probably wait an hour or so until all this has died down before I try and sneak onto a train. *Damn*, I feel vulnerable now. The crowd has thinned out, and if Michael and Gene are here they'll see me. I won't be able to get away from them. I look around, feeling my fear begin to mount, and I see the kid, and the anger in his face at what happened, but I also see the tremor in his hand; the fear that still quakes through him. He looks at me and frowns a little, like he can't account for what I did, though to be honest, neither can I. It has totally ruined my chance to escape on the early train, and now, through the Victorian arches, I can see the first shards of daylight slicing into the ground at the entrance. Soon the glass station will be filled with light and it will be harder to get away without—

'No,' I hiss to myself and kneel down, as if I'm pretending to re-tie my laces – but of course it's all so I can drop behind the row of seats and hide. I see Michael Vincent at the back entrance to the station. He hasn't seen me yet. He's level with the bank of ticket barriers, hidden behind the queue for Pret a Manger. I don't know how long he's been there, but if I had got to the barrier while he was there, he would have had the perfect view of me. If he sees me, what will he do? Follow me through and pull a knife on me, maybe even slide it in and twist it – I think he'd rather see me dead then get away from him a second time.

I dip down. I know he can't see me, but at the same time I can't get away. I'm trapped. I feel sick. I can see the transport police from here, maybe I should go and turn myself in to them. It would be better than being tort—

'What's up?' The kid stands behind me, his eyes slowly scanning the crowds ahead of me. 'Who d'you need to get away from?'

I don't turn round; I must not take my eyes off Michael Vincent, not for a second. 'The guy in the jeans and leather jacket, standing by Pret, and watching the ticket barrier.'

'Okay, I see him.' He nods. 'This is me paying back my debt. Okay?' and I hear him scuttle off. I watch Michael. I can see he's like a hawk, his eyes moving from person to person, looking out for me. They know that the train's the best option for me to leave by, but it isn't the only one. Gene might be at the coach station, as that would have been my other option, but it's harder to get on a bus without a ticket and a train is pretty easy. I hold my breath. My stomach grumbles with hunger. And then I see the kid. Somehow he's got past Michael and is in some kind of walkway that leads to the back of the station. I see him pause and then throw up his hands into the air as he shouts out: 'Daddy, Daddy. I knew you'd come on my birthday. I knew it.' He throws himself at Michael and wraps himself around his legs, burrowing his head into the man's stomach. It looks comical as Michael tries to lever the kid off him but the kid's arms are tight.

'I am not your fucking dad,' Michael yells and actually tries to pull the boy off him. In that moment, he loses sight of the barriers. I think about storming them, but I'm too scared to take the risk, and instead I rush for the exit. I have no idea where to go but I know I can't stay here. I have to get out and think. I have to get some air and—

'Well, well.' A hand grabs at my shirt and I look up into Gene Vincent's face.

'What a stroke of luck—'

'Stranger danger,' I scream. 'I don't want to see your puppies, and I won't show you my knickers.'

Gene drops me like he's been scalded. 'I don't—'

I pull back my fist and I punch with all my might. I punch him right in his private parts. He drops to the floor, tears already running down his face. From all around, concerned faces turn to me. 'You okay little girl?' someone asks, thinking from my height that I must be about ten, but I shake my head and I bolt, running as fast as I can through the entrance and down the hill. I have to get away... I have to.

'Here, over here,' the ancient-looking kid calls, and waves at me from across the street. I run towards him and follow him down a tiny alley at the back of the station and we disappear into the darkness.

Chapter Nine

My chest is heaving when we finally stop running and I can gasp for air. I am not fit, my god, I am sooo not fit. The kid reaches into his hoodie pocket and pulls out a half-smoked cigarette and lights it. The smoke makes me want to vomit, but he's calmed by it. I want to tell him not to smoke, that it kills, but you can't tell people what to do. I'm not like my dad. Instead, I cough and retch for a few seconds and then sit on a wall and look around. We're in a square with a little grassed area in the centre and two concrete table-tennis tables. On every wall surrounding us there is the most vibrant graffiti. There's Alien fighting Ripley on one wall, and on another there's some weird crocodile creature with a jewelled crown and gold teeth that gleam in the morning light. On another wall are superheroes, and a parade of dogs, and then some kind of cute Japanese garden. It looks more like an art gallery than a square in a city.

'Thank you,' I manage to tell the kid, before another round of coughing and retching hits me. He doesn't reply, he just watches the alleyway we came out of. I guess he's worried that we were followed.

'You got any money?' he asks after he's finished the cigarette and flicked the butt into the gutter.

'No, nothing. I'm sorry.'

He scowls.

'Those men—' I start to tell him what happened, but he shakes his head and goes to walk away. I don't know what to do, so I follow him.

'My name is—' I start.

'Don't care,' he calls back over his shoulder. 'Have you eaten?'

'Not since yesterday morning,' I tell him as I follow his back into another alleyway that opens up into another little graffiti-art square. On one side is a jerk-chicken stall, but it's way too early for that to be open, and on the other side is the back of an Aldi supermarket.

'There might be something for us in here,' he says. He pulls a crate over to the large skip-sized bin and stands on it, so he can peer over the edge into the bin. He frowns and then leans over and slides his hands inside and rummages around. 'Nothing good,' he says and jumps down. His arms are a little wet now, and there's a smell of rotting food coming off him.

He turns away from me, and trudges on, towards a church that's nestled into a triangle where two roads meet. I look up at the church, which is incredibly tall, with wonderful stained-glass windows that stretch into the sky. The kid heads to the front door, but as he pushes at it, nothing moves. It's locked; must be too early for sanctuary. Then he heads around to the side, where there's a small window. He stretches up on his tiptoes and pushes at the glass, which swings open. He puts his hands onto the ledge and pulls himself up; he's strong, even though he doesn't look it. He holds out his hand to pull me up too but I hesitate.

'It's a church,' I hiss.

'There's a food bank inside.'

'That's for really poor people.'

He looks at me, like I said the funniest thing ever. 'There ain't no one poorer than me, and you said you ain't got no money.' He laughs and then offers his hand one more time, and I take it and he helps me through the window. There's no light in here but the daylight makes the stained glass glow a little, so we can see something of the interior. The church isn't that fancy inside, but it does have really nice carved pews and there's a makeshift stage at the front with boxes and boxes of dried food on it.

'There's some fresh stuff at the side,' he tells me and we find a box of sandwiches and some crisps and oat bars. He fills his pockets. I take a cheese and pickle sandwich, and a packet of cheese and onion crisps. I feel bad, as I don't like stealing from a church. It feels like I should get hit by a lightning bolt or something. As I pocket the food, I straighten up and look directly into the face of a vicar, who is standing in the aisle watching us, a look of pity on his face. I feel my stomach shrivel.

'I'm sorry…' I start to make an excuse but he shakes his head at me, with such abject disappointment, that I can only drop my head and mumble another apology. I feel awful.

'Come on,' the kid says and takes my hand gently and pulls me away. We head up the aisle to the front doors and he pushes the emergency exit bar and we're out on the street again. I want to curl up and die.

'I'm leaving you here,' the kid says and drops my hand.

'No.' I feel panic surge; I need his help. 'Please, I just need somewhere to rest and think. I haven't slept in two days, please. I'll go once it gets dark. I can't do this alone.'

'I'm sorry, but no one gets to see where I live.'

'But you owe me.'

'The debt was paid.'

'Please… a few hours. Please. I don't know Brighton at all, I have no idea where to go. I would never tell anyone where you are – and I'll be gone from the city tonight. I need to lay low for a while, a few hours… please.'

He doesn't say anything, merely turns and walks away – but he didn't say I couldn't tag along, so I follow him, because this is better than nothing.

-

We walk for some way, out of the centre of town and into much more residential streets. The day has properly started now, as alarm clocks wake kids for school and a legion of freelance delivery people start criss-crossing the city with boxes of plastic and crap that we all desperately need. The kid keeps to the same pace all the time, and I start to find it hard to keep up as tiredness begins to sweep over me and – *oh hell* – I start getting flashbacks to Theo and…

'Wait,' I call out to the kid, as I'm sick in the gutter. When I finish retching, all I can do is stand there with my hands on my knees and feel my body shake with a total emptiness. The kid must be long gone by now, I guess. I feel tears well up and run down my cheeks. They aren't for Theo, I don't think they're for Drew, but I don't know who or what they are f—

'Here.' A handkerchief is thrust under my nose. It looks clean and really old-fashioned; it has a lace edge and flowers embroidered on it.

'Thank you,' I tell the kid and take it from him. I wipe the tears away and then blow my nose, loud enough to wake the dead. I hand it to him, but he looks at me like I'm crazy.

'I don't want it back.' Then he turns and starts to walk again. This time I walk alongside him like we're equals, though I keep quiet.

–

The building looks tall for Brighton, at least six stories, though it isn't as tall as the blocks in Camden. We go inside and head to the stairs.

'Is there a lift?' I ask but the kid smiles wryly and takes the stairs. My head swims a little, but I manage to follow him up three flights (just about) and then out onto an open balcony and... wow. There's the sea again, like it was when Theo first showed it to me yesterday... *Christ*, it's not even twenty-four hours since we got here, but everything's changed. I stand on the balcony and look out at the water, sparkling in the chilly sun; it's so beautiful. Maybe I should run to the coast next – not Brighton – but maybe the west coast; I would love to be able to see the ocean every day. I think I might be addicted to its salty tang now, even after just one day. I look down to ground level and can see the route we just walked from the church. It felt like we came a long way out of the city centre, but from up here I can see that we haven't really gone very far at all.

'In here,' the kid calls over in a low voice, and I see that he's standing in the doorway of one of the flats. He holds up a finger and rests it on his lips. I nod back to him, then we go inside.

–

The air in the flat is thick with old lady smell – potpourri and lavender – and I start to sneeze as my allergies go through the roof. It's gloomy inside, as the curtains are pulled close and there are no lights on. The kid walks through and opens a door at the end, into the living room. Lying on the sofa, covered in an old blanket, is a younger girl. She looks about seven or eight years old. Her face is damp with sweat and her hair looks a little greasy. Her cheeks are sticky, and her arm is curled around a stuffed toy, but I can't tell what kind of creature it is. Her features are slender and her hair is way lighter than the boy's, but he looks at her with such obvious love that I know she's his sister. He softly reaches out and brushes the lank hair from her forehead. He bends down and gently kisses her head so as not to wake her, then he straightens up and turns back to me.

'Come on,' he whispers, and leads me into the kitchen.

'Your sister?' I ask, but he doesn't answer. Instead, he opens the fridge, which is pretty much empty, and puts two sandwiches inside and a little pouch of juice. Then he sits at the table and opens his remaining packs and starts to eat them hungrily. I sit down next to him and open mine. Even though I'm thoroughly starved, I'm not sure I can eat it all, as my stomach still feels so upset. I take a small bite and chew thoroughly, but I can't swallow and have to spit it into the sink. I run some water and splash it across my face and then turn back to the kid and—

Blackout.

I open my eyes. My vision is blurred and my mouth feels like something crawled inside and died in there. I'm lying down. I try and raise my head but somebody stapled it to the… *oh Christ.* I retch, but there's nothing inside me to come out, so I dry heave for a few seconds.

'She's awake,' a small voice says and then a giant head looms into view. 'Would you like some tea?' the voice says and as I blink away the distortion I see the little girl who was asleep earlier.

'Yes please,' I croak, as my throat is parched. I sit up a little and she hands me a tiny plastic cup and then picks up a doll-house teapot and mimes filling my cup.

'Glup-glup-glup,' she says and smiles. 'One sugar or four?'

'One,' I rasp and she drops in an imaginary cube. I would die for a real cup of tea right now.

'Would you like a biscuit?' she asks.

'What kind do you have?'

'Chocolate digestives.'

'Yes please.'

She hands me a round piece of paper that's been coloured on one side in a kind of yellow, and on the other with thick black Sharpie.

'Yum,' I tell her as I sip the invisible tea and mime eating the paper biscuit.

'Who's Drew?' she asks, frowning a little.

'He was my husband,' I tell her.

'Then why is he a fucking—'

'That's enough, Aggs. What have I told you about your language?' the boy says as he comes into the living room.

'She said it. She said it three times when she was sleeping.'

'I'm sorry,' I say. 'I've had a very hard couple of days – a bad fifteen years, actually.'

The girl frowns. 'That's stupid.'

'Agnes.' Her brother is annoyed with her. 'Don't be so rude, she's a guest.'

'But it's stupid. A broken mirror's only seven years' bad luck and that's the worst you can have. Fifteen years is even older than you, Jordan.'

'No, she's right,' I tell the boy. 'I am being silly, it hasn't been nearly so long as that. I had a nice day last March.'

'Thank you.' Agnes rolls her eyes like she's the teacher and I'm the idiot student who finally got a maths problem right after an hour of trying.

'What's your name?' she asks me.

I pause for a split-second. 'Fran,' I tell her. 'My name is Fran. Nice to meet you, Agnes.' And I hold my hand out to her and we shake.

'Where's Drew the fucking—'

'Agnes,' her brother snaps at her.

'No that's fine, questions are good; it's how we learn stuff,' I say, and the boy rolls his eyes, like I just made his life much more difficult.

'Drew isn't here anymore, we aren't together,' I tell the girl, not wanting to bring the idea of death into the conversation.

'Did you have children? Are they with him now or are they fostered or in care?'

'N-no, we never had, I m-m-mean, we weren't ever lucky enough to have... you know,' I stammer. Her eyes are huge and beautiful.

'That's it with the interrogation, Aggs,' the boy tells his sister sternly and then turns to me. 'I am sorry for my sister. She'll be a policeman or a spy when she's older.'

'Police?' Agnes makes a *yucky* face, and I think that, even at her young age, she knows you can't trust them. 'No I won't, I'm going to be a make-up artist in horror films. I'm going to create an army of zombie pig-headed babies.' And with that, she slides off the sofa and leaves the room. The boy – I think his sister called him Jordan – looks concerned and then he too disappears, but he comes back a few seconds later with a glass of water.

'Thank you,' I tell him and the water feels good as I drink it. A part of me wants to splash it on my face but that would be too rude.

'I'm glad you're awake,' he says as he sits opposite me. 'When you fell I thought you might be dead. I've never seen someone collapse like that.'

'I'm sorry, I didn't mean to scare you – I mean if I did – and I didn't mean to impose on your hospitality. I just really need a place to crash and get some rest.'

He shrugs in a *no problem* kind of way, though there is a look of concern in his eyes that I find quite touching.

'What's the time?' I ask him and he looks over at an ancient-looking carriage clock on the windowsill. I follow his eyes but I can't believe what I'm seeing. It must be broken. 'It isn't really after four in the afternoon, is it?'

'You slept a long time,' he tells me. *Christ…* He's right, I've slept all day. I look past the clock and onto the wall. The wallpaper reminds me of Mum and Dad's old bedroom, except on this wall are loads of framed photos. There are at least four generations of some family, but none of them look like these two kids.

'Is this your house?' I ask, and I can tell by his shy smile that it isn't.

'Who——?' I start to ask but he scrunches his face and stops me dead, his eyes flicking to the door to see if his sister is anywhere close. Then he cocks his head, motioning me to follow him. We walk into the hall and he takes a key out of his pocket and unlocks one of the doors.

'I...' he starts but he doesn't finish as I see his jaw trembling. For a moment he looks like the ten-year-old I first took him for. Then, he pushes at the door and I step inside. I'm immediately overwhelmed by the scent of extra strong lavender, mixed with some super-sweet spice, like cinnamon or maybe it's cloves and... pine. It smells like Christmas. We go into the room and he locks the door behind me. Hanging from the ceiling, pinned into the plaster and wood, and covering every surface and stuck all across the walls are air fresheners – the kind you hang from the rear-view mirror in a car, but there must be five hundred of them in here. The smell is heady and sweet... it makes my legs go springy as I recall the scent of blood as Theo was... *calm down, breathe*... I tell myself as a wave of nausea hits me.

'Are you okay?' Jordan asks.

'Yes,' I tell him and shake my head to clear it. The room is gloomy. The curtains are closed but they're thin so they don't cut out all the light. I look around and can see that we're in a bedroom. There's a large antique wardrobe to one side and a double bed in the centre of the room. On either side are small tables, each with a lamp on them, but it is the centre of the bed that draws my attention. The covers have been pulled off the bed so that it is just a bare mattress, but on that is a large roll of plastic sheeting. I move towards it and—

'Maybe you shouldn't,' he says in a low voice. But I can't help myself, I have to see the roll. I push at the plastic and feel something soft and kind of squishy inside. And I see movement under the plastic, and hear a little rustling from inside the roll. I know what it is. A dead body. And I don't need to ask who it is; it's obvious that it's the woman who lived here.

I turn to Jordan, and even in this low light I can see the tears that sparkle at the corners of his eyes. I open my arms and he leans into me. A sob wracks his body, but only for one second, and then he pulls himself together. He uses the sleeve of his hoodie to wipe the tears and snot from his face.

'I told Agnes that Mrs Stevens went to visit her sister when she was at school.'

'And then you dealt with the body?'

He nods and I see the toll it's taken on him. *Christ*, I feel my heart miss a beat – he's had to grow into a man too early. He's just a kid, but he has to look after his sister and worry about her, care for her and carry such a big secret all alone.

'How did you get here?'

'We're cuckoos,' he tells me with his face half-turned away from mine, though I can tell from the colour of his ears that he's a little ashamed of what they're doing. 'We came here three months ago, after Mrs Stevens had a nasty fall and her carer quit on her. She needed help, so we became her new carers.' He turns back to me and I can see the distress in his eyes. 'We shopped for her, made her tea and looked after her. In return we lived here – it weren't bad, we didn't hurt her. She liked having us here. I mean she *really* did; more than a carer from the council. She loved the company and she would play tea party with Agnes for hours and never get bored. She gave us money for the shopping and sometimes a little extra for sweets or a treat. She didn't have any family, see, or at least not in this country. She had a son but he lives in Australia, moved there fifty years ago she said, and hadn't been to visit in years and years. She had six brothers and sisters, but they're all dead, she was the last one. And now there's nothing and no one.' He shrugs, but I can see that it isn't because he doesn't care.

'What about your family?'

'Family?' He drops his eyes from mine. 'I got my sister and…' He trails off. I wait for a few seconds, but I can see he's not going to add any more.

'Where are your mum and dad?'

'I don't—' He goes to move away but I grab his arm. I don't put any pressure in my grip, but it's enough to stop him for a second.

'Jordan, my dad used to hit me and—'

'It was nothing like that,' he blazes at me. 'My dad never touched me, not either of us, and Mum loves us, she does.'

He says that so emphatically that I know something terrible happened.

'Where are they?' I ask softly.

'They… Dad's in prison – he didn't do it. He took the rap for someone else. They said they'd hurt us if he didn't.'

'And your mum?'

Tears sparkle in the corner of his eyes but he doesn't let them leak out. 'Some men knocked on the door, they wanted to *talk*, they said.' He sneers at the thought of these men just *talking*. 'But she wouldn't open the door. Next day she sent us to school and… when we came home, she was gone.' His face crumbles. I feel butterflies in my throat, beating against my chest and trying to escape. I want to run, to take these kids and run.

'Why don't you leave here and come with me to—'

'*No.*' He pulls away from me. 'We can't go, we're waiting for Mum. She's coming back – if we go away she won't find us.'

I see the pain stitched across his face.

'I know she'll be back, she loves us more than the sky and the Earth.' He says that like it's a ritual, a declaration of love made so many times it becomes lore. In his head he can hear her voice say those words. 'And this is where school is. Agnes loves her class and I don't want her to fall behind.'

'And your school.'

'I go… when I can,' he says guiltily.

I sigh. I'm amazed by how incredibly strong this young man is, but I'm also scared for him and his sister. Their life is so full of peril. 'How long since your mum… since you saw her?'

He pauses and I know that his answer is going to be bad. His jaw tightens and his heart hardens. 'Four months.' He's trying to keep control of his feelings, but behind the mask I see a scared little boy.

'You should go to the police.'

'Like you're going to the police.' His eyes hold mine, they are level and burning. I'm impressed that, in such a short time, he's sized me up and seen what a fraud I am.

'You're right,' I tell him. 'I don't trust the police either. But four months is a long time for your mum to be gone.'

'I know,' he says bitterly. 'We've lived it.'

The room is stifling. The scent from all the air fresheners is curdling in my throat and the boy is giving off enough angry heat to power half of London. I look down at the body on the bed. I think I see things move through the plastic sheeting. These kids can't live like this much longer.

'What happened to your own house?' I ask him.

'We lived in another council flat, a block a few minutes' walk away. Not as good a view, but it was clean and the four of us were together…'

'Your dad, and your mum, and sister? A proper family home. That's really nice. I live by myself – except my hamster, Hobnob.'

'Aggs wants a pet. She'd like a dog but a hamster...'

'He's cute, but he's mostly up at night. Suits me, I work late and then we hang out when I get home. We watch TV and I tell him about my day and... you know. Pet stuff.' I shrug. There's silence for a moment and then I break it. 'So, your mum just disappeared? You didn't hear anything?'

'No.' He grinds his jaw hard for a moment. 'No news.'

'What did you do, did you ask her friends or—'

'At first we thought there must have been an accident – but I reckoned that if she'd been hurt, then someone would have come to tell us – the police or the social, but no one ever did. Then I thought she must have gone to see Dad or something, that maybe she'd be gone for a day or two; a week at most. So we waited. We stayed at home, but I made sure Agnes went to school. We waited, but days went past and then weeks. We heard nothing. I didn't want anyone to know we were alone, I was afraid they'd send someone... so we kept our heads down, didn't get into trouble.'

'You just stayed at home?'

'As long as we could. I cooked and made sure stuff was clean and all. But after a couple of months they cut off the power and the phone. None of the bills had been paid, and then the police started knocking on the door and...'

'You came here.'

'Yes, Mrs Stevens liked it, and I think she needed us as much as we needed her.'

'But then she died.'

'Yes.'

'When?'

'Week ago.'

A week. I look down again and see forces shift in the plastic once more, like eddies in the ocean, currents that go this way and that, until suddenly they erupt and force their way to the surface. 'She has to be buried,' I tell him.

'I know.'

'You've done a good job so far but—'

'I burned incense for her spirit and...' He starts to cry. Not giant sobs but more like little burps of tears; the soft and gentle tears of someone who knows they're doing wrong, but there's no alternative.

'I know she has to be buried; I know she has to be looked after. At night, I worry that Mrs Stevens will not find her way into the afterlife and she'll go to hell because of us...' A massive sob rolls through him and he rides the wave out before he continues. 'But I can't let Aggs go into care. We won't be kept together if the police take us to social services, I've seen what happens to kids who're cared for by the council. It's not good. They get hurt and broken, they get abused and hardened and... my sister is a good girl.'

'I know, I see that... I'm sorry.'

And the two of us sit on the corner of the bed in silence, keeping Mrs Stevens company, and we think about the future. We wonder if we have one.

–

After about half an hour (or maybe it just feels that long, as we're sitting with a dead woman) I start to tell him my story... at least a version of it. I tell him that my husband became involved with bank robbers and they got away with a lot of money, but he betrayed them and ran off with everything. Then he disappeared.

'Like my mum,' Jordan says.

'Yes.'

'Did you find him?'

'I...' I stop talking, seeing the hope in his eyes. He wants to know that sometimes people come home again. 'Sort of,' I say. I can't tell him that he's dead. 'But the men couldn't find him, and so they came after me and I had to run.'

'Your husband...'

'I lost him.'

'Oh.'

'But that was okay.' *Christ what a lie.* 'He got away, but the men kept hunting me. They're still after me, even now. That was them this morning.'

'But why?'

'They think I know where the money is.'

'Do you?'

I open my hands and half shrug. 'If I did, would I be eating stolen out-of-date sandwiches from a church food bank?'

He laughs. 'No, I guess not... but wouldn't it be amazing if you had it? Like finding buried treasure.' He gives a low whistle and I can see he's thinking about what he would do with the money. I see how it could change his life completely. I bet he'd use it really well, to care for his sister. What about me, would I use it well if I found it? I'm not at all—

Bang... Bang... Bang...

Someone hammers on the front door. Next to me, Jordan drops to the floor and whimpers. My chest hurts as every drop of air is punched from my body. How did they find me? I can't let them hurt the kids, I'll have to—

'Mrs Stevens?' a voice calls out. 'Enid... Enid Stevens? Can you hear me?'

Jordan shakes next to me. This is his worst fear, but it isn't mine, his fear is like electricity in the air but I can breathe again. It isn't the Vincent brothers. I get up off the bed and walk into the hallway. Through the frosted glass in the front door, I can see the shape of a man.

'Mrs Stevens, it's Officer Brennan here. We've been asked to call to make sure you're okay. Your neighbours have reported that they haven't seen you in some time.'

I head back into the bedroom. I want to ask Jordan what he wants to do but he's in a panic, rocking on his heels, as he squats down by the bed, the body of Mrs Stevens just inches from him. Under his breath he is mumbling what I think is a prayer.

'Mrs Stevens, if you don't answer I will have to come back with others and force the door.' The policeman calls through it. Then I hear him push the letterbox open and yell through that. 'Mrs Stevens?'

'Shit,' I hiss and then I turn and charge through the house. I get to the front door and pull it open.

'Jesus Christ, feller, we've got a sick woman in here,' I hiss at Officer Brennan, who turns out to be about sixteen years old with a pink baby face. 'She's only just got back from the hospital and she needs her sleep, not some drongo yelling through the letterbox at her,' I say sharply, trying to scare the baby policeman – and I appear to be using an Australian accent.

'Oh... sorry.' He scrunches his head into his neck like a tortoise might if he were scared. 'So who are—'

'I'm Mrs Stevens' granddaughter. My dad's at home in Sydney, he's not well enough to travel so he sent me over, and I'm mighty glad I did come. If I hadn't have got her to the hospital last week, she would have been dead by today. So, a fat lot of use this visit would have been.'

'Well I am... I mean we only react when...'

'Yeah I get it, but my grandmother doesn't need some fool trying to knock the door down; she needs rest and looking after; lots of liquids and soup. Now I'm here, we'll get her back on her feet.'

'Good... well, good... Miss...'

'*Mrs*. Bloody cheek. Are you trying to pick me up, think I might be a sucker for a man in uniform?'

'Oh god, no.' He turns a very bright shade of scarlet.

'What do you mean "God, no"? Am I that old and disgusting?'

'No, I didn't...' He turns even redder. I feel a bit mean.

'I should bloody well think not. All right, off with you, you can go back to the station and cross her off your list. She doesn't need you, she's got family.'

'Good, okay well...' He makes a strange kind of bowing movement, and then turns and trots away. I look out over the balcony and see him get to his car and drive off. I watch him as far as I can, and then turn back to the flat. Jordan stands in the doorway. I can see the beads of sweat on his brow.

'Thanks,' he says.

'It'll buy you some time, maybe a couple of weeks but they will come back... and I don't know that Mrs Stevens has two weeks.' I think of the insects spawning inside the tight plastic sheeting.

He nods. I can see the gears clanking inside his head, desperately trying to work out what his next move will be.

'Maybe we could put the kettle on,' I say and we both go inside and close the door on the scary world outside.

In the living room, Agnes is watching the TV.

'What have I told you about watching *The Walking Dead*?' Jordan says angrily to his sister.

'It's research.' She takes the remote control and puts it behind her back so her brother can't change the channel. On the screen, a man bites a woman's cheek off and I feel a little sick. Agnes looks appreciatively at the skill of the make-up person.

'I bet it tastes like chicken,' she says cheerfully.

Jordan scowls at his little sister, and I notice that he won't look at the TV. I think the zombies freak him out. 'Come into the kitchen,' he says and I follow him in. I am jonesing for a cuppa.

—

'I don't think you can take the coach out of town,' he tells me a little while later. 'It's too difficult to get on without a ticket, and if they find you onboard, then you're a sitting duck.'

'So that leaves the train?'

'It would be better, but you know they're watching it.'

'This morning they were, but there's only two of them.'

'They could hire someone to look out for you. Do they have a picture of you?'

I remember Theo making such a big fuss of taking a picture of me. After fifteen years of trying to keep a low profile I actually stood still and smiled for him. *Idiot*. 'Yes, they have my picture,' I confess to Jordan.

'So they can have people you don't know watching out for you.'

'And I wouldn't know them...' I feel empty. I want to fold and fold into nothing and escape all this. I want to, but I can't, I mustn't. They killed Drew, and then they killed Theo – they can't have me too. I have to fight them, and now I want to find the money too. I want to follow the trail that Drew left. I want to know about Aberdeen. I want to know everything.

'You have to be careful Fran.' He frowns, looking both ancient and wise in the same moment.

'What about hitchhiking?' I ask.

He pauses to consider. 'Maybe. If you could get out of the city and hitch a ride from the A27, that would be safer,' he says and then stops to think. 'How did you get to Brighton in the first place, was it by train?'

'No...' *In my mind, I flashback to seeing the sea for the first time*. 'N–no, we drove.'

'And the car you arrived in has gone?'

'No... I mean I suppose it's still there, where we left it.'

'Do you drive?' he asks and I scrunch up my face. I had lessons a lifetime ago. I took three tests and failed each one. The nerves used to eat me up, I hate exams and being tested. But maybe I could now; to save my own life, maybe I could.

'I suppose so, but it doesn't matter anyway – we don't have the keys.'

He smiles. 'That isn't the problem you think it is. Let me be in charge of making the car start.'

'But there's one thing,' I say. 'One massive problem. The car... it's parked only a few houses down from where they live.'

'The Vincent men?'

'Yes,' I shudder.

'Oh,' he says. 'That is something to think about.' Then he smiles at me again. 'You should sleep some more, we'll wait for dark before we leave.'

'Okay,' I say, wondering if I really should be placing so much trust in a fourteen-year-old boy.

Chapter Ten

We drink tea in the kitchen. I can see the light fade through the layers of net curtains as the day dies away. The air in the flat is heavy with anxiety. We sit for some time and finally he tells Agnes to go to bed. She complains, but does as she's told. She's a good kid, they both are. I wish I could... what? Be their mummy? *Christ*, get a grip, girl. I can barely keep myself alive, what use am I going to be for these two kids? They're far more resilient than I am. Instead of being their parent I should ask Jordan to adopt me. I bet he'd protect me from the Vincents better than I'd keep them safe from the council. We listen to Agnes clean her teeth and say her prayers, and then she lies down and we wait for her to fall asleep.

'You know where you're headed, when you leave here?' he asks in a low voice.

'Scotland.'

'You have friends there?'

'No.' He looks concerned at my answer; I didn't tell him about Aberdeen. 'But first I have to go to London, to my flat.'

He looks shocked, like I'm crazy. 'Why go there? They could be waiting for you. It's too dangerous.'

'Maybe, I...' I pause. I don't like to see the worry in his eyes. I'm not used to anybody caring about what I do.

'I have to go back, there's something there that…' I pause. 'I haven't told you the whole story, Jordan.'

In the near-dark his eyes flash.

'He's dead… My husband, Drew… he's dead.'

Around us both the night has frozen and died. There is no motion, no sound, except our words.

'The Vincent men?'

'Yes, he was killed because of the money.'

'I'm sorry.'

'But there's something else, something that just came clear. When Gene was asking me questions, he said something about my husband, from back then. He said that Drew went to Aberdeen fifteen years ago and hired a car, right after the robbery.'

'You think the money's there?'

'I… I don't know, but there's something about the place that rings a bell in my head… and on the day he died, something arrived in the mail from him. I never told the police, I knew they'd take it, and it had nothing to do with the robbery. At least, that was what I thought back then. But now…'

'Now you think it's a clue?'

'Yes.'

I feel my hand shaking like a fizzy drink bottle that's been shaken up, so when you open it, it explodes. Jordan puts his hand on mine and I can feel the tremor start to subside.

'Sometimes we have to put our heads into the lion's mouth,' he says gently. 'We have no option, otherwise we live as if we were dead.'

We sit in the dark, listening to Agnes's breathing get softer and shallower, until it turns to snuffling little snores. When I was her age I still had my mum to protect me from the bad man, and I listened, night after night, to her getting a beating. Sometimes it was her body, but other nights he just screamed foul abuse, the kind of messed-up stuff that is so horrible that I don't know how it got in his head. I loved my mum and she protected me... mostly. I miss her. I miss her every day. I hope these kids can find their mum, though at least they have each other. They love each other and that's something... that's really something special. It's hard to be on your own. So hard.

'It's time to go,' Jordan finally says. 'Agnes shouldn't wake up while we're gone.'

'You don't have to come,' I say. 'You can stay with her and...' my words fade as he looks at me like I'm crazy.

'I will help you,' he says firmly, like a parent would talk to a child. That's what I feel like – that Jordan's the grown-up one here.

'Thank you,' I tell him and we quietly make our way out of the flat.

We take the stairs, but after one flight he turns left onto the floor below Mrs Stevens' flat. Along here it smells strongly of dope, but also that horrible sweet sugary smell of vaping, like cigarettes and candyfloss. We go four doors down and Jordan taps on a metal grille drilled into the frame. He knocks with some kind of pattern or code. After a few seconds it opens a fraction and a dog growls at us through the gap.

'Hello Piglet,' Jordan says, and bends down to stroke the dog's muzzle.

'Oh come on man,' the dog's owner moans and takes the door off the latch to open it fully. 'This fucking attack dog is for shit,' he says as Jordan strokes the dog's ears and it licks his hand.

'Who's she?' the dog's owner asks and I step forward into the light.

'I'm Fran,' I tell him and he pokes his head back inside and goes to pull the door closed.

'We don't want to buy nothing, I wanna borrow Jimmy,' Jordan says.

'Fifty per cent of the take,' the man says.

'I don't think there'll—' he starts, but I talk over him.

'Fifty – sure.'

'We only need Jimmy,' Jordan says. I have no idea what we're asking for, or what I'm offering the guy. Jordan rolls his eyes at me and the man grunts and disappears. He comes back, a few seconds later, and thrusts a bag through the gap in the door. It's a weird shape, like a snooker cue and a bowling ball had a baby.

'I'll bring it back tomorrow,' Jordan tells the man. 'Bye Piglet, I'll try and bring you something nice when I bring Jim back.' He grabs my arm, and pulls me towards the stairs.

'Who the hell is Jimmy?' I ask as the fresh air hits our faces as we walk out of the block and head down the street back towards town.

'Meet my little friend,' he zips open the bag and pulls out a long piece of metal with notches cut in it.

'What does it do?'

'You'll see,' he tells me, and then he extends his stride and speeds up. I guess we have quite a long way to walk now.

'This is it,' I tell him and feel the butterflies in my stomach. I can see the house that Theo died in, the front door has some kind of metal shutter on it I think. And next door... that's where they live. I feel sick.

'Which car?' Jordan asks, and I point to the one Theo drove us down in.

'That's unlucky,' he says, and I open my mouth to ask why, but then I see what he means. Theo parked directly under a street lamp, so the car sits in a corona of sulphur yellow light. If we try and break in to the car, we will be in full view. I hold my breath; this is such a stupid risk, we have to find some other w—

'Okay, wait here.'

'No Jordan, I—' But he's off, down the street towards the car, keeping to the shadows, and I lose him as he seems to become a part of the darkness. I'm scared... My heart is pounding... I should forget this crazy idea. Going to Scotland is stupid, I should tell the police and maybe they'd believe me. Maybe? Or I could stay here, with Agnes and Jordan. Get a job, earn some money, and get the power back on. We could all live in the flat, like a family: Agnes, Jordan, me, and the slowly putrefying corpse of Mrs Stevens. Except none of that would happen. The police would find me and arrest me. Agnes would go into care and Jordan would get sent to juvenile detention; all of our lives would be ruined and... *Oh god*... I suddenly turn ice cold. What if Michael and Gene are inside the car already, waiting for me to try and escape in it? *No, don't think like that.*

'Fran!' he yells from the car. He has the door open and waves Jimmy in the air. He waves like crazy, for me to come over, so I straighten up and stumble forward. I can see that he's bent over in the front seat now, and he's pulled the dashboard off from under the steering wheel and is trying to jump-start the car. He told me back at the flat how he'd learned to do it – how he'd learned to twist the wires together – but he'd never worked that magic on such a new car. There might be problems with it, he might actually fail and—

No... the world comes tumbling down. I see a figure at the top of the street. It stops, in the halo of another street lamp, and I see that it's Michael Vincent, his arms full of grocery bags. I'm in the middle of the road; there's nowhere to run, no place to hide. I freeze. Michael stops. I think about Agnes asleep on the sofa, and her waking up to find her brother isn't there. That cannot happen.

I look over at the car and I see Jordan's back, as he squirms under the dashboard... then I look back at Michael, still frozen to the spot. Maybe he thinks I'm a mirage. But then his face breaks open – at least that's what the garish light makes it look like – I think it's actually him smiling, like the Joker about to catch Batman with his utility belt round his ankles. He opens his arms and the bags fall to the ground. There's an explosion of glass, and what looks like blood, but it's just pasta sauce.

'*Gene!*' he screams and leaps forward, like a starter pistol just exploded. I could run to the car, get in and lock the doors, but that puts Jordan in danger and he's having no luck getting the car started. Maybe he never will. I see Michael coming fast at me, like a demon on horseback; his body seems to twist like smoke as his coat flies behind him, the sodium streetlight making it crackle like flames.

'Fran,' Jordan yells at me, as he looks up and sees the man charging towards me and – *oh god* – Michael's hand glitters with the metal of a knife. In that instant I know what to do. I cannot see another person die because of me. I turn to the right and run. At school I was on the sprint team for a year, but as the others grew, and I stayed under five foot, I got dropped. But it's still in my bones, and I run, like I'm back there with all the other girls; I sprint for my life and for Jordan and for Agnes. I hit the pavement on the other side and I break left, towards the sea. I remember the light is worse there, if I can get across the main road maybe I can lose him... *maybe*.

'Gene,' he screams again, but this time there's a reply.

'I see her, Michael.' They are both hunting me, and it's to the death now. I will not see the day break if they catch me.

My muscles burn as I push myself as fast as I can go. I can hear the explosions of footsteps behind me, but I can't tell how far behind they are. I should scream for help, but my throat burns with the effort of running. Why aren't there people here? I saw a club on the seafront last night. Can I get there? But then, isn't that just like giving myself up to the police? I can't do that. I can't spend the rest of my life in a cell; that's the same as dying out here on the street, but if I get to the club, maybe I can lose myself in the crowd, or hide under the arches or—

'Michael!' Gene calls to his brother and he's close, closer than I thought, but he can't be running, not with the damage to his legs. I turn my head, and – *oh shit* – I duck, as he lunges towards me, and his fingers rip hair from my head.

'Bitch,' he hisses and I see him trip and fall onto his back in the street, coughing so hard a lung might come out. I keep running – Christ, I wish I'd done long distance at school now, but I always cheated and waited for them to lap me. Oh my god, my chest is burning and – damn – I'm falling, as I trip on a loose brick. I'm down, I feel my knee scream in pain and blood smears up my leg, but I roll and I'm up again and running – hobbling... *shit, it hurts*.

From behind I hear Michael stopping to ask his brother: 'You okay?'

'Don't fucking stop for me, go and get her,' Gene tells him and Michael starts to run after me again. I feel my strength start to ebb away, I can't outpace him; he's too strong. I feel for the foxes, as their hearts explode as the hounds finally run them to ground and rip them apart. Michael will pull my arms and legs off like a boy with a spider, he'll—

'*Fran.*'

The car squeals to a halt right in front of me, the engine stalling with a grating sound. 'Get in. I don't know how to drive.'

I leap towards the car. Jordan rolls out of the driving seat and I slide in, desperately trying to channel the *Fast & Furious* guys. Jordan does something with two wires and the car roars back into life. 'Go,' he yells as Michael's hands reach to the open window to grab me. I stamp down on the pedals and the car shudders forward. *Don't stall it, don't stall it...*

'Fuck,' Michael spits, as he tumbles over into the road behind us.

I gun the car and we roar ahead, leapfrogging up the road, as I can't get it out of first gear.

'This is a dead end,' Jordan warns, but it's too late.

'What do I do?' I'm panicking. 'I failed my test on the three-point turn.'

'He's coming,' Jordan hisses. 'We have to go.' Michael is running at the car, screaming and holding his knife like he's the star of some new slasher movie. He will kill us both and make our skins into hats. *Shit.* I start to turn, but hit the curb hard.

'Don't burst the tyre,' Jordan warns, as Michael is almost on us. I slam it into reverse and back up, as the knife hits the hood and scrapes down it, sounding like a million fingernails scratching down a giant blackboard.

'Go!' Jordan yells, and I reverse fast, all the way to the dead end. We're trapped. Michael is thirty feet ahead and running full pelt, like a madman.

'Run him down,' Jordan yells and I gun the pedal. We shoot forwards, the headlights catch Michael, we're playing chicken and I know he won't swerve. I see me hitting him, breaking his legs and throwing him up in the air – like Drew – his body crunching down onto the tarmac, the force of it shattering bone and tearing flesh. Doesn't he deserve it, for what he did to my darling boy? But I'm not a killer. I turn the wheel at the last second and screech past him. Up ahead I see his brother on the side of the road, but all he can do is watch as the car flashes past him. I screech into another street on two wheels and shoot up, away from the sea, heading north finally. We did it, we're free. We're safe, we're—

'Oh no,' Jordan groans beside me.

'What?'

'The light, there.'

He points to the dashboard and there is a blinking light in the shape of a petrol pump. I look at the gauge, and we're past empty, we're on fumes. There isn't enough fuel to get us anywhere. And as I think that, the car starts to shudder again as even the dregs of petrol fade to nothing.

'Damn.'

The fumes get us out of the city and onto the A27, but barely. I lose all power, but manage to cruise over onto the hard shoulder, before everything gives up the ghost.

'At least you've lost the brothers,' Jordan says, and even though I agree, I think this is pretty damn annoying.

'Up there,' he points a little way ahead, 'that's where trucks stop for the drivers to catch a few hours' sleep. Maybe you could catch a lift north with one of them.'

'Yeah, I guess that's a good idea,' I say, though I can feel my knee swelling and my leg has smears of blood down it. 'I'm not going to get a ride looking like this though.'

'No, maybe...' and I can see his brain is whirring, and he suddenly takes off his hoodie and his sweat pants and hands them to me. 'Wear these.'

'I can't.'

'You must. Look Fran, I have to go back, I don't want Aggs waking up and finding I'm not there.'

'But I can't take your clothes.'

'Don't be an idiot, give me your ripped joggers, I don't care about the blood.'

'I suppose... okay,' I say, and we exchange clothes. He looks a little scary in the bloody trousers. I'm so grateful, but also totally feeling, like I could just collapse.

'You have to go now Fran, before the traffic police come to see what's happened with the car.'

'Yes, you're right, I... thank you, Jordan.' I step forward and, opening my arms, I wrap them around him and pull him into me. I feel his bony chest against mine and, for a second, it's like our heartbeats fuse.

'Go,' he hisses.

'Okay, jeez.'

'Be safe, Fran,' he tells me with real warmth.

'It's…' I start to say *call me Rebecca*, but I've not been her for an age, and even though it's only a couple of days since I was Sarah, I already think that she's dead too. So maybe I am Fran now. I don't know anymore. Maybe I'm a treasure hunter now, a flat-chested Lara Croft.

'You're a good brother and a fine son,' I tell him, thinking he's far braver than anyone I have ever met. I wish we could… but wishes are for children. 'Give my love to Aggs.' I would like to say that I'll see him again, but I don't know that I ever will. Even if I keep clear of Gene and Michael and find Drew's money, how would I ever find these kids again? They'll leave Mrs Stevens' flat soon and be back in hiding somewhere else; two cuckoos in another nest.

'Be safe.' I walk away, and I don't look back.

Chapter Eleven

There are three trucks parked up on the slip road. Two of them look like they're refrigerated and have flashy graphics and text in some foreign language I don't know. The third is smaller, looks older and more battered. The side reads, *Brian Samuels Independent Haulage*. I don't know how to decide which one to take; maybe I should eenie-meenie-miney-mo, but the decision's taken out of my hands, as the smaller truck suddenly comes alive. Its headlights come on, like a dragon breathing fire into the darkness, and it shudders as it's ready to drive off.

'Wait,' I call and wave my arm as I run to the driver's side door. 'Stop, please stop,' I call and hit the door, slapping my hand on the metal as hard as I can.

'What the... who are you?'

'Are you going north?' I ask.

'I'm going to London, Battersea.'

'Can you help me? I need to get home. I really need to get home.'

'Where's home, sweetheart?'

'London, Peckham – but I can get there from Battersea. Wherever you want to drop me is great. I just need to get there quickly.'

'Why?'

A whole heap of lies fly through my head. I could tell him that my mum's dying, or my child's sick. I could tell him I need to get my medication or I'll die... but after so many lies I don't think I can keep the story convincing.

'I came here with a boyfriend but he can't take me home.'

'You not together anymore?'

'No... no, the relationship ended.' I actually feel a lump in my throat as I tell him that. It hadn't been a long relationship, but it had been real – or at least real to me. I had invested in it and... I feel my eyes start to moisten. Crap, I really don't want to do this. I step away from the cab and wipe the tears away.

'I'm sorry, I—'

'Come on round the other side,' he says and I run through the headlights and pull open the passenger door. I have to stand on the rim of the wheel to get up, and pull myself into the cab. I've never been in a truck before. I like being so high.

'Seatbelt,' he tells me, and I strap myself in as we sail off into the night. I look at the clock on the dashboard. It's eleven p.m. What a day. All around is darkness, but ahead the headlights blaze, showing us the way north.

'Do you like to drive at this time of night?' I ask.

'Oh yeah, there's not much traffic and the radio stations are better.' He pauses. 'Why are you out so late? I'd have thought hitchhiking was far easier, and safer, during the daytime.'

'I guess so, but this is the first time I've ever hitchhiked so I don't know.'

'You're a virgin, then?' he says and I look over at him for the first time. He's in his mid-to-late fifties I guess. Heavy, bordering on fat, with salt-and-pepper hair pulled back into a ponytail. He's wearing what I would consider to be pyjamas and on his feet are pink slippers. He has big glasses, like 1970s Elton John, and he's got a scrubby beard and fleshy lips.

'It's my first time hitchhiking. I wouldn't have done it today but my ride let me down and—'

'You have to get home.'

'That's right.'

'Okay then.'

I look ahead… it's about sixty or seventy miles to London and when I get there, I'll have to… *oh shit*… My belly suddenly cramps and I fold over in the seat.

'You aren't going to be sick, are you?' he asks.

'No, no I'm okay.' I sit back up and look through the windscreen ahead. I don't have my keys. I left them in the BnB. I'm going to have to break into my own flat. My own… *ohhhh*… my belly cramps again.

'Have you eaten anything today?'

'I had…' Then I realise the last food I had was the sandwiches we stole from the church, and even then I only had a couple of small bites before I was sick. The last *real* food I had was in London… but when was that? A million years ago. 'No, I haven't.'

He raises his knees to hold the wheel, and then reaches into the glove compartment and pulls out some dried stick of something that smells like meat, and a bottle of water.

'Here you go,' and he hands them to me. I take the top off the bottle and drink. It's pretty warm water but it still makes me feel better. I have the dull throb of a headache starting, and I know I'm dehydrated. Then I take a bite off the stick and have to chew and chew to get it down. It tastes gamey and bloody, but I feel it ease my tiredness a little.

'Thanks,' I say and close my eyes. For the briefest moment I see Agnes asleep. I lean down to kiss her; she smells like milk and biscuits.

'I'm Brian,' he says.

'I know.' He looks surprised. 'I read it on the side of the truck.'

'Oh… oh, of course,' he laughs. 'I thought you must be psychic or something.'

'No, I have absolutely no superpowers,' I tell him.

He smiles. 'So what's your name?'

I pause. Who am I? Am I staying as Fran or have I already tired of being in that skin? I'm heading back to London, do I return to being Sarah – or is she dead too? I could be a Jane or a Laura or a Lynne… anybody I want to be.

'Lisa, my name's Lisa.' I pluck from nowhere. Why Lisa?

'Huh, I wouldn't have thought you were a Lisa. No, not in a month of Sundays.'

I feel goosebumps crawl across my arms and legs.

'And I must say you look prettier in the flesh.'

I feel myself curl, like a hand clenching into a fist. I wish I had a pepper spray or a knife. At home I always have a rape alarm and a pepper spray in my bag. Sometimes I even have a razor blade, though honestly I don't know that I could ever actually use it, and right this second I wish I had something to protect myself with – but I didn't bring anything, because I thought I was going away on a romantic weekend. I didn't think for a second I would need to repel anyone – I thought my job was to attract someone.

'Why do you say that?' I ask him, trying to push as much cold into my voice as possible.

'The local paper, there in the bag.'

I open my eyes and look down. I see a newspaper curled in a bag for life. I stretch my fingertips down and pluck it out.

'Front page,' he says as he looks forward into the dark. I uncurl the paper but can barely make out what it says as the cab is in darkness, then the headlights of another car fill the air and… *Hunt for Laines Lover* is the headline, and to the side is a picture of Theo and me. For a second I wonder how the papers could have identified me so quickly and got a photo, but that's just me being slow. It was the Vincent brothers, of course they told the newspapers who I was and they have a photo of us. Of course they do. I feel dread encircle my heart.

'The paper says your name is Sarah,' Brian says, not looking at me. I hear a tone of accusation in his voice.

'Even that's wrong, I wasn't born Sarah either,' I say as calmly as I can.

The headlights of another car pulse through the cab, and then they speed past us and we fall into the dark once more.

'Are you going to turn me in?' I ask from the black depths.

'We'll have to see,' he says and pauses – maybe for dramatic effect, or to let the threat sink in – I'm not sure which it is. 'Before I decide what to do with you, I want you to do something for me.'

I hear the sound of a zip unfurling. 'Take hold of this,' he says as light streams into the cab once more. I dare not look across at him. I guess his cock is in his hand. I don't know what to do, but if he tries to put it in my mouth…

'Here,' he says and his hand touches mine. I look down and he's holding a bible in it. I look over at him, his pyjama trousers are intact but a small leather bag has been opened.

'Pray with me, sweetheart,' he says and pushes the bible towards me.

'My father made me pray with him, before he beat me,' I say as tears stream down my face.

'I'm sorry that happened,' he said. 'He wasn't a real man of God.'

'No, no, he wasn't.'

And I open the bible and read:

'*Those who say: "I love God," and hate their brothers or sisters are liars. Those who don't love their brothers and sisters can hardly love a god they have not even met.*' I finish and he nods emphatically.

'Amen, sister,' he says and then we sit in silence, the words from the bible hanging in the air like the air fresheners in Mrs Stevens' bedroom.

I turn my head and look out of the side window, as a car cruises past. I look in, and see Gene Vincent in the driving seat. He's a mere few feet from me. I'm too scared to move. My heart freezes. If he turns his head, he'll see me; there's no place I can hide. Instead, I watch him as shadows flicker across his face and I burn with hatred for him and his brother. I wonder about grabbing the steering wheel from Brian, and slamming the truck sideways and into their car... I could force them off the road... and maybe that would kill us all... but I hesitate too long, and Gene puts his foot down; their car speeds ahead, and is soon lost in the night. They're on their way to London. I expect they'll go straight to my flat to lie in wait for me. I feel sick. Maybe I should run, settle somewhere and hunker down again. I could even go back to Jordan and Agnes and… what? What would I do there, hide for another fifteen years?

'No,' I whisper to the night. I can't keep running, I must head directly into the heart of this darkness. I have to follow Drew's clue, even if it leads down the rabbit hole… I have to know everything about what happened all those years ago, and maybe, just maybe, I will be able to avenge his death.

'Do you like hymns?' I ask Brian.

'Who doesn't like a good hymn? Especially at Christmas. They say the Devil has the best tunes but I've never really agreed.'

'What's your favourite?'

He smiles, he doesn't need to consider the question, he has the answer. 'I love "Joy to the World".'

Together, we sit in the dark, speeding towards a dirty city where there will be two maniacs who want me dead, and we sing about rocks and hills and plains. We sound like angels, me and the haulage king.

—

After we finish singing, he tells me where to find the biscuits and a thermos of hot sweet tea. We sip and nibble and pass the time of night. He doesn't ask me anything about the murder and I don't ask if he plans to turn me in. Instead, he talks a lot about the 'bloody red tape' of getting to Europe now (haulage is not what it was, he tells me), and how he loves fishing. I don't really care about either topic – but it's nice to just sit and talk like normal people, sharing the inane chatter of life and not thinking about Drew, or Theo, or Agnes and Jordan, or the money… or even about how I might die.

Brian drops me close to the café where I work. He doesn't ask why I want to go there, and he doesn't tell me to turn myself in, or any of that. He's a kind man. When I get out of the cab he gets out too, to stretch his legs, he says, but really I think it's so he can hug me goodbye. Standing up he's short, still taller than me of course, but only about five foot five inches tall, and he might be the same width as well.

'I want to give you something,' he says.

'No, you really don't—'

'Here.' He gives me his bible, zipped back into its little carry bag. 'And I won't take no for an answer,' he says. 'If you throw it away as soon as I drive off, then so be it, but otherwise keep it. It helped me when...' He pauses. 'It helped me when I killed a man.'

'What?' I ask, shocked. Not by the fact that he's killed a man, but amazed that he would tell me that. I'm not used to hearing confession.

'He and my wife were... you know, while I was away working. They had an affair, but I found out about it. I went round to his house, I asked if he loved her. He said no, it was just a bit of fun. He might have thought that would make it better, but it was worse. Sex without love is a sin. So I hit him.'

He closes his eyes and I see the pain contort his face, and he starts to shake a little. I think it's the shame of remembering that time. There's a part of me that wants to reach out and put my hand on his shoulder, comfort him somehow – Christ, I'm going soft – but I don't. I watch as he's overwhelmed by the memories and the tears start to flow freely.

'I hit him,' he says. 'I kept on hitting him. He begged me to stop but my heart was black as tar. I wanted to hurt him and...' His words fall away for a few seconds as the horror of that moment rolls through him once more. 'I killed him, and I lost her anyway.' He shudders. 'Just like the great and much missed Meatloaf said, he'd do anything for love... but not that. But I did. I took a life. I did it *all* for love... but lost it anyway.' He wipes the tears away. His eyes are wide and bright, like a new-born's. 'So believe me when I tell you that I know all about pain, sweetheart. I know. What you have to do now is find a way to forgive yourself, there's no way back out of the dark if you can't,' he tells me. 'I'll pray for you,' and he turns away and climbs up into the cab. He doesn't look back, but drives away.

He reminds me of my dad, or at least of the man my Dad could have been, if he'd been able to quiet the anger in his heart. Brian looks like he's found peace with himself, but my dad could never let the rage die, so mum and I paid the price. For the first time in my life I feel some pity for him – I actually feel sorry for my dad – for the man so full of anger that he could never appreciate life and love. He threw away everything because of some bloody nonsense rules he imposed on himself and life. Stupid, stupid man. I'd like to forgive him, I wish I could shed a tear for him, but I can't. Even now, after all this time, I can't truly let my own anger go. Maybe one day I will. Maybe.

The haulage king has gone now, vanished from sight, and I'm all alone, in the dark. I close my eyes and feel the stillness of the night cradle me, and for the first time in days I can relax a little. I'm not in immediate danger, I almost have some control of my life again. I could run. I could disappear. I could. I hold my breath and open my eyes and... for a second I think I see a shooting star. I open my mouth to make a wish, but it isn't a star after all. I think it's probably the space station slicing through the night sky, a tin can in space, and you can't wish on a can of spamanauts.

I take a deep breath and think about the last couple of days. I was so happy then, and thought my life had turned around and... now Theo's dead. It wasn't my fault though, I have to keep reminding myself of that. I'm sad but I can't blame myself. Theo put his own neck on the line, though that isn't quite the same with Jordan. The boy put himself in danger, but it was for me, and I know I didn't ask him to, but I let it happen. I didn't stop him. If he'd been hurt, that would have been my fault. You'd think I would have learned a lesson from that, but I haven't, because I'm actually going to go even further now. I'm planning to put someone in life-threatening danger, and I can't lie to myself that this is their choice, because it won't be. I am going to risk Ayo's life and it's my choice and mine alone.

My stomach cramps a little at the thought, but *god forgive me*, I must have the package Drew sent me on the day he died. It's the answer to everything. It's in my flat, but the police and the brothers will be watching for me, I need someone else to go in and get it, and there's only one choice: Ayo. She's been going in to feed Hobnob, so she's the only one with a plausible reason to be there. If I want to know the truth, if I want revenge for Drew's death, then she has to put her head in the lion's mouth for me.

But I already know that the only way she'll do it, is if I lie to her. If I tell her the truth about the danger, she'd run a mile. So I will lie. I'll ask her as *a friend*, even though I've never treated her like a real friend. *Jesus Christ*,

I don't even know her home address; I have to go to the restaurant to get it, which shows how terrible a friend I am. When she leaves my sight at the end of our shift, she's gone and I don't think about her. What a shitty person I am. No wonder I don't have any real friends when I push away any who try, like Ayo has tried to make friends a number of times over the years and I've always avoided or ignored her. I thought she was a bit needy, too chatty about her problems with her parents' old age and with her daughter Tara and the man who was her father. She railed against him, and the fact that he could take Tara away from her, because he had a passport and he had a penis – which was white – while Ayo had no status and no rights because her parents were Windrush casualties, and the home office were hunting them and her. She told me all this, cried so many tears, but I never wanted to get dragged into her story. I tuned her out, too caught up in my own misery, and at some point she just stopped talking. First her parents slipped out of her monologues – I think her father must have passed away – and very soon after, her heartbroken mother joined him. Then it was just tales of Tara and school, and the problems of seeing her dad every other weekend and then… Tara just faded away too.

I am so ashamed of myself sometimes. Maybe I do need Brian to pray for me. Maybe—

'No.' I hiss to myself. 'Stop the bloody pity party, either do this properly – take the risk – or run away again, put your head in the sand and hide away from life. If you want to finally be free, then you have to play the game to the end. It's time to choose.'

Chapter Twelve

Tuesday

The sign on the restaurant door says *Closed for Renovations*, and below that, there's a phone number – scrawled in red pen – that I don't recognise. It makes me feel uncomfortable. There's no way that Lillian is paying to have any work done inside; that isn't how she is. The walls would literally need to be crumbling to dust before she'd spend a penny on them – something must be wrong. I press my face against the glass and peer inside. I can see the chairs are stacked on the tables, like any other night, and everything has been put away, but on the floor there's a pile of letters and flyers that haven't been cleared from yesterday morning's post. Does that mean the restaurant was closed all? Why?

At the far end, over the bar, I can see the clock, barely lit by a shaft of moonlight that comes through the glass and bathes it in a grimy glow; it shows it's just gone two a.m. The lights are out everywhere else in the building, including in the flat upstairs, where Lillian lives. She must be asleep, which is unusual as she's such a night owl. She says she can run on thirty minutes' sleep, and I'm not always sure that's much of an exaggeration. She's always been fair with me, and I know that she's no fan of the police. I hate to wake her but I have to, and I think she'll give me sanctuary, just a few hours to rest. I hope she'll let me have that, as well as Ayo's address.

I ring the bell, and wait. I count to thirty and then ring it again. No lights come on, and there's no sound of footsteps. Everything's dead inside. I push the bell again… and again… but still nothing. This is all wrong, she should be here, she's always here. *Oh Christ*… has this got anything to do with me? I can't help myself and I start to cry.

It takes a while for the tears to stop. I don't have any tissues so I have to wipe the snot on my arm. I look down at the sleeve – it's filthy, but that's me all over now. I would love a bath, and a cup of tea, and some cheese on toast… But Christ knows when I'll have any of that again. Hell. I have to think… *think*. I need Ayo's address, where else can I find it? But as I wrack my brain I realise there is no other place. I need Lillian's address book. I have to get inside, no matter what. *Hell*. I look up and down the street, it's all quiet, so I skirt around the side of the building and dip into an alleyway at the back.

'Sorry, Lillian,' I mutter and pick up a brick and smash the glass in the back door. It clatters down in shards and then I use the brick to knock away any loose pieces, before I reach inside and unbolt the door. From somewhere a dog barks frantically, but there's no other sign anyone heard the glass break, or that they'll do anything about it even if they did. There is a silent alarm, I know it rings and sends a message to the police, but I also know that they won't come. It's gone off twice by mistake in the last year, and nobody came either time. The police in London are too busy to deal with simple burglary, especially in a little café that doesn't have much to steal, unless you want an enormous coffee machine that takes four people to lift it.

So the police won't come and normally that would annoy the hell out of me, but tonight it's just tickety-boo.

I also know there are CCTV cameras in the office and the dining room, but the images are just stored on a machine in the office, nobody actually watches it live. I could turn it off and erase the memory, but I don't bother. I'm not here to steal anything, I just want an address and somewhere safe for a few hours.

I get inside and walk through the kitchen. It's pretty much pitch black, but that doesn't matter, I know the place so well. I head to Lillian's office. It's pretty poky and doesn't have a window, so I close the door once I'm inside and turn on the light switch and—

'*What?*' The desk drawers are pulled out and empty. The usual pile of books behind the desk has gone and I turn with growing unease to see the single piece of art that used to hang on the wall behind the desk has been taken down and left on the floor. Behind where it used to hang, the safe door swings open. It's empty. Lillian's taken everything. *What the hell has happened?* And then I see a single piece of paper on the desk. I pick it up and read it; mostly legal jargon and long words, but it's essentially saying that the restaurant's being closed down because illegal immigrants are being employed here and no proper records are being kept.

Until all accounts and operational books and bank statements are turned over to HMRC and the home office, this business will cease to trade.

Shit. Crap, shit, damn.

This is my fault. I've brought the wrath of god and the government down on everyone here. *Bloody hell…* I've worked with these people for years and now they might go to prison, they could even be deported, and all because

144

of me. I've ruined lives… I feel sick. I'm overwhelmed by all this, it's like a house of cards collapsing around my head. I only went away for a couple of days with someone, I just wanted some love and affection. It wasn't meant to hurt anyone. How did it turn so sour?

In the corner of the room is one of the CCTV cameras, I look directly into it and mouth: 'I'm sorry.' Then I say it in sign language – I know a little from a deaf neighbour – back when I lived with Drew. 'I am sorry,' I say with my hands, and it's bloody true, I am more sorry than I could ever show.

I turn the light off and go back into the restaurant, stopping for a moment by the big refrigerator. I open it up and take out a little pot of tiramisu. Just a little bit of sweetness to help me through the nig—

'Nyagh.' Something swishes through the air, aiming for my head but at the last second I sense the motion and move, so it crashes into my shoulder instead. *Hell*, it hurts and slams me to the floor. The light from the fridge illuminates some feet. I look up and see a broom handle about to swing down and smash my head to pulp.

'You bitch,' a voice says as the wood swings at me. I roll to the side and it crashes down where my head was a microsecond before. 'You killed him, you psycho. What the hell is wrong with you? He was nice.'

'Ayo?' I ask as it smashes into my shoulder. 'Stop hitting me!' I yell.

'What, so you can kill me too?'

'I didn't kill anyone.'

'We know what you did Sarah, the police came. And it's all over the news. You cut his throat and stabbed him in the heart.'

'I—'

'And then the Home Office came and they took people away, like it was Nazi fucking Germany.'

'I didn't mean for that to happen.'

'I thought we were friends,' she yells as tears break through the defences of her eyes and pour down her cheeks.

'Friends?'

She growls and swings the broom handle again, but this time I grab it and tug it out of her hands. I throw it away and it clatters into the corner.

'No.' She aims a kick at me, put I punch at her legs and tangle them up. She falls on me – *Jesus* – she's at least double my weight, and her knees hit my chest and force all the air from my lungs – *argh*. The only advantage I have is that she's scared of me – she thinks I'm a murderer – and I have to use that.

'Now I've got you down here I'm gonna gut you with my knife,' I hiss at her. 'Just like poor Theo.'

'Eeeee,' she squeals and rolls away, her eyes wide with fear, and she starts to scrabble away. I can't let her get out of the restaurant, she'll go straight to the police, so... *Oh god...* I reach down and grab the broom handle she dropped and I charge at her. I don't have a thought in my head except that I must stop her, I have to... I pull my arm back and swing with all my might as she gets up and reaches for the door. Her feet crackle as broken glass crushes under her heel. She half opens the door as my arms hurtle the wood towards her and—

Thunk. The broom splits in two, shattering as it hits the back of her head. She tumbles down, arms and legs and glass all knitting together. Blood seeps from her head. Oh my god, I didn't mean to hit her so hard.

'Ayo,' I drop down next to her. 'Ayo,' I whisper as I shake her, but there's nothing. She's limp, like I am when I leave my body. She's left hers, but I think it might be permanent. I think I've killed her.

Chapter Thirteen

I've finished all eight portions of the tiramisu from the fridge. They were really good, but now I have to actually do something with all the sugar rush energy.

My first thought was that I'd take the body upstairs and put it in the flat, but have you ever tried to move a body? Even with all that coffee and creamy goodness in my bloodstream, it's impossible. I'd need a forklift truck, because she's a dead weight and she has such a difficult shape to do anything with. I mean, in the past I've always thought she had an amazing figure, so good it made me jealous. She's tall and has these luxurious curves, and breasts you could fall asleep in. But now it's a long and heavy set of lumps that won't move. So instead, I've got the chair out of the office and I just about manage to get her up and into it. Then I tape her wrists to the armrests and find some string in the kitchen that the chef used for trussing up the chicken. I use it to tie her ankles to the chair legs, and then I go round and round her waist and chest to keep her in the chair. I wasn't ever a girl guide so I use my best shoe-lacing knots. When I'm done she slumps in the chair, but doesn't slide off.

Oh – I should say: she isn't dead.

Once I'm certain she can't move, I head upstairs to Lillian's flat. Lillian's in her mid-sixties, and at least six inches taller than me, but she's thin and has a young outlook. Anyway, I reckon I might be able to fit into some of her clothes (I can roll sleeves up) and at least get something warmer. I could really do with a nice thick fleece or even a cardigan. But when I get to her flat I find the cupboard's bare. Everything's gone – really everything – all her personal stuff, clothes, furniture (except one chair with a broken leg), art, books – *everything*. I don't know how she did it so quickly, but whatever happened, Lillian has run, and there's nothing left. I rummage through drawers, in case she's left a T-shirt or something, but there's nothing. I sit in the broken chair; it rocks a little but doesn't fall apart. What the hell do I— *Oh*. I see a biscuit tin on a high shelf. My mum used to keep emergency running away money in a biscuit tin. My dad didn't indulge in sweet things, so she thought she was safe, but one day he found it and burned the money and gave her the biggest beating. The memory makes me feel nauseous for a moment. I step up on the wobbly chair and, trying to balance, reach up and grab the tin. Inside there's half a pack of Jammy Dodgers, a couple of custard creams, an unopened pack of Garibaldis (dead-fly biscuits) and nestled in the centre is a gun.

'Help me. Help me, she's a killer. *Help.*'

'Shit.' I jump down and run downstairs as Ayo screams at the top of her voice. I should have gagged her, I knew that, but I was scared she'd choke, and after being afraid I'd killed her once, there was no chance I was going to accidentally kill her again.

'Help!' she screams as I get to her.

'Shut up, Ayo, I don't want to have to—'

'Murderer. Rapist,' she yells.

'I didn't rape anyone.'

'Okay, *murderer*,' she screams and there is nothing I can do but hold her face and force a pair of rolled-up socks into her mouth, I'll tape over them in a second and… 'Oh hell.' She gags on the socks until she vomits.

'Oh gross, Ayo, really gross.'

I get a mop and bucket. Ayo swears she won't scream again if I clean her up. Her eyes are all bloodshot and her lips are flecked with spittle and dinner. I sponge the worst off her clothes, while she bitches and moans, but she keeps her word and does it quietly. It takes a good half an hour to clean her and the floor up, and by the time I'm done, my fear of the police has gone too. If anyone was going to respond to her screams they would have been here by now. Bloody London, no one reports a neighbour screaming rape or murder anymore. What a city. Keeping my eye on her, I grab one of the dining chairs and I sit in that, opposite her.

'You bitch,' she says with absolute hatred for me. 'You killed him. He was really nice, he loved you and you stabbed him. I can't believe it – I thought I knew you.'

'You do,' I say, though I realise that's a lie as she doesn't know me at all. She doesn't even know my real name. 'I didn't hurt him.'

'You just said you did.'

'That was to scare you, so you'd stop screaming.'

She glowers at me. 'I know that's a lie, the police came. They have your fingerprints on the knife and eyewitnesses that saw you arguing and—'

'Ayo, it isn't true.'

'The police are sure.'

'But they're wrong.'

I can see from her frown that she doesn't believe me. 'Theo's dead. He was a good man.'

'He wasn't. He was a liar.'

She opens her mouth to yell something but pauses. 'Liar? How was he a liar?'

'He...' But I can't tell her. 'It doesn't matter.'

'I knew you were lying, you should rot in jail.'

'No I shouldn't, and I won't. That's the thing that isn't happening. I'd rather be dead than that.'

'And you'll pay for what you've done, and not only for poor Theo, but we've all lost our jobs and Lillian's on the run. Poor Simi was arrested and Anton and Dev are in hiding. They came to check the papers of everyone here, and not just to give out fines, but deportations and criminal charges. Everyone's gone, the restaurant is dead; the Home Office know our names and addresses now. I've got four days to take my paperwork to a police station and after that they'll hunt me down. I'm in the system now, and they won't stop, you know I don't have the right papers – I told you all about my mum and dad and how they never got what they were promised. Even now the Windrush families are afraid of being deported.'

'Yes, yes I—'

'Will you untie me?'

'I... I'm sorry.' I feel really bad but I don't trust her. 'I can't... not yet.'

Her jaw sets hard and she looks at me coldly. 'Well, if I have to stay like this, then at least you have to tell me what happened in Brighton. How was Theo a liar?'

'He... I...' I don't know what to say, it can't be the whole truth. 'Theo, he had a gambling problem – an addiction, I guess. He owed a lot of money, forty thousand he said. Men were trying to collect, and that was why we had to get away. It wasn't a romantic mini break, we were in hiding.'

'Jeeez-sus.' She whistles through her teeth, shocked by the revelation. 'So what happened?'

My stomach falls away. 'I… I…'

'Did you go to bed with him?'

'Yes,' I say in the tiniest voice.

'About time, was it good?'

A part of me – a massive part of me – wants to tell her yes, the sex was great and he said he loved me – *he loved me.* And I said I loved him too, and we were so happy… for a few seconds, but I can't bear to relive it. I don't want to recall that I was happy, even for a moment.

'It was over quickly,' I say, unable to meet her eye. 'Then the men arrived, the ones he owed the debt to. They killed him, Ayo. They did it and…' My shoulders start to shake and tears cascade.

'It's okay, shhhhh, it's okay. You're safe now,' her soft voice tells me, but I know differently. I'm not safe as long as the brothers are out there, because they won't stop until I'm dead. *Christ*, I can't stop sobbing.

'Who are they, these men?' she asks, trying to cut through my tears but I barely hear her. Instead I collapse into myself and I slide to the floor where I curl into a ball. I can't hear anything. It's like when I leave my body, but this time I'm not leaving – instead, my consciousness collapses from the strain. I curl into a ball of grief and the pain takes over. In my head I scream and scream, until I fall into unconsciousness.

―

'*Drewwwwwww!*' My own scream rings in my ears as I suddenly snap back into the world.

'Easy,' Ayo says and she lays her hands on my shoulders while I shake. 'Calm down, calm down,' she tells me as she slowly rubs my shoulder and back until I stop shaking.

'Good,' she says, and her hands slide off me. My stomach is wrapped in knots and I don't know where I am. I look around, there's a pale light coming from somewhere and... the ground is soft. I'm on a bed, but there are no sheets on it, and I'm naked.

'Where are my clothes?' I desperately grab at some kind of throw and wrap myself in it like I'm mummifying myself.

'In the washing machine downstairs. They stank like hell and we don't have anything to change into,' she says and sits on the end of the bed. I look around; we must be in Lillian's bedroom.

'How did you get untied?' I ask Ayo.

'You are joking. They were the most useless knots I've ever seen. You couldn't even truss a roasting chicken like that. I know you weren't no girl guide.'

'No... I... how'd you get me up here?'

'You don't weigh nothing, I carried you.' She moves and the light catches her and I can see she's naked too. I turn away, embarrassed (and a little envious, I have to admit). I remember her clothes had sick all over them. Her skin is bronze and smooth in the half-light. I look like a ghost in comparison.

'Who's Drew?' she asks.

'What?' I feel my hackles rise like a wolf warning off a hunter. 'How the hell do you know about Drew?' My fingers curl into claws.

'You called his name in your sleep – well, nightmare, I guess.'

'Oh,' is all I can say.

'Budge up,' she says and makes to lie down with me again. I tense up and she sees that and stops. 'You're the one that tied *me* up, remember.'

'I… I'm sorry. It's just that the last time I was in bed with someone, they were killed.'

'Lightning can't strike in the same place twice.'

'Yes it can, and it does. There's a guy in America, he was a park ranger and he was hit by lightning seven times.'

'Get out.'

'It's true.'

She shrugs. 'Shit. Okay, so I guess we could get murdered in Lillian's bed.' She pauses, thinking for a second. 'But we need some sleep and I'm willing to risk it. Plus, I'm having the bed, so if you don't want to sleep next to me, then you can have the floor.' She looks at me, her eyebrows raised.

'This will be fine,' I tell her.

'And no more nightmares. Okay?'

I don't respond to that. I can't promise anything. I wrap my mummy's shroud even tighter around me. After a few seconds I turn away from her, but she doesn't turn the other way. Instead, she moves into me like spoons in a spoon drawer. My body curves into hers and I feel the warmth of her skin. Her arm comes over me. I feel safe for the first time in… I don't know how long. I remember my mum doing this to keep me calm when he was at his most angry. It feels… good. In a few seconds I'm dead to the world.

–

I wake up to some great smells and sizzling sounds coming from downstairs. I know I should go down but I'm naked and there's nothing I can wrap around myself.

'Ayo,' I call softly down the stairs.

'Come and get some very late breakfast,' she calls back.

'I don't have any clothes,' I answer and she responds with a kind of giggle and then comes up with my clothes, mostly Jordan's clothes really, in her arms. They look more pink than I remember. I don't think he'll want them back now.

'Here,' she throws them at me. 'Come down.'

I put them on. They look odd but I love how they smell, like a new-mown field of wild flowers. I used to do all my laundry in the sink at home, mostly I used dish-washing liquid that I snuck out from the café, so having nice-smelling clothes (which are actually clean) is a real treat. I go down to the kitchen.

'We can't eat out in the restaurant,' Ayo says. 'Can't have people seeing us, but we can eat back here. Lucky that it all happened so quick and the fridge has been left well stocked. We could live here for a month.'

Her words make me panic a little. 'No. As soon as it gets dark I have to go.'

She looks at me, her head cocked. 'Where the hell are you going to go?'

'Home, I need to go home.'

'Why?'

'Hobnob.'

'Come on Sarah, what do you take me for? I've seen the two men.'

'Wh-who do you mean?' I feel cold curl around my heart.

She scowls at me. 'You know – the scarecrow and the rottweiler.'

I feel myself shake a little; she's seen the Vincent brothers. 'Wh… where?'

'My place, why else do you think I'm hiding out here?'

'Wh… what happened?'

'They came last night, about midnight, maybe. They knocked on the door and I said nothing, but they knew I was home because the lights were on. They called out my name. They knew me.' Her eyes flare, as dark as hell. 'They called out your name too, told you not to be scared, that they just wanted to talk.'

'My name. They wanted me?'

'Yeah, they were looking for you.'

'At your place? But what did they want?' I ask, afraid that Ayo might know about the money. I actually think she might be helping them like Theo was, maybe it's all a trap. I feel myself shrink away from her. She sees me do it and her eyes cloud over a little.

'I didn't stay to find out what they wanted. I climbed out the back window and went down the fire escape. But when I got across the street I looked back and the blinds were down.'

'The blinds?'

'Yeah, I couldn't see into my flat, but when I left the blinds were up.'

'They'd got inside your place?'

'That's what I figure.'

'Oh god.' I feel dizzy and I can feel sweat leaking out of my pores, making me smell even worse.

'What have you done, Sarah?' she asks, not in anger but with real genuine concern. I close my eyes. What have I done? What do I tell her? Do I go back to the beginning?

Do I tell her the truth and drag her further into this? A few hours ago I was willing to put her in real danger, but I can't. Not now I know the Vincents have already targeted her and know her name – this is all such a mess.

'Tell me Sarah,' she says, but I can't tell her the truth. I stick to the half-truth about Theo's gambling.

'Theo owed these men a lot of money and they think he has the money to pay them, and that I know where it is.'

'And he doesn't – didn't.'

'No, he was broke. He had some crazy scheme to win it, if he could get some seed money. He thought I had it.'

'Christ, he was an idiot. But these men think you know where a lot of money is?'

'Fifty thousand pounds, and they're prepared to beat it out of me.' I feel bad about lying to her, but the truth doesn't set us free, it makes everything more complicated.

'You have to go to the police,' Ayo insists.

'No, I can't. I... I'm wanted for something else.'

She frowns, 'Wanted for what?'

'It doesn't matter, it's from years ago, but it means I can't go to the police. I can't Ayo, I need to lay low and...' I let the rest sit in the air like noxious smoke.

'So what's the plan?' she finally asks.

'I have friends in Scotland. I'm going to visit them until this all blows over,' I tell her, and hope it's convincing. She looks unsure for a second; maybe it's too big a lie – that I have friends anywhere.

'Maybe I could come with you.' She drops her eyes away from mine. 'I can't stay here.'

'I... yeah maybe,' I say, but that's the last thing I want. I can't take her along to Aberdeen with me. I only need her help retrieving the clue from my flat, then I have to say goodbye and never see her again. I have to.

'We could go at first light,' she says.

'Yes… but before I do that I need to get something from home.'

'Your flat?'

'Yes, you still have the key, don't you?'

'But the police and…' She shudders. 'The two men.'

'Hobnob needs to be fed, they can't stop you going in.'

'A hamster, you'd risk everything for a hamster?'

'Sort of.'

'You're crazy.'

'No… that isn't the whole reason to go into my flat, I need something really important.'

'What is it?'

'A box… a music box.'

'What?'

'It was… it's important.'

'You want to risk everything for a music box?'

'And a few other things. Please, Ayo. Please, I need you to grab a couple of trinkets from my flat and then we can go.'

She looks at me oddly. I think for a moment she knows I'm lying; that she's realised that I plan to have her get the things from the flat and then in the middle of the night I'll sneak out on my own and run away from her. But then that wariness dissolves.

'Okay, I'm in.' She even smiles. I wish she wasn't so nice. I feel guilty, but I'm selfish, and I need her to get into my flat. I need her to risk her life.

'When do we go?' she asks.

'We'll wait until it gets dark.'

Chapter Fourteen

She gives me a phone. It isn't the one she normally uses, and I don't know why she has two. It's an old model, not a smart phone, and has these little jewels stuck on to it, like the phone of a fairy princess who fell on hard times. I turn it over and see a name written in silver pen.

'Tara's old phone?'

She closes her eyes for a moment but ignores the question. 'If there's any problem I'll call you,' she tells me and waves her mobile phone at me. 'You can use one, can't you?'

I roll my eyes, I may never have owned one but I know how the damn things work. She shrugs her shoulders and half-smiles. She's avoided talking about her daughter and I have to respect that – and to be honest, I'm glad. One thing at a time.

'Okay, so I'll go in and feed Hobnob and then—'

'In his cage, hidden in a small plastic blue house that's full of sand, is the music box. Tip the sand away and you'll find it. Please grab that – and by the front door on a little Ikea bench there's a tin box, please get that, too.'

'Anything else?'

'No… I think… well, some music would be nice. There are some mixed CDs, they should be on the same shelf as the tin box, can you bring the pile?' I ask and I flash a smile to cover the facial tick I seem to be developing from all this lying.

'Okay, wish me luck,' she says with such a sweet smile that I almost stop her, but I don't. I'm not a good person.

'Good luck,' I say and hug her. She squeezes me tight for a second and then she pulls away and heads to the bottom of the road. I follow behind her, and as I get to the end, I can see my building ahead. My flat is on the sixth floor. It's completely dark inside. I feel my heart start to beat a little quicker.

I watch Ayo as she pads across the street, tall and calm, like a dancer. There's no moon tonight, and the clouds hang low and oppressive like thugs at a football game, ready for violence at a moment's notice. She reaches the front entrance and pulls the door open, just as the rain starts to fall. *Damn.* It's hard and heavy, quickly filling the holes in the road, and then drumming on the puddles it makes. I hold my hand over my eyes and try to squint through it, but my vision is cut by at least fifty per cent, and I can barely see my flat now as a mist has swung in, and overhead storm clouds skirmish. I hope the lift is working. Six flights of stairs is not fun at the best of times. I hold the phone tight and hope she won't call, but I'm ready if she does. Is it too late to call this off and go to the police? I don't—

Click. I see the light come on in my living room. I feel like I've been plugged into the national grid as my body trembles with at least 220 volts running through it. I grip the phone harder, straining to see through the falling rain. I hold my breath… It should only take a few seconds, she only has to—

Rinnnnnnnng Rinnnnnnnnnng…

I start to fold – escape as fear overwhelms me. I feel the phone in my hand get heavy, I almost drop it.

'Not now, not anymore,' I whisper to myself, angry that I immediately want to run and hide from life. That won't get me what I need – no more running. Instead I pull my soul back into my body and touch the green button on the phone.

'Ayo?' My voice creaks like my throat needs a squirt of WD40. 'Are you okay?'

'I can't find anything, you should come up.' It's her voice. But what if they're holding a knife to her throat, what if this is a trap?

'W-why?' I stammer a little, the fear sprouting in my chest.

'Someone's ransacked your place, everything's broken and I can't see what you need.'

'Is it safe?' I whisper.

'What?'

'Are they there?'

'No.'

That's all she says – I expected a few lines, something to calm me down and persuade me, but all I get is *No*. I'm supposed to have faith that she's telling me the truth, but how the hell do I do that when I know how easy it is to lie? *Christ*, I've lied to her for six years. But I don't see that I have any choice in this, so I tell her that I'll be right up.

I step straight into a puddle and feel the water squish around my foot, cold and slimy. *Great*. I run across the street, and in just a few seconds the downpour threatens to wash me away. Bloody global warming.

I get to my building, my hand is out to push at the door – but I hesitate. I could run – forget the whole thing, hide again. I can feel the rain running down my spine, pooling in the small of my back. It's cold... like me. I think I might be crying but with the rain it's impossible to tell for sure. I'm so scared. If Michael Vincent is up there – if he gets his hands on me again – he will tear me apart, and laugh as he does it. I'm shaking. As a kid, I used to get into my wardrobe when Dad was yelling for me. I'd hide in there, close my eyes and pray, promise I'd be good... and sometimes I was safe, but mostly he found me, and dragged me out and hit me. He hit me and hit me and...

'*Stop it,*' I hiss to myself. '*Get a grip.*'

The Vincent brothers have stolen so much from me and I can't let them have more; I have to keep something for myself. I close my eyes, stretch out my hand and push the door open. I'm going upstairs. I'm facing the fear.

I walk to the lift. My legs are shaking far too much for the stairs. I call the lift and wait. It only takes a few seconds, and thank god it's empty. I ride it up to my floor and get out.

'There you are,' Ayo calls as soon as I walk out of the lift. She's standing alone in the hallway.

'I'm sorry,' is all I can say. My voice is trembling. I walk past her and into my flat. My home. I want to cry when I see my hamster, I'm so happy he's alive.

'Hello Hobsy.' I open the door and scoop him out. He's so soft, and I hold him to my cheek and feel his whiskers snuffle me for a few seconds.

'My beautiful boy,' I whisper to him, but I know I have to say goodbye. He can't come with me. I walk him into the kitchen and pull a chair over to the big cupboard. I hoist myself up so I'm level with the top of it, and I put him up there. There's a hole in the wall, I dug it out ages ago. I push a nut treat inside and then stroke him for the last time. 'Good boy,' I say and he sniffs at the hole and then goes inside. I hope this is the beginning of an awfully good adventure. 'Be safe,' I whisper to him. 'I–I...' but I can't finish the word *love*. I can't even tell a hamster I love him. *Jesus Christ*, life has done such a number on me.

I jump down and go back to the living room. I can see that Ayo has taken Hobsy's house out and shaken the sand away. She holds a little box in her hand. 'Is this what we came back for?' she asks, waving it at me.

'Yes, that's the answer to everything,' I tell her. 'You hold onto it until we get back to the café.'

She nods.

'I want a jumper and a coat,' I say and pull off my soaking clothes, still embarrassed to be seen undressed, but the fear is making me not care about the small things – torture and death are taking up most of my panic-stricken brain, but it does mean that Jordan's never getting them back, sorry. I stand there, naked for a few seconds, while I scan the floor. I can see that all of my things have been pulled out and scattered. I grab some jogging bottoms, an old hoodie and a raincoat. It has a hole but pretty much everything I own does. And I think it's time to say goodbye to my wonderful Doc Martens boots. They saved me in Brighton but they are a bugger to run in. I grab an old pair of trainers. They're worn and soft; I can run fast in them. Then I see my treasure box. I reach down and open it, taking out my old Discman, which has been my constant friend for so long. Inside are the few notes Drew wrote to me, and a strip of photos of me and my mum. It's from a photo booth in the Arndale centre, taken on a day we played hooky and went shopping... it was my birthday. It was a treat, maybe the best birthday I ever had, and I look so happy. We both look so happy. I can't remember that many days when we actually laughed together. My mother is radiant and her skin is soft and there are no bruises. I recall a childhood of so many bruises. I kiss her face. Stupid. It's only a piece of plastic-coated cardboard, it isn't her. She's gone. They're all gone. There's no one to kiss.

I take everything from the box and push it carefully into my pockets.

'I want some music to listen to, can you grab the pile of CDs, there by your feet?'

She looks down and sees them, picks them up and lobs them over to me. I catch them and take a quick look. All my favourites are there, and I stuff them in my pockets.

'Ready now?' Ayo asks.

'Yes, and don't lose the box,' I tell her. 'It's really important.'

She nods.

'Let's go.'

We take the stairs. My legs have stopped shaking just enough that I can use them, and I feel safer on the move. I don't want to be trapped in a metal box. We get to the ground floor, and I can hear the rain drumming on the glass, maybe even harder than before. It's a dark and stormy night.

'Are you ready?' I ask and she grabs my hand and squeezes my fingers briefly. She pushes the door open and steps into the rain. I'm stuck there for a second, too scared to move. 'Come on,' she says and moves away. I follow and step into the street. The rain is harder, my vision is blurred, like it's smeared and breaking up and I look for her. I see her step onto the road and—

'*It's them!*' I scream as I see Michael Vincent rushing at us.

'*Run!*' Ayo calls and I hear the whoosh of someone close. I duck and pirouette, like a dancer or figure skater, and feel a fingertip glance off me, as a hand grabs at me from the dark.

'Argh,' a voice grunts in anger and frustration and I duck away from a shadow. I run, turning to see Michael Vincent – his face a mask of hate as a car's headlights catch him.

'Turn the fucking lights off, Gene,' he howls with rage at the driver of the car, and the light on him dies.

'Ayo,' I call and start to run. We planned for this; we said back at the café that if we saw them, then we were to run to the tube station. It's so close, and a train leaves every couple of minutes. We can jump the barriers and be on the platform in seconds. It's busy, they can't touch us in that crowd and we can either get away – or turn ourselves in if it looks certain they'll catch us.

So I run, like the hounds of hell are coming for me. I run for all I'm worth. I run on fear and hate. I hear them behind me. I pray that Ayo is free, that she's running too, but I can't look back – I dare not look back. I zig and zag, around people and across the road – cars screech to a halt and blare their horns at me; I don't care. I slip on the wet greasy road but right myself, and run on. I have to duck under umbrellas, but that's okay because I know it's slowing them down, too. My lungs burn. I think I hear someone stop – Gene can't keep this up, not with his illness. I can make it… I can…

'Stop.' I hear a moan behind me and know it's Michael, but he can't run anymore. I think I hear him throwing up. I don't look back and I don't slow down. I can see the light of the tube station. It's so close, I leap off the pavement into the road. I don't look, I just run and—

Brakes screech, a car clips me, I can't keep on my feet and I fall. Trying to stay in control, I put my hand out and feel it cut and shred, grit and stones ripping my skin and forcing into the flesh. 'Aghhhh,' I scream and careen sideways but I keep going, and right myself. I know there's blood. I put my hand into my armpit and – *Jesus Christ* – I see stars. Everything tilts, but I have to keep going. I can see the sign, like neon – it's bright and garish – and past it, in the tiled hall, I see the ticket barrier. I jump, sail like a bird and land on the other side on my tiptoes. I nearly fall, but I don't. I stop and look for the sign to tell me where to go, but I'm lost, as everything spins. My head is like a roundabout. Where's the Northern line? Where's Ayo? My head is turning, the pain in my hand is burning through the adrenaline high.

'Look out, behind you,' a voice yells from somewhere, and I spin round and there's Gene. Behind his head I see the arrow to the Northern line, but he's blocking my way.

'End of the line,' he says. He looks like death, his face is bloodless and his chest heaves with the effort of running. There's spittle on his mouth and a tremor in his hand as he holds it up. 'Give us what we want and you can go free.'

'No,' I hiss and I pull Lillian's gun from my pocket. 'Move to the side,' I yell and from behind me a woman gasps and pulls back from us.

'It's okay, just a joke,' Gene calls to her, trying to fake laugh, afraid she'll call the police. He knows time's running out for him. He looks scared for a second and then his eyes droop. He opens his arms and pushes his chest out. 'Do it,' he says, but he isn't daring me. It's more like he welcomes it; he looks too tired to live. 'Do it,' he yells. 'Shoot me, if you can.' And he raises his eyes, now dark and full of chaos. 'You're no killer, Rebecca, you don't have the guts.'

'You don't know me.'

'I know you're too scared to—'

I pull the trigger. I want to erase his leering face, and I do – for a tiny moment – but the gun just clicks. There are no bullets in it. I don't know if I knew that, or whether I would actually have killed him, but it doesn't matter. I can use that second of his fear. I run at him, hurling the useless lump of metal. He manages to move his head, but it still hits him hard in the shoulder and knocks him to the side. It gives me the time I need to leap forward and past him. He throws out a trembling arm but I brush it aside and run to the Northern line. Behind me I hear his hacking cough as I run.

'Keep going,' Ayo yells from somewhere, but I can't see her. Instead, the crowds swirl around me, tutting and complaining as I bounce through them, like I'm in some giant pinball machine. 'To the left, to the left,' she shouts and... *yes*, I see the Northern line board: *Train Arriving*. I take the stairs down two at a time as ahead of me, the train fills up with passengers. It will be ready to leave any moment now... I can get on, but where is Ayo?

'Sarah,' she calls and I turn, to see her still on the stairs. Oh god, she looks exhausted. Her chest is heaving. Behind me the door is closing. I can jump on. I can get away. But Ayo...

'Sarah,' she yells and I catch the edge of the door and I hold it so it can't close.

'Let the fucking door go,' someone shouts from inside the train, but it opens again. She's almost here. 'Come o—'

'Bitch,' Michael Vincent spits as he lurches towards me from out of nowhere, his head butting into my shoulder and throwing me off balance, so I smack into the carriage and fall onto the platform. He howls and kicks at my head, hard enough to explode it like a pumpkin, but I move at the last moment – I feel it graze against my shoulder – and he smacks against the train. Some man grabs at him, pushing him away from the train doors, giving me the vital seconds I need. I see the fury contort Michael's face. I think he'll kill the man who pushed him, but I don't wait to watch. I turn and yell to Ayo. '*Run.*' Time is almost out.

'Forget her, the black girl has the box,' Gene orders from the top of the stairs. 'Go after her.'

Michael snarls at the man who pushed him off me, but then turns and runs at Ayo, like he's going to rugby tackle her to the floor.

'No, leave her alone!' I scream. 'She doesn't know anything. She doesn't even know my real name.' He's like a bull charging Ayo, but she sidesteps him and jumps for the train doors. She is almost here, I can see the joy in her face and then… Michael throws out his arm and grabs her, plucks her from the air and drags her back, his hands lacing around her throat. I feel the doors closing at my back. Ayo is lost and I will be too if I don't…

I fold, quicker than ever before, my spirit is out of my body and my limp form falls backwards, through the closing doors and I hit the floor of the carriage. My body's on the train. My soul is still on the platform, looking at Ayo, her eyes wide. I see the pain in them, but it isn't from his hands on her neck, but my betrayal. Her eyes say: *why don't I know your real name? I trusted you with everything, why didn't you trust me?*

My soul falls back into my body as the train starts to pull away from the platform. Around me people look at me like I'm some feral animal, they back away and I see someone eye up the emergency button.

'It's okay, I'm not dangerous or crazy,' I hold my hands up to show that I've got no weapon and I'm not going to hurt anyone. I stand slowly and I feel the tension in the carriage bleed away as people go back to what they were doing. I look out, onto the platform, and I see Ayo and Michael with his arms around her throat. Behind them both, Gene Vincent comes hobbling down the stairs. He looks as pale as a ghost. Then I see Michael dig a knife into Ayo's side and take the box from her pocket. The box she took from Hobnob's cage.

The train pulls away and the three of them get smaller and smaller. Before they disappear, I see Michael hand the box to his brother. Then they are gone. My chest constricts, and I feel like I'm having a heart attack. I burn with shame. Ayo is lost, probably dead any second now. I can't breathe. I hold onto the door as we slow down and come into another station. I have to get out, I need air. I can't breathe. I stagger off and up the stairs. I am free of them and yet... the price of that freedom. The price is astronomical.

'Are you okay, do you need...' some kind person asks, but I can't cope with compassion now. I wave them away and keep moving. I have to keep moving, can't stop. Must not stop. At the top of the stairs I squeeze through the barrier with a woman and her pram. She gives me a dirty look but says nothing. She must think I'm homeless – which I am – and she sees the blood smeared on my hoodie from my hand and wrinkles her face at me. I head away from her. I see the exit and follow it, like it's the star guiding me to Bethlehem. I step into the rain and tip my head up to it. I need it to cleanse myself. I need it to… I'm sick in the gutter. The woman with the baby rolls past me, I hear her *tut*. I expect she'll tell her book club all about this junkie loser she saw. I fall to my knees and can't stop the tears as I cry and cry.

She'll be dead by now. They'll open the box and see it has nothing inside but my wedding ring. *Forever. Rebecca and Drew* it reads on the inside. I would have liked it back but it doesn't matter. I can live with that loss… but Ayo. Ayo. She was so good to me and I killed her. I used her. I knew they would be listening, and I used her like a decoy. I made it sound like the box was important, that it held the key to where the money was – the crucial clue I'd kept hidden where no one would find it. But it was all a red herring, the MacGuffin. I have the real clue, the real reason I had to get back into my flat. I put my hand to my pocket and squeeze. I feel it there. I have it. The last mixed CD Drew ever made me. I've played it a thousand times and often wondered about the cryptic title. *Four Minutes Past Aberdeen*. That's what he scrawled on the CD in Sharpie. Then he wrote. *Forever, D.* It arrived the morning he died… was killed. It will explain everything. It will solve the mystery and I'll find the money and be revenged. I will win. I will, but the cost is so great. Losing Ayo and—

'No,' I suddenly realise there's something else I've lost tonight. I pull everything out of my pockets, but it's gone, the photo strip of me and my mum, the only picture of us together, it's gone. I must have lost it running from the brothers. Now I've got nothing to remind me of her. I have nobody and nothing. Life sucks. Everything is so bloody shit.

I start to walk. I pull the headphones out of my pocket and put them on. I want to lose the outside world, quiet the screams and yelling. I want... I want this to all be worth something. I need answers. I need the truth. The CD goes into the Discman and then I hit play. I fast forward through the songs to the last one. 'Aberdeen' by some weird American indie band I'd never heard of. I'd always thought it was a strange choice, as Drew liked electronic music and not grunge. I never knew why it was important... but now I listen intently. The song plays and when it ends there is silence. I walk in the rain listening to the sounds of silence. I listen for 240 seconds... *four minutes* past 'Aberdeen'. Then I hear his voice.

> *Hi Becs. I hope you like the mix, I know the last track isn't great but there wasn't much to pick from. I guess that you're hearing this after getting my letter and so something bad's happened – but maybe not, maybe we're both old and happy and rich and we're listening to this together to remember how lucky we were. Maybe. I hope.*
>
> *I'm recording this in a car, it's like three a.m. and I think the police are after me and... I don't know if I'm going to get away. I don't know what'll happen. I'm sorry. It's all been too quick and... I'm going to send you this and I'm gonna leave a letter with the Rev. Remember how he helped and never judged us... well, I'm hoping he'll help me now, when I need him. When it all dies down go and find him. Okay. I told you I bumped into him... I'm sure you remember. Okay. Bye, Becs. I care for you and... bye.*

I stop the disc and take the headphones off. The sound of the rain swamps me and great wracking sobs devour my body. *I care for you...* he didn't say he loved me. Not even from the fucking grave... and the Rev... he went to the Rev but not to me. I don't understand. And he said maybe we were old and happy and... *Christ*, Drew, did you love me or not? Were we going to live happily ever after or... or what? I have to know. I have to know if I've ever been truly loved. I have to keep going to the end of this.

Chapter Fifteen

'Ten quid for a blowjob darling. You can pay me more if you like.'

He leans over me, his breath dark with booze and his eyes a mix of lust and loathing, he leers – thinking it's fun to scare women – to show them who's boss. But I don't shrink away from him. Instead, I hold his gaze and imagine I'm gutting him, sliding in a knife and pulling out his innards. He pulls away from me, not sure what he sees in my eyes, but he knows it isn't friendly. He stands straight, if a little wobbly, and takes a step back. He's much stronger than me, but the booze would make him slow. If I had a knife I could... but I turn away and ignore him. He isn't who I want to kill.

'Dyke,' he spits, and rolls away towards the escalator, chuckling at the wittiness of his comment. He thinks he's Stephen bloody Fry. I shiver, but it's from the cold, not fear. It's bloody freezing in this station concourse. The floor's marble and the walls are metal and glass. I turn back to the giant screen that hangs from the ceiling, and watch the breaking news continue to scroll across it. I'm hoping for something new, desperate for it to have changed, but it still has the same headline it's had for the last three hours.

Two dead and four injured in tube station knife attacks. Manhunt across London for the killers.

And then there are the six pictures of the victims. The first is Ayo – she looks really pretty and she's with a kid who must be Tara. I haven't seen a picture of her before, or at least I didn't look if one was shown to me. But now I do look… I see the poor motherless child, and that's all because of me. *Christ*, they both look so happy, the perfect mother and daughter team – of course that's the best copy for the newspapers and TV: happy people who are now dead and everyone around them is devastated. It doesn't matter that it isn't real, that Ayo's family had been destroyed years ago – but that isn't the story that gets the public angry and scared and buying more newspapers. That isn't what sells.

After Ayo and Tara, there are two CCTV pictures, they're lousy – fuzzy and blurred – but I can see it's them: Gene and Michael Vincent, though the police don't know that yet. All the police seem to know is that two men stabbed six people and escaped. They think it might be an act of terrorism – they always think that – it's obvious that the police don't know much, so all the press has is idle speculation and *experts* who say whatever they think makes a good story. Then the next headline crawls across the screen.

> Two men escaped the scene. If you see them do not approach them but alert the authorities. These men are armed and dangerous.

'God help you,' a woman says and she drops a pound coin in the cup in front of me, then moves on without catching my eye. I watch her as she walks away. She's wearing a Burberry raincoat that probably cost as much as a small car, but for a pound she can buy a conscience balm to salve any guilt that festers in her expensively styled head. I should throw the pound back at her, patronising bitch, but I keep it. Beggars can't be choosers – literally. I have seven pounds eighty pence now, enough to get some food before the last place closes… but not enough, not nearly enough, to do what I need to do.

I'm stuck. I went to the information booth when I first got here, a good few hours ago. The last train to Aberdeen goes at twelve thirty-five a.m. from Euston, which is about a fifteen-minute walk from here. The train takes almost thirteen hours to get to Aberdeen with three changes. The cost is forty-six pounds something. In the morning it will cost a hundred and sixty something. I haven't got the money for either. And if I was Gene Vincent I'd have someone at Euston looking for me, somebody I don't know but who has my picture. *Christ*, that thought burns my stomach. So I'm here at King's Cross, watching the giant screens and praying that they've been arrested. Praying they get caught, and that a part of the nightmare can end. At least then, I'd only have the entire British police force to hide from – okay so the police and the psychos and bastards that prey on women who're alone at night in the city. What a terrible fucking life this must be if you're homeless or on the streets, basing your very existence on the kindness of strangers – when we all know there isn't nearly enough kindness to go round now. These days you can't even trust a policeman to direct you home.

I look down the concourse again. I remember when King's Cross was an absolute pit of a place, wretched with prostitution and drugs, the depths of humanity available for anyone with a few quid. Every shop sold porn, the pubs had women stripping from lunch until closing time, and almost every one you saw had the pallor and dead eyes of a zombie. It was gruesome. But now it's been cleaned up and gentrified. You can get fancy pastries and hardback books, and even visit art galleries – that's the closest you'll get to a nude down here now. Though it doesn't mean the debauchery's gone, merely been moved on elsewhere. The council has created a slightly more *safe* zone here, but the drugs and destitution are still out there, women still have to open their legs for... *No*... it's not good to get this worked up on an empty stomach. And I'm starving. It's eleven thirty, and most places are closing down, as the last of the late-night drinkers gets the train home. I should probably get something with my seven pounds eighty... after all, what else will I do with it?

I have less than an hour for the last train tonight and if not that, then what do I do? Do I sit here all night watching the screen? Will I keep begging and at some point say yes to some drunk fuck who wants me to— *no*. I shake. I'm scared. I'm so bloody scared. And I'm so bloody alone.

Then from further down the concourse I hear a clattering sound and open my eyes to see two police officers walking through the concourse. They prod at a sleeping bag, waking someone up. There's no sleeping on the station, no homeless people allowed here. The poor man stands. He looks filthy and lost. The policewoman jabs her finger aggressively at him, and he cowers from her and grabs his worldly possessions up into his arms and staggers off. The police move on, coming towards me. My first instinct is to shrink away, roll into the shadows or maybe run... but I can't – there's nowhere to go. I need to brazen this out. I'm not homeless, I'm waiting for a train... waiting for friends... waiting... I sit as tall as I can and wait for them to reach me.

The news hasn't shown a picture of me. I'm not linked to Ayo – at least not yet. I have some grace. Maybe it's a day, maybe it's two, I don't know, but as the two police officers pass me, the woman stops and sizes me up, her eyes scanning me up and down. I stare back at her, I don't take my eyes away and I don't blink – not even when she sneers at me. Finally she has to pull her gaze from mine, but she does it with a comment to her partner that makes him look across at me and laugh. Bastards. They have no respect, not even pity for the people they see on the street. Where's their empathy? Shit, any one of us could fall one day... any one of us. Then the two officers turn and walk away, I'm invisible to them again. Good. I watch them, moving two others off the concourse and then they're gone.

I turn back to the rolling news. I have to know if they catch Gene and Michael. That's why I'm here, for the screen and the free toilets, as at least I did manage to wash in the station bathroom and get a drink of water. If they catch the brothers, then I might have choices. Then I could get to Aberdeen without the fear that they'll step out of the shadows and grab me – that's the problem with them knowing where I'm going. Aberdeen is their clue, but that's all they know; they don't know about the Rev.

The Cornish pasty shop has started to sweep up, maybe they would sell me a cheap pasty. I don't want to blow five pounds on something to eat, but I would love some hot food. I should go and ask. I get up, feeling the hours sitting cross-legged take their toll and I'm unsteady for a few seconds. Then I stop wobbling and head over to—

No.

My blood runs cold. I hadn't thought that was a real thing, just something cheesy that terrible writers say, but it actually happens. I feel cold, deep in my body as the rolling news screen finally does break the pattern of the last few hours and there is a new headline and a new photo – but fuck, why does it have to be a picture of me?

> Latest update on Tube attack. The fatal stabbings tonight are linked to a murder in Brighton on Sunday, police now believe. They are looking for this woman known as Sarah, though she was born Rebecca Waite. She is believed to be highly dangerous and may be armed. The public are warned not to approach her but to call for help.

Then it cuts back to the studio for another talking head. *Christ*, they know me... it must be Gene and Michael. They're trying to smoke me out. I feel... *oh god*... I have to hold onto the wall, I'm so dizzy. Everything's falling apart... I'm damned. Damned.

I stagger across the concourse. I don't even try to get a price cut. I blow every penny on a scalding pasty and a hot black coffee. I wolf them down, not even caring that they strip the lining off my throat. I head to the toilets and once inside I'm sick, which is a total waste of the food I just bought.

I throw water on my face, and then try and style my hair to look different. I head back up but stop as I take a step onto the concourse and see the two police officers again – they're searching, disturbing everyone and shining a torch in their faces like the Gestapo looking for Anne Frank. I think they must have recognised me. They might have called it in, there could be other officers here in minutes... *Christ*. I let them go past and then I run.

I head towards St Pancras, I have no choice now. I look ahead to where the Eurostar train comes in; around the entrance there are ATM machines. If I had any faith I would offer something up – come on, God, throw me a bone for you-know-who's sake. I speed up, and as I get close I see a man stumble slightly and then head to the cashpoints. He's dressed in a nice suit, but he appears to be wearing only one shoe. He gets to the ATM. He slides his card in and punches the numbers in. I have to time this to perfection.

'What's with the one shoe?'

'I'm sorry?' He turns to me. His eyes are huge, all black pupil, and I realise that he isn't drunk but stoned. He moves his head around a little, trying to get me into focus.

'You and me could find somewhere to go and party, I have a friend too. More than one, girl, boy, mix of both, whatever you—'

'I want to…' He hits at the ATM as his money comes out. He's disoriented and looks scared of me.

'I can hurt you… if you like that.'

'No,' he turns to run.

'Don't forget your cash,' I tell him and he turns back, desperately trying to focus on the machine. I can see that the beeping is hurting his head.

He grabs at the cash and backs away.

'Bye,' I say and he turns and runs. As he goes, I lean forward and pull his card from the machine and it stops beeping. I don't have long before police will surge through here.

I run.

I break onto Euston Road and can see the station a little way ahead. A clock tells me it's twelve fifteen. I have to hurry. There is no time to worry about whether Gene or Michael will have someone posted at the station. Now that my photo is live, every fucking man, woman and child in the country could spot me. I have to roll the dice and get on that train.

'You idiot,' a cabbie yells at me as I hurtle past him, making him slam on the brakes. My chest hurts, it burns, and my stomach complains. I have to ignore all that. I have to reject everything except the fact that the train will leave soon. I can see the station ahead. The air is cold and stings me a little. My throat burns. I doubt there will be a snack trolley on the train, but there's no time to buy anything.

I race into the station and see a bank of ticket machines. Thank god they raised the level on contactless payment. I hit the buttons to get a single to Aberdeen and hold the card against the payment window – I really do whisper a prayer this time. Where the hell does that come from, what deep recess of my mind contains actual prayers? The clock above me says twelve twenty-one – two minutes until the train goes. *Come on*. The machine starts to print all four of the squares of cardboard I will need. I beg it to hurry up. Finally the last one drops down and I run forward. One minute… oh my god. Platform seven – all the way over there. I run. My lungs burn. The train is there but the whistle's been blown.

'Wait,' I yell, but there's nobody there. I see it start to move. No, I'm too late. Goddamn, this is not fair. I reach the last carriage but it's moving ahead and none of the doors can open. I'm too late. I'm too bloody late. Why does God hate me? Why does—

'Come on then.' An arm stretches out as the last door opens. A man in a uniform grabs my hand and pulls me up, as the train starts to gather real speed.

'Oh my god, thank you, thank you.'

'No problem, no problem at all,' the guard says.

'Here's my ticket,' I wave it in front of his face.

'It don't matter at this time of the night. Where's your final destination?'

'Aberdeen,' I tell him and for a second I think I see a flicker of something in his eyes.

'Aberdeen, that's a long journey. No case?'

'No, my things got sent ahead. I'm moving up there for a new job so I can travel light tonight.'

'That's exciting, new start?'

'I hope so.'

'Great, well, sit where you like.'

I walk away from him. I get to the end of the carriage and then something makes me turn around, and I see that he's on the telephone. His eyes have followed me down the carriage and he's talking to someone. I think he's talking about me. I hold up my hand and wave at him, hoping I'm wrong. He waves back, sweet as pie.

Then I find somewhere to sit. I have a table to myself.

'You have to stay awake,' I tell myself. But as I slump down into the seat, and feel my head rest against the window, I know I won't be able to do that. I shall have to trust my life to the kindness of strangers. I feel my eyelids get heavier and heavier. I stuff my hands into my pockets and grip the Discman and CDs. They are all I have now, and they contain the secrets of where I'm going and what I'll do. I'm going to follow Drew, follow the directions he left me all those years ago. I'm going to find the Rev.

—

'The Rev,' I whisper to myself. Why him? He was a teacher at our school. He was a kind man... what was his real name? I stretch my mind back, years and years and… Hanley. David? Daniel… He'd been a vicar somewhere, but had kind of lost his faith and come to teach history and religious studies at our school. He was kind and funny, though often sad. He drank sometimes, and we caught him drunk once, he was totally shit-faced, so we helped him get home and cleaned up. After that he was always so friendly, but when my dad died and Drew and I got together, he was more than wonderful. He was the only grown-up who helped us, who understood us. We owed him so much for his kindness then, so It makes complete sense that Drew would go to him. Complete sense. Though it hurts that he didn't turn to me. He didn't trust me… He didn't love me enough to share the bad times with, and he didn't want a family with me. *Oh my god*, that hurts. That hurts so much.

I want to talk to him, ask him questions… but he's gone. My only hope is that he talked to the Rev about how he felt about me. Maybe I'm not merely looking for what happened to the money, maybe I'm looking for the truth about what happened to my life. The truth about Drew leaving me. Maybe the Rev can answer all my questions. Maybe I'll find out why my life exploded. Maybe the truth is in Aberdeen. Maybe.

Chapter Sixteen

Wednesday

'Northampton.'

'Wha—?' I swipe my hand across my face and feel something wet; *oh my god it's blood*. But when I look at the back of my hand it's only drool.

'We're in Northampton, this is where you change trains.' The guard that helped me onto the train is standing there. I look around. There's a few travellers, mostly asleep, bent over the tables or wedged against the windows.

'We'll be pulling out any minute. I think you should—'

'Yes, yes, thank you.' I get up and stumble towards the end of the carriage. I feel hollowed out by hunger and the desperation to sleep more. If I could, I'd hit the snooze button fifty times and fall back into the arms of the Sandman, but it's not an option.

'Careful.' An arm reaches out to take mine as I threaten to topple out of the door and face-plant into the concrete of the platform.

'Don't.' I snatch my arm away, scared for a moment that it's Michael, but it's no one I know, just some middle-aged man in a cagoule who looks shocked by my response to his kindness. 'Sorry, I mean thanks,' I mumble and stagger off the train. He probably thinks I'm drunk. I wish I was. I yawn, hard enough that my jaw almost dislocates. A giant clock hangs down from an archway – it's a little after two a.m. I only had an hour and a half sleep, no wonder I feel so bad.

I look around for someone to help me, or an inform-ation kiosk as I don't know when the next train is. My head and stomach start to complain about how badly I'm treating them. 'I know, I know...' I tell them but it doesn't stop their bitching. The platform is empty and the station's like a ghost town. I walk up a set of steps and follow the arrows to the way out – that's where I should find someone but there's nothing, only a big green button that says 'information'. I press it. Nothing. I press it again, holding it in for a few seconds and then there's a squawk of sound.

'Yes,' the voice sounds as sleepy as I am.

'I'm heading to Aberdeen, I—'

'Five-twenty train to Crewe.'

'That's more than three hours.'

'That's why the ticket was so cheap.'

Oh, I had wondered about that.

'Is there anywhere to eat?' I ask.

'I don't know. I'm at London Euston, I've never been to Northampton.'

'Well don't bother coming, it's not Las Vegas, not at two in the morning anyway.'

'When you get to Crewe, you get on the Edinburgh train and then at Edinburgh—'

'Jesus Christ, this is round the houses.'

'It's a long way.' He pauses. 'Why are you going there anyway? Sorry that's a bit personal.'

'Yeah it is,' I tell him.

'Bit bored I guess, sorry. I don't get many actual conversations in this job.'

'No big surprise,' I tell him. I think it's funny, to talk to a disembodied voice in the wee small hours. I can't see his face so it's kind of like a confessional.

'I'm on a pilgrimage,' I tell him.

'Oh,' he sounds disappointed. Now he thinks he's flirting with a religious nutjob.

'Not a churchy thing though, my husband did this trip years ago, visited an old friend before he died, so now I'm making that same journey.'

'Your husband died?'

'Yes.'

'I'm sorry,' the voice tells me.

'No need to be sorry, it was a long time ago.'

'Our dog died.'

'Oh.'

'Every year, on the anniversary, we do his favourite walk. Makes us remember him.'

'Yeah. That's sort of what I'm doing.'

'That's… oh, sorry. I have another help point flashing. I have to go.'

'Thanks, it was nice to talk…' but I know he's gone already.

I walk around the station, looking in every nook and cranny but there's nothing here. Not even a vending machine with overpriced stale crisps. I even go to the exit to walk outside and look down the street – all closed.

I go back inside and find a bench that's in shadow but has a good view of all the entrances. If Gene or Michael try and get me, I'll see them coming and I can scream my head off. I don't know if that will do me any good, but I won't go down without a fight. *Feel the anger, not*

185

the fear. That has to be my mantra now. *Feel the anger*... I do. I feel it so deeply now. I didn't even get to go to my Drew's funeral because of those bastards. They forced me to run away before my Drew was even put in the ground. I've never visited his grave, not seen the headstone. I don't know what his parents wrote on it, I don't know if they buried him in love or in shame for what the police said he did. I don't know if they're alive still. He had a sister, Amy, she was younger and cute – how the hell did she react to a bank-robbing dead brother? I never even tried to get in touch with her. Instead I ran away. Bloody hell, I'm just such rubbish at life. And I'm so tired I think I just have to close my eyes and hope.

–

I wake with a start. My head throbs and my stomach growls. I need to pee, but the toilets are locked, so I have to squat in the shadows at the end of the platform. It's still dark, I feel like I'm in perpetual night, and have been since Theo died; like I'm a vampire, hiding during the hours of daylight and then awake and running in the night. I'd like to stop, I'd like to feel the sun on my face again and not be looking over my shoulder, but that might not be for a while. I look up at the clock and see that my train's due soon. There are a few people on the platform now, yawning and shivering in the cold morning air. One of them has a newspaper and I sidle up to them, hoping to see the front page, but I can't really see anything without making it bloody obvious what I'm doing. There are still no shops open or places to eat. Maybe when I get into Crewe I can get something – though I'll need to use the debit card again, and I don't know how many times I can do that before I get found out.

As the clock ticks over to five-twenty a.m. I slide into the shadows at the back of the platform. I'm scared that Michael and Gene might be on it. Spending three hours here has robbed me of my head start, and I need to keep aware of the police and of CCTV cameras. They know me, they've got pictures of me, and come the dawn, there will be dogs out baying for my blood. That's the problem with today's world of social media; nobody can hide for long. If they want to find me hard enough, they will.

The train pulls into the station – lit up like an amusement park. I watch the carriages slide past and look for faces pressed against the glass. I don't see anyone that looks suspicious; no one seems to care about who's getting on the train in sleepy Northampton. I slip from the dark, and head into a carriage near the middle, close to a toilet and the end of a carriage. My head is down, my eyes scan the floor and my shoulders are hunched. I walk with a pronounced limp, I have no idea why – bloody stupid if you ask me, but once I start I'm committed to it. I sit opposite the loo and slink into the corner. I'm so tired but I can't afford to sleep. There's less than two hours on this train anyway. I have to stay awake. I have to.

At Crewe I drop the limp, but keep the hunched shoulders, head-bowed depressed look. It's a little before seven a.m. and there's only fifteen minutes until the Edinburgh train. I see a Boots open and run in there. I use the stolen credit card to buy paracetamol, some scissors, eye shadow, some hair colour, a sandwich, a bottle of water and a packet of crisps. It's risky, but I don't think the stoned guy will even have missed it yet. When the train pulls in, I watch it carefully, but I can't see anyone I know.

I get on, close to the toilet again, and immediately head inside. I open the packet of scissors and start to saw at my hair. I cut it in clumps, like I'm punk and then I dip my fingers into the hair colour and brush it through my hair, trying to keep it off my scalp but that isn't easy without a brush and comb. It looks pretty crappy but that doesn't matter, as long as I look different. Then I take the make-up and draw a line across my face – I imagine it might look like the robot in *Blade Runner*, but it doesn't. It looks more like a woman with mental health problems did her make-up in the bathroom of a swaying train carriage – so pretty much the truth, then.

I go back out and sit at a table that has a school kid and her mum already sitting there. I open the water, take a sip and then two paracetamol. I devour the sandwich, though a bit too much like a lion eating a gazelle. I can tell the kid's mum wishes she'd sat elsewhere but the kid's eyes are like saucers as she takes in this crazy-looking woman. I might smell a bit ripe too.

I look ahead and can see a man across the aisle has dropped his newspaper on the seat next to him.

'Could I have that?' I ask with a weird accent. I didn't know before it came out of my head that I was going to do a new voice too – and I don't know why I'm now a Russian that's been living in South America with a family from Nepal. I point at the newspaper and hope that I can communicate only in mime from now on. The man nods and hands the paper over. I open it slowly, scared to see—
No.

Gene Vincent opens the connecting door at the end of the carriage, a phone held to his ear and his eyes scanning the other passengers. I can't breathe. I could get up and go to the loo, but what if he looks up at that second and sees me, or waits to see who comes out? Anyway it's pretty much a moot point, as my legs are trembling so much I don't know that I could walk. I'm stuck here. I watch him get closer and closer to me and—

'Do you want a banana?' The little girl asks and jabs it towards me.

'No, Carrie, don't talk to the lady.' The mother grabs at her daughter's hand. I think she's afraid that if the kid touches me, she'll get infested by a goth-punk virus.

'That's sweet, kid. I'm Anastasia,' I tell her and open my hand to accept the fruit, not caring about how annoyed her mum looks. I peel the banana and put the flesh into my mouth. I make it look like I'm giving the banana a blow-job, nice and slow, as Gene's eyes roam across our table and… they move on quickly, embarrassed by the rude young woman. Ha! I knew he'd be a prude like my dad. Both of them would look away and blush at anything they thought was un-ladylike. I watch him as he gets to the end of the carriage and opens the door to the next, and he's gone. I think it was a brilliant idea, but I can see from the look of horror on the mum's face that she thought it rather inappropriate to deep-throat a banana in front of her child.

'Carrie,' the mum squawks, grabs the kid's hand, and pulls her out of the chair with a jerk. She drags poor little Carrie down the carriage and pretty much throws her into an empty seat. I wink over at her, and bite the banana in two. Then I hunker down into the corner and close my eyes. Gene didn't recognise my face but he might remember my coat, so slowly, and as surreptitiously as I can, I slide my jacket off and drop it onto the floor. Now I pray he won't come back, as I watch as the first rays of light kiss at the horizon.

When we reach Edinburgh, I watch the brothers. They get off the train and wait at the top of the slope, just before the ticket barrier. I can see them scanning the hordes of commuters that trundle through. They watch as everyone gets off and then wait a few more minutes for any stragglers, but I can see they're antsy as the train to Aberdeen will leave soon. They wait as long as they can and then, with less than two minutes to go, they turn and run for the Aberdeen train. I slip off and follow them, but when I get to the platform I can see that it's no use. It's only four carriages. If we all get on, there's no way I can stay hidden from them, and so I have to watch the train pull away with them on it. Damn. I run to a train guard and start crying as I tell him I missed my train and that I can't afford another ticket. I really pile it on, I cry so much that he takes pity on me and issues a ticket for the next train for free. I have an hour to kill, so I get some food and buy a new coat. I will arrive in Aberdeen at ten to two, but now I know for sure that the Vincent brothers will be there to meet me.

Chapter Seventeen

The Lady Vanishes... that's the film set on a train where an old English governess disappears, and all the train staff insist they never saw her. Somebody writes on the window, and later on it steams up and the writing reappears. The hero reads it – and that's the proof the old lady was real... I think. That's what I remember anyway, I think it was a Hitchcock. I breathe on the glass and write *help me.* Maybe someone will read it later and... stupid. I rub at it with my sleeve, erasing my plea for help. There's no hero coming to save me, this isn't the movies.

I watched a lot of films when I was a kid, though of course we couldn't tell my dad. I'd stay home from school, say I was sick and my mum and I would curl up on the sofa and watch some old film. That was mostly on days when he'd hurt her, or not been careful enough and the bruises showed – then she would call in sick at work, and stay home until she healed. I loved those days. I loved any time when *he* wasn't there, days when it was just the two of us. That's why I love old films.

And I'm trying to remember a film where someone jumps off a train, but I can't recall one. It probably wouldn't help anyway; I doubt it would give me practical tips. I guess I protect my head and bend at the knees... and hope I don't kill myself. I look out and I can see smoke spiralling into the air in the distance. I'm guessing that's the outskirts of the city. We're due to arrive soon, but I can't be on the train when it pulls in. They'll be waiting for me. I've looked at hiding places on the train, but there aren't any that will work. If I ride all the way into Aberdeen, then Gene or Michael will find me and… the thought of what they'll do to me makes me feel nauseous. I look out through the window again and follow the snake of the tracks ahead. I'm lucky because this is an old train and not a new one where you can't get any air. In between the carriages there's a way to squeeze out and jump. I'll have to be quick, I can't delay – no *umming* or *ahhing* – no fear; it will have to be a leap of faith. If anyone sees me jump, then they'll pull the emergency cord and the police will come.

Across the aisle I can see my own face as it glowers out at me from the cover of the newspaper. *Face of a Killer – The Brighton Airbnb Murderer.* Where the hell did they get such a mean-looking picture of me, it must be from CCTV. I look like the Kray twins' hench little sister. I'd like to read the story, but I daren't ask the man to lend me the paper, I don't want to draw attention to myself. I know my hair looks different now, but I don't want to risk it.

Ahead, it looks as if the train will have to slow down for one of the banking turns that the tracks take as they head into the city. That's when I'm going to have to jump. If it isn't then, it'll be never, and I'll be caught. My heart is starting to race, I can feel the train start to slow as the driver applies the brakes. I have to time this to perfection. I can't hurry – that will draw attention – I have to get up quietly, walk slowly and evenly, no noise, no sudden movement. I'll get to the door and open it as the train slows... then I'll close the door behind me and dodge to the left and jump. I won't even look down. *Ready?*

I feel the train slow a little more and bank to the right. I can do this... I have faith that I can do this... I reach out to the door and twist it. I go through, closing the door softly, and I stand between the two carriages and feel the cold air on my skin. Winter is coming. I feel it bite, I really don't have the right clothes, I— *shut up, Rebecca/Sarah/Fran whoever the hell I am today. Shut up and stop thinking, let your brain rest and do something simple.* The cold makes me shiver – it's just the cold – not fear. *Jump.* I'm in no man's land here. I love you, Mum... I'm coming to find the truth, Drew. I take a leap of faith. I jump from a moving train. I am so dum—

-

'Aaargh.' *Snap – Christ*, is that bone or twig breaking as I hit the ground? Pain drives through my ankles, into my legs and hips – I twist like Chubby Checker, and something hard smashes into my side. I scream, but I can't hear myself. I bounce, and tumble and roll – I hit and hit and hit. I can't stop moving, falling and tumbling. I'm careening down a bank; it shifts under me like marbles. My legs flail and my arms cartwheel like Wile E. Coyote in a *Road Runner* cartoon.

'No.' A sinewy trunk grabs at my foot, pulling me sideways – my hip drives into the ground and then I'm flipped up and I'm head over heels, like that cheese they bounce down the hill in Gloucester. I try and put out my hand to stop myself, but I feel a ripping of skin, and pain flashes up my arm.

I hit a tree and everything turns bla—

You deserved that, child, you must learn to follow the orders of your elders and betters. You will never amount to anything good with your attitude. You are nothing... NOTHING.

–

There's the sound of water splashing. I might be peeing myself, I can't tell. My head hurts, like a bomb went off in my skull. My whole body aches; it's like the opposite of when I leave my body and fold into nothing to escape the pain. Now the pain is everything. I'm fully in my body and it's on fire. Then something is placed against my head and—

'Ow.'

'Sorry,' a soft lilting voice says, and then there's the sound of more water and then something wet is pressed against my head again, and the pain spikes through me once more.

'Please don't,' I manage to moan. I try to open my eyes but I think they've been sewn shut – they feel like they'll tear if I do open them.

'We should call a doctor,' the same voice says, but not to me. I think she must be talking to someone else... but there's no sound from them. No sound at all.

'I don't need a doctor,' I say and try to open my eyes. 'Oh my god.' The pain stabs through my head, I feel like I'm on a rollercoaster, and I retch.

'Grab the bucket again,' the soft voice says, and I feel something plastic push into my chin. I want to vomit – I really do, I think it would make me feel a whole lot better – but I can't, there's nothing to come out. Instead I dry heave for a while, before collapsing backwards. I feel terrible. I try and raise my head but—

'Don't try and move, you have a lot of bruising, cuts and abrasions.'

A glass is pushed to my lips and my head is gently tipped forward.

'Try and drink,' the woman says. It isn't water, or not pure water, anyway. There's a bitterness to it – sharp – like lemon juice.

'Here.' A couple of tablets touch my lips and I open my mouth. The liquid is tipped in too, and I force myself to swallow the pills.

'Good, that's good. You should start feeling a little better soon. The pain will pass. Everything ends eventually,' she says. I manage to nod and then an inky black seems to surge around me and over me, and I drown.

—

The next time I come back into the realm of the living, I think I can hear a low whistling, but it might just be my brain dying.

'She's awake, I think she's awake.' The same woman's voice as before, comes from close by. A damp cloth is placed on my forehead and someone feels my wrist; I assume they're checking my pulse.

'Would you like something?' the woman asks. 'There's soup.' And some hands grip my back and shoulders, and pull me back onto the pillow so I'm propped up. I wince a little at the pressure on my skin, as I feel like I've been flayed alive. In response there's an apologetic grunt.

'Here you are,' and a spoon is held to my lips.

'I can feed myself, I'm not a child!' I snap, and the spoon is pulled away and I hear the liquid being tipped back into the bowl.

'Chicken noodle,' the unseen woman says. 'I hope you aren't a vegan.' She says *vegan* like she means *crazy*.

'No, I'm not vegan – even though I hear it's good for you to…' but my words fall away as I finally mange to tear my eyes open and see where I am. It's like I've gone back in time, or been dumped into a Hobbit house in Middle Earth. I'm in an old-fashioned cottage. There are wooden beams above my head and whitewashed walls. There's no natural light; heavy curtains cover what must be a window. I'm in a bed, or a day-bed, more like, though it's really low to the ground – and actually that's the weirdest thing: the height of all the furniture is wrong, like it's all been made for a child's doll house. I move my head from side to side (which makes tiny little bombs explode in my head) and I can see that the walls are covered with framed cross-stitch scenes and quotes from the bible. The biggest one is of Homer Simpson on the cross – no, it can't be him – I guess it's Jesus, but he's pretty yellow. In the corner there's a large, old-fashioned radio, like my grandmother had. It's sitting on a small table that's so low it's almost on the floor.

'You need to eat you know,' the lilting voice tells me, and I realise I can't see her. Then she pushes forward, into my line of sight, and I see she's in a wheelchair. No wonder everything in the room is at an odd height – it makes perfect sense now. Behind me another person moves. He comes round and stands behind her, and I can see that he's in no way a hobbit – more of a giant. He's big and solid, dark and… well, the word that springs to mind is *meaty*.

'Where am I?' I sound like a rusty hinge.

'Our farm.'

'How did I get here?'

'We found you.' She pauses. 'Unconscious. We didn't know if we should call an ambulance or the pol—'

'No.' I cut her off. 'No need to bother anyone.' I try and give her a *you find unconscious people that look beaten up every day* smile.

'The soup smells amazing,' I say, and I'm not lying, because it really does – but it also serves to change the topic of conversation – though to underline how good the soup smells my stomach begins to rumble, and I think I actually start to drool.

'Then you should have some,' she says and I feel my fingers move as a spoon is placed between them. I try to grip it – I really concentrate – but it clatters to the floor. The man bends down and retrieves it.

'I'll get another,' the woman says and wheels away.

'Five-second rule,' I say. 'It'll be fine, but maybe I do need some help after all.'

'Leonard, could you?' she says to the man and I feel his hand grab mine and mould my fingers around the spoon.

'Oh,' I whimper, and start to shake. I can't help it – it feels exactly like Gene moulding my fingers around the knife that stabbed Theo.

'Leonard,' the woman chastises him, as if he's been too rough with me.

'N-n-no…' I stammer. 'It isn't him…' My hand is shaking uncontrollably. I can see the concern on both their faces and know that they'll call an ambulance if I don't pull myself together… *oh god*… I stare at my hands and force them to stop shaking. 'I'm okay, really I am,' I tell them. 'I am hungry, though.'

Leonard reaches over and helps me lift the spoon, now full of broth and a lump of moist chicken. He leans forward to blow on it, and then helps bring it to my lips. I slurp it down. It's a little salty but it tastes so good.

'Yum,' I say and he slowly feeds me the entire bowl.

When we're done, I let myself fall back into the softness of the pillows. It was quite an effort to keep my neck forward and I feel a wave of tiredness wash over me.

'We should let you rest,' the woman in the wheelchair says. 'I'm Hannah, by the way. And this is Leonard. He doesn't speak, except a little with his hands.'

'Oh,' I say and turn my head so that I can see him. He turns a little red and won't meet my eye. I lift a hand and wave at him.

'He isn't deaf,' Hannah says. 'He just can't speak,' and Leonard moves away, into the shadows so I can't see him anymore. I look back to the woman in the wheelchair. 'I'm…' I dry for a second. 'I'm Jane.'

'Hello, Jane,' she says and smiles thinly. 'We'll let you rest.' And with that, she wheels away and Leonard follows her.

Once they're gone I sit up in my makeshift bed, which isn't easy, but I force my aching body to do what I tell it. This is no time to sleep; the police and the Vincents will be searching for me, so I can't stay here, I'll be a sitting duck. I have to… *argh*… pain jags through my side and up my back and into my head where it explodes in a firework display that's better than the fourth of July and New Year's Eve rolled into one. I grip the bed with both hands. I breathe hard, trying to… *huh*… and as the pain calms down, I realise that I'm not in my own clothes. I'm wearing pyjamas: striped men's pyjamas that remind me of a prison uniform. *What the hell? Why do people keep undressing me when I'm unconscious?*

I swing my legs over the side of the bed and slowly put them down onto the floor. I feel a creaking in my hips and my side feels heavily bruised. I try and raise an arm but it only gets to about shoulder height before I want to start screaming. I slide off the bed and onto the floor. The flagstones are cold. I gingerly step over to the door and see there's a mirror. I look at myself and barely recognise the woman there. My face has been scrubbed clean, so all the make-up has gone. It looks like my hair has been washed and set. Some of the dye has come out and the contrast of the stripe is less pronounced now – I don't look quite as much like a badger on heat. I look alive at least, my eyes burn bright. I look like I want to get something done – and I do. There have been times over the last fifteen years when I've looked in the mirror and seen nothing – literally nothing, like I was invisible, with nothing to live for. But that's changed now, as I have a mission. I give myself a wink – cheeky I know – but it makes me smile. I like my smile. I wish I did it more.

There is the lightest tap on the door, which opens before I have a chance to say anything and a wheel pushes through it. 'I thought I heard you get out of bed. This is an old house and you can't go anywhere that people don't know it,' Hannah says as she rolls inside. 'I really think you should rest more.'

'I want to get up and stretch my legs, I don't want to lie down anymore. How long was I out for?'

'A while,' she says enigmatically – which is really annoying.

'What time is it?'

'It's late afternoon.'

'Then I shouldn't sleep, I have to get moving.'

'Of course, if you feel up to it.'

'I do, but my clothes, I was looking—'

'I washed them, they're hanging up to dry now. I'm not sure they're quite done.'

I look down at the pyjamas I'm wearing and feel a little blush creep through me. They're fine pyjamas – silk, maybe – but they're far too big and I can feel where they hang off me and gape open, so that anyone can see through to my naked skin. I don't feel comfortable in them.

'I'd really like to wear something...' I flounder for the right word, not wanting to embarrass either of us.

'Warmer?' she asks and I nod gratefully. She tells me to wait a moment and wheels herself off. After a little while she comes back with a pair of jeans, a T-shirt for some band I've never heard of, and a thick Aran jumper that's beautiful. For a second I don't see any underwear – then she drops them down. There're thick cosy socks and a pair of knickers that are tiny and revealing, like a thong, and won't cover much of anything.

'I'm sorry, your underwear is still wet and this is all I have,' she says. 'These are... unworn.'

'Thanks, I'll...' I nod my head to the door, wanting privacy while I change my clothes. She looks me up and down for a moment. I feel her eyes scan my body and appraise me; there is a flick of her tongue against her top lip, just the tiniest movement, and then she nods, and wheels herself backwards. I close the door, noticing that it doesn't have a lock, and then I strip off the pyjamas. Naked, I see the bruises that cover me, they're all shapes, sizes and hues of purple and blue – I'm a bloody mess.

I put the clothes on, even the skimpy panties. I can't imagine Hannah in these clothes. Not only in terms of style but I can't see them ever fitting her. I pull the Aran jumper over my head and it's bliss. I have never worn anything so soft, like strapping a whole hutch of angora rabbits to my chest and cuddling them. The socks are the last thing I put on and they're chunky, almost like boots. I couldn't possibly wear them with shoes, but they're so toasty on the cold flagstones.

Feeling almost human again, I open the door and walk out into the rest of the house. I follow my nose to the kitchen, which is warm and buzzing with herbs and spices. I can immediately see that the entire room has been adapted to accommodate Hannah's wheelchair. The Aga has been lowered from its normal height – maybe the floor was dug down, so that the hotplates are at wheelchair height. The sink's also lower than I would have expected, and a ramp goes all around the walls so that the larders and cupboards are within easy reach. There's some kind of pulley system too, so that pans can be lowered down or hoisted up to the ceiling.

'This is very impressive,' I say as I walk in.

'Yes, after my accident Leonard adapted the entire house to accommodate my new situation.'

'It looks great, very professional.'

She smiles. 'That's good to know, but it still doesn't allow me to open a jar.' She holds up some kind of preserved fruit and I take it off her. I try to unscrew it, but the top won't twist. So I hold it firmly, and whack the metal lid hard onto the sink top. There is a little *farp* sound and the centre of the lid pops up and I twist it off.

'Thanks, who needs a husband when you have such a pretty guest?' she says and I feel myself blush a little.

'What are you making with the...' I point at the red-orange fruit.

'They're apricots. I was going to make a crumble. Traditional. Do you like custard?' she asks and I nod, trying to look enthusiastic, when really I'm not a great custard fan. I think it was school that put me off it, all those heavy suet puddings with yellow water sitting in the bottom of the plate – yuk.

'Can I help?' I offer.

'No, that's okay...' She pauses, and her eyes appraise me again, this time more coldly. 'I don't need help, *Jane*. Thank you very much for the offer. Dinner will be in a couple of hours. I think it's time for a nap, you know, you still don't look right.'

'Did you undress me?' I ask but she doesn't answer. Instead, she cuts herbs and scatters them in a pot. 'And I think I was washed.'

'Bathed, my darling,' she says. 'And then we treated your cuts and bruises. I was a nurse once – long time ago now – before...' She makes a motion towards her chair, and then she goes back to her pot. She can't have undressed me; it must have been Leonard.

'I should get going,' I tell her. 'You have been wonderful hosts but—'

'That won't do, child,' she says and shakes her head. 'Not now, not tonight. The weather's bad and it will be a miserable night. I don't trust that head of yours too, you need a night of observation.' She makes a clucking sound like a worried hen.

'I'm sure my head's fine.'

'Well let's be careful. I don't think there's a concussion but it's better to be safe and not sorry. So, I'd like to keep an eye on you.'

I frown, a little unsure. 'I guess that's okay.'

'Tomorrow morning we can drive you into town.'

'Aberdeen?'

'Of course Aberdeen, where else?'

'I don't... I mean, thank you. That would be kind.'

'Was that where you were going when...' She doesn't finish her sentence. She looks at me, wide-eyed, waiting for me to fill in the gaps but I don't say a word. I don't know what to say. Finally, she can't wait any longer and asks: 'Did you get lost?'

'Yes... yes, I was lost. I was out on a hike.'

'You were out hiking?' She frowns.

'Yes.'

'In those beaten-up trainers?'

I set my jaw, knowing I am going to have to brazen this out. 'Not the ideal footwear but I'm in training, and it's for charity.'

'Charity?'

'Yes, last year I ran the London marathon in stilettos and I'm going to hike across Scotland in heels.'

'What's the charity?'

'Save the Children,' I tell her. It's a pretty good lie, I think; nobody is going to challenge Save the Children. Everyone loves children.

'I was hiking but I got lost, then I heard the train and was following the tracks into town, but I slipped and tumbled down the bank.'

'Hmmm,' she purses her lips. I don't know that she believes me. Then she shrugs. 'Well those trainers are ruined, the sole is breaking away and there are so many holes in them I could use them to drain pasta. I think we might have something better suited. By the front door there's a shoe rack. Go have a look. I don't need...' and she looks down at her feet, nestled below her on the bar at the base of the chair. 'It would be good if someone actually used them.'

I nod and smile at her, before heading to the front door. The hallway is dark and oppressive, with low ceilings and exposed beams. At the front door there's the shoe rack she mentioned. The men's shoes are on one side and then a series of women's shoes, but each pair seems to be a different size. It's really odd. It's as if four or five women live here. The last pair on the rack are my old and battered trainers. I can see that Hannah's right; they really are wrecked.

I stand in the hallway and look at the front door. I reach out. It's made of heavy wood, I want to say *oak* but actually I'm terrible with this kind of thing, and it could be pretty much anything. It's solid and there isn't a letterbox. I want to open it, and at least see if it's day or night out there. But when I grip the handle and pull, nothing happens. It's locked and there's no key that I can see.

'Everything okay?' Hannah calls out from the kitchen. 'Did you find any shoes that fit?'

'Yes,' I call back and pull out a pair of walking boots that look my size. 'I'll try them on.' Inside, written in sharpie, I see the name *Tina Bray*. They fit.

'Who—'

'Can you help me with some jam?' Hannah calls out.

'Coming,' I call back. I don't finish my question. Maybe I don't want to know about Tina Bray.

—

After I help with the jam, Hannah has me peeling potatoes, and then together we light fires in the sitting room and in a small bedroom.

'This will be yours – for tonight,' she tells me, as I kneel down to light the fire. On the walls there are posters for films and pop bands. I don't know the bands, but one says *The Sweet*, and in the centre is a blonde man with a swirling silver shirt.

'Is this your daughter's room?'

'No,' she says with a colder voice than before. 'We never...' She pauses, and I can see that she's wrestling with something, but I have no idea what it could be. 'God never blessed us with children.'

'Oh... I'm—'

'No matter,' she says brusquely, like she really wants that to be an end to it, and then she wheels off, leaving me alone in the room. To the side of the bed there's a window, with a heavy curtain in front of it. At least I can look outside and see if it's still day. I pull the curtain aside and look at a wooden shutter. It's been nailed shut and then for good measure, the nails have been painted over.

'What's the time?' I call out.

'Nearly dinner time,' Hannah yells back.

'Okay,' I say. I feel lost in time without being able to see the outside world. I look to the bed, which is small but looks comfy. I suppose I should stay here tonight and leave tomorrow. That should be okay – shouldn't it? I look at the door. I can see where there used to be a lock on it, but it's been taken off. The screw holes are still there, bare and ugly, but no lock. I head back to the kitchen, feeling anxiety start to prick at me with each step.

–

Dinner is pork. It smells amazing, roasting in the oven, and I can see a sauce bubbling on the stove, releasing sweet heady notes of apple and cinnamon.

'Sit, sit...' She motions me to the table.

'Is there anything I can—'

'No, just sit.' She makes it sound like there's nothing I could possibly do that would match her skills, so why bother. I'm sure she's right, so I sit and watch her get the pork out of the oven and put it down on the table. It spits a little, as the oil and fat sizzle.

'This was Amy,' Hannah tells me proudly. 'She won a rosette – Leonard slaughtered her on Sunday. You can't beat fresh, home-grown pork.'

'He killed her here?' I look around the kitchen, afraid that I'll see a bucket of blood and some trotters or something hanging from the side – but there's nothing gross.

'She had a good life, we loved her,' Hannah says simply.

'And now you eat her?'

'She gave herself willingly; it was always her destiny to feed us, but for two years she had the best life a pig could imagine. She was happy. Content. Apple sauce?'

I nod and she starts to slice and spoon and stir... I'm actually too hungry to show any real vegetarian morals, so I let her pile my plate high with slices of Amy, roast potatoes, cabbage, runner beans and carrots. There is also an amazing mushroom gravy. While she makes up the plates, Leonard comes in and I see him properly for the first time. He's older than I first thought, probably in his late fifties, about the same age as Hannah. He's tall and dark, with a long face, and has a criss-cross of scars along his neck and throat. It looks like they were done some time ago, as scar tissue has built up around them. They look like they would have been nasty, maybe even life-threatening, all he needs is bolts in his neck and there would be something of the Frankenstein monster about him.

'Hello,' I call out in as friendly a voice as I can muster. 'I'm Jane, I haven't said thank you for finding me and bringing me in.' He doesn't even look at me, but goes to the sink and washes his hands – which are black and crusted, like he's been digging into the mud with them. I watch the water turn a red-black as it swills through his fingers and fills the sink with what looks like blood.

Once he's done, he sits at the head of the table. Hannah hands him two plates and he places one before me, and the second he puts down in front of himself. Then he bows his head as if in silent prayer.

'Please feel free to say Grace, Jane. Leonard still feels the need to thank God but I don't. Not anymore.' She pours the gravy.

–

The food is amazing, though the conversation is a little stilted and awkward. Leonard doesn't open his mouth all the time we sit there, and Hannah asks no questions, merely answers those that I throw out to her, with as few words as she can. I think I catch Leonard making movements with his hands, saying something in sign language to Hannah, but I could be wrong. It might just be a nervous wringing of the hands or something.

'So, you can take me into Aberdeen tomorrow morning?' I ask Leonard, but it's Hannah that replies.

'Surely, Leonard wakes at four a.m to tend the animals and breakfast will be at six. Then we can drive in to town.'

At that, Leonard jumps as if an electric current has been shot through him.

'It's okay, you can… you can do that… Leonard can drive again, Leonard can drive to town,' she says to him in a sing-song voice, the kind that you would use with a baby or frightened pet.

'If it's a problem—'

'It isn't,' Hannah pretty much snaps at me. 'He's just nervous as he hasn't driven much lately, not outside the farm… not for quite some time.' She smiles at me, but it feels false. 'He needs more practice, then his confidence will come back.'

'Yeah, I get that. I just drove for the first time in years and… it was quite a ride,' I tell them.

'I'm sure,' she says and then turns away from me and her voice drops and becomes more calming as she reaches out and strokes her husband's arm. 'Nothing to worry about, it's all going to be fine.'

'I would really appreciate that, but I don't want to put anyone out.'

'But you aren't putting us out. We're glad you are here, I've been praying for you to come…' Her eyes twinkle for a second and she looks a little like a crazy Christian or David Icke acolyte, then she smiles and looks normal again. 'I mean that we hoped someone like you would come.' She puts her hands together in a prayer-like gesture. 'Leonard needs help, you see, and you are just what he needs.'

'O-kay… I mean, of course I would help, but I do have to get to Aberdeen tomorrow,' I say, feeling incredibly awkward. I really hope this isn't going to turn into some weird sex thing. I feel my hands curl into fists, my fight or flight response triggered, and I estimate the distance to the door if I were to run. Obviously she couldn't chase me, but what about him? He looks slow and lumbering but that's how they are in horror films. Like Frankenstein or zombies or Jason – they all lumber after you (okay so modern zombies can sprint to eat your brains, but Leonard doesn't look like a zombie Usain Bolt) but they never get tired. It's like the tortoise and the hare – if the tortoise is a homicidal maniac and the hare is a scantily clad teen with a scream that only dogs can hear.

'You misunderstand me, I don't mean that we need something from you,' Hannah says and lays her hands down on the table and clasps mine. Her hand is warm, and she squeezes mine for a second. 'No we don't need anything, it was more that we've missed being able to help someone, to feel needed. Finding you unconscious and bringing you back here, that was what I had hoped for. To feel like we've done something worthwhile and connected with the outside world again – it's pretty lonely out here, you know. And Leonard only has this old cripple for company.'

'Nyargh,' he groans, but I can't tell if he's agreeing with her or chiding her.

'Well, I'm glad to be... I mean that I'm lucky you found me,' I stumble through my thanks as I'm a little confused and more than a little freaked out by Hannah's intensity. 'It's good to have hot food, I can't remember the last time I had actual home-cooked food in a real home, all I usually do, is boil a kettle and pour it into a Pot Noodle. So thank you,' I tell them both as I look from one to the other. Hannah's eyes glitter but Leonard won't meet my gaze. There's something up with him and I don't know what it is. I'll be glad to get away from here. No matter how grateful I might be that they found me and brought me in, I still don't want to spend any more time here than I have to. They make my spidey senses tingle.

'Do you want to have crumble right away or have it later?' Hannah asks as I hand my plate over to her. I have literally licked it clean, it's the best meal I've had in years and I'm actually in pain because I've stretched my stomach close to breaking point.

'I think I need to lie down, I'm feeling a little groggy. I could wash up and then—'

'No, you should go to bed and get a good night's sleep. Leonard will do the dishes. You are our guest. You don't need to do anything.'

'Thanks.' I get up and feel a little dizzy. 'That was a lovely meal, Hannah.' I walk to the door like I'm drunk.

'Good night, Jane,' she says sweetly. 'Though it's funny, but you don't look like a Jane, I would never have guessed that you were one, and I'm normally so good with people's names.'

I stop in the doorway and have to hold onto the frame as my legs are a bit like jelly. I know the safest place to be in a house during an earthquake is in a doorway – but what if the earthquake is inside you? I turn and look at Hannah, she has a quizzical look running across her mouth.

'Who do you think I am?'

She frowns. 'I would have said you were a Sarah.'

I feel my jaw tighten so hard it might snap. The intensity of my tiredness dips a little as I watch her face, but there's no knowing smile or any tick; she looks as if she just plucked a nice name out of the air.

'Sarah?' I say, looking her deep in the eyes. 'No I don't see myself as a Sarah. I wasn't born a Sarah and I don't think my mum even liked the name.'

'Oh well, Jane is nice.' And she turns away from me, to stack the plates. 'You should get some rest,' she tells me over her shoulder.

'Yes… thank you,' I say to her back, and then I lean my hand over to the knives that hang from a knife block.

I take one that's long and sharp. I slide it into my waistband and then fold my jumper over it.

'Goodnight,' I say as I leave the kitchen. I feel my heart beating fast and a wave of nausea hits me. I feel giddy, like I'm at altitude and I can't get enough oxygen. There is a slight shift, like the world suddenly slants to the left and I can hardly stand up. It's all I can do to walk to my room, as with every step, I shake more and more. I know there's no lock on the door, I wish there were, but it's too tiring to do something about it. I manage to get to the bed, and pull the blankets up and over me before the dark sea crashes back down on me and I lose consciousness.

—

'You're a slattern.'
　　'I'm not, don't say that I am.'
　　'You're a whore.'
　　'No.'
　　'A harlot, a jezebel.'
　　'No.'
　　'A murderer.'
　　'Dad?'

—

I feel the cold before anything else. It's on my legs and belly. Cold between my thighs. My legs are naked – I don't know what happened to my trousers… and my chest is bare too, where is my soft, warm jumper? In the cold my nipples are erect, and I'm angry with them for betraying me. The covers have been pulled away and I'm completely naked. It's so dark, and I pat around my body for the clothes or the covers… but there's nothing. And then I hear a kind of guttural growl and a dark shape shifts in the air above me, and hands grip my ankles.

'*Nyargh...*' I moan and try and pull my legs together but they won't go, they're held and then I feel breath on my legs and thighs as a weight moves onto me. I hate the dark; the shadows twist and my mind imagines monsters – worse than a man, though in reality there is no monster worse than a man. Leonard is between my legs. His breath is hot and heavy with booze. He's naked too, I feel his skin on mine as he forces my legs wider apart. I turn my face away. My arms are free and my hand feels under my pillow to where the knife is. My fingers curl around the hilt. It's thinner than the knife that killed Theo and not as sharp. This knife isn't meant for butchering; it won't go through flesh like butter. This knife will get caught on ligament and sinew, will bounce off bone. I will have to use force, I will have to channel hate and anger and... I feel his weight on me and between my legs, forcing them wider apart. He growls and I swing the knife forward. It's a guess – I can't see him but I have a vague sense of where his heart is.

'Get off me,' I hiss, as I press the tip of the knife into his skin. 'I will stab you. I will. I will kill you if you don't let me go.'

I pull my other hand over to hold the knife – I'm shaking. He doesn't grab at my arms but he thrusts his groin into mine. I go to push the blade, deeper and harder. I could thrust it through his heart – skewer him like a pig. Like roasted Amy. A knife into his heart before he forces his manhood into me. I push the blade in and feel his flesh give a little. I could kill him, but... but... he doesn't have a hard on. He pushes against me again and growls. I can feel that he's naked, I feel his penis against me, but it's soft.

'Get off me or I'll kill you,' I spit, my voice full of venom. But he doesn't get off me; instead he pushes against me harder, like he's dry humping me – but instead of a growl, the sound is more like a whimper and then he gurgles a word that sounds like *please*. Then he whimpers again, and he stops moving and slumps on me. His whimper turns to a rhythm of noises deep in his throat – and I realise it's a prayer. The knife has cut into him; I feel a drop of blood fall onto me. Just one, warm and thick.

'Leonard, get off me,' I say in as calm a voice as I can, and I pull the knife away from his chest.

'Urggh,' he moans and his hand grips my wrist and pulls the knife back to his chest. '*Please...*' he gurgles, from deep in his chest, and then I feel warm drops on my skin but now they aren't blood, but tears like a spring rain. They fall onto my chest and start to form rivers that run down my stomach to pool in my belly button. He's sobbing like a child, like a lost little boy who knows he will never get what he wants; a boy that has suddenly come to know the unfairness of life.

'I'm sorry, Leonard.' Hannah's voice comes out of the dark and I hear her wheelchair move forward.

'What the hell is going on?' I yell, pushing at his head and shoulders, trying to get him off me.

'I told you she wouldn't do it. I said I didn't think she could,' Hannah says. 'I thought she was good, deep down.'

'Do what? What wouldn't I do? Jesus Christ, what perversion is this?'

'Kill him, child, I told him you wouldn't kill him.'

'Kill?'

'Yes, that's what he wanted from you. It is a sin to take one's own life, but for it to be taken by the violence of another... He wanted you to be his executioner and deliver him to heaven.'

'Why the hell would he think I'd kill him?'

'Because you're a killer, Sarah. You murdered your boyfriend Theo.'

In the dark I can't see what her face is doing. I can't see anything of either of them. I feel cold, like a snowman was just built on my grave. 'I didn't kill Theo,' I say low and clear.

'You're not a killer?' she says and actually sounds disappointed.

'I... I didn't kill Theo,' I tell her, which is the best answer I can give right now. I think the jury's out on Ayo. I try and get up, but Leonard's weight still pushes down on me. He doesn't move, a dead weight. I'd think he *was* dead if he wasn't still crying silent tears onto me.

'I don't know what you think happened, but you're wrong and I sure as hell can't give you what you want, Leonard. I can't kill a man. I'm sorry.'

I feel the rain on my body increase, but the weight shifts and Leonard gently levers himself off me. His tears move across me and away, to fall on the bed and then the floor. I can hear them pitter-pat, and then the light suddenly snaps on and I can see Leonard as he staggers out of the room, leaving Hannah staring at my naked body. I feel very vulnerable and try to cover myself.

'Get dressed and come into the kitchen,' she says. 'I'll make us some hot chocolate. Maybe I'll put some brandy in it.' And she wheels herself away.

–

I dress. I even put my new boots on; I want to be able to run if I need to. Then I stick the long knife into the waistband of the jeans and pull the jumper over it again. I feel overwhelmed by all of this, like my brain is too full of stuff and will explode. I've had fifteen years of boredom and loneliness and now I'm fitting a century of excitement into a few days, and I still have so much more to do before I can stop running. It's crazy, when the hell am I going to get a break?

In the kitchen the overhead lights are off, but the stove range is open, casting light into the room, and from there I can see Leonard on his knees, his head in his wife's lap as she strokes his hair. She looks up at me and tears mark her cheeks too.

'Suicide is a sin,' she says, her voice soft but tired. 'That's why he can't do it; he can't end his own life, though he dearly wants to.'

'But, I'd nev—'

'You're all over the news girl. They say you killed a man by the seaside. Stabbed him through the heart after you slept with him. The police say you're dangerous.'

'I'm not, it wasn't like they say…' I tell her, though I'm not really sure that I can explain it to this woman. 'How did you know? I haven't seen a television here.'

'We have the internet, we aren't in the dark ages.'

'Oh… I didn't think.' I sit down, my legs a bit wobbly.

Hannah continues to stroke the man's head, like she might a child, and she hums a tune for a while before she speaks again.

'There is a lot of pain,' she says, not looking at me but at his head as she strokes him. 'Pain, both in his soul and in this house. Terrible pain, and it has got too much to bear.' She pauses, and her fingers dig into his head to disappear amongst the salt and pepper roots. She leans down and kisses the top of his head lightly, then looks up to me.

'Truth be told, I think it has been too much for Leonard to bear for many years. When you came he hoped...' A single tear escapes the levee around her eye and falls down her cheek. 'We both hoped that you would show him some mercy. He thought you'd been sent to save him... we both did.'

'Save him, by killing him?'

'Yes.'

'I'm not a murderer.'

At that I see Leonard's shoulders shake all the more as his sobbing increases.

'Aren't you?' Hannah leans forward in her chair and her nose twitches. 'You reek of death.'

I feel like I've been slapped by her words, though in some strange way I don't think she meant it unkindly. Maybe she's right and I do have the stench of death on me; in my hair, my clothes. Hanging over me like a pall, as if my aura is red with blood. Maybe she can see such things, like some old witch of the woods – I don't know. But she's right. I can't deny that Theo is dead because of me, and so is Ayo. And Drew... maybe I pushed him to his fate too. I have ghosts circling my head like carrion birds. But even though I have held their hands and walked them to the gallows, I didn't take their lives.

'I can't help you – not like that, I'm sorry.' I tell them both.

'Yes,' Hannah bows her head, and strokes his hair again, as she whispers something to him that I can't quite catch, and he continues to weep.

I watch them both for a while, until the tears are finally gone and then Leonard gets to his feet. He bows to me, and then rummages in the cupboard and brings out a small caddy labelled *chocolate*. Then he takes a pan and gently heats some milk on the stove. As the milk warms, he takes down a couple of mugs and spoons chocolate into them, then pours in a little of the milk and stirs each one to make a rich chocolate paste. Then he pours the steaming hot milk in each cup and stirs and stirs until the chocolate is rich and creamy and has a little foamy head on it.

He hands me a cup, and the heat of it nearly makes me drop the whole thing. 'Thanks. Why—'

'Chocolate first,' Hannah says, accepting a cup from her husband and slowly sipping. 'A little sweetness,' she says with the tiniest hint of a smile.

'Okay.' I sit and blow on my chocolate and think about everything that has got me here, to this point, to a man who wants to die at my hand. Christ, it is so messed up. But this is the best hot chocolate I have ever tasted. *Oh my god.*

—

We sit in silence and I guess about an hour passes while we drink hot chocolate and Leonard opens a tin of fruitcake. He cuts three thick slices and hands one to me.

'What about a plate?' Hannah says, but I take the slab from him and bite into it. I don't need a plate. The cake is amazing; the fruit is so plump and it's full of glacé cherries that must have been soaked in booze for years. It's so good I almost want to cry. At Christmas my mum would make a Yule cake, and it would be full of fruit. I helped with it; I would stir it with her, every day for a couple of months – but instead of being joyful it was a time when she was fearful. One year, when I was little, the cake wasn't good enough, wasn't fruity enough. *How could you do this, we couldn't serve this to Joseph and Mary if they came here from*

Bethlehem. He screamed and hit her. He broke her jaw. The cake was always packed with fruit after that, but it was never as tasty. I found it a little bitter, even though my dad praised it to heaven every year afterwards. But some days, while we stirred the fruit, I saw her weep into the batter, and tears don't make for great cakes. I think Mary Berry said that.

–

Once the cake is gone, and the hot chocolate has been drunk I ask: 'So, are you going to tell me the story?'

'It's late…' I can see the fatigue in her face, but I still need to know.

'Is it late? I have no idea even if it's day or night here,' I tell her. 'There are no clocks and I haven't seen the outside.'

'It is ten past three in the morning.'

'So Leonard has to be up in less than an hour to deal with the animals.'

'Yes, I suppose he does.'

'So tell the story, I'm not tired.'

She closes her eyes for a moment, as if to gather herself together and then her hand reaches out and grabs his. Their eyes meet and she silently asks him for permission to tell their story. He nods his assent and she begins.

'It happened a long time ago, fifteen years.'

'Fifteen?' I repeat. I feel a tingle in my fingertips, which runs like electricity around a circuit, and fills my entire body with an inner hum.

'Yes… it's fifteen years since… since the accident… since our lives were turned upside down.'

'Fifteen…' I feel like I want to fold into myself and leave my body. I am full of fear. The electric hum makes me shake. 'W-when exactly?' I ask, but I already know the date. Somehow I know what she'll say.

'November seventeenth,' she says, her brows knitting as she sees the effect this is having on me. 'Are you okay?' she asks.

'I... please tell me what happened.'

'I don't think I can, we have never—'

'Please... November seventeenth. All that time ago, please tell me.'

She drops her head and whispers something to Leonard. I can't hear what she says but he makes a few motions with his hands in reply. She nods her head and closes her eyes, as if she is going to meditate.

'I will tell you what happened that night, though for it to make sense I will have to go back a little more – maybe even back to the beginning.' She sighs. 'This is our story, Leonard's and mine.' She looks to him and gives him a watery smile. In reply, his eyes crinkle. I think he wishes she could stay silent but knows deep down that their story must be told. They have kept quiet for so very long. Too long.

'We didn't meet until we were that bit older, the first flush of youth was gone and we were both a little lonely. For Leonard it had been the farm. He had worked alongside his father until the old man died and then he was alone, caring for a place that was far too big for one man. I, on the other hand, was stuck at home caring for my mother who battled dementia for the longest time. Romance was impossible, for either of us, and so we were well into our thirties before we met each other and... I suppose we saw some sort of kindred spirit in the other. We married and we were happy – at least we were content to be in a new stage of life. Leonard sold off parcels of land, made the farm more manageable, and actually I was able to help him more around the farm and...' She laughs, sadly.

'I lied to you earlier – at least I embellished. I said I was a nurse, and I sort of was, in that I looked after my mother. I sometimes call that nursing, but I was not a professional. I was making myself out to be something I am not. The sin of vanity.' Hannah takes a deep breath.

'So... as I was saying... the farm was enough for our needs and we loved each other, but there was a...' She pauses and a deep sadness settles in her face. 'There was a hole in the world... in my world, I suppose.' She takes a deep breath. 'What we were missing was a child. I had pushed away all my motherly desires while I cared for my own mother. She was a full-time job and there was the violence and anger – she could explode at the slightest provocation – it was frightening. It was no environment to raise a child in, and anyway, when was I ever going to find the time to meet someone? When I married Leonard the thing I wanted most was a child.' She looks across at him. 'And it wasn't only me. We talked and both agreed.'

I look across at Leonard and see the same depth of sadness in his eyes as I see in hers. 'But God did not grace us with a baby. I don't know why, but after ten years I couldn't keep the disappointment and sadness at bay. We went to the church and spoke to the father there, and began to take in foster children. Never a baby... no, we received older children, even teenagers who were exceptionally needy, often those who had been the victims of crime and...' She blushes and I understand what had happened to those kids.

'Our farm was seen as a place of security for those children, away from the temptations and seductions of the city, a place where they could heal and find a new way of being that was slower and safer. It wasn't always a success... some of the children ran away, wanting to get back to London or Manchester, or whatever urban hellhole they had come from. A couple of them came with addiction problems, and that was not easy.' Her eyes drop for a second and I can see the terrible memories rise and crash through her mind. 'Some only stayed a few days, while others came for months and months.'

I remember the boots in the hallway with the name *Tina Bray* inside. I understand all those shoes and coats now.

'And it was nice to have young people around the farm. Nothing was ever dull and it gave us both a sense of God's purpose. We were put upon this earth to care, for the soil and the animals, but also for the young people who've lost their way. We loved it, and all the children. Until a girl came to us – a foster child who was older than most we had seen before then. She was fifteen, almost sixteen and she set our lives on fire.'

I see Leonard drop his head, as the shame and guilt radiates from him like a fire.

'She was difficult... she could seem much older one moment, and then be a young child the next. I know there was a worry that she would turn sixteen and be lost, fall into some unscrupulous hands, so she came to us.' Hannah shakes her head sadly. 'We were supposed to keep her safe but... it was my fault. I couldn't cope with her you see. She could turn on the waterworks one second, and flirt like a concubine the next. She walked around the house practically naked some days and when she sunbathed in the top field, boys came from miles around to watch her. That excited her, to see the effect she had on men; that gave her power. And when she turned sixteen... well she didn't listen to us anymore. Some days we couldn't find her, she would disappear. And men would come to the door... she was like a drug to them.' Hannah stops and her eyes flick towards Leonard, who sits stock-still. His head is down and I see a single tear run down his cheek. In response I see Hannah's jaw tighten and twitch.

'She was just a child, I know that, but she knew how to get under my skin... she drove a wedge between us. Between Leonard and me and...' She shakes her head, as if clearing the cobwebs from it.

'Well, enough of that. Suffice to say, it damaged our marriage. We began arguing, which we had never done before, and Leonard started drinking. Heavily.'

I hear him whimper, low and under his breath.

'And one day it came to a head... one awful, awful day that left me like this.' She waves her hand to indicate her wheelchair. 'And left Leonard unable to speak and...' She closes her eyes. They both sit with their heads bowed and I think they are praying silently.

'And that was November seventeenth?' I ask to break a long silence.

Hannah slowly opens her eyes; they're red-rimmed now. 'Yes, fifteen years ago, it was a foul night. It rained so hard and there was news from up river that the banks had burst. I put on my rain gear and went out in the storm to find Leonard. He was up at the dairy shed.'

'You could walk?'

'I wasn't in a wheelchair then... not yet... but...'

I see the pain etch into her face and feel my stomach clench. I'm a little lightheaded, as I can see the strands of my own life story are coming together, knitting into a larger work; somehow it is entangled with these people.

My own story intersects with theirs. I don't understand how... but it does. It must. I feel it in my bones. We are all linked by some over-arching misfortune, by the darkness of the past. We are the victims of a shared tragedy. November seventeenth – the night so much happened – the night that broke this couple and the night my Drew died. The night *I* died, or at least Rebecca Waite died. For a moment I think I might faint. I have to reach out and grab hold of something.

'Tell me... tell me about that night. Tell me everything.'

Chapter Eighteen

November 17th, Fifteen Years Ago

Hannah's Story

Hannah closes her eyes and drops her head. I keep quiet, not wanting to disturb the memories that are swarming through her. She moves her head and shoulders, suddenly seeming to loosen up, become more free. It's almost as if the years drop away from her. She tips her head up and opens her eyes – they are full of ghosts. She opens her mouth and starts to tell me what happened all those years ago.

All I can do is listen, and be transported back in time. These are her words:

-

'Tina!' I call into the howling storm. Opening the door, even for a few seconds, makes the hallway run like a river. The rain is thick and juicy, and the wind takes it and whips it so hard it stings. I'm worried. I've been worried for days now. Everything seems so perilous, like it's balanced on a precipice and ready to fall. I curse the vicar for bringing her here, like a virus, infecting our home and making us sick. I feel like I want to damn him… but then feel guilty for that. It is not a Christian act – I do not like to hate, but I can't help but detest what she has done to us, the discord that she has brought into our home.

I kick at the shoes piled by the door. The walking boots we gave her are still here, as are the trainers she insisted we buy, but she never wears them. Her coat is here too. I don't know where she is, if she is out in this rain then I worry for her, and if she has found someone to shelter her – then I worry for them. I want to cry, to add to the slop of water inside the doorway, but I must stay strong. We will ask the vicar to find her another place to live. She has to go, we must not back down this time. Not like before when we asked her to leave and she begged us to let her stay. She said we were the best family she'd ever been placed with and that she loved it here; she told us the last foster family used her, that she was their skivvy. She wept and pleaded, she swore on the bible that she would change, and of course we reconsidered our decision, we showed her sympathy and mercy because we are people of god. We were stupid. Naïve fools that let a spit of a girl wrap us around her little finger. I doubt any of what she told us was true. I don't think anything that comes out of her mouth is real; she exists in a world of lies and fantasy. She is temptation, she is both Eve and the Devil in a child's body. She has stabbed our marriage through the heart and left it bleeding.

I don't know all she has done, the depths she has dragged my husband to, as Leonard won't talk to me, won't even look me in the eyes. He is a different man now, his drinking has become a problem and he neglects the animals, they will die if he continues to do nothing. He cannot see the world around him, all he seems to do is play and re-play something in his head – something that *she* did to him, something so shameful that he cannot get past it. He's trapped in the quicksand of that memory and it is pulling him down and it will smother him. It will kill him. It will—

Riiiiiiinnnnnnngggggggggg… Riiiiiiinnnnnnngggggggggg…

The telephone drags me out of my reverie. We rarely have callers, as neither Leonard nor I have family. He has an aunt in Canada, but she has only ever telephoned when someone has died, and the only one left to die now is her and—

Riiiiiiinnnnnnngggggggggg… Riiiiiiinnnnnnngggggggggg…

I lift the receiver with a shaking hand.

'Mrs Fleetwood, Hannah, is that you?'

'Vicar?'

'Yes, yes, it's me. I'm glad to hear you're inside the house, this is not a night to be outside. I have never seen such a storm as this.'

'What has happened, Father?' I ask, knowing he would not be telephoning me if there wasn't something amiss. 'It's her, isn't it?'

'I don't want to worry you—'

'I haven't seen her all day. We had words and… where is she, Father?'

'I had a call from the police station in Aberdeen.'

'Aberdeen?'

'They were checking on her. It seems that she was a witness at some fight… though…'

I hear the concern in his voice. There is more involved here; she was not merely the witness to some crime.

'She gave them your telephone number, you were the one the police called?' I ask him.

226

'I don't know about that, but they ascertained that she was a foster child placed by the church and so the call came through to me.'

'And what did the police say?'

'They said they would hold her until her legal guardians collected her.'

'You think we should go to Aberdeen for her.'

'Well, the storm is pretty bad, so you might want to wait a while. I daresay a little longer at the police station might not be such a bad thing. But I wouldn't want her to have to stay the night.'

'I'm sorry, we can't.'

'What, I didn't hear you, Hannah, the wind is so loud against the windows. I keep thinking they'll blow in, or that a tree will get uprooted and smash through one.'

'I said *we can't*. I'm sorry but we don't want her here. I think a night in a police cell would be exactly what the doctor ordered.'

'Oh please, Hannah, you have to have more—'

'No… no, I'm sorry, Father.' And I put the receiver back in its cradle. I close my eyes and I pray, but not for her. I pray for myself and for Leonard; that we can come through this ordeal. Then I turn and head to the door. As I do so the phone starts to ring once more, but I ignore it. I know it will be the Father, but I won't talk with him. I won't be persuaded into giving her another last chance. My marriage is more important.

I put on my wellington boots and my longest rain coat. It has a hood which I put up and hold at my throat, knowing that the wind will try to whip it from my head the second I open the door. I take a breath and open the—

'Sweet Jesus.' It is a maelstrom outside as rain slashes down hard, and the wind cuts and thrusts like a rapier, twisting and turning one way and then the next. I step into it and feel it try and lift me like a kite. In only a few seconds I feel the water pierce my waterproof coat and begin to drench my clothes underneath. Even my socks start to get wet as the water runs down me to collect in my boots.

'Leonard,' I shout with all the breath of my lungs, but the word is grabbed by the wind and torn into strips. I am made mute by the weather. I even walk like a mime, fighting against the wind, taking one step forward and half a step back as it buffets me. I head to the barn, hoping that is where I will find him and not... not... not broken and beaten in Aberdeen. That's my fear, you see; that he drove Tina there and the fight was with him and some nasty thug she has tried to manipulate and seduce in the city. I have to know he's safe. I hope I will find him in the barn. Maybe he's drunk or sleeping it off, I don't know, but as long as he's still here, we have a marriage we can fight for, but if he is in Aberdeen with her... then we are lost. That is why I force my body forward with all my might. My boot is sucked down into the mud and I stumble and go down on my knees, like I am in prayer, but this storm is not an angry god to pacify with prayer.

I get up, my trousers now muddy and soaked through to my skin. I feel like I weigh double my normal weight as the water soaks through me. I keep going, keep moving and as I turn the bend I can see the barn, but it is dark. If he is with her... I feel my heart harden in my chest. If she has taken my Leonard, if she has poisoned him against me, then I will kill her. I'm sorry, Jesus, I am sorry to let hate into my heart but...

I reach the door to the barn. It rocks back and forward in the wind. I release the catch and the wind drags it out of my hand. It smashes against the wall and wood splinters and buckles. I move inside.

It's cold and dark in here. The rain drums on the roof and the wind howls through the countless gaps in the walls. He's been fixing this place for years and years, but it's still no good. The job is too big for one man, and he's too small-minded to ask for help. He isn't here. That must mean that he's with her and that we are over. I let that sit in my chest for a few seconds and suddenly I feel a little clearer. I think I know what I must do. I know that, in this barn somewhere, I'll find rope and there will be a ladder that will reach to the rafters. I am proficient enough in knots that I can make a hangman's noose. I am no Albert Pierrepoint, but I should be able to perform the service for myself. That way he'll find me in his barn, dangling before him. Maybe the wind will make me dance. That will be my final gift to him, to cut down my body and—

'Errrggghhhhh...' There is a moan from the back of the barn.

'Leonard?' I call and squint into the darkness, but I can't see anything. Damn, I hiss to myself and reach my arms out, trying to find the light switch near the door. My hands roam across the wall, and I get a splinter. It's deep in my flesh, but I continue to search for—

Yes, I find the switch and we have light.

I see him, sprawled in the dirt and hay. There's an empty bottle of cheap supermarket whisky by him and I can smell the booze from here. I feel sickened.

'Get up,' I shout at him.

'Wha—?' he groans and rolls onto his side but then falls back again, like a turtle unable to right itself.

'Get up... get up... get up... GET UP!' I scream at him and – lord help me – but I kick at him, at his foot.

I am so angry that he has crumbled like this, showing so much weakness.

'What?' he says as he gets himself to his feet. I can see from the way his eyes try to focus but keep sliding in and out, that he's more drunk than I've ever seen him.

'She's gone,' I tell him. 'That bitch has finally gone.'

I expect him to laugh or say *good riddance*, but instead his face crumples and he says: 'No, she can't. She has to come back.' And in that moment I know why everything has gone wrong with us. He loves her and not like a father or an uncle, but as a man. As a lover.

'Have you...' I start to ask but the horror in my soul won't let me finish.

'Did you send her away?' His face curls with anger at me – at me.

'She ran, I didn't send her. She's in Aberdeen and she isn't coming back.'

'Liar.'

'The vicar called.'

'He's a stupid bastard.'

'Leonard.' I'm shocked by such language towards a man of the cloth. I can't believe my sweet husband would talk like that – except he isn't my sweet man any longer, not since she dug her claws into him and turned him all inside out.

'She wouldn't leave us... leave me.'

I feel my heart shrivel in my chest. I wish I had hanged myself.

'Then why don't you go and get her?'

'I don't know where—'

'In jail. She's in bloody jail in Aberdeen, the little bit—'

And he hits me. He pulls his hand back and lashes out. I fall to the ground, though it's as much from shock as the blow itself.

'I have to go,' he says and staggers to the door and out into the storm. I should let him go, see how far the idiot would get without me, but I can't. I can't let him leave me.

'*Leonard.*' I follow him into the tempest.

I catch him at the house. He's soaked and looks insane, like Lear out in his storm. He has the keys to the Land Rover and I think he's planning on driving to the police station. I can't let him go, he's too drunk, it's crazy.

'You can't drive in this...' I scream but I don't know if he can hear me through the storm. He's heading down the path and I run after him and grab at his shoulder.

'Not now, Hannah,' he yells.

'Go tomorrow,' I tell him. 'A night in the cells won't hurt her.'

'Go home, she needs me.'

'I need you,' I yell but he doesn't respond. I hope he hasn't heard me, but I fear he has and just doesn't care.

—

Hannah stops talking for a moment and the years pile on her again; she looks as old as time, and full of the pain of the ages. I open my mouth to say something, to tell her that she doesn't need to continue with her story, but I don't get a word out as her eyes flash at me and she holds up her hand.

'I will go on,' she says. And she continues with her story.

Leonard gets to the car and opens the door. I will lose him in a few seconds. I can't do that. I rush at the passenger door and pull it open as the engine roars into life. I jump into the passenger seat as the wheels spin and the car shoots back, mud squirting out as he throws the car into reverse.

'You can't come,' he shouts and pushes at me.

'I'm coming. You owe me that.'

'I can't choose you over her, you know that. I can't. I'm sorry,' he yells over the howling wind.

'I know,' I say soft and low as I close the door and sit in the passenger seat.

'Don't say I didn't warn you,' he says and pushes the car into gear and heads off. He grinds his foot into the pedal from the first moment. I hear the strain of the engine but I know he won't listen. A curtain of water covers the windscreen; the wipers strain to get rid of it, but it's too strong. The path from our farm to the main road is a mile and a half, and is difficult at the best of times, but now it has been partially washed away. There will be flash floods down in the valley and many animals will be drowned tonight. God is angry. Just like I am.

'Slow down, Leonard,' I say but he doesn't listen. Instead, we bump and bounce from rut to rut as the track crumbles and collapses around us. It will be better when we get to the main road but then he will want to go faster and faster. He's already at forty-five miles an hour and the road wasn't built for that.

'Please slow down,' I beg, but he is crazy and pushes to go faster and faster. The windscreen is like frosted glass, impossible to see through and we are blind in the darkness as our headlights illuminate trees, making them look like soldiers returning from the war. I'm scared, maybe I should get out. We are close to the main road now, our last barn is up ahead, the outbuilding where the machinery is kept and—

CRASH.

Something smashes into the wing of the car and flips up, hitting the windscreen and shattering it, so that a broken fingerprint stretches through the glass. Just before it happens, I see a man's face, then the glass cracks and the car slews to the right.

'What was that?'

'Deer, I...'

And we're leaning as the horizon shifts and we slide over, hurtling forward. The car's on its side; there are sparks and an explosion of sound that comes from hell, as we slide on the river of mud and hit a tree hard. I am slumped against the passenger window. My seatbelt holds me in place but Leonard is in freefall, nothing holding him in, as he hits the windscreen and then topples sideways and falls onto me.

Then there is nothing, only the wind and the rain. And my tears. I cry that I'm still alive and that God sent something to stop Leonard going to her. God has kept my husband with me and given me a second chance. He loves me. He has rewarded me... but then I see the cut on Leonard's forehead where he struck the windscreen, and blood smears his face.

'Leonard are you...?'

He moans softly and my heart flips. His eyes open and they're wild.

'What did we hit?' he asks as he tries to move, but can't work out how to raise himself off of me. The passenger's side of the car is on the ground, so I'm slumped against the door and he's curled and twisted on top of me. He tries to move, but his knee hits me in the face.

'Be careful,' I say and he grunts.

The driver's side door is now a hatch in the roof. He reaches up to push at it, and the wind grabs it and whips it back with a squeal of metal. The rain starts to fall on us both as Leonard levers himself up and through the hatch, out onto the top of the car. Then he half slides and half jumps to the ground, his legs buckle and he lands in the mud with a grunt. He pauses for a few seconds, swaying like a baby giraffe, and then starts to walk away from me.

'Help me out too!' I yell and he turns back and leans into the car to pull me out. The rain is lashing down. The ground is waterlogged. Somewhere, not too far away, a lightning bolt hits the ground and there are sparks and that metallic smell in the air.

'What the hell did we hit, was it a deer?' he says.

'I don't think it was a deer,' I say and point back down the sodden path. It's hard to see anything but there is a crumpled heap a little way back on the rutted track.

'I thought, for a second...' but I don't say what I thought. That would be crazy. A man? Where would a man come from? This is our farmland, our private road. The main road is not far, but there are no cars, there is nothing. It has to be an animal; it must have been a trick of the light; my anxiety playing tricks on me. I couldn't have seen a man's face on the windscreen – I couldn't.

'There's a torch in the back,' he says and after a struggle, he gets the hatchback to open. It leans a little drunkenly but allows him to rummage about and find the little toolbox he keeps back there. Inside is a small torch and he turns it on. The beam of light it produces is pretty weak. It makes the rain look like a swarm of locusts ready to devour us. He walks forward and I slip into his wake. The torch beam bobs about, making the rain sparkle and then... *oh my god*.

'Is that...?' We stand in the howl of the maelstrom and our breath is stolen from us as we look at the body of a man. The torch beam starts at his foot and slowly moves up his body – a body that lies broken, in an unnatural shape – twisted and bent. The man is dead. Everything seems to get darker. Above our heads the clouds twist and turn, lightning cuts the night sky and thunder crashes... and suddenly it ends. The rain stops and the wind no longer howls. All is quiet in the eye of the storm, as the torch beam reaches the man's face. I think for a moment he is an angel. He looks as though he's sleeping, his beautiful dark hair swept back off his face, his chiselled jaw and perfect features utterly still. We stand there, struck dumb, filled with awe at the majesty of the dead man as the heavens are silent... and then the torch light dies as the battery gives up the ghost, and the angel is swept up by the darkness. The rain begins again as the wind howls and the eye of the storm passes over us.

'How the hell did he get out here?' Leonard asks and for the first time tonight he sounds sober. I guess taking a human life will drive the alcohol right out of your system.

'We have to call an ambulance,' I say and turn to go back to the house.

'No, no ambulance, and no police.'

'What the hell are you saying?' I am suddenly so angry with him. I want to hit him; he's ruined our lives and killed a man, and all for what? All for a stupid kid... all for her... his *lover*. The thought makes me shake. I have tried to keep it out of my head, I have tried to imagine that something else has happened, that somehow she has unlocked a paternal streak in him, but I know that's a lie. And Jesus hates a liar. I know what she's really unlocked in him, and it's all about his desire and... he... he made the beast with her. She has transformed him into a base animal, stolen what little sense he had, and now he is just her puppet. He's in her thrall – and when she's done with him she will drop him, cut his strings like he's a marionette, he will fall and she will trample him into the dirt. That is what a girl like her does – but he can't see it, and now his blindness has led to this poor man's death. I can't be a part of not reporting it. The truth must win out; only that can set us free.

'I'm going to call the hospital.' I have made up my mind. I won't let him deflect me from that and there is nothing he can say to me now. I know I've lost him. I start to walk to the house, purposefully, striding out as quickly as I can.

'No... no you will not, Hannah. You're my wife and you'll—'

'Your wife? Really, am I still your wife?'

'Yes, you are Hannah, and you'll do as I say.'

'No, I will no longer do what you say.' I speak so low I know he can't hear me, but I say it anyway and it's the truth. He has taken me for granted and now he has to suffer the consequences. He keeps talking and keeps ordering me to do what he says, but I don't listen anymore. Instead, I carry on walking through that evil night; through the dark and the storm towards our home. There is nothing we can do for the man now, he's dead but he needs to be seen to by a funeral director; his body needs to be treated like it's sacred. That can't be delayed. So I walk as fast as I can, while still being careful I don't fall, as the very earth beneath my feet starts to crumble and mini mudslides slip past me. I finally get to the house, I don't know where Leonard is, he disappeared a hundred yards or so back. Maybe he's gone to find another bottle of cheap scotch to guzzle down before he sobers up and realises what he's done. I know that tomorrow my Leonard will hate what he did tonight, he will hate the—

'Argh.' Someone grabs me and lifts me up. I try and twist in his hands but he has me tight and he puts one arm around my throat and the other round my waist. I struggle and kick back. I feel my shoe snap into his shin and he stumbles but does not let me go. He holds me tighter. I feel lightheaded – I can't get any oxygen. He kicks the door open and we stagger inside. I want the phone, I can see it there by the door, but he drags me past it. I can't breathe – my body is shaking from how hard his forearm is pressed into my throat. I feel like I'm passing out as he carries me towards the kitchen.

'No, no…' I manage to gasp as he lets go of my throat and I manage to drag some breath into my lungs. My vision is blurred and pops of light explode as synapses deprived of oxygen suddenly burst into life again. He uses his free hand to open the door to the cellar.

'No, Leonard,' I rasp but he doesn't seem to care.

'Stay in there. Do as you're bloody told, woman.' And he drops me onto the top step. There is no light; the cellar steps stretch before me as my vision twists and concertinas. My legs wobble from lack of oxygen and I try and turn back. I reach out to the door. He can't lock me in here. My fingers get to the doorframe to stop him closing it on me but he grabs my hand and pushes me away. He slams the door, and I'm in total darkness. The momentum of his push still runs through me – if I hadn't been gasping for breath and already dizzy I would have been fine, but

I can't right myself. My body weight keeps moving back and back... I reach out, but in the darkness I merely claw at the air as I fall back and topple down the stone stairs. I feel the concrete smash into my head and there is the wetness of blood and then a snap, like a giant elastic band being cut and then...

—

'And then?' I ask, but Hannah looks blank. She's still trapped in those memories, still lying on that cellar floor where she fell, still lost in the grief of that time. She can't see me, let alone answer my questions. I turn to Leonard and see his eyes are red with tears, but he cannot answer my questions either. All I can do is sit and wait for Hannah to find her way back from the labyrinth of her memories and to resurface in our time.

I know what it's like, to fall into the rabbit hole of memory, all the *what ifs* and *whys* and wishing you could go back in time and choose another path. That night, fifteen years ago, both our lives changed. While she lay on that cellar floor, I was hearing that my husband was dead.

I watch Hannah for a long time, as the cycle of pain revolves through her. I doubt that she allows herself to think back to that night very often – it would be far too painful for her. She's only gone into those memories because of me, so I feel both thankful and guilty. Before tonight she may even have treated that time as if it were a dream, something she partially recalls but isn't sure was even real; a nightmare that she's integrated into her life story... maybe. But it is clear that killing that man changed everything for them, and for me too. Because I think since that moment, our lives have became entangled, wrapped around each other's throats, like Japanese knotweed, throttling the life from each other. That moment in the rain changed our lives forever.

—

The three of us sit in silence for the longest time… it feels like hours… and then, finally, Leonard rises and leaves us. I guess the animals will be desperate to be fed. I feel hollowed out. My stomach rumbles loudly and in reply, Hannah lets out a soft breath and her eyes open. For a second she doesn't know where she is, and then she comes back to herself.

'Are you all right?' I ask and for the first time, I see a genuine smile on her face.

'I haven't thought about that night in so long and actually, I do feel a little better. Like pulling a plaster off a cut to let the air in; it hurts but the wound can heal at last.' She sighs. 'At last the wound can heal,' she whispers to herself.

'Your fall… that night into the cellar… that's why you're—'

'Crippled,' she says and her hands drop onto the wheels. 'Yes, the fall broke my back, severed my spinal column. Perhaps if I had got treatment right away… but that wasn't what happened.'

'Leonard dumped the dead man's body.'

'No… not then, anyway. What he did was get the truck and drive to Aberdeen. He went to get *her*.'

'And did he find Tina?'

'No. She had been collected from the police station by her *father*.'

'Her father, didn't you say she was an orphan in care?'

She shrugs. 'I don't know the truth of what happened, either way she was gone; that was all the police could tell Leonard when he arrived. He called the vicar but the church had no idea where she could be and confirmed she had no living parents. For an hour he drove around the streets looking for her, but then he came home and...' Pain cuts through her face. 'He came for the body, the dead man. He didn't come to find me. He left me on that hard cellar floor screaming in agony for him... for him to help me or for God to let me die. Leonard didn't come for me. Instead, he got the body and drove him away and—'

'Left him,' I say, my voice like cold steel. Behind me I hear the front door again and Leonard comes back to the kitchen. I see there are tears frozen on his eyelashes.

'Leonard drove the man's body as far as he could – he drove until dawn, and then he took the body and dumped it behind a wall,' I carry on, my voice cold and low, emotionless.

I watch Leonard's face, as all the blood drains from it.

'It was found hours later by a couple who were hiking. They called the police and—'

'How do you know all of this?' Hannah asks, her eyes wide.

'The police found the body. It was all twisted and broken. They knew it had been hit by a vehicle – they knew it was a red Land Rover – I don't know how they were so sure, something about the height of the side lights, I think. They thought the man had been struck where he was found, knocked into the air and over the wall. They didn't think he'd been dumped there.'

Leonard is shaking. Hannah leans forward in her chair; her eyes blaze. 'How do you know this?' she asks again, this time even more insistently than the first.

'His body was taken to the morgue where he was identified as Andrew Waite.' I pause. Leonard is gripping the table to stop from falling. Hannah has clamped her jaw so tight I think it will snap.

'Two police officers were dispatched to tell his wife that he was dead.'

I see the truth flower in Leonard's eyes... he knows. Hannah's mouth shrivels, like she's sucked a boxful of lemons.

'They knocked on my door. I knew it was bad news because they held their hats in their hands. They had come to tell me my husband was dead. A hit-and-run accident. My Drew...'

Leonard sinks slowly to his knees, his head bowed. He can't look at me. Hannah is shaking, she thinks that retribution has finally come for them; that the crows have come home to roost, to pick at her flesh. She thinks I'm the angel of death.

'What happened to your throat?' I ask. Leonard won't look at me. I lean forward and take hold of his chin, then I tip his face up so that he can see me. I ask again. 'What happened to your throat?'

'He—' Hannah starts.

'I asked him,' I spit. I want him to tell me.

With abject fear in his eyes, still on his knees, he mimes breaking a mirror and taking a shard of it and sawing at his own throat, trying to cut through it.

'I thought so,' I say and let go of his chin. His head sinks down once more, as if he's offering his neck to the guillotine.

'You thought I was a killer.' I look from husband to wife. I see them both burn with shame. 'But I'm not. I'm the victim. Your victim.'

They both close their eyes, I think they would both like to die now.

'You thought I could help you end your life,' I say to Leonard. 'Because you can no longer live with the shame and guilt of what you did. Good, I hope your heart burns in your chest for all time. You don't deserve a moment's peace for what you did to your wife, for hurting someone who loved you.'

Leonard's eyes move across to Hannah, full of tears.

'And my poor husband? For his death, I can't take your life; all I can do is… all I can do is forgive you.'

He looks up at me, uncomprehending.

'You didn't kill my husband,' I tell him.

'You weren't there,' Hannah says dismissively.

'You said he came from nowhere, like he jumped in front of the car?'

'That was what it looked like; the rain made it impossible to see more than a few feet ahead.'

'He was thrown in front of your vehicle.'

'What?'

'He was already dead, or close to it. He'd been tortured.'

'No.'

'He was held by two men who wanted to get some information from him.'

'That isn't what happened.'

'And one of them took it too far, so they had to get rid of the body and they found a patsy. You.'

'They threw him? But if we hadn't struck him…'

'Leonard would still talk and you would still walk. I'm sorry, but the truth isn't what you've thought for fifteen years. You aren't murderers. In a way, you're both victims too.'

'But you can't know what happened that night.'

'I can. I do. They're the same men who killed my boyfriend in Brighton. They're the men who have ruined my life and made me live like a cockroach for fifteen years. They stole all of our lives. And they're still chasing me. They won't rest until they find me, and when they do... they'll kill me.'

Chapter Nineteen

Thursday

The ground is wet and there are frozen puddles on the path. Hannah offered to come down with me to the old barn, but I said no, I want to go alone. She said they haven't been inside since the night of the accident, so it should look exactly as it did that night. Something in my belly is telling me I have to see it, because if Drew came from somewhere close to where they hit him – if he was held and *tortured* somewhere – then it was most likely in this derelict barn.

I continue down the path. A low mist clings to the ground, waiting to be burned off by the sun. The trees are bare and brown. Everything looks ugly, like I imagine a war zone to look. Bleak and dead.

I reach the barn and can clearly see how the years have taken their toll on it. The roof is broken in places and sags and dips in others. There are holes in the planking of the walls, and it looks like it's only spiderwebs that keep it from collapsing. I put my hand on the door and push. I have to put my shoulder against it and strain with all my might, until finally it gives and shudders open. Inside, the barn smells of must, damp and the sweetness of animal droppings, like the base note of a fancy perfume. It's pretty much just mud and straw and cut-up sacks on the ground, but in one corner I see a glint of metal, and my stomach dips like I just corkscrewed on a rollercoaster. I take a deep breath and walk over. It's a chain. It was probably used to hold an animal in place, perhaps while a vet examined it or a blacksmith shod it. I pick up the chain and drag it through my fingers, at the end is a metal hoop, like a collar, and caught inside that is a brown boot. A man's boot I think, though it's waterlogged and mouldy, so not easy to be sure. When Drew's body was discovered, the police report noted that only one boot was found at the scene; they guessed that the force of the car hitting him had sent one of his boots flying and it was lost. But now I know that wasn't right, this is his missing boot, I just know it is. I pick it up, even though it feels wet and slimy. If I were going to call the police, then touching the evidence would be dumb, but I know I won't, because I can't prove the connections here. There's no way of implicating Gene and Michael, and the whole story sounds crazy. But more importantly, I realise that I don't want Gene and Michael arrested. I want a deeper and more satisfying revenge on those two. I want to make them watch me find their money, and then I want to hurt them. I don't know how yet, I'm not sure how you hurt men with no souls. But I want to see them squirm in front of me. I want some payback for what they've done to my life. Wow, I didn't realise until this second, but it's true, I want them to feel pain. I want revenge.

I drop the boot and kick at the straw around the chain. I almost don't see it, as the wood is so discoloured by the advancing elements, but low down at the base of the wall there's something scratched into the surface. I lie in the dirt and get close enough to see what it is, some initials scratched into the wood: *AW*.

I lie still, not breathing. The smell of the straw's quite overpowering but I stay there for some time, as questions boil inside me. So many lives were destroyed that night but why were they here? What brought the Vincent brothers to this farm and how, all this time later, did I get here? What the hell is going on? Why did it take all these years to get to this point? Why the hell didn't the Rev send me my letter from Drew fifteen years ago? Why did I have to sit in my pain and distress for all that time? Drew was dead, but why did others have to be dragged into this macabre dance – Theo and Ayo? Why are they dead too?

Why? I scream and wail at the top of my lungs. I kick my feet into the ground and beat the floor with my fists until they bleed and still I scream until my voice is shredded and there is nothing left. Then I roll into a ball.

'I will make them pay, I swear I will.'

–

An hour or so later, we pull up in front of a church. I had wanted to be dropped on the outskirts of town but Hannah insisted they brought me all the way in. She said they both need to pray. I didn't complain – actually, I was happy with the thought that I wouldn't be alone if I saw Gene or Michael. And if I do see them, I hope they won't see me, or at least that they won't recognise me, as my hair is black with a side parting smoothed down with gel. I'm wearing black-rimmed glasses that make me a little giddy but are pretty mild in terms of prescription. I've got waterproof trousers and a big yellow cagoule that is so bright and garish, it's like you've looked at the sun too long and melted your eyeballs. I also have a bobble hat and scarf in my pocket if I want to look like *Where's Wally?*.

Leonard gets Hannah's wheelchair out of the back and then lifts her into it, while I chomp at the bit, eager to get in there and find the priest.

'Minister,' Hannah tells me, as Leonard pushes her forward. 'In the Scottish Presbyterian tradition you call him a minister. Or Davey.' And we enter the church.

I don't recall the last time I was in a church, I guess it was for my dad's funeral. Of course he was High Church, so there was a big do. They took care of everything, including the wake, so that was good. I nodded a lot and shook some hands. A couple of creepy old people wanted to hug me and I did that, even though it made my skin crawl. Drew said he'd come but I told him not to. At that point I wasn't sure he'd cope with the guilt – the last thing I wanted was for him to start blubbing and telling the truth. So I sat alone, the unhappy bereaved daughter, and let the masses come to me.

What a gentleman your father was… He was the salt of the earth… What a true man of God… You must miss him so much… and on and on the tributes came. But nobody said what a great actor he'd been – a saint at church and a devil at home. I could have told them a thing or two about that great man, but I didn't. I nodded and tried to smile and took all their crap. I also took all their frozen lasagnes and hotpots and the money they collected to help out with the bills. It was a little over five thousand pounds. Hallelujah.

'There,' Hannah points out a man in his mid-sixties. What's left of his hair is white and he looks like he enjoys his food a little too much. 'He was the one who arranged the foster placements, and after the accident he came and saw us every week without fail. He's a good, kind man and he's cared for his parishioners here for thirty-something years. If anyone knows your reverend, then it's him.'

'Thanks, Hannah.' I head towards the white-haired minister. 'Father?'

'Call me David,' he says with a lilting voice, so soft and comforting I could imagine being sent to sleep by his sermon within a minute or two.

'Hannah told me to talk to you.'

'Yes I saw you come in with her.' He looks me up and down. 'Not a relative, I think?'

'No, a lucky meeting. I was lost and she found me.'

'She's a good woman.'

'I'm searching for someone, a man you might know.'

'If he's a man from Aberdeen there's a fair chance.'

'I don't know where he came from originally but I know he lived here. He was a vicar, a long time ago, and then he was a teacher. Hanley was his name.'

A shadow flicks across the minister's face. I see it and realise this isn't going to be a simple request.

'Daniel Hanley?'

'Yes.'

He looks at me with a little frown on his face. 'So why would you be wanting to find the man?'

'It's... could we talk more privately?' I look around and see a woman with no teeth waiting patiently to get her time with the minister.

'I'm sorry but I have parishioners to see all this afternoon and this is the time I have.' His eyes are steely now.

'He was my teacher,' I say and watch as the minister's eyes narrow. 'He was the best school teacher I ever had.'

'Where was this?' he asks.

'St Paul's, in Salford, Manchester. It was about twenty years ago now. I wasn't the happiest of children. I had problems with my father and Mr Hanley was a great comfort. Especially after my dad died, he was a real rock, to me and my boyfriend – who later became my husband. We called him "the Rev", it was a joke name, but we both liked him very much.'

I see the minister's brow furrow, and then he looks past me to the toothless woman. 'I'm ever so sorry, Bess, can I come and see you this afternoon? I really should talk to this young woman now. Is that okay with you?' He smiles and she grins toothlessly back at him. He puts his hand on my arm lightly. 'Come with me into the vestry, I think I might even have a bottle of sherry.'

He leads me to a series of private rooms behind the public part of the church.

'I do know Daniel Hanley,' he says as he pours two glasses of sherry. I've never had sherry and think of it as a little old lady's drink, but I don't want to refuse his kindness.

'A tragic man in many ways.' He shakes his head and hands me the glass.

'He came to the church later than some, after hard times. He was married, did you know?'

'No… I…' I realise I don't really know much about him at all. 'I'm sorry, I only knew him as the Rev, a man who was incredibly kind to a teenager who had been made an orphan.'

'Yes of course, he would have been a great friend to turn to in your hour of need.' He knocks back his sherry in one go. It looks like he's used to harder liquor. He pours himself another and looks at me levelly. His eyes are a very light blue and for a moment I can imagine him as a cheeky schoolboy.

'Daniel Hanley lost his wife in an accident,' he tells me.

'He never said; he didn't talk about himself. Not to us kids, anyway.'

'No, no, of course he wouldn't. It was a road accident and she was driving. Their son was in the back seat and he was badly hurt. It was the accident that sent Daniel into the church. But it was also the same accident that dragged him out of it, made him question himself.'

'What do you mean?'

'He was a priest for ten or so years, and all that time his son was growing up and dealing with the after-effects of the accident. He was badly injured and he had been put on a lot of pain medicine. He slowly became addicted to the drugs, and as he moved into young adulthood it progressed to a stronger addiction and then to drug dealing. He was arrested and sent to prison. He was in his early to mid-twenties I think, and it was at that time Daniel Hanley left the church and became a teacher.'

'I didn't know any of that.'

'No reason you would.'

I bow my head, feeling pressure begin to build. I'm scared this is all going to be a wild goose chase. 'I'm hoping you can tell me where to find him.'

The minister knocks back the second sherry and lifts the bottle to pour another but stops, I can see a little pucker of distaste run across his mouth. He gets up and opens a little cupboard and takes out another bottle. He pours a tumbler full from this, but doesn't offer me one. I think it's whiskey.

'Can I ask why you want to find Daniel after so many years? Are you wanting to say thank you for what he did back then?'

'No. No something else has happened and...' I dry up. I don't mean it to happen but I feel a tear run down my cheek. 'My husband died.'

'I'm sorry,' he says. Opening a drawer, he fishes out a box of tissues and I take one.

'It was some time ago, it was a hit-and-run accident.'

'That's awful.'

'Yes, yes it was, and it happened a long way from home. My husband was here; he had hired a car in Aberdeen and I never knew why until just this week when I found something he had written... My husband had come to Scotland to visit the Rev... Mr Hanley.'

'I see.' The minister frowns. 'When was this?'

'Many years ago, fifteen.'

'Yes... yes I suppose he was here around then...' the minister says, more to himself than to me. 'But what do you think Daniel can tell you now?'

'I want to know why my husband went to see him.'

'Maybe you would be better not knowing.'

'I have to know. I must talk to the Rev – he's the last man who saw my husband alive. I need to ask about what he said and...' I could tell this man of God the truth; that I need to know if my husband told the Rev where he'd hidden eight hundred and seventy-five thousand pounds. But I don't. 'Please, help me. Do you know where he is, is he still alive?'

'Alive? Oh yes he's still with us, though he is rather a recluse nowadays. *Off grid*, the youngsters might call him.'

'You know where?'

He looks concerned for a moment. I think he's scared to unleash me on the old man. I remember him saying that Daniel Hanley had come through bad times. 'How is he?' I ask.

'He is...' The minister thinks long and hard about how to describe the man. 'He is sad, I think that's what best describes him. He has many demons.'

'From the accident?'

'And from after.'

'His son?'

'Yes, I think the hardships of the boy's life weighed very heavily on Daniel. He came here, to Aberdeen, but he found it too noisy and brash. I helped him find somewhere quiet. He brought an old farmhouse, somewhere the son could come to when he left prison. I think Daniel thought that good honest hard work was what he and his son needed. He wanted them to grow honest healthy food. But the son didn't go to live there. He visited a few times – mostly when he needed money – but otherwise he went back to his old life in London.'

'What does he do?' I ask.

'He was musical – at least he wanted to be in music. He was a club DJ, I think that's the right term, and at some point he was successful. He made money and was well known, but that made the problems worse. The money meant he could buy more drugs and there were many hangers-on, piranhas that attached themselves to him and fed off of his success like parasites.'

'That's awful,' I say, and the priest nods.

'My poor old friend was beside himself. He said the fame and the money were destroying his son... and then, one night, his son took his own life.'

He pours himself another drink and we sit in silence for a while, as the sad story drifts in the air between us like the pall of death.

'What happened?' I finally ask. 'To Daniel Hanley, I mean; what did he do after he lost his son?'

'He closed his life down, he meditated in the wilderness.'

'All alone?'

'He has a woman who does for him, a housekeeper. I have only visited him once in the last few years. I should have gone more but his house is the saddest I have ever known, it's very upsetting to see such a good man brought so low. So very low.'

'But you have visited him, you can give me his address?'

The minister sighs. 'You will not hurt him?'

'No,' I say genuinely.

'You won't stir up an uncomfortable past?'

'I can't say that. For me it's a terrible time, but I have no idea what it might mean for him. I think he might be glad to see me. I really was very fond of him, you know.'

'Huh,' the old man says and I can see him, like the scales of justice, desperately trying to weigh the good versus the bad here. Perhaps if he were fully sober he would have told me to leave, but he has drunk enough to poison himself with nostalgia, and he goes to a small desk and pulls out a beaten-up address book.

'Skye. He lives on Skye,' he tells me, and then takes a pen and jots down an address on a piece of scrap paper. 'Here,' he says and hands it over. I hug him and leave.

—

Outside the sky has brightened and the sun is actually trying to break through the fug that hangs in the air. Leonard stands on the pavement by his truck. There's another man there and they seem to be talking in sign language. As I walk over, they shake hands and the other man leaves.

Leonard points at the church and moves his hands open as if to say *what happened*?

'I have an address for my missing reverend.'

He smiles in reply.

'Maybe I can get some answers now. For both of us,' I say, and feel a little guilty that I have not been totally honest with Hannah and Leonard. I've told them about the Vincent brothers and what they did to Drew, but I haven't mentioned a word about the bank robbery, or the money that's out there waiting to be found.

'Thank you, Leonard,' I tell him and he delves into his pocket and takes out a notebook, like the kind a reporter might have, and a small pen. He writes: *I can take you.*

I shake my head. 'No, you've done enough already. I'll be fine.' I hold his gaze. 'Hannah needs you here. I'll do what I need to do, and then I'll be back in a few days.'

I can see he doesn't trust me to return, but he also knows that Hannah can't be left alone, and with the best will in the world, she can't come on the journey. It isn't safe for her. It probably isn't safe for any of us. Leonard nods once more and then from his pockets, he pulls the car keys and his wallet. He opens it and takes out some notes, then hands them to me.

'I can't.'

But he presses them into my hand. And then he opens my palm and sets the keys in it and closes my fingers around the fob.

'No, really, I can't,' I tell him but he nods his head and grips my hand, squeezing hard. 'I'm a terrible driver, I really am,' I say, but he shrugs and writes something on his pad and holds it up.

> *You have to get them to pay for what they did to you and to us. If I can't come with you, then take the truck. Make them pay, Sarah. Please.*

'Okay,' I tell him. He squeezes my shoulder and walks past me and up towards the church. I think that Hannah must still be inside and he's going to find her. Maybe they'll take a taxi home or— but I can't concern myself with that. I have to get to my old friend in Skye. I have to know what happened when Drew went to see him and where my letter ended up. I have to know the truth.

Inside the truck are map books and a large road atlas, which I open to find out approximately where I am, and where I'm going. It's about two hundred miles, but it's mostly *A* roads all the way, so it could take hours.

I'll need to stop somewhere to get fuel and some food. I look towards the church but I can't see Leonard anymore. I pull away from the curb and head out. In the cab, sitting shotgun beside me, is Drew. Behind me sit Ayo and Theo.

'Okay, let's go and find some answers,' I tell them and then pause. 'And let's take some revenge.' I listen hard for any reply, or any sign that they're with me, that they forgive me. But there's nothing. *Okay.*

My eyes flick to the side, but Drew has gone. I look in the rear-view mirror and Ayo and Theo are gone too. I'm alone. Just me. Rebecca, abused by her dad, Mrs Drew Anthony, Sarah scared to have friends, Fran all alone and Jane lying to everyone she sees. All the different parts of me that have skulked in the dark, hidden inside each other like a Russian doll prison of hopelessness. Fifteen years of despair... but that must come to an end... one way or another. I drive.

–

The two hundred miles of the journey are torturous. The road winds and turns; it's never straight, but circles around hills and banks, always following the path of least resistance. Occasionally a spear of sunlight lances through the clouds, but that never lasts long as the clouds regroup and plug the hole. It takes hours, and I only get close to Skye as the light starts to die – and yet that is the most beautiful sight of all, as the sun dips below the misty clouds sending shafts of gold and ochre, of rust and bronze and even scarlet, out over the shimmering water. It really is a shepherd's delight (and that thought makes my stomach grumble as if it's complaining that my throat has been cut). I look over at the seat beside me. The food I bought before I left Aberdeen remains untouched, so no wonder I'm hungry.

Ahead of me is a bridge, it looks like the one that arcs up to the Norse heaven of Asgard. It is an incredible shape as it fires out into the water and then turns to the right and over the loch. In my head I hear… *carry the lad that's born to be king, over the sea to Skye.* The sun drops onto the water like an egg sizzling on a grill and then the light starts to die.

I pull over just before the arc of the bridge and park on a grass verge. I watch the light fail. It shimmers in the air like a billion fairies, before the dark begins to take over. I feel exhausted by the drive and I remember how hungry I am. I lean across and grab the food, opening the cheese and potato slice. I wish it were hot, but it's still good. It reminds my body that I'm still alive, and tells my bladder that it needs to pee. I climb out of the cab – oh my god, my lower back screams at me and I have to stretch it out before I squat behind the wheel arch. It isn't very ladylike but—

What's that? On the road behind me, suddenly appearing from a twist in the road, is another vehicle. I haven't seen another car for a while, so it feels a little odd. Then its headlights disappear. It must be another twist on the road, and I watch, expecting the lights to reappear any second… but I wait and I wait, and there's nothing. The lights have disappeared. It's possible the car has turned off the road, but I can't remember seeing a turning for miles and miles, and there are no buildings that I can see. Did I imagine the whole thing? Was it a ghost car? I suppose I could have been wrong, maybe it was something else… but it feels weird, and cold fingers run up and down my spine.

I pull my trousers up (I don't have any hand sanitiser or anything so I can't clean myself, but I was very careful not to splash) and get back into the cab. I sit for a while, looking in the rear-view mirror, but there's nothing there. No car comes past me and there are no lights… and all the time the air gets darker around me, the sky closes me in its arms and hugs the heavens until there's nothing but darkness. No moon, no stars, no light… nothing. *I must have imagined it*, I tell myself. All this time alone is doing crazy things to my head.

I put the car into gear and head off. I'm close to the end now, I know I am, I can feel it call to me; but I'm scared the truth isn't out there. I'm afraid there will be no closure. No answers. Nothing to make up for fifteen wasted years.

–

I pull onto a private road about ninety minutes later, and to be honest, this part of the journey should only have been about thirty minutes, but I've been very lost. I have visited two farms already, one of which was friendly and the other threatened to call the police, and actually set the dogs on me. I only just managed to get away, without major holes in me. But at last I'm finally here – I think. The map doesn't have any of this area in enough detail to be able to find individual buildings or homes but, by a process of elimination, I think this must be where I'm going to find the Rev.

The road is pretty rutted and I'd think it was unused, if it wasn't for the bright and shiny mailbox at the turning to the main road. I drive up slowly; this is the kind of road that can break a crankshaft or lacerate all four wheels if you aren't careful. After about half a mile of bone-shaking progress, the surface suddenly gets firmer and I coast up to a low-slung building. The only light is from my headlights. I drive in a semi-circle so I can see the lay of the land. There's a fence all the way round the property, topped with razor wire that makes it look like a high security prison. At the front there is a double gate, with a camera phone set into the wall. I get out of the cab and walk over, the headlights still blazing the way. It isn't at all where I imagined the Rev might live, am I in the right place?

As I reach the gates I push an intercom button, and I hear a little buzz from deep in the darkness ahead of me, but there is no answer. I push it a few more times but nothing stirs in the house. I push it again and I can see that there's a grille below it. I speak into it.

'I'm here to see the Rev, I mean Reverend Hanley, Daniel.'

I lift my finger off the button and wait. Still nothing. I push it again.

'It's… it's Rebecca. Rebecca Waite, do you remember me? You were so kind and I need help. Men are after me, dangerous men, two brothers Gene and Michael Vincent... please let me in. It's Rebecca.'

I look to the house, hoping a light might come on somewhere, but everything's dead. Maybe there's nobody here, or they can't hear me, or they're asleep. It's past midnight. To say I'm disappointed is a huge understatement, but there's nothing I can do now. I walk back to the car. My mouth feels gritty and I could do with a shower, but that's not an option. I step up into the cab, stretch, and then I lie across the seat and quickly fall asleep.

Chapter Twenty

Friday

BANG, BANG, BANG...

I don't know where I am. I look around for Drew –
he was just here with me... I try and hold onto his voice;
I heard it so clearly in my dream, but it's already faded. I
try and remember what he said – but that's gone, too.

BANG, BANG, BANG...

A hand slaps on the windscreen, and then rattles the
driver's side door.

'Who the hell are you?' An angry voice cuts through
the cold morning. I squint through the steamed-up
windows, but I can't make out who's out there. The voice
is coarse and the accent's thick and burred with cigarette
rawness. I see a dark shape, I think it's wrapped in a coat
or maybe it's a cape with a scarf and hat. A gloved hand
hits the windscreen again.

'We've got dogs, I'll get the dogs.'

I reach over, unlock the door and then push it open.
The person outside has to step back quickly. I can see they
limp pretty badly. The cold rushes in as soon as the door
opens, and I feel myself gasp as it attacks my lungs. *Christ*, I
want to pee. I slide out and down onto the frozen ground.
My hips feel crunchy and my back hurts.

'Who are you?' a woman asks, she is not friendly. I see a mass of dirty blonde hair and a scar that cuts through the left side of her face. I don't know if her left eye works at all, it seems to be a little milky, and it certainly doesn't seem to move like the right one does.

'I came looking for the Reverend Hanley, Daniel Hanley.'

She looks at me like I'm the VAT man who's arrived on a shock audit. For a second I think she might spit on me. 'Reverend.' She rolls the word around her tongue like it's poisonous. 'The mister ain't here.'

'But this is his address, isn't it?'

'He ain't here.'

'Are you his wife?'

'Wife?' She makes that sound poisonous too. 'I do for him,' she says and then turns away, heading towards the house, like this conversation is done.

'So this is where he lives – when will he be back?'

She stops at the gate, her back to me. Now that there's some light, I can see that I was wrong about the fence, as in places the chain-link is broken, and the razor wire is rusted from the almost-constant rain. It looks like the fence was put up years ago – maybe there was some threat back then, but times have changed, or someone's just got lazy and the fence has been allowed to rot away in places and sag in others. The woman turns back to face me. She looks like that hell hound with three heads that keeps people out of the Devil's business.

'Why do you want to see him?' she spits. 'Why can't you leave the man alone? Ain't he suffered enough?' She heads to the house.

'Suffered... I don't know anything about that,' I call over to her. 'I haven't seen him in a very long time, more than twenty years. He was my teacher.'

'Teacher?' she says, looking confused. 'Mr Hanley's never been a teacher. He was a man of God.'

'He taught at my school, religious studies. When my father died he... he was very kind to me.'

'You got the wrong—'

'Let her in, please.' A voice comes from the intercom. The scarred woman turns towards the house for a moment, and then her shoulders sag a little. She looks as if she's weighing up whether to ignore her master's voice, but then she turns and opens her arm, like a fern unwrapping itself for the sun, and she motions me inside, her one good eye blazing with anger.

'Thank you,' I say as I walk past her. I look closely at the house now, and see that it's set into the side of a hill at the back, and the front has huge windows that look out over a dip to see the woods fall away below. It reminds me of a medieval castle, fortified against the marauding hordes, and I wonder who Daniel Hanley is afraid of... or was afraid of some time ago. Maybe fifteen years ago?

I step across the threshold and am immediately taken by the smells of baking. I sniff... cinnamon and cardamom... nutmeg and clove... maybe mace too. There's the smell of fresh coffee as an earthy undertone, and bread baking. In the restaurant one of the chefs was a proper baker and he would make cinnamon knots and teacakes and currant buns. My mouth is watering at the thought of them.

'Excuse me,' the scarred woman says and I realise I've blocked the hallway.

'I'm sorry, the bread smells amazing,' I say but she doesn't react, just pushes past me, and heads to a door that she disappears through. I stand in the hallway, unsure what to do or where to go. I take a deep breath and walk forward, towards the light that spills around a half open door and— '*Oh my god.*' The light explodes in front of me. I'd seen the large windows from the outside but walking through to the heart of the house is like walking into the sunrise. The entire wall is made of glass and opens onto a vista above the treeline, looking out over a small wood. I can see forever. I can't tear my eyes away from the view and as the sun rises I can see the glass darken ever so slightly, like a pair of Reactolite sunglasses.

'Rebecca?' I hear my name, my birth name, spoken for the first time in many years by someone who has the right to use it. I turn and see him. I wouldn't have recognised him in the street, as he looks so old now. Twenty years have taken a heavy toll on him, and I wonder about what the housekeeper said: *hasn't he suffered enough?* He's thin, clothes hang off him like they might off a scarecrow made from broom handles. He has no hair at all on the top of his head, but a scrubby beard on his chin, which is steel-grey. His skin is sallow and covered in age spots like freckles on a redhead. He stands holding a cane that's got three tennis balls at the base like a tripod.

'Rev?' I ask, and he smiles, rolling back the years. I suppose he was in his late fifties back then, but he seemed so much younger in outlook than the other stuffed shirts who taught us. When my dad died he actually knew what to say to a bereaved teenager, and how to act around me. There wasn't just the obligatory 'sorry for your loss', and he didn't offer a frozen lasagne, or a bouquet of flowers with a cheesy poem stapled on. No, he took me and Drew ten-pin bowling. He bowled three strikes, one after the other, and said nothing about my dad being a great

Christian man, like so many others did. He said nothing about time healing wounds or about God's will – he showed me how to get a couple of difficult splits and he gave me my first espresso coffee. He let me smoke in his house, even though I could see he didn't let others and... he was a good man. He didn't judge me. I wish I'd had him with me when Drew died. I wish...

'Rebecca,' he says softly and opens his arms, which I can see is quite a feat of balance for him. I walk forward and let him put his arms around me. He smells of mints. He feels like home. He feels like a dad should, he feels like love.

'You're all grown up.' He puts his hand to my chin and tilts my head slightly so he can see my face fully. 'I can see the child still,' he says and then lets me go, and steadies himself with his stick.

'Do you need to sit down?' I ask him.

'In a moment, let's watch the sunrise first. It's the best part of the day, I don't like to miss it.'

We turn to the window and watch the sun rise and spread across the horizon, setting fire to the small clump of trees and making them glow with a rust and gold haze, so that the air dances around the tips of the branches. We watch for five minutes, until the Rev slumps a little, and I help him across the room and into an ancient leather armchair that looks like it has his shape moulded into it from years and years of sitting there. To the side of the chair is a table and on it are a pair of field glasses and a copy of *Birds of Britain*.

'I have become a birdwatcher in my old age. A twitcher.' He smiles and I hear a rasping breath in his voice that doesn't sound good. He must see the concern in my face because he says, 'Emphysema, and I didn't even smoke.' He gives me a sad chuckle. 'I blame all those hours in teacher lounges; they all smoked like chimneys back then.'

'Can I get you something?'

'No, Mrs Dearden can get us some coffee. You still drink coffee, I hope?'

'Strong and black, like you taught me,' I say and he laughs again, but this time like a wicked uncle.

'Can you hand me…' and he points at what looks like a plastic cup on the table, with a tube that comes out of one end. I pass it to him, he puts it over his nose and mouth and flicks a switch on a box by the chair, suddenly an electronic hum fills the room. He breathes deeply into the cup and sucks some medicine into his lungs – or maybe it's pure oxygen – I don't know. The plastic distorts his face for a moment and makes him look like a demon, then he pulls it away and offers me a half smile.

'Could you be a dear and go and ask Mrs Dearden to bring some coffee? My mouth is always gritty after I use this stupid machine.'

I nod and go off in search of the kitchen, following my nose on the spice road. When I open the door I find she has her hands in a bowl, working something that could be pastry or bread – I'm not sure which.

'Em… sorry to interrupt, but Reverend Hanley asks if it is possible to get some coffee?'

She doesn't look up, but keeps working whatever is in the bowl. 'You won't hurt him?' she says. 'I won't let you hurt him.'

'No, no. I'm not here to cause anyone any pain. As I said, he helped me a long time ago. I owe him a lot.'

'He isn't well.'

'He said he has emphysema.'

265

'And the rest, but that ain't the half of it. It ain't just the physical problems – don't get me wrong, they'd test the fortitude of a saint – but it's the emotional pains that are the worst.' She looks up at me, her eye flashes like a she-wolf warning predators away from her children. 'His son…'

'The DJ.'

'DJ…' She curls her lip in disgust, at the memory of the man. 'Like that's a bloody job. Meth-head, junkie, thief, leech and waster, that was him. He was in and out of prison, and every time he got out he swore on the bible that he'd changed, but it was a lie. He never altered his ways, no matter how the good father prayed for him, no matter how he suffered or what befell him – the boy got worse and he drove a good man mad.'

'I thought he made it big,' I say. 'I was told he had hits and was flying around the world, bought his own club.'

'In the end maybe, after he'd lied and cheated for years. Maybe at the end he got all he ever wished for. After a lifetime of chiselling and stealing, he finally had money and fame and women and enough heroin to blow his head off. Once he got success – after that first big hit – he was dead – it only took him six months to fry himself.' She looks like she wants to spit on his memory. 'At least being poor and unknown kept him alive. What a waste of oxygen he was.'

She pulls a tea towel over the top of the bowl, and puts it into a cupboard to rest or prove or whatever they do. Then she starts to make the coffee. It's pretty fancy. She opens two caddies of beans and spoons some from each, which she weighs until she has the right amount. Then she tips them into an electric grinder and reduces them to a powder. She tips that into a glass flask and then adds boiling water. She swirls them together and sets a two-minute timer. I watch as dark tendrils swim through the curling water like seaweed at the bottom of the ocean, slowly turning everything dark and silky. Then, when the timer cheeps, she pours it through a cone of filter paper into a coffee pot. It smells like smoke and chocolate and toffee. Then she opens a tin of home-made shortbread biscuits, and carries them through on a tray. I follow, and as I get back into the room I see that Reverend Hanley is sitting with his eyes closed and his head tipped back so the sun warms his face. He looks very ill. I look across at Mrs Dearden and she flashes me the evil eye, then touches his shoulder ever so softly and he opens his eyes. He was asleep.

'Sorry, little cat naps.' He smiles and, for another moment, the years fall away and he is once again the man who was so kind to me... to us... all those years ago. When the world was young.

'Do you need anything else?' Mrs Dearden asks in a low voice.

'No, that's fine, maybe you could leave us for a while.'

Her good eye flicks over to me and I can see the mistrust in it.

'Please, Mrs Dearden, I really am in no danger from Rebecca here. You can go.'

She gives him what can only be described as a little bow, like he's royalty or something, and then she leaves.

'I apologise for Mrs Dearden, she is fiercely loyal and...' He pauses. I can see bad memories swirl behind his eyes. 'But she is not a bad woman, she was in trouble and I helped her. I helped us both really, and she was grateful. So she stays and looks after me and she does that very well.'

I stay silent for a moment, wondering if he'll carry on and tell me about how he helped the woman, but he doesn't.

'Shall I be mother?' I say, and immediately feel uncomfortable. *Mother.* I haven't thought that for a while. Drew and I would say it as a joke sometimes, but it was always bittersweet, as deep down I wanted us to have a child, but it was too soon for him. He felt like we were still children, playing at being grown up, and that at some point the real adults would come and tell us off for pretending. He thought children couldn't possibly have children of their own, but I didn't and I'd wanted a child. I really did but... you know, shit happens. Or doesn't.

I pour the coffee. It's really good – dark and bitter but creamy too, like dark chocolate and figs. I close my eyes as I swirl it around my mouth. *Christ*, there is so much I want to know – so much I *need* to know – but we say nothing, instead we just sit and drink our coffee as the sun beats through the glass and warms us. It feels good to stop running and just *be*.

'This is what keeps me alive,' the Rev finally says, so softly I almost don't hear him. 'It isn't the drugs or the machines... it's the warmth of the sun as I sit here.' He puts his hand up to his face. The skin on his palm is like tracing paper, translucent, so I can see through it to the bone and blue veins. He strokes his cheek. 'My blood is so cold it barely moves around my body now. So I bask, like a reptile.'

'A snake,' I say and even I don't know if I mean it as a joke or an accusation. I want to ask about Drew but I just know that if I start down that road I will be screaming in seconds, so instead I take us back to the enigmatic Mrs Dearden.

'She doesn't like me, your housekeeper. She sees me as a threat somehow.'

'That isn't...' he starts but can't finish that thought. 'She sees herself as here to protect me.'

'That's nice, to have someone who cares.'

'Is it? I sometimes think I'm cruel to keep her here, like I'm the Beast and she's—'

'She's no Beauty,' I say callously.

'But she was, before her face was cut, it was... and she is young, though you can't see that. She...' But that sentence slips away from him as pain crosses his face. He looks up at me and his eyes are red-rimmed. 'Her face, the scar – my son did that to her.' He lets out a sob and his whole body shakes, as he scrambles on the table for the oxygen mask. I'm scared for him, I don't know what to do; he's turning a horrible purple colour.

'Mrs Dearden,' I yell. 'Mrs Dearden, please come.'

She rushes in, like she was standing behind the door ready, listening to us, and rushes to him. She grabs the mask and holds it over his nose and mouth, then she switches the machine on and slowly he catches his breath, his chest jagging up and down. She coos to him, *that's right, that's good* and after a minute or so, his colour is back to normal, he's steady, and his hands have stopped shaking.

'What the hell are you doing, getting him all riled up?' Mrs Dearden hisses at me as she secures the mask around his head with a length of elastic, and then gets a glass of water and some pills from the sideboard. All this time I've been rooted to the spot, watching what's happening, and... I'm ashamed to say that I'd begun to fold into myself. When he needed me I was useless.

'You need to go,' Mrs Dearden spits at me. 'We don't need trouble here.'

'I'm sorry, I—'

'No… no please don't go, Rebecca,' the Rev says, his hands flailing a little as he tries to reach me. He wants to pull me back to him. 'Let me get my breath back and then we can talk. Maybe you could walk around the garden for ten minutes and then come back. I don't want you to go. We have to talk.'

'But Father—'

'No, Mrs Dearden. I don't want her to leave.'

'Of course I won't, I'll walk outside for a few minutes. I'll come back,' I tell him with a smile and a nod, and head to the front door. I'm shaking, and I can feel the tears in my eyes. I walk into the cold of the morning. The glass only lets the warmth through, not the biting chill of the wind, but outside, it cuts like a billion tiny knives. I walk to the back of the house, and look out across the wood, seeing the trees sway. I close my eyes and the wind blowing through the trees sounds like the sea.

You could run… Drew's voice is in my head.

'No. No more running.'

Good, a voice says and I think it must be Ayo.

–

'He's ready for you to come back.' A yell from behind me cuts into my thoughts. I don't turn back towards her, at least not right away. I want to feel the sun for a few seconds longer, and I think I've decided that whatever happens here, I won't run again. Maybe I'll go back to Brighton and find Jordan and Agnes, or maybe I'll join a commune or something. Christ, I could even be a nun… maybe… I don't know. But what I do know is that I don't want to be alone anymore. Oh god, I want to be normal.

I open my eyes and the sounds of the sea fall away, as I can see it's only the wind in the trees. I turn around and wave to Mrs Dearden. She looks less scary now. I get that she's really protective of the old man, and that's nice, I'm glad he has that. I guess I'm glad that they have each other.

'I'm coming,' I call back, and head into the house.

When I walk back inside the gorgeous living room I see the bookcases properly for the first time. I'd been more intent on the wall of glass before, but now I see its counterpart is a wall of bookcases. In his chair, in the centre of the room sits Daniel Hanley, this time more erect, I think he must have a couple of pillows wedged behind him. I sit down opposite and see new coffee is steaming in cups on the little table. There is a small, delicate milk jug to the side and a sugar bowl.

'I'll be mother this time,' he says and pours the coffee. He takes his coffee black with one small spoonful of sugar. 'And you?' he asks.

'Very milky with two large sugars,' I tell him – I'm guessing I might need something to make the medicine go down. He sits in his chair and this time he has something in his lap, a square of white paper, and I recognise the writing even after all these years. I feel a lump rise in my throat, like a giant bullfrog wants to explode, but I bite my tongue and sit still, cupping the hot coffee in my hands. Outside, clouds draw in, they wrestle on the horizon and steal away the sun. With its warmth gone, my skin feels chilled.

'I know why you are here,' he says, and his hands go into his lap and he holds up the sheet of paper. 'Andrew came to see me.'

'I know.' My voice is like ice. 'That was a long time ago.'

'He left this with me.'

'To send to me?'

'Y-yes.' There is a tremor in his voice. I can see the struggle in him; he doesn't know what to do or say. 'I waited too long and...' His head drops and he slumps forward, his head in his hands. Slowly, I reach into his lap and take the paper, then I read the letter that has been lost to me for fifteen years.

If you're reading this Becs, then something awful has happened and I didn't make it back to you. I guess that I'm dead. Shit. I'm sorry. That's the best I can say – sorry. You've handled the last year so brilliantly, I am inspired by how you've been able to adjust to life after the money ran out, but I can't live like this. When we had your dad's insurance I was happy. That sounds crass and stupid, but it's true. Living the life of Riley is what I'm made for; I can't do hand to mouth, I can't have a small, nothing life. I'm not like you. I can't have a crappy job that I do and live for the weekend. I can't do it. I would rather roll the dice on this, and put everything on hitting the big time.

I never intended to steal, and I wouldn't have started down this path but for being approached by two men – the Vincent brothers. Honestly, Becs, you need to stay away from them, and tell the police if you see them. This is all because of them. They came to me and offered to make me rich. I'm not a thief, you know that. I'm not really a criminal – you have to believe me – but this was too good to miss.

But if you're reading this then it has ended badly and I'm sorry. I'm sorry for not being around

and I'm sorry I couldn't give you what you wanted.
I know you want to be a mum, but I didn't want to
bring a baby into this world when we had nothing.
My mum and dad lived in a shit hole with me and
my sister when we were tiny; they made me a bed
in the bath and my sister was in a desk drawer for
six months. I won't have that for us. I won't be
so poor, and I won't work all the hours that God
gives, just to earn a crust to feed a family I never
see because I'm always working at a job I hate.
I'd rather be dead than that. Or in jail. I'm sorry
that I don't love you enough to be poor. I'm taking
the coward's way out, and stealing the money we
need. At least I'm not mugging old ladies for their
pensions. I've asked the Rev to post this if he hears
that anything has happened to me. Anything bad,
I mean. I've posted you a new mix CD. Listen to
it. Listen to it all… and remember me. Remember
our favourite song, and our favourite place, and
our favourite film. Remember. I'm sorry I let you
down.
  Drew

I finish his letter and fold it. Funny. There are no tears.
Maybe I cried them all out already. The Rev looks at me.
I remember that look from years and years ago, when I
told him about my dad; no judgement, only acceptance
and love. It makes my stomach turn over.

'I should have posted it immediately but I waited and
waited and—'

'I'd already run,' I say.

'I'm sorry,' he says in a voice so low I can barely hear
him over the blood coursing through my veins at warp
speed.

'I ran, Rev… and ran… and ran… you had no right. I should—'

Mrs Dearden rushes in with a poker. 'Stay away from him!' she screams.

'Mrs Dearden, I am not in danger.' He waves his arms at her.

'She needs to go, leave you in peace,' the housekeeper hisses.

'Mrs Dearden… please…' and the two of them continue to talk but I can't listen any longer. Instead, I curl into myself but I do not fold. I don't escape the pain. I feel it claw at me, but this time I don't run. I let it bite me, I need to feel my pain, and remember that this is my own fault. I hear a pathetic whimper, and realise it must be me. I don't know how long I'm curled into myself, but finally I hear my name being called. The voice full of concern, and slowly I uncurl.

'Rebecca… Rebecca, are you all right? Should I call a doctor?' the Rev asks kindly, worried by how I hold my stomach.

'No I… I'm fine, I'm just overwhelmed by all of this.' I pause for a moment. Mrs Dearden lifts the coffee pot to refill our cups. 'Fifteen years ago, on the day that I heard Drew was dead, I ran away. From my memories and from my grief, but most of all… and worst of all… from two men who attacked me. I ran from them, but they have chased me like dogs hunting a fox ever since.'

'But who—'

'Gene and Michael Vincent.'

The coffee pot shatters on the floor.

'I… I'm… so sorry.' Mrs Dearden is shaking and has turned pale.

'Are you all—'

'I'll clean it up. No problem.' And she turns and scampers from the room.

'I'm sorry for that, Rebecca, please carry on. Who were these men who hunted you?' the Rev asks.

'They were the men who robbed the bank and dragged Drew into this. They killed him fifteen years ago.'

'The news said it was an accident.'

'No, he was murdered, and those two men have kept on killing. They killed two people on the London Underground, and killed a man in Brighton. Both times I was the real target and I barely got away with my life.'

'Oh my dear, that is awful,' he says, shocked.

From the door Mrs Dearden speaks, as she comes inside with a cloth and a floor cleaner. 'I saw that... I saw the victims on the news...' Her face turns so pale I think she might faint.

'Mrs Dearden, maybe you could find some brandy. For shock, you know.' She slowly nods her head at the Rev, and staggers out of the room, leaving us alone again.

'I should have...' he says and begins to cry. 'Andrew came for my protection and—'

'Don't blame yourself. These men are evil, wicked.'

'I didn't know how to help him,' the Rev says, pathetically. 'I tried, but I didn't know what to do... I was scared and...' The tears overwhelm him.

'Drew made the decision to become a criminal, and that was what hurt him. You didn't make him rob a bank.'

'No... no, he came to hide. He said he had been betrayed; that the men he was working with planned to get rid of him and take all the money for themselves; so he decided to betray them first. He thought he had it all planned out, but it didn't go as smoothly as he hoped and he had to find somewhere to run to.'

'And he came here, he looked for you, even though it was years after we'd last seen you.'

'I don't know why exactly. I think it was more about chance, because he'd bumped into me a few weeks before. I was fresh on his mind.'

'You were back in Manchester?'

'No. I was in Aberdeen visiting an old friend. It was strange. Andrew was coming out of a shop and—'

'In Aberdeen? A few weeks before the robbery? That was when he was working for the bank.'

'Maybe they sent him here.'

'What day of the week was it?'

'A Saturday, I think. I was visiting a priest there and... what's wrong?'

'There was a weekend when we had a fight and he stormed off. On Friday when he got home from work there was a blazing row and he didn't come back until Sunday night and wouldn't tell me where he'd been. I cried all weekend, worried for him because the argument seemed crazy, like he'd made it happen out of nothing, as if he'd engineered an excuse to leave... and now I know I was right. But why did he come to Scotland?'

'I don't know... I mean I can't help with that, but a few weeks later he was here, at my house. I'd given him my address when I saw him. He arrived in the midst of a terrible storm. It rained for days and days, I remember, there were floods all over the country. I certainly wasn't about to turn him away – not even after he told me what he'd done.'

'Helped rob a bank,' I say flatly.

'And then robbed the other thieves.'

'Did he have the money when he arrived here?' I ask.

'I...' He scowls, as if trying to recall. 'No, no he'd left it somewhere between Manchester and here. What he wanted from me was sanctuary, a place to wait out the storm and think. I could not deny him that.'

'Of course not.' I look at the old man and I don't understand why Drew came here, if it wasn't to hide the money? He wouldn't have come all this way only to talk to the Rev, would he? 'What did Drew want from you?' I ask.

'I think...' He pauses and I can see his mind whirring through an ethical dilemma. 'I think he came to talk about you, I think he wanted advice from someone who knew you both.'

'Why?' I feel cold.

'He was feeling guilty.'

'About the robbery?'

The old man doesn't answer. I feel a little light-headed.

'Why did he want to talk with you? Was this some big confession or something?' I look at him, waiting for the Rev to speak but he says nothing. 'Tell me, what was Drew's big secret?'

'The robbery... the two men who planned it.'

'The Vincent brothers.'

'Yes, the two of them planned it, but there was also a woman, the girlfriend of the younger brother, I believe. They used her as...'

I watch his skin darken as embarrassment sweeps over him.

'She was a kind of bait, a sweetener, I believe, to get Andrew interested. They used her to get him entangled with them and then... compromised.'

I feel like I'm made of stone. I wish I could sink through the floor and keep going, down and down into the molten core of the planet and be melted like the wicked witch of the west. A pretty face trapped him in this dumb plot, a pretty face and a cute ass; a honey trap. He was just a fucking stupid, horny fly.

Suddenly a glass of water is pressed into my hand. I look up into the Rev's face and I see the concern and the sorrow. 'I'm sorry.'

'Did he bring her here?'

'No.'

'Was he going to run away with her, if he had the money?'

'I... I don't...' but I can see the truth in the pain in his face. Drew was going to leave with the money and this girl. I never fitted into his plans.

'I wish I could have saved you all of this, Rebecca,' the old man says and I can see the earnestness in his face. 'I tried to change his mind. I tried to turn him away from the course he had chosen, but nothing I said had any effect.'

'He couldn't bear to be poor,' I say and I hear the hollow ring in those words. 'He didn't see me as worth anything.'

'I don't believe that's true.'

'But it is.' *It is.*

I can see the old man is starting to shake. He looks exhausted and hangs his head, as if deep in thought. Maybe he's thinking about his own son and how he ended his life. We have both lost the person we most loved, that should bring us together but I think it will probably do the opposite; we will both be lost in thought while we drift away from each other, like dinghies in a storm, floating away from the hull of a broken ship as it sinks. Drew is my broken ship.

I look out at the view. The sun has disappeared and shades of grey and green wash before me as rain starts to spit down. The clouds move fast above us, chasing each other across the skies.

'He didn't say where he was going after here?' I ask and the Rev shifts in his chair slightly.

'No, he stayed one night and—'

'Was he here the entire time?'

'I… no, he went out for a walk, maybe an hour.'

'He could have hidden the money.'

'No, I mean he had nothing with him. He had a coat and I loaned him an umbrella, but that was it.'

'Huh,' I say. 'But he was gone for an hour.'

'About that, I'd say.'

'Was it just you here?'

'Yes, I lived alone, and the house was different then, smaller.'

'No Mrs Dearden?'

'No, she came to me later.'

'And your son?'

He pauses, a sadness deep in his eyes. 'He was in prison at the time… that was really why I came here, out in the hinterlands of society. I wanted to prepare somewhere he could come to when he got out of prison, somewhere he could learn another way of being, away from the temptations of the city. I thought we could tend the land together.'

'Nurture and growth to help his troubled mind?'

'Maybe… something like that. I hoped I could help him back from the brink.'

'But it didn't change anything,' I say.

He doesn't answer. I guess it didn't. Just like all the love I offered Drew wasn't enough. For some people it will never be enough; they will never be sated by love from another person, because they can't love or understand themselves. Some people need to keep falling on their face until one day they either don't get back up, or they'll finally learn a lesson. I think I've learned that I need to do something a little different from now on.

'Can I use the bathroom?' I ask.

'Of course, upstairs, use my private bathroom.'

'Thanks.'

I leave him in his reverie of guilt, and I walk upstairs. I wonder... I wonder... In his note to me Drew says I should remember our favourite film. It's *Charade*. In it there's a robbery – wartime gold, I think – and one of the robbers betrays the others and takes it all. The robbers kill him but they can't find what he stole, so they kill each other off, but they never find the money because the betrayer hid it in plain sight, by buying a stamp with it. A stamp that was worth millions. A stamp that he put on a letter and kept it in his pocket. I imagine Drew walking out with the Reverend's umbrella. He had no big bags with 'SWAG' written on them, but he could have had a stamp. Or an ancient coin, or even share certificates. He could have left here and dug a small hole with his hands and pushed it inside. He could have done that so easily.

In the bathroom I pull my down trousers and a musky smell floats up. I could do with a shower. I sit on the toilet and think some more. I try and remember what was found in Drew's clothes. When I was at the morgue they gave me a bag. Was there something in that bag worth eight hundred and seventy-five thousand pounds?

I sit and wait. All this running around scared, has made me a little constipated but... finally... I can go. Good, because I need what's been stuck in my insides for the last few days. I want that little plastic capsule with Gene's mobile number. It's time this stopped. So I poop.

When it's out, I look into the bowl. I don't normally do this, but I reach in and... yuk. I have Gene's phone number.

—

I wash my hands really well. I scrub so hard I might even have taken my fingerprints off. I walk down the stairs and out into the day. Hell, it seems only a few minutes since the sun rose but it's so grey now it feels like twilight. I wonder if they have the northern lights here. I would love to see them, almost more than anything else. That would be awesome. I open the capsule and unfold the tiny piece of paper. Then I take the mobile phone that Ayo gave me and I dial.

Be strong... be str—

Rinnnnng Rinnnnnnnnnnnnnng...

My blood turns to ice. From a little way off, in the treeline where the wood starts I hear a phone ring. *Jesus Christ*. Then the call is answered and I hear his voice.

'It's too late to make a deal, Rebecca, we're already here,' Gene says and then hangs up.

My stomach churns and I think I might throw up. I see something move in the treeline ahead of me; a grey blob shifts and I know it's them. They found me. They're here and they'll kill us all. Oh my god, they'll kill us all.

Chapter Twenty-One

'They're here. *They're here.*' I scream as I slam the door behind me. There's no key… I look frantically around but there's nothing I can use as a barricade or anything. There is nothing to keep them out.

'We have to run. We have to run.'

I dash into the kitchen, where I find Mrs Dearden by the back door. It's open and she's anxiously looking out of it, with a phone in her hand.

'They're here, the men who attacked me. The men who are chasing me. They're here and we need to run. *We need to run!*' I yell at her, but her one good eye is cold. No fear, only contempt.

'Mrs Dearden you have to believe me. These men are killers, they will hurt you and the Rev too.' I move forward, but she steps away, keeping the kitchen table between us. 'You don't know them, they're monsters.'

She smiles, she actually *smiles* at that. Like she thinks it's all a joke and I'm trying to trick her.

'You can't possibly know the danger we're all in!' I yell at her.

'Not us – you,' she says.

'There's no time, they will be here any…' My words die away as I look at the phone in her hand.

'Who are you calling?' I ask as dread starts to creep through me.

'Wouldn't you like to kn—'

I leap at her, across the table like a cat would. I'm quick and I manage to grab at her coat as she tries to move away. My fingers curl into her collar and grip hard as her arm flails at me, the phone hitting me in the temple.

'Leave me alone, you bitch,' she screams and twists like a snake, pulling out of my grip so I'm left with her coat in my hand. She runs off shrieking and I hear her burst through the front door.

'She knows she knows... Michael, she knows...' she yells. Then there is a clap of thunder and the rain begins to fall.

Oh my god, oh my god... She called them, is all I can think. She knows them. I look at the coat in my hand, and see that it's rubberised. I should put it on and run out of the back door, into the rain. I open it up and I see a cloth tag stitched inside. A name tag like you get in school... and the name reads: *Tina Bray.*

Oh god, Hannah and Leonard's foster child. How can that be true? How can she be here? How can Mrs Dearden be Tina Bray? I don't know, but she is. That woman is Tina Bray. She must have called them the moment she saw me. Christ, I said my name over the intercom last night, and that the Vincent brothers were after me. Did she call them then? Oh Christ, but it doesn't matter – because all that matters is that they're here and they want to kill me.

The rain is lashing down. I hear voices, but my legs are in cement, I can't move. The door rattles in the wind, and then slams as it blows shut.

'Michael,' a voice yells and I feel sick to my stomach. It's Gene. He's inside the house, they both are. I can hear them moving through it, like rats through a rubbish tip. I reach for the back door. The coat feels slick in my hand;

it's red and shining, like blood. I open the back door, as a fork of lightning spikes the air and seems to strike the ground in the distance. It lights the trees and the rain like a flash photograph and I can see a million individual drops of rain in the air. I could run, maybe get lost in the wood and hide but—

'Rebecca.' His voice is faint; he's old and frail. He's in the living room and the brothers must be with him. I imagine a knife at his neck, like Michael held that knife at Ayo's neck… and I could have saved her. I could have pulled the emergency cord. I could have let him take me instead. I could… *Oh Christ*. I feel myself start to fold and bend, I want to escape—

No… I can't. No more running. I have blood on my hands. Theo's blood and Ayo's blood and—

'Rebecca…' he calls again and this time I hear total fear in his voice. I can't let him die for me. I have to give myself up to the brothers. No more blood can be shed for me.

'Rebecca, you should run. *Run*. R—'

'Fucking bastard,' I hear Michael spit and there is the crunch of fist on bone as Tina Bray screams.

'Don't hurt him. You promised me. Take her and leave us alone. You swore to me, Michael!' Tina yells at him. And I hear her grunt, I imagine she is trying to keep him away from the old man and then I hear the sound of Michael Vincent hitting her, swatting her back like a fly. The rain is like a curtain and another fork of lighting illuminates the night. He told me to run, the Rev commanded it… but no. It's a good day to die, I think, while the heavens weep for those lost in the storm. I throw the door closed and turn away from it. I won't run, never again. I drop the coat on the floor and head towards the men who will kill me.

'Don't hurt him,' I call out. 'Don't touch a hair on his head, you bastards. I'm coming.' I walk towards the living room, but before I get there I take a right. I find myself in Tina Bray's room. I want a weapon. I see a comb with a long metal handle like a knitting needle. I slide that into the waistband of my— *oh my god*. There are two photographs taped to the mirror. The first is of Tina Bray, her face still unscarred, holding a baby – she is beautiful, and so young. The second is of her with a boy, maybe he's ten years old, and he must be the baby, grown up. Her face has the scar now. But it isn't her that attracts my attention, it is the boy who, even at ten years old or so, towers above his mother. He looks into the camera, no smile, and I know his father. There can't be any doubt as to who made Tina Bray pregnant.

'Where the fuck are you?' Michael Vincent screams for me.

'Coming,' I yell. 'I wanted to brush my hair.' I leave the room and its secrets, and head back into the living room. My jaw is set, my teeth grind together. I promise myself that I will not be scared, I will not run. I will not escape my body no matter what. I will never leave someone to die or be hurt again, not in my name, not for me. I will take my own medicine. I am prepared to die.

The Reverend is sitting in his chair, his eyes red-rimmed with tears. There is a bruise like a giant egg on the side of his head, and a trickle of blood has traced down his face and fallen onto his shirt to blossom like a red rose on the white linen. It looks as if he has a poppy pinned to his chest. Gene is standing, leaning against the bookshelf. I see him first, reflected in the glass across the room. He looks shrunken, like a ghost, his eyes way back in his head and I perceive a tremble in his hands, maybe even his whole body.

On the floor lies Tina Bray and her mouth is a mass of broken teeth and cut flesh. I imagine Michael punched her directly in her once beautiful mouth. Her one good eye is closed and the bad eye is open and a tear runs from it. The last person I see in the room is Michael Vincent. His face is flushed and alive, a total contrast to the vampiric look of his older brother. Never have I seen siblings who look less alike than these two men. I can see that it's now Michael who's in the ascendancy. So I turn to Gene.

'I telephoned you,' I tell him, trying to keep my voice level and calm.

'Forget him, look at me,' Michael yells angrily at me, but I keep my eyes on his older brother.

'I'm talking to the organ grinder,' I say, calm and low.

'What the fuck did she say?' Michael spits at his brother.

'Calm down, Michael, let's not turn this into—'

'Look at me, you whore. I'm in charge here. I'm the one who can end this bastard's life. So fucking talk to me.' He swings the knife towards the Rev's throat. But I don't turn and I don't let the fear eat me up. I stay looking at Gene. 'So is he the boss now?' I ask.

'No,' Gene says and Michael explodes, pulling the knife away from the Reverend's throat and bounding over to his brother. His hand extends to grab him, lifting him up, almost off his feet. I see Gene wince as pain rattles through him.

'Michael, she's trying to—'

'Who's in charge now?' He leans his face into his brother's so their noses almost touch. I can see how Gene tries to hold his brother's stare, but he can't.

'What are you gonna do, Gene, piss yourself again?' Michael gloats and lets him go. The older man almost falls and has to grab onto the bookcase to steady himself. I walk briskly over to the Rev's chair and kneel down.

'Are you okay?' I ask quietly as I take the sharp comb and slide it under his leg. He opens his eyes wide, in surprise.

'You should have run,' he tells me.

'Run... I think it's time to stand up for what's right.'

'I'm old, I'm not worth saving.'

'Who said I was coming to save you? I'm saving myself, I can't live on the run anymore. Anything is better than that.'

'Really, anything?'

'I think so,' I smile. 'We'll find out.' I stand and turn back to Tweedledum and Tweedledee.

'Okay, so there's been a change at the top, I see.'

'Shut up, this is the time for you to answer questions and not ask your own.'

'I called you, didn't I? I wanted to talk and share, but not like this. Not with this man as your hostage. Let him go and I mi—'

'Don't you fucking tell me what to do.' Michael leaps forward and screams in my face. But I am no longer afraid of him.

'If you want the last fifteen years of searching and scratching around to mean anything, then you will talk to me like a regular human being and you will stop playing the crazy gangster and—'

'Argh,' he yells as his fist flies at me. I start to duck but there's no time and his fist hits me in the eye. I hear a click and feel pain shoot though me. Something is broken in my face and I—

Black.

—

I come to with a jagging pain that scrambles through my left temple and up into my eye where it does the Macarena. I have no idea how long I was out for, it could have been seconds or the full Rip Van Winkle. I try to move but my arms don't budge. I think I'm tied into a chair. My right eye opens easily but my left one does nothing. I move my head, so I can see myself reflected in the glass of the— *oh god*. The left side of my face is bloody and I look like the elephant man. One punch from that animal and my face is black and blue.

I look down and see I was right; my wrists have been cable-tied to the chair. They're pulled so tight that no blood is getting through to my fingers, but that's the least of my problems. I twist as far as I can to see the rest of the room. Reverend Hanley looks as pale as a sheet, still in his chair. Michael is in the centre of the room and talking to Tina, who looks a little shell-shocked. I don't see Gene anywhere. That worries me.

'Tina, you take the old man down into the cellar and lock him up in there while I talk to—'

'No,' Gene says, but I can't see where he is. 'I just found an interesting letter, brother.'

'What the fucking use is a letter?'

'But this is very interesting, come out here with me, I need to talk to you.'

'We don't need talking, Geney, we need—'

'Give me a couple of minutes, bro. Come on.'

'Two minutes, then we come back. We wake her up and I start extracting teeth. Okay?'

'You're the boss of extraction,' Gene tells his brother, who then turns to Tina – 'Clean up her face, it's making me feel sick looking at it,' – and the brothers leave. I pull at my wrists, but it just makes the ties dig deeper into my flesh.

'Don't struggle. Pull it tighter and it'll cut your arm off,' Tina says as a sponge is pushed into my face and water leaks across my chin and down my front.

'Don't bother playing the Florence Nightingale act for me, Tina – though you're good. I actually thought you cared for the old man.'

'They weren't supposed to hurt him,' she says, as she wipes blood off my face. 'That was the deal, to leave him alone.'

'You don't mind them hurting me, though.'

'You deserve it.'

'Why?'

'Because snitches get stitches.' She sounds like a kid in a playground.

'What the hell are you talking about? I didn't snitch. I didn't know anything about what was going on, so how the hell could I snitch?'

'You grassed on 'em, in Brighton.'

'Brighton – that wasn't even a week ago. Hell, Tina, they have been ruining my life for the last fifteen years.'

'Fifteen? Don't be stupid.' She squeezes bloody water into a bowl.

'Yes, that's when they first attacked me. Years ago. I had no idea who the hell they were. And the joke is that they didn't tell me; all they asked about was money. They wanted to know where the money was.'

'Money,' she parrots as she pushes herself away from me.

'And I had no idea what money they were talking about. But they'd robbed a bank, and I was supposed to know where the money was.' At those words Tina drops the sponge into the water with a splash. She looks scared.

'I don't... I mean why did they think you'd know anything?'

'They said my husband robbed them.'

'Husband?' she says it raspily, like she can't understand the word itself. 'I don't... I never...' sh dries up.

'My husband was missing and then the police found him dead and that night the Vincent's turned up at my house and tried to beat information out of me. But I had no idea what had happened, I just knew that my husband was dead.'

'You're his wife...' she says it like she's in a dream. 'You're Drew's wife.'

And finally the ball drops, and I know who she is in this mess, I know how she links all of this together.

'You were the bait, the hook to get Drew into the gang,' I say. 'Gene and Michael used you to seduce my husband.' And I can see it in my mind. He must have got the job in the bank and as soon as they saw him they knew he was what they'd been waiting for. A man who could be tempted, a man who was corruptible, so they sent in their very own Lolita, in the form of Tina Bray. I know what she looked like back then, I know from seeing the picture on her mirror, the one with the baby. She was beautiful.

'You got Drew to agree to help with the robbery, didn't you?' She doesn't reply. She looks back at me with her one good eye, full of fear and loathing. 'Of course he wouldn't have been able to resist you; he must have fallen hard.' I can imagine she would have made him drool. 'I assume you batted your eyelashes and wiggled your hips and he was your slave.'

She laughs at me. 'It was more than that; he said it was boring at home. The Mrs wasn't sexy, didn't turn him on… that's what he said.' She leers, but she can't rile me. She might have been beautiful then, but now she is scarred and scared. Maybe Drew *was* bored by our love life. I know he craved excitement; he wanted to be James bloody Bond, and this would have been perfect for him: a teen femme fatale, shady brothers planning a heist, crosses and double-crosses, bags of cash and hidden treasure. It would have been like an action movie, and he was always so immature.

'You hooked Drew, and he agreed to help Gene and Michael carry out the robbery.' She nods, looking miserable. 'But something went wrong, didn't it? You got dragged away from Manchester, because you were underage and in foster care. I assume the police found you and dragged you back to the farm.'

Her eyes turn black. 'How the hell did you know that?' she hisses.

'Living on a farm must have been hard for you – I bet you hated it there. The smell of the animals and the chores, so you flirted with the farmer. You tied him around your little finger, didn't you? He was in love with you, and would do anything you wanted.'

'How do you know that?' Her eye twitches and she takes a step away from me. 'You're a witch.'

'He let you do whatever you wanted, didn't he… poor Leonard.'

She gasps and makes the sign of the cross. It makes me want to laugh. She really thinks I'm a witch, but I'm far worse than that. As far as she's concerned I'm the Devil, and I'm about to steal her soul.

'You had Drew and Leonard on a string, like they were your puppets and they'd do anything you wanted. And maybe that's what gave you the idea to betray Gene and Michael.'

'No.' She shakes her head and her eye darts to the door. She's petrified one of them will come back in and hear what I'm saying. 'You decided to take all the money for yourself. That's right, isn't it, Tina?'

She whimpers, and pulls back further, pushing herself against the bookcases. She's afraid – and I like the look of it, because her fear shows me that I'm right. She was the one chattering seductively in Drew's ear, persuading him to play a part in the robbery in the first place and then, when he was hooked, she put the idea in his head to betray Gene and Michael and take the money himself.

'The two of you worked out a way to get the money from under Gene and Michael's nose and then spirit it away. And of course you thought about the farm. It was the perfect place to hide it, and I'm guessing that Michael and Gene had no idea about your foster family. Did they even know how young you were – sixteen – you were just a kid.'

'I was never a kid. I've been stealing and picking pockets since I was ten years old. I was never a fucking kid.'

'Boohoo, my heart bleeds for the poor street urchin,' I say with ice in my veins.

'You have no idea,' she says.

'Some… I have some idea of growing up in fear.'

She shakes her head and spits on the floor. But I won't get caught in some misery pissing contest with her.

'So what did you do then? Did you plan to meet Drew at the farm to share the money? Maybe after that you were going to go to Spain or Greece or somewhere… but he didn't turn up at the agreed time, did he?'

Her eyes flash black and hard. She doesn't say a word, but I know I'm right. I can feel it in my bones.

'You didn't know where he was, did you? So you waited, but he didn't come and then you got really scared. You thought he'd taken all the money and that Michael and Gene would hunt you down and kill you.'

'He was a bloody thief. It was his idea, I went along with it. I—'

'Don't lie, Tina.' The Rev's head is still bowed but his voice is clear as a bell as he calls to her. 'I don't think any of us are getting out of this alive, these men will kill us. I think it's time to tell the truth at last. Only the truth can set us free.'

'I am telling the truth…' she tells him, her eyes full of tears. 'None of you have any idea, when you're so poor that you'd lick someone's shoes or suck their cock for ten pounds, then you're past caring what's true. Just staying alive is everything. Michael and Gene would have killed me.'

'So you gave them Drew to save yourself.'

'You don't know what they were like.'

'I do know what they were like, I've still got the scars on my body from back then, because you set them on me. You told them Drew had run away with the money, and you told them that he was supposed to be on the farm. You sold him to them.'

'I had no choice.'

'That's crap, you always have a choice – especially if it's someone you love. But you never really loved him, you just used him. You don't know what love is.'

She stares at me. I don't think she's ever actually thought about what she did back then; she doesn't strike me as someone that's aware of what they do. She just acts on base instinct.

'He was supposed to meet me with the money but he didn't, so I called Michael and told him that Drew wanted to meet me at this old farm. I thought it was the only way to stay alive.'

'And he finally arrives there but without the money.'

'He should have been there the day before,' she says.

'And you didn't tell him that it was a trap; that Gene and Michael were on their way.'

Tina drops her eyes away from mine, and maybe I see some shame in them. 'I bet you tried every one of your womanly wiles to get him to tell you where the money was, but he wouldn't.'

'No, but he still wanted me – to go away with me, he still chose me over you.'

Her words sting me, as deep down I know what she says is true; he would have gone away with her. But after the money ran out and the sex wasn't new and exciting… what then? Would he have stayed with her? I don't think he would. Perhaps he would have come back to me, with his tail between his legs, or maybe he'd have tried to rob another bank or find himself a rich older woman. I think the life of a gigolo would have suited him well.

'Maybe he did choose you, Tina, I don't know,' I tell her. 'But it didn't matter because Michael and Gene found him and…' I remember the cigarette burning my skin, his fingers digging deep into my flesh and… and it would have been so much worse for Drew. I bite the inside of my mouth, needing the pain to bring me back from the horror of my thoughts. I can't get lost in the past.

'You fed him to the lions, sacrificed him so you could escape, and you ran. Aberdeen was it?' I ask her, but I know that was where she was when the police called Hannah.

'You were desperate for money, all your plotting had backfired and you must have been petrified that Drew would give you away. Your life would have been worthless if Michael had known what you planned to do.'

Her eye blazes with hate.

'You wanted money so you could get away, hide yourself – but what happened? Did you offer a blowjob to the wrong man or try and steal someone's wallet? The police picked you up for something and they called the farm for your foster parents to come and get you. And when they drove out in the rain, they hit Drew. They thought they'd killed him but he was already dead.'

'How do you know all this?'

'Do you know they crashed their car that night trying to get to help you?'

'No.'

'Leonard almost died and Hannah was left in a wheel-chair.' I lie a little, just a little. 'But that didn't stop Leonard getting to you. He left his wife and got to Aberdeen but you'd flown the nest.'

'I was scared in the cells, so I called Michael and he came and got me.'

'Why the Mrs Dearden act?'

'It isn't an act. He was my husband. I married him later, after… after this.' And she touches the scar that bisects her face. 'I fucking hated him, but what other man would

295

have wanted me? And not only me; I had an infant son to look after.'

I remember the picture of her and the baby on her mirror.

'So I married a man for security and a roof over our heads, and he married me for… for what all men want, and ugly old fat men only get when they pay for it.'

'I'm sorry,' I tell her, and I mean it. She's still young, she's only in her thirties, but the way she holds herself is like an old woman; she's been sucked dry of her youth by all the men who've used her. She sees that I'm genuinely sorry for her, but in a strange way that makes her hate me more. She thinks it's pity, and that makes her angry.

'I don't care what you think of me. I did what I had to do to protect my son. But it didn't last… he died.' There's a glint in her good eye as she says that, and I wonder if she killed her awful husband somehow. Poison, maybe? But she won't tell and I won't ask.

'But it turned out that he left everything to his children in his will, and they hated me, so my kid and I was out on our ears. I had a little bit of jewellery to sell but not much. The boy was three, and I was desperate, so I went to the church. The minister there said he had work for me. A job as a housekeeper in the middle of nowhere, but somewhere clean and safe for my boy.' She pauses, maybe remembering the day she first arrived here and breathed in the clear air.

'I would never have imagined actually liking the countryside, I was always one for the bright lights and big city, but being here saved me. He saved me.' She looks across at Reverend Hanley and I actually see some affection in her face.

'A pity you brought those two killers into his home, then.'

She hisses at me, like a snake. 'I didn't mean to get Daniel involved, I just wanted you gone.' She points at me with a stabbing motion of her thin, bony hands. 'I didn't know you was his wife, all I knew was what you said last night on the intercom. Two brothers chasing you; Michael and Gene Vincent you said – so I called them. All I wanted was some money, something to tide me over. I thought they'd pay for news of you. I thought they'd be in Manchester or even London… but they were in Aberdeen. So they came and…' Her voice drops and she looks broken. She looks across at me and I see the hate in her eyes.

'Please don't tell them what I did back then… not for me but for my boy, he needs his mum… please don't.' She begs me and I know that I have to push home my advantage now.

'Okay, Tina, I'll keep quiet about what I know, but in return you're going to get two knives from the kitchen and give me one and keep the other. With that knife you'll protect the Rev with your life.'

'But if they catch me getting the knives—'

'I have total faith that you can steal anything from under their noses. But you need to remember: if you sell me out, or let the Rev get hurt, then I will feed you to them. I'll tell them everything and Michael will chew you up and spit you out. Then what will your son do, go into foster care like you did? End up like you have?'

'Not my son, he won't end up like me.'

'I hope not; his father wouldn't have wanted that.'

She gasps, and I see the shake in her hands.

'I saw his photograph in your room, Tina,' I tell her.

She whimpers a little, and her hands come together like she's imploring me to save her boy. 'He's at school, on the mainland, he's only a child.'

I open my mouth to say something else, but at that second Gene and Michael return. A chill settles in the room, total silence. I watch them as they come in and I sense that the power has shifted between them again, as Gene walks tall and Michael is a little hunched over, his jaw tightly wound, like it could snap.

'Tina, take the old man and lock him in the cellar. He can have a couple of blankets and a pillow,' Gene tells her.

'What abou—'

'Shut up,' Michael screams at me, cutting me off in mid-sentence, his face a mass of fury. I think he'd kill me for the fun of it right now.

'The old man will need some food,' I say softly and slowly, my eyes hooded slightly and lowered, as if I'm bowing to the alpha dog.

'He doesn't need any fu—'

'If you want the money, then he has to be fed,' I say this to Michael but then I tilt my head to Gene and look him full in the face. 'You have no idea how to find the money without me.' My eyes are still on Gene but it's his brother that answers.

'Then we can cut the fucking truth out of you.' He is like a volcano of hate and anger, his eyes like molten lava.

'You tried that, remember?' I say, as I meet his angry stare. His eyes are wild, like my dad's were after a massive prayer meeting when he was all full of the holy spirit and puffed up on his own righteousness. The two of them are cut from the same cloth. Both bastards.

'Give the old man something,' Gene says and he points at Tina like she's their skivvy, 'and make me and Michael some food too. What do you want, Michael?' Gene cleverly asks his brother to choose, taking the sting out of being the one ordering Tina about.

'Burgers... and chips. Proper chips, not the bloody thin ones, not fries. I want fat chips. Crispy. No fucking lettuce or tomato, just ketchup. And jelly and ice cream.'

'Good choice, bro,' Gene tells him and then looks directly at me. 'She gets nothing – understand?'

'That's okay, I'm on a diet,' I tell him with a smile. I don't care about food for me; I don't need to eat, even if it might be my last meal. Not eating will keep me sharp, and I'm going to need to be fast and furious if I'm going to stay alive.

'Take the old bastard into the kitchen, feed him there and then lock him up,' Gene tells Tina.

'Don't worry, Rev,' I call over to him and he turns his head to me, but his eyes are dead. I don't think he has any hope.

'Look after him,' I call after Tina as she guides him out, but she doesn't look back. I can only trust to her seeming affection for him, and her sense of self-preservation.

The two brothers whisper to each other and I look out through the glass and see the lighting jag again and... I see something else, in the trees. I remember the lights that seemed to be following me yesterday evening. I thought I was imagining them back then, but now I know I wasn't. Behind me I hear Michael hiss something to his brother, and then he goes out, slamming the door behind him like a toddler having a tantrum.

'And then there were two,' Gene says and pulls the old man's chair over towards me. I look at the chair. I'm struck again by how it's perfectly moulded to the old man's body, I don't suppose anybody but him has ever sat in the chair.

It fits him like a glove, until Gene drops into it, his own frame obliterating the Rev's impression in the fabric – like a bomb going off and erasing all evidence he was ever there. Gene leans forward in the chair and his eyes slowly scan me up and down, like he's sizing me up for a casket. He frowns and pulls a knife from his pocket. It's sheathed, but he pulls it clear from the leather pouch and it makes a *schwing* sound as it seems to cut the air. Outside, a jag of lightning illuminates his face and catches the blade. Both light up, one sharp and the other dull. Gene Vincent looks old and tired. I remember the scars on his legs and the catheter bag. Cancer.

'Don't move,' he says and the knife slashes at me, cutting through the cable ties and releasing my hands, which fall like dead weights. I can't feel them at all for a second and then massive pain shoots through them as the blood forces through once more, making them burn, like lava running through my veins. I can't help but wince and my eyes tear up, but I won't give him the satisfaction of moaning with the pain. He sits back in the chair. He looks tired.

'Flex the fingers,' he tells me. I try but it hurts. My hands don't feel like they are a part of my body anymore.

'I've been reading this.' He holds up Drew's letter. 'It's very interesting.' He leans forward again. He hasn't shaved since I last saw him and the stubble is grey and powdery. 'So all those years ago, when we came to your house that night, you didn't know a thing about it, the robbery?'

'No. Nothing.'

'Huh.' He drops his eyes from mine for a moment, almost like he's praying. 'So all that was a waste of time,' he says, though he speaks more to himself than me. 'We were trying to force you to tell us what you didn't know.' He laughs, but without a trace of humour. It's a hollow and joyless sound. His eyes swing back to mine; he looks like a lost kid. 'But you ran, you disappeared and you didn't go to the police. Why the hell would you do that if you hadn't been a part of it? That's what I don't understand – why did you run?'

'I ran because…' And I open my mouth to lie to him, but I find that I can't. Not anymore. I want to tell the truth and not run away, not ever again. 'Back in Brighton you asked if my dad used to hit me. He did.'

Gene doesn't say a word, he looks at me, cool and calm.

'He hit my mum too. He was a devout man, a man of God and we were sinners… so he hit us. A lot. After my mum died he… it got worse. Outside, he was well respected, a great man of the community but at home—'

'He was a bastard.' Gene finishes my sentence with a look of contempt on his face. I don't know if it's for my dad or for me, for letting the abuse affect me.

'It got worse as I got older.'

'Did he fuck you?'

'No… no, he wasn't like that. He thought I was unclean somehow. Being a woman made me a whore in his eyes.'

'You ran away from him?'

'No, I killed him.'

Gene opens his mouth to say something but nothing comes out. Instead, he looks puzzled.

'I made a plan to get away. I tricked a guy into coming to the house and I made my dad think we'd just had sex.'

'What happened, did he have a heart attack?' Gene smiles, thinking he's really clever.

'The doctors thought he had an embolism and dropped dead but that isn't what happened. When my dad exploded in anger, the boy didn't know what to do, he hadn't seen a grown-up so angry before. And when my dad tried to grab me and beat me, he held my dad off me, stood in his way.'

'This boy—'

'It was Drew, yes. He tried to calm my dad down but he was raving, threatening to kill me, and he tried to do it. My dad wanted to kill me, so Drew held him, grabbed his arms so he couldn't hurt me. Drew kept telling him to calm down but the old man got crazier and crazier – screaming that I was a whore and a jezebel. He said I was like my mum. He said my mum was a whore… but my mum was an absolute saint to stay with an abusive man like that, and I wouldn't hear him say a bad word about her.'

'So what did you do?'

'I got Drew to push him down onto the floor and hold him there, while I ran and got a pillow. I sat on his chest and I pushed the pillow into his face – I pushed with all my might and I felt him struggle underneath me. Drew wanted to let him go – *he's learned his lesson*, Drew kept saying – but I knew that wasn't true. The second we let him go he would start screaming at me again. And the moment Drew left, he would beat me close to death. It was who he was, his nature. His heart was full of hate.'

'Yeah… I know anger like that…' Gene says, but I don't know if he's talking to me or is lost in thought.

'I screamed at Drew to keep holding him down, and I pressed all my weight onto his face and that pillow. I could feel it moulding to the contours of his face. Trapping the nostrils and mouth. I could feel his lungs beneath me, struggling to fill with air. His heart was racing. I pushed myself down and down and down. This time I wasn't escaping him, not folding myself into nothing and allowing him to beat me. This time I was hurting him.'

'You wanted to kill him?'

'With all my heart.'

'And you did?'

'I felt it... a flutter, like a bird in his chest. His last breath leaving him, his soul uncoupling from his body and flying away. And even after that I kept pushing and pushing until Drew finally pulled me off him. Then I wrapped myself around Drew and I cried and cried... and he did too.'

'You made him complicit in a murder.'

'I didn't think—'

'You trapped the poor boy, tied him to you. I was right all the time; there was something bad in Drew Anthony, but it was you that put the *bad* in him.'

'I didn't—'

'No wonder he was ripe for us when we came to him.'

I feel a sob in my chest... he's right. It wasn't Gene and Michael that made Drew a criminal, it was me. I stole his innocence that day and I brought his silence with my dad's insurance money. I bought Drew anything he wanted, and as long as the money held out I could keep him, but when we'd spent it... I lost him, because he was never really mine.

'So you're a proper murderer, like in cold blood and everything.' He whistles through his teeth, like he's impressed. 'And that's why you ran.'

'I wanted to be someone new and—'

'Liar, you didn't want to be someone new – you wanted to be punished. You didn't start again, you put yourself in a kind of prison, your own little purgatory to pay for what you did.'

I want to say no, no... you're wrong... but I can't. I think he's probably right. These fifteen years of being alone and scared, I wasn't hiding from Gene and Michael but from myself. My guilt at what I did to Drew and my dad. I'm a killer. I shouldn't be allowed in society and I've proved that by letting Theo die and then betraying—

'Ayo,' I groan, and I feel the tears run down my face. I am such a user.

'Who?' Gene asks and I hate him for that, not even knowing the name of the woman they killed.

'My friend, the one on the tube that—'

'Yes,' he bows his head. 'I'm... I'm sorry. Michael is—'

'Psychotic,' I spit. Gene looks genuinely pained.

'He hasn't had a good life and... he's my brother.' It sounds like a prison sentence when he says it. 'He's a lot younger than me, nearly twenty years, and my mum...' He pauses. I can see the memories flood him. 'My mum drank, a lot. She shouldn't have had another child really, and if she'd been able to get an abortion she would have done, but she didn't know she was pregnant for a long time. When he was born he was damaged. Foetal alcohol disorder, that and neglect, I guess. I was in prison – fucking story of my life, eh? He was put into care and... shit...' Tears flow down his cheek. He looks embarrassed and wipes them away with the dirty sleeve of his suit jacket. 'I got him out.'

'You adopted him?'

'Christ, they wouldn't let a man like me adopt anyone. No, I just took him from the foster home. Nothing legal, but Mum made me promise I'd look after him.'

'You raised him?'

'Yeah. Not very well, but yeah.'

'But you can't control him.'

He looks at me with hate, but that crumbles and slides away like the banks of a river washed away by a flood.

'I don't know what to do with him, with the anger,' he says, sounding lost. Then he turns away and walks to the giant glass wall and looks out into the oncoming night. I must have been unconscious for longer than I thought.

Nothing's said for a while. I watch the back of his head. A couple of lightning bolts light the scene, but all I can see is his reflection in the glass. A ghost in the machine. He's like me; his spirit has left his body and it floats in the air outside the window, not feeling the cold or the pain of the flesh. Then suddenly he laughs, loud and hard. The sound is hollow and full of pain.

'I blamed you,' he says. 'I hated you... really hated you. I would dream about finding you and killing you. I was going to hurt you... make you pay for how you ruined my life.'

I don't reply; I can hardly breathe. All the air has been forced out of the room by the strength of his words. I can feel it burning the oxygen from the air... and then it just falls away as he drops his head and looks old again, like Methuselah, forced to walk the earth for a thousand years. I watch him as fifteen years of hate and loss and wretchedness spirals through him.

'Cancer,' he says. 'Fucking cancer. Took her five years ago, my lovely Maggie – she was my everything, you know. Bloody saint to put up with me, and all my shit... and her reward? Cancer. Cancer that spread through her, slow like water torture getting through the cracks with that *drip, drip, drip*... When she died she'd been in pain for years and years, so it actually felt almost like a blessing. A blessing? To lose the woman I loved, Jesus Christ.'

'I'm sorry,' I say, but I don't think he can hear me. He's locked inside something, outside of time. I see his hand squeeze the air, and I think he's squeezing her hand. Maybe in his mind they're young lovers on a first date, or partners for years and saying goodbye – or maybe it's all of those moments. Maybe he's seeing every time he and Maggie ever held hands, all rolled into one memory running through his head.

'I was inside, in prison again, when she got the diagnosis. She had to deal with all of that alone, because I wasn't there... because I'd been forced to do another robbery because Drew took our big haul.'

I can't say anything; I just watch as pain cuts him in half. Some of it is mental – emotional pain – but most of it is real, and in his body, twisting the knife in him. He really is near the end.

'I have spent half my life in prison – maybe even more than half. I was never home for the important stuff.' He pauses.

I can barely hear him now, he's speaking so low. It isn't to me but someone else. Maybe he's talking to his wife. Or maybe it's to God, I don't know.

'We had a baby, a boy...' Gene continues. 'He was born when I was on a seven-stretch, thirty years ago maybe... might even be more, I can't tell nowadays – time isn't what it was – but he was wonderful. He was what we'd dreamed of, something that could heal us, make life work properly at last. Maggie had prayed for him, lit so many candles, we could have bought our own church with all that money. Beautiful little thing he was, and always smiling and laughing. She sent me photos, loads of photos, but he couldn't come and see me in there, not in that flea-pit jail. He wasn't strong, the boy, he had a hole in his heart.' He stops talking; maybe he's listening to the beat of his own heart. 'We named him Robert... he was dead at ten months and I hadn't even seen him. Not once. They let me out for the funeral, but even then...' Pain lacerates his face and he has to make a superhuman effort not to just fall in a heap. 'I was handcuffed to a bloody guard the only time I saw him... I couldn't even sit alone with his little body. My boy.' He stops talking. I see his shoulders shake a little. I look past him and out into the cold night. Rain hammers down and lightning cuts through the sky, but Gene isn't affected by the maelstrom only inches away; he's back in that moment with his son.

'It was supposed to be the last job for me. I promised her, one last job – the big one – and then we were done. It was gonna be enough money to take Maggie to Spain. We were gonna get a little bar and live there. No more thieving, no more crime. Michael was giving me his share, it was all gonna be mine. My nest egg. The retirement plan.' He turns around, the tears have dried, but I can see the tracks of them down his face. 'But it all turned to shit when your husband screwed us over.'

'He screwed you over? Just like you planned to do to him?' I ask and see his righteous anger falter. A frown creases his brow and his lips purse.

'You planned to have it all, didn't you? You said Michael was handing you his share as a gift, but Drew wasn't, was he? He barely knew you and wasn't bonded by blood. He was doing this for the money, so you planned to ditch him and take it all. You might even have sold him out to the police and scarpered to the Costa del Crime. That's right, isn't it?'

He doesn't answer, but I see from his eyes that I'm right.

'There's no honour among thieves, Gene, it's more Old Testament than that – an eye for an eye – and it looks like Drew did to you what you would have done to him.'

Gene opens his mouth to say something and then stops. Slowly his face changes, as if a truth is dawning on him for the first time, as if he sees the light for the first time in his life.

'Maybe you're right. Maybe I'm just mad because he beat me to the punch but none of that matters now... He took the money and when we caught up with him—'

'You tortured him to death.' I glare at him.

He drops his eyes away from mine, and I see the shame burn in there for a moment.

'I... am not a good man.' He says it like a confession; maybe it's the first time he's ever really thought about how he's moulded his own life. I don't know – I'm no priest – I don't hear confession and I sure as hell don't give benediction.

There's a moment of silence. I think I see pure hate in him for a second, and then he laughs, he barks with laughter, a real belly laugh. 'And we thought you were running with the money.' He wipes a tear from his eye. 'I have hated you for fifteen years.' The laugh dies in his voice. 'I blamed you for... for her. If we had the money maybe it would have been different. I blamed you.' He sags and walks over to Reverend Hanley's chair and drops into it. There's silence for a while and then he speaks again.

'I piss in a bag,' he says. 'For two years now, pissing in a bag. The cancer came to me after I buried her. I think it's the grief, it gets in the bones. It's all over me now, in me and through me. I don't have long. Eighteen months, they said, but I think that's generous.'

'I'm sorry,' I say and I actually sound like I mean it.

'I just want some comfort, at the end. I want clean sheets and care. I'll pay them all the money, just to die like a king. That's all I want, to go out in style. Is that too much to ask?'

I don't reply, I don't know what to say. He holds up the letter from Drew.

'You know where it is, don't you? You know where he hid the money.' Lightning jags close by as a clap of thunder fills the room. We are almost in the eye of the storm.

'Yes,' I tell him and Gene Vincent closes his eyes. A smile plays across his lips and I imagine he's planning how to make his last months on earth special. He's imagining just how a king might die. 'I only got the letter today,' I tell him. 'Reverend Hanley hadn't sent it as he promised Drew he would, so I only found out the truth today.'

'Where is it?'

'With the letter was a map.'

'Where?' His eyes spring open and they flash, reflecting the lightning that strikes close by. We are in the eye of the storm and suddenly all sound drops away. The rain is gone and the wind – there is nothing but the sound of my own blood pulsing through my body and the rasping breath of a dying man, clinging to the hope of being rich in his final days.

'I destroyed the map, after committing it to memory.'

'No.'

'The money isn't far. I'll take you to it in the morning, but only if you swear that nothing bad will happen to Reverend Hanley and Tina Bray.'

He's silent, watching me for a minute.

'Of course,' he says finally, and I want to believe him... but I don't.

'We'll go in the morning. It will be about a thirty-minute walk,' I say. 'You'll need shovels to dig, and a map and compass. You will leave the Rev and Tina here, they can be locked up. When you have the money you can tie me up and drive off with it. That will give you time to disappear. I won't call the police. I'm not going back – there's nothing to go back to, anyway. You killed Rebecca when you killed Drew and you killed Sarah when you murdered Theo and…' I pause for a split second. '…when you killed Ayo.'

He nods slowly. 'Okay, I agree. We won't hurt the Rev or Tina, as long as you lead us to the money.'

'And when you're free and safe, you'll send the police the film that proves I didn't kill Theo.'

'You have my word,' he says as he stands. 'Now, I'm going to tie you up again, and you can get some sleep on the sofa.' He ties my hands and feet, but not as tight as Michael did, then he goes to leave. But before he does there is a flutter of something, and a strip of paper lands on my chest. I pick it up, with some difficulty. It's the photostrip of my mum and me, the one I lost when I ran through the tube station with Ayo. Gene must have found it and… I look at the pictures. I see two fearless women, daring to go and have fun even when my bastard dad had forbidden it.

Fearless… I must remember that tomorrow.

Chapter Twenty-Two

Saturday

Morning is breaking. Tendrils of heavy fog inch across the ground to worm into the trees, like the world is on fire. Somewhere the sun kisses the horizon, but the grey fingers wrestle it, smothering it in a blanket, so it feels more like twilight than morning.

I haven't slept a wink. Instead I've watched the night, and then as it slowly morphed into a milky-grey morning, I tried to gauge just where I think he is. Leonard is out there. I'm pretty sure that's what I saw, illuminated by the jag of lightning last night; a shape, a hulk, something like a man. But it was only for a fraction of a second. I'm gambling everything on this one last throw of the dice: that Leonard followed me here; that it was his headlights I saw in the darkness on my drive. This is my last and only hope. If I'm wrong, then I'm going to die this morning. And even if he is out there I still might die, but at least that will only be me, I can save the Rev and Tina.

I've been thinking all night, weighing up my worth in this life and I find myself wanting. I'm worse than the two men who hold me captive – not that they aren't the dregs of humanity, they are – but it was me that corrupted my Drew. I sowed the seeds of his death. I let Theo die, even though I'd told him I loved him, and Ayo... I sacrificed her. Christ, *sacrifice*, what a fucking lie of a word. That's what politicians and generals say when men are led into slaughter, or when armies pack up and leave, allowing those who gave them succour to die. I betrayed Ayo. I let Michael kill her so that I could escape. The last thing she heard me say was that she didn't even know my real name. Michael may have stabbed her in his anger at me, but I killed her, and it was in cold blood. I am a monster. All I know is how to run and how to be alone. That must end.

'I need the toilet,' I call out, and after a few seconds of swearing, Gene appears with a knife and cuts the bindings off my legs and hands. I don't thank him. I have to massage my feet and ankles, rubbing life back into my calves and up to my thighs before I can move. I go to the toilet, wash my hands, splash water on my face and clean my teeth with toothpaste on my finger. If I do survive today, then the first thing I have to do is buy a toothbrush and scrub my mouth really well.

'Are you done yet?' Gene shouts through the door.

I don't reply, I just open the door and step out. Gene goes to tie my wrists again.

'No,' I snarl like a she-wolf protecting her pack. 'There's nowhere to run. I just want to watch the sun rise.'

He looks at me, first with a look of distrust and then that shifts. He nods. I think we both know a final request when we hear one. Neither of us thinks I will be alive to see another sunrise. I walk over to the wall of glass and look out. I can't see anything. In the distance the woods stretch away and into the mist, was I mistaken? Am I crazy?

From the kitchen I can smell bacon frying and I guess that Tina has been brought up from the cellar to cook. I tùrn towards the glass and try and angle my body so that anybody walking into the room could only see my back. And then I start to sign as I mouth the words.

I know you are out there, Leonard. I will lead the two killers away from the house. Wait ten minutes and rescue the Reverend. He is locked in cellar. Take him and get police. I will keep killers busy as long as I can.

I repeat it three times, slowly. I don't know if I am making any sense; I have not signed in a long time, and it was never very good when I did. I pray he understands. I don't mention Tina Bray, I honestly have no idea what he will do when he sees her again. I don't—

'What are you doing?' Michael demands, his voice sharp like broken glass.

'There are kites and eagles out there, the birds of prey are—'

'Shut up.' He grabs my shoulder and spins me around. Then he ties my wrists tight so that no blood can get past the rope. I wince, but he doesn't care, and I don't complain. If I did say anything, I think he'd do it even tighter. I think he wants an excuse to hurt me. I think he'd like that. When I look in his eyes I see no chance that I can make it through the day; he'll kill me out of spite. All I can hope is that it'll be quick.

'We're going soon,' he says. I see the grease on his lips and can smell the smokiness of the meat on his breath, and…

'Coffee,' I say.

'You won't get a fucking drop of anything. We're in charge.'

'A cup of coffee,' I say as Gene enters.

'Give her the coffee,' he says to his brother.

'Gene,' Michael squeals like a little kid told he can't have a chocolate bar.

'Give her the coffee, it'll keep her going. Just for a little while longer,' he says and all three of us know what that means. With a grumble Michael goes to the kitchen. Gene walks over to me and looks at my hands. He pulls a knife from his pocket and cuts the cord.

'Thanks,' I tell him. His face is blank.

Michael comes back a few minutes later with a coffee. No milk or sugar but I think he must have spat in it, as there is a film of froth in the centre. But I don't care, I still drink it and it tastes amazing, toasty and bitter like strong, dark chocolate. The warmth of it in my hands feels good, bringing life back to my fingers, and as I drink it down, it seems to cleanse me, like the blood of Christ. I'm ready for this.

Gene takes a long rope, loops it around my waist and ties it, like I'm a dog on a lead. 'So you can't make a break for it,' he whispers in my ear.

'I don't intend to. I'll stick to my side of the bargain as long as you'll stick to yours.'

'I won't touch a hair on their heads,' Gene says. I can hear the escape clause in his words. He won't hurt them but Michael might – I know that. I guess their plan is to dig up the money, then kill me and bury me. Then they'll come back and kill the Rev and Tina. She'll beg for her life, she'll squirm and plead, but they won't want to let anyone live that could turn on them. We will all be silenced and then they'll drive away. Gene will pay some Harley Street specialist to tell him how long he has left and… but I don't care what happens then.

All I can do is lead them out into the woods and we'll dig for the money. Oh, and just to be clear about this

– I lied to Gene. There was no map in with the letter that Drew left me, but I've worked it out. I know exactly where the money is. I know what happened back then.

'Come on,' Gene barks and I head out of the house.

I shiver as the cold hits me. Behind me, Michael hisses *fuck this* as his coat is not nearly thick enough for this biting wind. I wait in the cold while he runs inside and takes a coat and scarf off the back of the door. He wraps them around himself and comes back out. I have to stop myself from laughing, as the scarf is a ridiculous pink pastel colour, with angels embroidered on it.

'Go on,' he orders, and I start to walk out, heading for the woods.

'Make a move to run, or fuck with us in any way, and you will be begging for us to kill you quickly,' Michael says, and I have no doubt that's true. We walk. Behind me the two brothers follow, carrying shovels. As I move, my eyes dart from side to side, looking out for Leonard or any indication he's here, but there's nothing. I'm walking to my death and I am very much afraid that it will be meaningless – all of this is to save the Rev and Tina. If Leonard can't do what I asked… I feel tears run down my cheek, as I walk into the woods.

–

'You dig,' Gene tells me and throws the spade down at my feet. Great, I'm actually going to be digging my own bloody grave too. The sun has burned away some of the fog. I can't be sure, but I think it's been about forty minutes since we left the house. I'm going to stretch this out for as long as I can and then tell them the truth and… well, it will be what it will be. There's no escape from here. I pick up the spade and—

'Christ.' I slam the metal face into the ground, but I can't pierce it. All that happens is that it shudders out of my hands and springs up like a jack-in-the-box and the handle hits me in the shoulder. The brothers laugh so hard I think they might wet themselves.

'Sit down, you're fucking useless,' Michael says, still laughing as he starts to dig. I guess making him dig an enormous hole before I tell him there is no money down there, will just about drive him crazy. I should probably tell him now, but I want to give Leonard enough time to rescue the others. I could—

'There's no need to keep digging.' A voice comes from out of the mist and then a body steps through it.

'Rev,' I yell, my eyes staring past him, hoping that police officers will breach the fog too, or at least Leonard and Hannah with shotguns... but all I can see is Reverend Hanley, leaning heavily on his walking stick, coming into view. 'Rev... no... go back!' I shout as I start to fear the very worst.

'How the hell did you get out?' Gene spits. I can see that he's looking into the mist too, searching the woods for the police that won't come.

'It doesn't matter how – you just need to know that Tina has gone for the police. It will not take her very long; we are not as backward a community as you think we are. You have very little time if you're going to escape incarceration.'

'Gene, we gotta—'

'No!' the older brother screams. He is shaking so hard I think he'll collapse. 'We came for the money. It's ours. It's ours, Michael.'

'There is no money, this isn't Treasure Island... look around you, man.' The Reverend raises his voice like he's addressing the church with a sermon. He stands upright and looks more alive than I have seen him all this time. 'Rebecca guessed, I'm sure.'

'Rev,' I call out. I want him to stop speaking but he waves me away.

'No, Rebecca, this is my time now. Confession is good for the soul. I am speaking my truth unto God, and you and these men can listen.' He looks directly at me and leans on his cane for support. 'Andrew came to me fifteen years ago and I let him down.'

'Did he have the fucking money?' Michael goes to grab the Reverend, but Gene stops him.

'Michael, let him talk, damn it,' Gene yells. Michael shrieks like a crazy person and squats down on his haunches, shaking and rocking. As I look into his face I can see that these last years have worn away at him too, just like his older brother. When I first saw him he looked like a boy. He was probably twenty-five but with a baby's face and a shock of thick hair. Today, the face is leaner and the skin has weathered badly. His hair has thinned and his boyish looks have turned feral. He looks wild and demented. The brothers both look as if they've been in a padded cell for a long time. In age they are only about forty and sixty, but they look ancient – both eaten up by their greed and hate.

The Rev pauses for a second and then carries on. 'Andrew arrived in the night without warning. I was alone. He had the money and was scared and upset. He told me that he had only wanted his cut of the money, but when Tina told him that he was to get nothing, and be turned in to the police, he took it all. I said he should give it back to the bank, but he still thought he would go to jail and that the two men who had actually robbed the bank would have him killed in prison.'

'And we would have,' Gene says with a snarl.

'His biggest concern was for you, Rebecca. He said he was sorry that he'd left you in danger. He couldn't decide about the money, but he knew he had to return to warn you, get you to safety somehow. I think his plan was to bring you back here.'

'Was he meeting anyone on the way?' I ask.

'Yes, there was someone who was helping him; he was collecting her en route.'

'That was Tina,' I tell him.

'What?' The Rev looks confused. He had no idea she was involved.

'She was in it from the start. She was Michael's girl-friend, and they used her to hook Drew, to seduce him into the gang. But she was the one who was the greediest; she wanted Drew and her to take all the money. She probably would have dumped him later too – but when he went missing and came here to see you, she panicked and told Gene and Michael that Drew had betrayed them. She told them about Hannah and Leonard's farm; she said that was where they could find him, and they did, and they killed him.'

'But I didn't know Tina then,' the Rev says.

'No, you met her later, after she got into deeper trouble, and I'm guessing that she met your son in London. That was a crazy coincidence. Karma, maybe or—'

'I don't fucking care about any of this crap,' Gene screams. 'Where's the money?'

'He left it with me,' the Rev says. 'I hid it in my fireplace after he'd gone and I waited for Drew to return.

He left me a letter to send to Rebecca… He said he would be back in less than a week. I waited a week but he didn't come.'

'But someone else did,' I say and the poor Rev drops his head and begins to cry.

'Who the fuck came?' Gene demands.

'His son,' I reply. 'The Rev's son was released from prison that week. He was an addict and small-time hustler with dreams of being a DJ and owning his own club.'

'No.' I hear the whine in Gene's voice. He's desperate to be wrong but deep down he already knows what I'm going to say.

'He came home, didn't he Rev. He either found the money or you asked his advice.'

'He was my son and he swore he'd changed. I'd moved here to make a safe space for him. But Drew's visit had shaken me and I asked for Christopher's help and…'

'That was how he afforded the club. It wasn't a huge success, he didn't have hit records, it was the money from the robbery.'

'He took our money?' Gene asks as if he's in a daze.

'He threw wild parties, gave drugs away to whoever wanted them and paid for studios to record an album – but he had nothing to record. He was not a talent – he just had the money. Three years… that was what it bought him, then it was all gone,' the Rev tells them. I can see the shame in his face as he talks about his own flesh and blood.

'Gone… all of it?' Gene sounds sick and his skin looks green as he sits on the ground.

'He was broke again and he came back, but it was just for more money. He was convinced that I had held onto some of it.'

'Had you?' Gene asks.

'No, no. I wanted nothing to do with it. It had ruined Andrew's life and it had exploded my son's. Maybe he wouldn't have settled down here, maybe it would have been too dull for him, but he had no chance when all that money fell in his lap. It was evil money. It corrupted and killed.'

'What happened when Christopher came home?' I ask, feeling a little light-headed.

'He came with a girl in tow.'

'Tina Bray,' I say.

'Though she said she was Tina Dearden. She didn't know about the money, only that they were coming to rob an old man. When she found out I was his father and a man of the church she baulked and tried to stop him. That was when he cut her.' The memory shocks him even now. 'I would never have thought him capable of that. Not my boy. As a child he had been so caring; when his mother was ill he would pick flowers for her. How did that boy turn into a man that would carve his girlfriend's face and... and... he tried to stab me. She stopped him, she saved my life and he ran off and... he hanged himself. He hanged himself.'

And the Rev begins to sob. He cries for his lost son. He weeps for Andrew and for Tina and for all of us. The wind starts to build again and there is a spit of rain in the air, as the four of us stand in the woods and listen to the beating of our own hearts and mourn all that we have lost. Nothing is said for the longest time as the realisation that all of this has been for nothing sinks in. And then.

'Aaaargghhh,' Michael screams and leaps at the Rev. A blade flashes and blood spurts and... oh my god, he just stabs and stabs and stabs, like he's crazy. A hundred times the blade flashes as Michael laughs like a maniac. He stabs and stabs and… I close my eyes and curl into a ball. He will kill me next. I want to pray but I don't know the words. I want to fold and fold… but I can't. I mustn't.

'Stop it… stop it… calm down, Christ, kiddo, calm down.' Gene wraps his arms around his brother and squeezes him tight. Between them the body of the Rev lies, his blood soaking the grass and the two men's clothing. 'Come on, come on, kiddo,' he whispers into his brother's ear. 'The police will be coming.'

'I don't want to go back, Geney, not back inside.'

'We won't, Mikey, but we have to run.'

'We need to kill her.' Michael looks at me with total hatred, his face splashed with blood so he looks like the Devil. I have never been so scared.

'H-h-hostage,' I stammer.

'Yeah, yeah Mikey, we need her as a hostage.'

The rain starts to fall. Michael is dripping with blood; the rain makes him look like a melting candle. Gene grabs my arm and pushes and pulls me and I let myself get blown like a leaf on the wind. I am still in my body but it's an effort to hold on. I feel like only my fingertips are anchoring me in the world; a gust of wind could whip me out of my body and tear me into tiny pieces, and then I will never be able to get back to myself. I would be gone… I am on the cusp of losing myself forever.

'Come on,' Gene yells and tugs at me harder as we get within view of the house. Their car is still there. I had hoped that Leonard might have thought to let the tyres down or disabled the engine but no. Gene pulls me to the car and throws me into the passenger seat.

'I always get shotgun,' Michael whines like a kid.

'The police will need to see her, then they won't dare shoot at the car,' Gene tells his brother. Muttering angrily, Michael climbs into the back and Gene floors the pedal and we shoot off. I'm scared that we'll catch up with Leonard. He's in an older vehicle and he doesn't drive fast. If we catch them then Gene will kill them both and then kill me. I lean forward to rip out the keys or something and Gene slams his hand into my jaw. Just like my dad that first time he hit me. Bastard. My head snaps back and hits the side window.

Ninety-nine bottles of beer on the wall…

My jaw is killing me. I could fold and be lost, but I won't. I will see these two men burn… and I have another reason to live now. Tina's son. I saw the pictures of the boy as a child and I have seen Drew at pretty much the same age, and I know that he's the boy's father. It hurts me a little, that Tina could have a son with him when I couldn't, but it's too late to feel jealous or angry; but I want to meet Drew Anthony's son.

Gene drives like the Devil is on our trail. The car slides from side to side and the tyres screech on the poor road surface. He does not let up… does not slow down as we eat up the countryside. Up ahead I can see the mainland, and once again there is that beautiful bridge that arcs and curves over the water. It is still amazing, like an umbilical cord of steel, connecting Britain to its baby Skye. Light suddenly pierces the cloud and there is a rainbow. It looks like it meets the bridge, like we could drive all the way to heaven from here. Then the rainbow fades and there is merely the bridge. It curves over the water, like a woman arching her back. Then my eyes follow forward and I see something flicker in the distance. A light, but not like a rainbow. This is not a natural occurrence but man-made.

'Gene,' Michael says from the shadows of the back seat, his voice scared and small.

'I see 'em, Mikey,' he replies, and then whispers, so that only I can hear him, 'I'm sorry, Mum, I tried to keep him safe.'

'I don't want to go back inside,' Michael whimpers from the back seat.

I look ahead and now I can see them too, flickers of red and blue light and soon I will hear the mournful wail of their sirens. The cavalry is coming.

'What did I tell you, Mikey?' Gene asks in a soft, singsong voice.

'That I wouldn't have to go back there.'

'I promised, didn't I?'

'Yes.'

'I swore it.'

'Thanks, Gene, you always look after me.'

I see the tears well in the corner of Gene's eye and then he guns the car at the bridge, faster and faster. We hit the bridge at warp speed. I see the curve up ahead. *Oh god…* I start to fold myself, I can save myself the pain of—

Gene leans across me, the weight of him on my body, and I feel the press of his catheter into me. I feel the swoosh of the liquid. He's so scared he's wet himself. I feel him unclip my seatbelt and then unlock the passenger door.

'She isn't dead, your friend, the waitress,' he whispers into my ear. I think he might even smile.

'Why are you—?'

'I need something for Saint Peter to chew on. Even devils can do good deeds,' he says and then pushes me savagely and I am falling sideways and—

323

'Aargh,' I scream, as I hit the hard tarmac of the road and tiny stones tear at me and I skid and roll and crash. I feel like I'm burning, but I'm alive. I stop rolling and try and sit up. I can see the police car in the distance, and finally hear the faintest trace of the siren in the air and then Gene and Michael's car gets to the arc towards the mainland.

'*No.*' I scream as the car barrels straight on, not bothering to follow the road, and breaks through the barrier. I am up and staggering forward, I forget the pain and the blood that's running down my arm. There is no sound, the car is in the air, all I can hear is the rushing of blood in my ears, and then it hits the water and a flume explodes. For a moment the car bobs and then it sinks, fast and furious. In a few seconds there is only a churning of the water and then even that evaporates, and there is just a series of ripples that flow outwards from the eye of the storm. Otherwise there is nothing else.

I run to the bridge and get to it at the same time as the police car gets to the other side. They stop there to create a barrier. I am stuck in the middle, watching the ripples. Someone is calling to me but I keep walking until I get to the broken barrier. The metal is twisted. It looks like modern art. I look down into the water, as the rain starts to fall again. There is nothing to see down there. Nothing floats to the surface. They're dead. The brothers are gone. But Gene said Ayo was alive. Was he being cruel or... or...

I see more police cars and an ambulance in the distance. I look down and see the blood still dripping from my fingers. And now I feel the pain, but it feels good. It proves I'm alive. I'm alive.

Chapter Twenty-Three

Five Days Later

I feel like the Mummy. I'm wrapped in a lot of gauze and bandages – really, a lot. I was in hospital in Aberdeen for four days while they checked me over. Three broken ribs, glass and stones embedded in my hip and right side, chipped vertebrae that could cause me lots of problems in later life – but the fact that I am actually going to get a later life did take the sting out of the news. I had a mild concussion, but that was on the top of a pretty big one, so they kept me in and did lots of tests and brain scans.

The worst thing is that two teeth were broken, and need to be removed, but as soon as the dentist saw the state of my teeth she went nuts. I have not flossed in fifteen years and there were months when I hardly cleaned them. I think I will spend a lot of time with sadistic dental hygienists in the future.

I had visitors – I know, me getting actual visitors. Hannah and Leonard came, and they'd left Tina and her son downstairs. They're all living at the farm now, and the pain that I'd seen in Hannah's face has gone. Leonard was lighter too; he walked taller. I was happy for him. They brought me home-made jam and some bread. I couldn't eat it because of my teeth but I cooed at it and said *thank you* and when they were gone I gave it to the nursing staff, who said it was the best toast and jam ever.

Hannah kissed me and Leonard shook my hand – rather formally, I thought, for someone who had lain naked on top of me. Then they left and Tina and her son came up. His name is Andrew and he looks so much like my Drew that at first I thought it could be him – you know, some sort of reincarnation, but he isn't. He was polite, told me a little about school and then Tina told him to go and find Hannah and his dad. *His dad*. Tina is pretending that the boy is Leonard's and... I don't care.

'You know the truth, but please—' she began to plead for my silence but I waved it away.

'I won't tell, Tina. For the boy's sake and for Hannah and Leonard. I won't tell.'

Tears ran from both her eyes. 'Thank you, oh thank you,' she said, but there's no need. I have no claim on the boy. It's actually a little painful to see him, as he's so much like Drew when I first fell in love with him. I'll have to be content to be the coolest 'aunty' to him, one that sends him great presents at Christmas and really lavish ones on his birthday – but rarely sees him in real life. I can cope with that, just about.

'He spoke of you,' Tina said as she was leaving. 'Drew, I mean. He loved you... he didn't want to hurt you.'

'I know,' I told her.

'And... and... back then I was wild, I didn't know that what I was doing was so wrong... it was all I'd ever known.'

'I know. You were so young, I don't blame you.'

'But I—'

'And you mustn't blame yourself. You were only sixteen,' I tell her. I don't tell her that when I was sixteen I murdered my own father. Shit happens, it's how you deal with it that matters. It's taken me twenty years to deal with what I did.

'Thank you,' she said one final time and then she left.

I heard her voice in my head for a long time after she'd gone… *He loved you… he didn't want to hurt you…* But actually I don't think it was true. He never really loved me, not with a passion. He felt sorry for me, and my father's death tied us together… but that is very different to love. I know that now. I think I know what love is now.

Finally the doctors said I could leave the hospital. Then I had to spend a day telling my story to the police, but they believe me now. They know the truth; they know all about the Vincent boys.

They pulled their bodies out of the water about six hours after the crash. I'd been ferried away by then, so I didn't see their water-logged corpses rise like Excalibur from the lake. I won't go to their funeral. There might not even be one for them; they had no one, after all. It sounds sad, put like that, but I don't feel sorry for them. The police also went to the Rev's house and found his body out in the woods. I will go to his funeral.

I have even received an apology from the police – they didn't treat me *with compassion* fifteen years ago, they said I was questioned as a *hostile witness* and they don't do that anymore. The officer who delivered this apology looked like he would have been a toddler fifteen years ago. I nodded and said thank you. I was informed that I might even receive compensation, but I don't care. I just want all the attention to stop so I can be alone to figure out who I am now. Am I Rebecca? Do I want to be Sarah again? Or Jane, or Fran, or someone else? Am I going to start again somewhere new, or do I stay and… I don't know.

But there is someone I need to see. No, that isn't quite right. There is someone I *want* to see. I want to see her very much.

–

I take the train. The guard is very helpful and he moves a couple of people around for me as, even though I have a seat booked, I need more space to accommodate my enormously bandaged arm and crutches. Someone has organised a hotel room for me for two nights in London, and then my flat should be ready to move back into. Gene and Michael had made quite a mess of it, but there's a budget somewhere for it to be re-decorated. I can't believe I get to stay in a hotel, for me that's total luxury. I am totally stealing all the toiletries. But when I arrive in London I don't head to the hotel. No.

–

I arrive on the ward at seven forty-five p.m. Visiting hours end at eight and I think she'll turn me away after what I did. I wouldn't blame her. So I arrive late, that way the nurses can ask me to leave and save her the embarrassment. I know she won't want to see me but... you know... I live in hope.

I stand in the doorway of her room. I read an article in the paper that said she lost so much blood they had to put her into an induced coma. She almost died, and certainly would have if there hadn't been a paramedic on the platform. He'd been running for the train and he missed it; that's what saved Ayo's life.

But two others died on the platform. One was described as a have-a-go hero, an ex-soldier; an older man who jumped at Michael and tried to take the knife off him. Michael stabbed him and ran. The paramedic might have been able to save his life but he was with Ayo. I'm so sorry for the man, but I am glad the paramedic picked Ayo to save – that's awful, isn't it? I am such a terrible person. The second person to die that night had a heart attack when he saw the blood on the ex-soldier. Both deaths are my fault.

Her back is to me. I think she might be asleep and I wonder if I should just turn around and walk away. She almost died because of—

'Are you coming in or not?' she asks. I can't see her face. I can't tell anything from her voice. It's low and clear, but emotion runs through it like electricity through a cable.

'I...' I start but I have no idea what to say. I shuffle inside. One step. Two steps. I walk up to the bed. I'm glad I can't see her face. I feel shame burn me like I'm a witch in Salem. I can't remember what I wanted to say or why I really came.

'Ayo...' I start, in little more than a whispered croak as my mouth won't work properly. 'I just... I wanted to... I– I'm sorry.' I wait for her to reply. I hope she'll turn to look at me, I want to see her lovely face, but there's nothing. Her back seems cold and stern.

'That was... I mean... you're probably tired, I should—'

'Why did you come? I mean, really, why?' she asks, still turned away from me.

'I... I hurt you. I saw it in your face on the tube platform. I can't forget it, and I thought he'd killed you and it was my fault and…' I dry up. She doesn't move. I don't deserve her forgiveness, I know that, I just hoped she might be a much better person than I am.

'I had to tell you I was sorry, that I'm ashamed of myself and… and…' I falter. There's a lot more I want to say, I've practised it for hours, but here in the hospital room it feels like too much to dump on someone. Especially someone I almost killed. I think I should just go and be alone. She's better off without me. Everyone is.

'You're right. You did hurt me,' she says. Then she shifts and moves onto her back. I feel the pain in her voice as she winces and I step forward. Her face is pale, her mouth is tight as she tries to get comfortable. I help her sit up and push another pillow behind her head.

'You told him I was nothing to you, that I didn't know you, that I didn't even know your real name.'

'I know, I said it to make him let you go.'

'Really? Was it just that?'

Our eyes lock for a second and then I drop mine away.

'No, it was true. I hadn't told you anything about me and… I don't know what to say. I don't know how to… I mean, I don't have friends and—'

'Why are you here?' I hear a brutality in her voice that makes me shrink inside.

'I just… I… Rebecca… I was born Rebecca. I wanted to tell you my real name.'

'So is that what you want me to call you?'

I open my mouth to answer but actually I have no idea. 'I'm not… I mean… I haven't been her for such a long time now.'

'So you're Sarah?'

'No, I don't think I'm Sarah anymore. I was Fran and then Jane…'

'Jane?' she asks, like she can't believe it.

'I know, it's hard to imagine.' She laughs, and I shrug half apologetically. 'I've had too many names this last week. I don't know who I am anymore.'

'Okay, so you're the girl with no name?' she says. 'Cool, I like that.' And she smiles, and my stomach rolls a little as I allow myself to think that she might forgive me. I really need a friend right now.

'I have some gossip,' I say. My stomach is full of butterflies. 'I thought you might want to know.'

'You know I like gossip. Is it about Lillian?'

'No.'

'One of the cooks?'

'No.'

'Is it someone from the restaurant?'

'Yes.'

She frowns and thinks hard for a moment, then she looks annoyed. 'I nearly died last week so just bloody tell m—'

'I'm pregnant.'

Her eyes widen but when she opens her mouth nothing comes out.

'They did tests in the hospital, you know because of the beatings and the crash and everything. A blood test came back that... I mean it's only ten days. The thing's only like a speck inside me. It might not even survive but—'

'You want it?'

I feel a kick inside. 'More than anything I ever wanted before.'

'It's Theo's?'

'Only guy I've had sex with in fifteen years.'

'Oh my god. And then he was...'

'Yes.'

'Oh my god.' She pauses, looking horrified. 'That is the best gossip ever.'

'I know.' I laugh.

'Sit down,' she says and she pushes a pile of clothes and books and junk off the bed. It clatters on the floor. 'You have to tell me everything.'

'Everything?'

'Everything.'

And so I sit on the end of my friend's bed, and I start my story. I go back to the beginning.

A letter from P.D. Viner

Novels are just like buses, you wait ages for one, and then two turn up right after each other. This is my second (fabulous) book this year – after a few years were barren – and like with kids it's really frowned upon to show favouritism (I only have one actual human child, but I still tell her she's not my favourite sometimes, just to keep her on her toes). So, I have to say that I love *The Call* and *The Choice* equally... but *The Choice* is newer and fresher and... *oh god*, it's my favourite. Damn, you made me choose. I am soooooo happy with it and really enjoyed telling the story of Rebecca/Sarah/Fran/Jane – she got under my skin and I ran with her all that way, just hoping that she would find the answers she was looking for. I also particularly liked writing about the kids, Jordan and Agnes, and I'm dying to know how their story ends, so if you would like to know more about what happens to them, then let me know by contacting me though my website at www.pdviner.com.

You can also go there to sign up for a newsletter, see what I'm up to, and send a message. If you want, I'll talk to your book group, read at your wedding or send you Edan's tiramisu recipe. Just get in touch.

I assume, as you're reading this, that you have finished the book – I hope you liked it (actually I hope it was incredibly stressful and you had to hide behind the sofa at times), but that means *you* need to decide on your favourite book of mine too (it isn't just me who gets to play favourites).

So, you should read *The Call* (also from Hera in 2022) if you haven't already done so, and there are my previous books: *The Last Winter of Dani Lancing* and *Summer of Ghosts*. There are also two novellas, which are free to download: *The Sad Man* and *The Ugly Man*. FREE. That's crazy.

I would also urge you to try out the audiobooks of *The Call* and *The Last Winter of Dani Lancing* as I directed them as unabridged audio drama, with some great performances. Sorry – I know that's shameless self promotion, but that's what happens when you're a writer. You spend a year crafting something and then you get a couple of months of activity and excitement (and revenue making) and then you're back on the laptop nursing a bucket of coffee and dreaming of the next time. I'm already in the storyworld of my next book – and it's a doozy. Come and join me soon.

Thanks
P. D.

Acknowledgments

If I was a famous crime writer, then this page this would be full of product placement for all the stuff I want, like Moleskin notebooks (I use nothing else) Apple laptops (mine is knackered and I could really do with a new one) and Taylors of Harrogate Java Lava coffee beans (I have a little addiction problem), but unfortunately I'm not well known, so I'm not gonna get any of that stuff. Instead, I should just count my blessings, and forget about blagging freebies (but if some bags of coffee are past their sell by date... I'm always here).

I am a very lucky man. I live by the sea in a town I love, with a wife who is really out of my league, and a daughter who is a joy.

I get to write, which is at least 50% drinking coffee and looking wistfully out of the window, and I have the support of other fantastic writers and lovers of books. My deepest thanks go out to all my Beach Hut writer friends in Brighton, and the wider community of writers and book bloggers who have been so wonderful and supportive. But I have to single out two other writers who read my first draft and gave me wonderful feedback: Jane Lythell and Laura Wilkinson.

Writing can be a lonely life, and for all writers out there, who are yet to be published, I say *good luck* and *keep going*. Until an agent or a publisher takes your book and tells you *we love it*, you have to just believe that moment will arrive, and be your own cheerleader and life coach. I am really lucky that I have a great editor in Keshini Naidoo at Hera/Canelo who challenges me and helps me write better than wot I would rilly rite if I had know editor and was left to my own Devizes. Nobody wants that. So I thank her and everyone at Hera.

And of course I want to acknowledge YOU the reader. Thanks. And tell your friends, and even your enemies, to read me and write a fab review somewhere (even the bathroom wall helps).